THE RADICAL ELEMENT

12 Stories of
Daredevils, Debutantes,
and Other Dauntless Girls

EDITED BY

Jessica Spotswood

CANDLEWICK PRESS

Compilation and introduction copyright © 2018 by Jessica Spotswood
"Daughter of the Book" copyright © 2018 by Dahlia Adler
"You're a Stranger Here" copyright © 2018 by Mackenzi Lee
"The Magician" copyright © 2018 by Erin Bowman
"Lady Firebrand" copyright © 2018 by Megan Shepherd
"Step Right Up" copyright © 2018 by Jessica Spotswood
"Glamour" copyright © 2018 by Anna-Marie McLemore
"Better for All the World" copyright © 2018 by Marieke Nijkamp
"When the Moonlight Isn't Enough" copyright © 2018 by Dhonielle Clayton
"The Belle of the Ball" copyright © 2018 by Sarvenaz Tash
"Land of the Sweet, Home of the Brave" copyright © 2018 by Stacey Lee
"The Birth of Susi Go-Go" copyright © 2018 by Meg Medina
"Take Me with U" copyright © 2018 by Sara Farizan

First paperback edition 2019

Library of Congress Catalog Card Number 2018936969
ISBN 978-0-7636-9425-8 (hardcover)
ISBN 978-1-5362-0866-5 (paperback)

19 20 21 22 23 24 MVP 10 9 8 7 6 5 4 3 2 1

Printed in York, PA, U.S.A.

This book was typeset in Adobe Caslon Pro and Caslon 540.

Candlewick Press
99 Dover Street
Somerville, Massachusetts 02144

visit us at www.candlewick.com

For all the radical girls,
past and present,
who fight for change

CONTENTS

INTRODUCTION
IX

1838: SAVANNAH, GEORGIA
Daughter of the Book – Dahlia Adler
I

1844: NAUVOO, ILLINOIS
You're a Stranger Here – Mackenzi Lee
25

1858: COLORADO RIVER, NEW MEXICO TERRITORY
The Magician – Erin Bowman
46

1863: CHARLESTON, SOUTH CAROLINA
Lady Firebrand – Megan Shepherd
74

1905: TULSA, INDIAN TERRITORY
Step Right Up – Jessica Spotswood
102

1923: LOS ANGELES AND THE CENTRAL VALLEY, CALIFORNIA
Glamour – Anna-Marie McLemore
128

1927: WASHINGTON, D.C.
Better for All the World – Marieke Nijkamp
156

1943: OAK BLUFFS, MASSACHUSETTS
When the Moonlight Isn't Enough – Dhonielle Clayton
179

1952: BROOKLYN, NEW YORK
The Belle of the Ball – Sarvenaz Tash
207

1955: OAKLAND, CALIFORNIA
Land of the Sweet, Home of the Brave – Stacey Lee
236

1972: QUEENS, NEW YORK
The Birth of Susi Go-Go – Meg Medina
257

1984: BOSTON, MASSACHUSETTS
Take Me with U – Sara Farizan
282

ABOUT THE CONTRIBUTORS
305

ACKNOWLEDGMENTS
309

INTRODUCTION

———

I N 2015, when I finished editing *A Tyranny of Petticoats: 15 Stories of Belles, Bank Robbers & Other Badass Girls,* I knew I wanted to edit another feminist historical fiction anthology. *Tyranny* was—and continues to be—the best, most joyful, and most satisfying collaborative experience of my career. So I cast about, searching for a theme, and hit upon the idea of girls who were outsiders in their communities. Searching for a potential title, I found a quote by President Rutherford B. Hayes: "Universal suffrage is sound in principle. The radical element is right."

And so *The Radical Element* was born, shifting the focus slightly—and I think empoweringly—from girls who were *outsiders* to girls who were *radical* in their communities, whether by virtue of their race, religion, sexuality, disability, gender, or the profession they were pursuing.

Merriam-Webster's definitions of *radical* include "very different from the usual or traditional" and "excellent, cool." I like to think our heroines are both. Our radical girls are first- and second-generation immigrants. They are Mormon and Jewish, queer and questioning, wheelchair users and neurodivergent, Iranian-American and Latina and Black and biracial. They are funny and awkward and jealous and brave. They are spies and scholars and sitcom writers, printers' apprentices and poker players, rockers and high-wire walkers. They are mundane and they are magical. They yearn for an education in Savannah in 1838, struggle with Hollywood racism in 1923, and immigrate to Boston in 1984.

There is power—a quiet badassery—in girls taking charge of their own destinies. Our heroines follow their dreams, whether those dreams are a safe place to practice their faith or an elusive pair of white leather go-go boots. These girls will not allow society to define them. Instead, they define themselves, claiming their identities even though it was often not historically safe—and, disappointingly, is not always *currently* safe—to do so. They learn to love themselves in all their perfectly imperfect beauty—which, as some of our heroines learn, might be the most radical act of all.

At the Texas Book Festival, a teenage girl in the audience of my panel said she was, with the encouragement of her teacher, trying to read about history from many points of view, not just that of the cisgendered heterosexual white men who have traditionally written it. We panelists applauded. We need empathy now more than ever. We need to read stories about, and especially by, voices that have been traditionally silenced and erased from history. We need curious, open-minded, open-hearted teenagers (and adults!) like you.

I hope you will see yourself reflected in at least one of these stories. I hope they will make you question what traditional history lessons miss and inspire you to seek out more radical girls. Most of all, I hope this collection will provide an impetus for you to *be* the radical element in your own community, dreaming big, loving yourself fiercely, and writing the next chapter of history.

Thank you for reading.

JESSICA SPOTSWOOD

DAUGHTER OF THE BOOK

DAHLIA ADLER

R ebekah threaded in.
      Rebekah tugged the needle out.

Rebekah had never been so bored in her entire seventeen years. At least not since yesterday.

"Beautiful, Miriam." Mrs. Samuels flitted around the one-room schoolhouse like a butterfly. Or, in her muted tones, perhaps a moth was a more appropriate comparison. Like Rebekah, she wore a simple cotton gown she'd stitched herself that covered every inch of skin from collarbone to wrist to ankle, but as a married woman, she also wore a shawl that covered her hair. Rebekah wondered if the shawl somehow kept Mrs. Samuels cooler, because she didn't seem to be perspiring through every stitch the way Rebekah was beneath her long chestnut curls. It made her feel like a poor imitation of a Georgian that she could barely tolerate the Savannah sun in these brutal summer months. But then, she was Jewish first,

American second, as her mama and papa never tired of telling her. "Look at Miriam's stitchwork in those clouds. It's so nice against that beautiful blue. Like tekhelet."

Rebekah smiled to herself at the mention of the holy turquoise shade, sported in the fringes of her father's tzitzit. It *was* a beautiful color, but just a few weeks ago, Caleb had taught her that true tekhelet dye came from an honest-to-goodness snail. "It's called a chilazon," he'd told her in that tone he always took when he was educating—the one that let everyone know he would be a wonderful rabbi someday. Her father would never have shared such knowledge with her, but Caleb Laniado continued right on, imparting what he'd learned from studying the Talmud with some of the other men from Mickve Israel.

Rebekah knew this scholarship wasn't meant for her ears, that the Talmud was for men alone, and she wished more than anything that she found it dull. That she could echo Caleb's sister, Naomi, or her own best friend, Deborah, when they teased him for babbling on about the legendary arguments between the rabbis Hillel and Shammai or why they couldn't blend wool and linen to make their garments as the gentiles did.

But she wanted that knowledge, thirsted for it, drank it down like the last dregs of kiddush wine. She didn't know if Caleb noticed, and she'd be mortified if Deborah or Naomi did, but she loved when he shared his lessons—and not just because of the way passion lit up his brown eyes and sent his strong hands flying into gestures. There would be a time for truly noticing that someday, and someday soon, she knew. Someday the challah cover she was stitching would be on her own Shabbat table, and it would be her husband commenting on the needlework.

Someday, but not yet.

She had so much to learn first.

✕ ✕ ✕

The sun was high in the sky when Rebekah finally found a few moments to escape the kitchen that afternoon. She didn't even have to think about a destination; ever since she'd figured out that Mama was too distracted by baby Abigail to pay her much mind once the lunch dishes were rinsed, she'd let her feet drag her to the same place. She'd been barely six years old when a fire had burned down the old wooden synagogue, but people still loved to talk of the miracle of the Torahs and the Aron Kodesh that had somehow been spared. Her little brother, Jacob, had had his bris at the old synagogue, and they had thought they'd see him read from the Sefer Torah for his bar mitzvah there. But this new brick building they were erecting in its place would be the site of his coming-of-age ceremony instead.

Better than Caleb had. Jacob would have a proper ceremony, including a celebratory feast for the entire community, but Caleb's bar mitzvah had been in his home, which did not fit even the forty or so men of Mickve Israel, let alone the rest of the congregants.

"Miss Rebekah? Is that you?"

It was as if thinking about him had made his long, lean figure appear out of thin air. "Caleb Laniado. What have I told you about calling me 'Miss'?"

His slight grin and the crinkle of his long-lashed eyes made him look boyish despite the shadow of a dark beard that could never stay away for long. "My mama would have my hide if I didn't, and you know it."

She knew it was immodest, but it was impossible not to smile back. Besides, Caleb was as holy a boy as she knew. He wasn't being improper with her; he was absolutely serious that Mrs. Laniado would be mad as a cottonmouth if he were more familiar. "Amazing how the new building is coming along, isn't it?"

"It is. The committee's been working nonstop. Dr. Sheftall wants it complete by next year and says they have all the funds to do it without needing to ask for more from anybody."

That was good to hear. She knew that if money was scarce in her household, it would be her own meager education that would be the first to go. Mrs. Samuels's instructions came at a fee, and though she taught little more than basic sums and sewing, losing them would be cutting one more tie to the community. It was hard enough to see how many congregants were already breaking away—marrying outside the faith, abandoning their traditions, adopting gentile business practices, and even buying slaves in an effort to blend in with their neighbors. But Rebekah's family did not blend in more than absolutely necessary, and she knew the Laniados did not—would not—either. Besides, other than Mama's lessons on keeping a kosher kitchen and properly observing the Sabbath, Mrs. Samuels's classes were the only education she received. It wasn't much, but it was better than nothing at all.

"It'll be nice to have, when it's finished." She fanned her cheeks with her hand and cursed herself for leaving her parasol at home. "I'm sure you'll be happy to have a new place to study." Her words were simple enough, but they burned hot with jealousy. Caleb's cheder classes had ended at fourteen, but he and some of the other boys still received private personal instruction, and it did not involve needlepoint. "What did you learn today?"

"The Shulchan Aruch," he said, and it made her heart ache a little. The answers used to be things she knew from prayers and holiday services and Mrs. Samuels's rudimentary parsha classes— stories of the Patriarchs and Matriarchs and the twelve tribes of Israel. The Shulchan Aruch was a book she knew by name only, as something her father studied.

"Can you tell me the story of Ruth again?" It was her favorite, after the story of Esther, which was too long for right now; Mama would no doubt be calling her any minute, if she wasn't already.

"We should get home." Caleb took one last look at the synagogue before turning back to the tree-lined cobblestone street. "Anyway, you've heard me tell it a hundred times."

"You could tell me for the hundred and first time on the way."

He sighed, and she knew he'd do it. He couldn't resist the opportunity to teach a willing student, and he was the only one she still trusted to ask. Unlike her father, he never rebuked her for doing so; his reserves of patience seemed truly endless.

"It was in the time of the Judges, when there was a man named Elimelech and a woman named Naomi, and—"

"Which judge?" Rebekah interrupted.

"Pardon me?"

Yes, he'd told her the story one hundred times, and she heard it read aloud in synagogue every spring during the Shavuot holiday, but new questions always seemed to spring up like dandelions. "You said the story's in the time of the Judges, right? So who was the judge during this time?"

A smile slipped over his face, quick as a shadow. "That's a good question, Miss Rebekah. I don't know the answer."

"But you have a thought, surely."

He gave a cautious nod, just a dip of his chin, the kind he gave when the answer lay beyond the Torah. She used to try her hardest to wheedle it out of him, but now she just waited patiently, fixing her attention on the way the light breeze swayed the Spanish moss dangling from the oak tree branches and swished her blue cotton skirt around her ankles.

"In the Talmud, it is stated that Ibzan was Boaz, and Rashi explains that this refers to the judge Ibzan. As such, many believe he was the judge at the time."

Ibzan. She tucked the name away in her treasury of those that appeared only once or twice and which no girl would likely ever hear. "Ah. All right, then. Go on."

"Elimelech and Naomi had two sons, named—"

"Makhlon and Kilion," Rebekah finished before she could stop herself.

Another shadow smile. "Right. And Makhlon and Kilion were married to . . ." This time he left a space for her to fill in Ruth's and Orpah's names, as if he were in fact a teacher and she a student. They continued like that until they arrived at her porch, where her little sister Sarah was standing with her fists on her hips and a suspicious glare.

"You're in trouble, Rebekah Judith!" she called. "Mama's fixin' to send you to bed without supper!"

Rebekah sighed. "Thank you for the lesson, Caleb. I had better get inside. But . . . perhaps I'll see you tomorrow?"

He tipped his hat. "Perhaps you will. Have a good evening, Miss Rebekah."

"Where on earth have you been?" Mama asked the moment Rebekah walked through the door into a warm kitchen smelling of peppery fish and buttery corn bread. "Have you forgotten your chores? Sarah had to shuck the corn for you. Say thank you to your sister."

"Thank you, Sarah," she mumbled.

"You promised you were only calling upon Deborah for an hour," Mama continued as she pointed toward the shelf of cornflower-blue dairy dinner dishes. Rebekah took five of the earthenware plates from the stack—baby Abigail was still just feeding off Mama—and spread them around the wooden table, knowing exactly what was coming next. "Your papa will be home soon and what a fine thing for him to work a hard day and come back to an unprepared supper!"

"I'm sorry, Mama," she said, louder than a mumble because she knew she'd simply have to repeat it otherwise. But she wasn't really sorry; she wouldn't take back her lesson with Caleb for anything.

"You'll do all the washing tonight," Mama said in a voice that brooked no argument.

"Yes, Mama."

Rebekah had hoped to leave it at that and continue setting the table in peace, but of course Sarah had to pipe up. "She was with that strange Laniado boy," she crowed.

"Sarah! What a thing to say. Caleb is a nice young man." Mama turned to Rebekah. "Or perhaps not, if he's spending time alone with you, with no talk of marriage. You are not children any longer, Rebekah."

"It was a chance meeting, outside in full daylight." Rebekah laid out the dairy forks, sparing a glare for Sarah. "Don't spread lashon hara, Sarah. It's a sin, and it's unbecoming, besides."

Sarah stuck out her tongue.

"Don't do that, either," Mama said. "What have I told you about respecting your elders? Both of you?" she added pointedly.

"But I—"

"I don't want to hear it, Rebekah, and I do *not* want to hear tales of you being improper with a boy, either, do you hear me? Especially not with the Laniado boy."

Rebekah wondered what exactly Mama's objection was to "the Laniado boy"—that he'd be particularly repulsed by impropriety, given his piousness? Or did Mama fear him as a prospect, knowing he dreamed of being a rabbi and teacher someday and would never bring in the money that the men dealing in dry goods or trading cotton did? Or perhaps it was that he was Sephardic—the

Laniados had come from Portugal a generation ago—and Mama secretly hoped her eldest daughter would marry a boy with German blood like theirs and raise a family with their Ashkenazi customs.

In any case, Rebekah knew better than to ask. "Honor thy father and thy mother" may have been the fifth commandment in the Torah, but it was the first in the Wolf household. Anyway, Papa's large, lumbering frame walked through the door then, turning all talk to his day at work and his upcoming annual trip to New York. When he brought up the subject of the synagogue's progress, though, Rebekah couldn't help but ask another question.

"What of the school once the synagogue is built, Papa?" she asked, ladling out fish stew.

He regarded his eldest daughter over the rims of his spectacles. "Cheder will return to the synagogue building, of course. I'm sure your brother will be delighted to have his studies in a proper Beit Midrash."

Jacob nodded, but Rebekah knew he didn't give a fig where he had his studies—not his religious studies, anyway. All Jacob ever talked about was how he was going to be a merchant like Papa, dealing with visitors who traveled from all over Georgia and South Carolina to purchase his textiles and making the long trip up to New York once a year to replenish at good credit rates. Jacob cared for sums far more than he would ever care for David and Goliath or the Exodus. More than once, she'd lingered outside while he studied with Papa, watching him yawn or clean dirt from his fingernails while envy burned in her like the candlelight that flickered over their texts.

"But . . . do you think . . . might there be room for girls to study in a proper Beit Midrash, too? Separate from the boys, of course," she added hastily, as if such a thing even needed to be stated.

"For what purpose?" Creases formed between Papa's light-blue eyes. "Does Mrs. Samuels not teach you that which you need to know? Does your mama not show you how to keep a kosher home?"

Rebekah swallowed hard, suddenly not at all hungry, although she continued to dish out the stew. Mama taught her the most important things—the blessing over the candles to welcome Shabbat just before sunset every Friday, how to boil eggs for the Pesach Seder and braid golden challah bread for Shabbat and holidays, that dishes like roast ham and oysters were for their gentile neighbors, but no pig or shellfish would ever grace a kosher table.

But she didn't teach the story of Esther, or of Ruth, or of Deborah. Her mother didn't teach her how Rebekah—her biblical namesake—saw that Jacob was the son chosen by God, and not his twin, Esau, who was preferred by Isaac. Those bits and pieces had all been gleaned from nagging Caleb or eavesdropping on Jacob's lessons.

"Of course she does. I just meant . . . it would be nice to learn more Torah. I know Mama is very, very busy with Abigail, and—"

"Do you not learn Torah in your studies with Mrs. Samuels?" Papa's voice had risen just enough for Rebekah to know he did not like this conversation.

"Mrs. Samuels does teach us the parsha every week," she said carefully as she took a seat with her own dish. "I simply hoped to learn a little bit more—maybe the Prophets and the Megillot. Perhaps even Hebrew, so I might study them for myself."

"You do not need any such instruction, child," Papa said firmly. "Our Sages are very clear that it is most important for the women of Israel to focus on nurturing a family and maintaining a kosher home. How can you have time to learn everything you need to know in order to be a proper Jewish bride and mother if you're filling your head with other things? If you marry a scholar, how will you support his Torah study if you do not learn the skills needed to maintain a boardinghouse or store?"

A hundred answers rose in Rebekah's throat, and she swallowed them all down. None were proper for a young southern lady *or* a daughter of Israel. "Yes, Papa," she said around the lump they formed.

"This is the nonsense the Yankees are spreading," he muttered. "That Gratz woman is shaking up Philadelphia with that new school of hers. Can't leave well enough alone."

"New school?" Rebekah had not heard any word of this, not even from her most gossipy classmate, Miriam. "What kind of new school?"

"It's foolishness," her father assured them all, buttering his corn bread with a firm hand. "A free Hebrew Sunday school for boys and girls. It seems Miss Gratz does not think our current educational system is sufficient."

What educational system? Rebekah wanted to ask, and she had to clamp her teeth down on her lips to keep from doing so. She knew she herself was lucky to have a mother who would teach her the ways of a kosher home, and Mrs. Samuels to teach her other matters; some did not have even this. It was no wonder so many of their Jewish neighbors were turning from Halakha and discarding the ways of their faith.

"And who is teaching in this school?" Mama asked. "Miss Gratz herself?"

"Among others." Her father stabbed his corn bread with such fierceness that Rebekah knew he was anxious to end the discussion, but she could not have been more enthralled. A school full of teachers? A school that would give equal education to boys and girls? To Rebekah, it sounded like paradise. "And the school trains new teachers as well. As if more women need to be distracted from their homes and children with this pointless pursuit."

Rebekah's heart beat a frantic tattoo. *A school that trained new teachers.* What if she could not only receive a better Jewish education but impart one as well? Her father's annual trip to New York was coming soon, and her entire being burned with the desire to join him on the journey north and stop in Philadelphia along the way.

But of course she could not. She would never see the inside of Miss Gratz's school, never teach in one of her own. She would remain in Savannah forever, bearing children and running a boardinghouse so her husband could continue the studies she could not. There would be no time for the "pointless pursuit" of her own studies.

They made the blessings over their food, then ate the rest of their meal in silence.

For the next week, she did not talk to Caleb even once; instead, she watched with envy from her porch as he went to learn with the men. Nor did she ask to attend services with Papa on Friday night, as he occasionally permitted, instead staying home to set the table for Shabbat dinner and help Mama put Abigail to sleep. He had been unusually irritable ever since the conversation about Miss Gratz's school, and she feared if she did not behave as a model daughter of Israel now, the few-and-far-between favors he granted would vanish completely.

But when Papa left for three months in New York with several of the other merchants from the congregation, Rebekah felt impatient to expand her education again. She was not brazen enough to try to intercept Caleb on his way to class, but she did walk past the synagogue again in the hopes he would be there. He wasn't, that first day. Nor the second. It wasn't until the third day that he appeared, his ill-fitting vest highlighting how rapidly he'd been growing this past year—too quickly for his mother's arthritic fingers to keep up. Rebekah wondered idly just how improper it would be to stitch him a new vest in between her work on table-cloths and aprons, and had to acknowledge that she already knew the answer.

But then, it wasn't any more improper than the favor she was about to ask.

"Caleb Laniado."

He seemed surprised to see her, but no less polite for it. "Miss Rebekah." He tipped his hat. "Rabbi Yehuda HaLevi's *The Kuzari*, before you ask. We talked about *The Kuzari* and other works of medieval Jewish philosophy in class today. It was fascinating."

A light flush filled her cheeks, and she prayed it was shadowed by her parasol. "I wasn't going to ask," she lied, or, well, it wasn't really a lie. She wasn't going to ask *that*.

She was going to ask something much bigger.

"Caleb, you are fond of teaching, are you not?"

"I am."

"And you're good at it."

Now he was the one to flush. "I just share that which God enables me to."

Modesty—the most notable of the great prophet Moses's virtues. Her father was fond of making sure she internalized *that* lesson. "Do you think God would enable you to share more? With me?" Her face promptly flamed at her inelegant phrasing. "Would you teach me?"

He furrowed his thick, dark eyebrows. "Teach you?"

"I know to teach me Talmud or Kabbalah would be forbidden," she said quickly, fiddling with the cuff at the elbow of her green cotton dress. "But Hebrew. Torah. Prophets. I just want to know more about our people, our history, our language. And nobody wants to teach me that. Nobody thinks women deserve to know anything but how to make challah and bless the Shabbat candles."

"A woman's role in the home is very important, Rebekah," he said, his voice patient but firm. "Men would not be able to both learn and provide for our families if women didn't—"

"I know." She exhaled sharply. "I know. I hear so much about the woman's role in Klal Yisrael, and I know it is important. But Papa learns *and* works, and so do the other men of Mickve Israel. If you all have time to do both, why don't we?"

"Because caring for children—"

"I don't *have* any children, Caleb." She was supposed to be demure, to know her place, but she'd had it with everyone deciding her place but her. If her biblical namesake had stuck to her place, the warlike Esau might be their forefather instead of the peaceful, learned Jacob. If Esther had stuck to her place, the Jewish people might not exist at all. Jewish history was not made of women who remained willfully ignorant in order to sew tablecloths. "But when I do, God willing, I want them to be learned. I want my boys *and* my girls to know our traditions, our words. I want them to see why observing our laws and sharing our history matters. There is so much more women could be doing in our community, if only we were allowed."

There was a long silence as Caleb stroked his angular jaw while contemplating her words, and then, mercifully, gave one stiff nod. "All right, Rebekah. I will teach you. But—"

"I won't tell anyone," she promised.

"I am not sure that is for the best. The laws of yichud forbid an unwed man and woman from being alone."

She knew this, but she also knew that if anyone had an inkling they were engaging in this private study, she'd never be permitted to leave home again—not for lessons or any services at which women's presence was merely optional, not even to call upon Deborah for social visits. And if word spread to the matchmaker that she was stubborn and immodest, not only would it be more difficult to find her a match, but possibly more difficult to find one for Sarah as well.

It was so much to risk, but it didn't feel like a choice; she needed this knowledge the way she needed air. Maybe she couldn't be trained in Miss Gratz's school, but this could be another path for her to learn everything she would need to teach others. "Surely there must be a way. Caleb, think what a difference it would make if the women in the community had someone to teach them to love our religion and laws instead of simply abiding by them. Think of all those we've lost from the congregation—what if this is the way to bring them back? To keep future members close?"

There was another long silence, but, finally, the spark of an idea flashed in his dark eyes. "We must find a place that is both public and private. As long as people are freely able to enter and see us, I think that would be halakhically permissible."

A place both public enough to keep with Jewish law and private enough that they would not be spotted . . . "Why, I reckon we could use the Gottliebs' carriage house, same as Mrs. Samuels teaches us in. They don't lock the doors after hours. We could leave them open; there'd be no reason for anyone to come looking."

Judging by Caleb's pinched expression, he still wasn't entirely convinced of the propriety and wisdom of Rebekah's plan, but he nodded. "We'll try it. Sunday evening."

"I'll bring a candle," she promised, praying to Hashem her mother did not keep careful count. "I'll see you Sunday evening, after supper."

He agreed, and she left before he could change his mind.

$\times$ $\times$ $\times$

"So Deborah was not the only female hero in Judges," Rebekah said with no small amount of satisfaction as they ended their session for the evening. They'd been studying together for weeks now, and as night began to fall earlier and earlier, they'd cut their lessons from two evenings a week down to just one, fearing her mother would notice if she snuck too many extra candles. "I cannot believe no one speaks of Yael."

"A woman who lulled a general to sleep and then stabbed him through the temple with a tent peg is not generally considered a topic for polite conversation."

Rebekah laughed at Caleb's dry wit, careful to keep her mirth quiet. She hadn't known Caleb *had* a strong sense of humor, but he routinely made her laugh, and she loved the way his dark eyes twinkled in the candlelight. He would make a wonderful teacher someday, and what's more, he inspired her to want to be the same.

It made her wonder how Miss Gratz taught in that school of hers up in Philadelphia.

It made her wonder about that a lot.

"Simply because she was whispering her prayers, Eli thought she was drunk?" Rebekah was flabbergasted. They were making steady progress in the Prophets portion of the Bible and were now studying the book of Samuel. "But we pray silently every day. I was punished with an entire week of extra chores for speaking aloud during the Amidah."

Caleb smiled, even as he gestured for her to keep her voice low. "Yes, we pray silently now, but our Sages point to this very source as evidence that we did not always. If silent prayer had been commonplace at that time, surely the High Priest would not have questioned Hannah. And so we must infer that it was not."

"So then Hannah is responsible for the way in which we now pray?"

His smile widened, just a little bit. "Arguably, yes, she is." He looked back down at the book in his lap. "I suspected you might like that."

She did not need to confirm for him how correct he was.

They continued through Kings and learned of Ahab and the queen Jezebel, who ordered the death of hundreds of prophets. Of Athaliah, a woman so violently stricken with ambition that after her son was killed, she murdered her entire family so she could reign. Of Jehosheba, the righteous princess who managed to rescue a single child of that family and protect him until he was old enough to reclaim the crown, therefore salvaging the Davidic line of monarchy.

They learned until Rebekah could slowly, slowly read the letters of the Aleph-Bet, until she could recognize the different forms of the name of God, until she could spot her own name in the book of Genesis, and Caleb's in the book of Numbers.

They learned until the night a shadow filled the door of the carriage house and covered the pages of Caleb's open Bible.

They never made it to the book of Ruth.

"What were you thinking?" her father raged. Her mother had been too preoccupied with baby Abigail and preparing the house for her husband's return to notice Rebekah's regular absence, but he noted it almost immediately. He'd only been back from New York for a week before he came looking in the carriage house. It felt like everything happened in seconds then: her and Caleb jumping apart as if struck by lightning. Her father's voice thundering in her ears. The candle flame being extinguished, although she had no idea who actually plunged the carriage house into darkness. Her father's demand that she and Caleb march in front of him around the corner to the Laniados' house. And now they were in the Laniados' simply furnished parlor, her fingernails digging into the wood of her armchair as if it might anchor her when everything else was spinning and it took every ounce of her strength to meet Caleb's father's gaze.

Haim Laniado's quiet nature made him all the more imposing, and Rebekah knew her father was ashamed in front of him now—ashamed of *her*, his rebellious daughter.

Nothing made her father angrier than feeling ashamed.

"I just wanted to learn," Rebekah said quietly. "There was nothing improper between us."

"The entire arrangement was improper." Her father's normally pale complexion was ruddy with anger, his knobby hands slicing the air as he spoke. Only his determination not to be heard throughout Savannah kept his voice at a fierce whisper. "The two of you? Alone? You know this is forbidden. You *both* know this."

"We were not in violation of yichud," she said, stealing a glance at Caleb. He would not meet her eyes, would not look at anything but his hands folded over his dark breeches. "The door was always open. Always."

"How can we believe a word you say?" Mr. Laniado's voice was as soft as his demeanor. "My own son—my *only* son—hiding with a girl in secret." He took a deep breath. "You were taught better than this, Caleb."

"She's telling the truth, Abba. All we did was study, and the door was always open. She asked me to teach her Torah, and I did. But I am sorry I did it in secret."

"No one would have let us if we did *not* do it in secret," Rebekah pointed out, earning glares from all the men. She pressed on anyway. "If you don't believe that we were studying, then test me. Ask me about the Judges or Kings. Ask me to read from a Torah scroll. Ask me about something I would never learn from Mrs. Samuels. Ask me and I will know."

"That is not the point, Rebekah. What did I say the last time we discussed this?"

"Did I not help Mama with chores these past few months? Did I not find time for both? I know my place in the Jewish home, Papa. But I think I have a place outside of it, too." She took a deep breath. "You and Mama have taught me so well to preserve our traditions, to put being Jewish first. You have warned me of all the dangers of turning from our path. But what of those who have not received such teachings? The nation around us holds such temptation to blend in. How can those resist it who feel they have nothing in our own beautiful Jewish nation to grasp? How can we continue as a community if we do not educate enough teachers within it?"

Papa snorted. "You view yourself as a teacher? Anavah, Rebekah. Midat Moshe Rabbeinu. Our greatest leader possessed modesty above all."

She winced; he could not have injured her more had he slapped her. But memories of the women who'd come before her, who'd believed they had more to give than men expected of them, drove her forward. "So I'm permitted to learn the virtues of Moses, but I'm not permitted to learn the story of him receiving the Torah at Mount Sinai? Doesn't that sound silly?"

Every man in the room sucked in a breath at her insolence, and she wondered if she had gone too far. But what did it matter now? Her father's respect for her was already gone, and surely Caleb would no longer speak to her after this. She would never be allowed to attend Mrs. Samuels's class or Friday-night services again.

What did she have left to lose?

"Tell me, Papa," she pleaded. "What do I have to do in order to learn? All I want is to be a learned daughter of Israel. I don't want to disobey you and Mama. I don't want to hide. I certainly don't want trouble for Caleb. But I want to learn. There must be a way. If he cannot teach me, will you?"

"I do not have time for this nonsense, Rebekah. I have a son who needs to learn Talmud, as does Mr. Laniado. The community has decided what you need to know, and you need to trust your community. Kol Yisrael arevim zeh lazeh—all of Israel is responsible for one another. You need to accept that your elders know what is best."

Caleb shook his head. "I do not think they do," he said, and Rebekah snapped to attention. "You are of course correct that Kol Yisrael arevim zeh lazeh, but does that not include being responsible for the women of the community, too? For their knowledge and education? Rebekah is very clever, sir. And she is interested— far more than most of the young men with whom I have studied. I do not believe it is in the interest of the Jewish community to deprive her of an equal education. I think she would have very much to offer Mickve Israel, especially since the new synagogue will be finished soon."

Rebekah was stunned to hear Caleb defend her, but he wasn't finished. He remained calm even though her father's jaw was clenched tight enough to crack a pecan. "I would like to keep teaching her. She is the most insightful study partner I have found in Savannah, and I think our learning has been beneficial not only for her education but for mine. I believe she could be a wonderful teacher someday."

The rest of the room fell silent as Haim Laniado stroked his long graying beard. Rebekah had never heard Caleb challenge an elder. It warmed her from head to toe to have him stand up for her and for their partnership—to hear anyone stand up for her at all. For the first time since her father had marched them into the parlor, Rebekah relaxed her grip on the wooden armrests.

"You cannot be alone as an unwed man and woman," Mr. Laniado said.

"With your permission, we can study on the porch," Rebekah said quickly. "In full view of everyone who walks by."

Mr. Laniado shook his head. "That would certainly not look proper. As Yossi Ben Yochanan teaches us in Pirkei Avot, 'Al tarbe sicha im ha'isha'—one is not to engage in excessive conversation with a woman, for he will neglect his own study. This is said even for a married couple, but for an unwed pair . . . I cannot allow it."

"Nor can I." Her father tugged at the cuffs of his linen shirt, the way he always did before making a proclamation. There was no space for either her or Caleb to argue that this wasn't the sort of idle chatter in question, that it *was* study. There was barely any space to breathe at all. "I see how arrogant these studies have made you already, not to mention how little regard you have given to your sisters' futures and the reputation you will give our family. I cannot tell another man what to allow in his home, with his wife, but I will not have a daughter living under my roof behaving in this manner."

With his wife . . . She had known, deep down in her heart, that this suggestion would arise, but hearing the words spoken aloud made her wish she could shed her skin like the serpent of Eden. "Papa, I . . . I do not feel . . . I am not . . ."

"You want to someday wed, do you not? To fulfill the mitzvah of Pru U'Rvu and bring more children into the Jewish community?"

Rebekah nodded numbly. She did. But not *yet*.

It was not that she did not care for Caleb; she did. He was

kind to her, and he was intelligent, and she did not mind that he would not earn a merchant's salary. He was nice-looking, too, with his strong, dark features and lean build. In truth, she had long suspected he would be her future; while many of the Jews in the South were marrying gentiles and working their hardest to blend into Savannah, the Laniados were like the Wolfs in their commitment to marrying within and observing the faith.

But she was not ready for a home of her own yet, and what time would there be for her Torah study once she had one? Once she had children of her own who needed to be fed and clothed and watched every spare moment?

Marriage was simply a different way to keep her from her education.

"What about school?" she pleaded, taking one last chance. "You mentioned Miss Gratz's school in Philadelphia. . . ."

Her father laughed, and his mirth had never sounded so cruel. "You reckon your mama and I would send you away from your home and family to study under the tutelage of that woman? I think not. I am kind enough to give you a choice here, Rebekah. You will speak to the matchmaker tomorrow, or Mama will ask Mrs. Baron to take you as an apprentice at her boardinghouse; I am certain she could use plenty of assistance with her sweeping and washing, and you would learn some much-needed skills in return. It seems I made a poor choice in your education once, and I will not make that mistake again."

Perspiration snaked down Rebekah's spine as she waited for Caleb to speak up again.

He did not.

It was his father who broke the silence. "It has been a long night, Benjamin. Let us discuss this further tomorrow. It is best we all get some sleep."

Rebekah's body moved as if pulled by the strings of a marionette. If she did not make a choice soon, she would cease to be given one. But what choice could she live with?

"Are you certain this is what you want to do?" Caleb's voice was so scratchy, it hurt Rebekah's throat.

"I am as certain as I have ever been about anything." She smoothed down the full skirt of her coffee-brown cotton dress with trembling hands.

Again, that shadow smile. It made her heart ache to think how long it might be before she saw it again. "I believe in you and what you have to offer the Jewish people, Rebekah. I think you will help change our community's future."

"You don't know what that means to me." She wished she could embrace him, feel the sturdy support of the only person who believed in her. But propriety and modesty reigned, now as ever. Running away might be her biggest act of rebellion, but she was determined it would be her last. Well, aside from asking Caleb to assist her in hiring a stagecoach that would take her to Charleston for the first leg of her journey north to Philadelphia. "I'll be back, Caleb. God willing, I will. It's not just me I'm going for; I'm hoping that it's for the future of Mickve Israel, too."

"What do I say to your family?" he asked, glancing over his shoulder as if they were lying in wait. Or maybe he was avoiding her gaze, the same way she'd found herself doing many times that day. She'd known leaving her family would be difficult, and she'd cried when she'd left the good-bye letter to her best friend, Deborah, but she had not expected that leaving him would be as hard.

I will return, she reminded herself as his gaze returned to hers. *I will return, and I will return to you, if you'll have me.* He hadn't said a word about marrying her, but he had come today, and that felt like as much of a sign from Hashem as anything. "I told you, I left a note. They'll know where I am."

"But still, they will ask if I knew. What do I say when they want to know how you could leave them behind?"

She had thought about this many times since she'd made the decision to leave, as she'd sold all the jewelry she'd inherited from her grandmother in order to afford the trip. And every time, it came back to the one thing she knew her family might understand. "Tell them I'm Jewish first."

⚙ AUTHOR'S NOTE ⚙

I was privileged to have excellent Jewish education my entire childhood at schools that valued girls learning all the same things our male peers were, including Talmud. However, this isn't the case across the board at Orthodox schools even now, and it certainly wasn't in Rebekah's time, when education for girls was barely a consideration at all.

Accessibility of Jewish education to boys and girls, rich and poor alike, can be accredited to the work of Rebecca Gratz (1781–1869), who founded the first Hebrew Sunday school in Philadelphia in February 1838. She was a fierce advocate for Jewish women and economic equality, and her life and work are skillfully documented in *Rebecca Gratz: Women and Judaism in Antebellum America* by Dianne Ashton, which was of great use to me in my research.

I chose to set the story in Savannah partly to highlight one of America's great early Jewish communities with tremendous devotion to preservation of their early history (as I warmly recall

from a visit to Mickve Israel nearly a decade ago), and partly
to send Rebekah on a physical journey to obtain the education
she sought. Of course, she had no way of knowing how soon
Savannah (and a number of other cities, including New York
and Charleston) would follow suit in picking up Gratz's school
model, and that by the time her baby sister was old enough for
religious studies, she would have no need to travel at all.

YOU'RE A STRANGER HERE

MACKENZI LEE

They shot the prophet!"

I hear Minnie Gadd shouting before I see her. When I look up from the row of type I'm laying out, she's flying past the print-shop windows and down the high street, her hair coming undone from its plaits and flapping behind her like a pennant from the rigging of the ships back home in Liverpool. Her face shines when the sun strikes it, like it's brushed in gold leaf, and it takes until she's nearly to the Taylors' house before I realize it's 'cause she's crying. Big, broad, unmovable Minnie—who had the boy who slapped my rump on the way out of the social hall swallowing his teeth for a week—has got tears running all the way down her neck and into the gingham collar of her school dress.

"They shot them!" Min screams, her feet slapping the dry road, sending tulips of dust blooming around her ankles. "They shot Joseph and Hyrum!"

At the press, Brother Coulter drops his mallet, and it strikes the floor so hard, it tips onto its side, leaving a half-moon of black ink stamped on the planks. My heartbeat starts to climb.

"They're dead!" Minnie stops running in front of the gunsmith's, but she goes on shouting, the horror hanging in the air like a heat haze and thickening with every word. "They're dead in Carthage!"

I'm at the door of the print shop now, almost before I know I've moved, the typeset pages of the Book of Commandments abandoned behind me on the desk.

Eliza, our schoolteacher for as long as I've been in Illinois, comes barreling out from the Lyon Drug Store across the road and seizes Minnie, one hand on her cheek, while the other strokes the wild frizz of Min's collapsing plait from her eyes. Minnie's shoulders shake as she tries to breathe—I can see it even across the road. "Say it slow, now, Minnie," Eliza says, and then Minnie's full-on sobbing, her chest heaving like her ribs are trying to claw their way out of her.

"Joseph's dead," she chokes out. "Hyrum too. They shot them in Carthage. Men with their faces painted black, they broke in and shot them dead on the jailhouse floor."

Behind me, Brother Coulter lets out a short soft cry.

Someone else is screaming from up the street. A man's voice. A woman's heaving sobs from the Scovils' bakery. People are starting to shout to one another over their garden fences. Doors slam. Nauvoo is rippling, the whole city torn up like roots, tumbling the soil as they scratch their way to the surface, with the news that Illinois has been watered with our prophet's blood.

Minnie still can't get her breath, and the words come out in great gulps. "I thought . . . we were . . . safe . . . here. Ain't . . . this . . . Zion?"

Eliza presses Minnie into her, like that'll smother the crying, but the sobs are multiplying up and down the street as the news spreads like fire through dry kindling. "Come with me," Eliza says, her voice a little frayed but strong. She looks up and sees me standing at the print-shop door, both hands pressed to my mouth. "Vilatte," she calls across the street. "Get your ma, then run up and get the ladies together in the Markham parlor." She starts to herd Minnie up the street toward the Markham house, where she rents an attic room, but turns back to me, like she knows I ent yet budged—cold fear is dripping through me like the icy dribble that would spill over the lips of the clams my sisters and I used to shuck back in Liverpool.

"Go, Vilatte," Eliza barks.

I go.

Down from the print shop, around the block, and down Wells Street. I can hear the hammers from the temple grounds, and when I look up to the spire, still wrapped in scaffolding, it sparkles where the sun strikes it. I careen into the guesthouse where my mam and I have been renting a room from the Risers and pull her from the kitchen—she ent heard yet, and I got to be the one to say it.

"I don't know" is how I start. "I don't know if it's true."

When I say it aloud, it near collapses me. Mam's face goes out, as if a refiner's fire has purged her features of anything that ent grief, and what's left is hard and cold and spare. But then I say, "Eliza wants the women." And some of the life comes back to her. She takes my hand, and we stumble onto the street—at the corner, we split, Mam one way down Main and I toward Partridge Street. I fetch Sister Ruby, who comes to Eliza's with a baby hanging from each of her feet. Sister Kimball and Ethel Tremont and the twins from Manchester who I ent yet learned to tell apart. Mary Ives climbs down from the ladder leaned against her house—she's been the deputy husband of her family since Brother Ives lost his leg at Crooked River in Missouri. They all follow me. That's what Eliza Snow's name does—it makes the women come.

By the time I get myself into the front room of the Markham house, they're all crowded inside. The women I sit with at church and in the social hall. The women who smashed their china to mix into the plaster for the temple walls so they would sparkle. Who stand at the dock to wave in the *Maid of Iowa* whenever she chugs up the Mississippi, bringing new saints to our City on a Hill. The women who beckoned me and my mam off that steamship when we arrived, our whole world at our backs, two of my sisters wrapped in sails and buried in the sea between Liverpool and America and my aunt behind us in New Orleans with only a lecture to remember her by.

"You want Vilatte married off when she's ne'er ten?" she had demanded—she'd been baptized alongside us in Liverpool by the American missionaries, but the crossing had sobered her. "The fifth bride to some leery Mormon cove?"

I had only been eight then. I were small, with no mind of my own about God, so when me mam said come, I came. When she said America, I held her skirts and went. And if Mam had married me off to some leery Mormon with a harem of wives, I would have had ne'er a say in that, neither.

"You're a foolish lass to follow the Mormons, Rose," my aunt had told Mam, then looked right at me at her side when she said, "They ent a church made to last."

I weren't old enough to know properly what we were doing then—was still clutching me mam's hems and suckling off her faith—but my auntie's words burrowed in my mind and chewed away like aphids on a rosebush as we made the last limb of our journey up the Mississippi River. I were too small to think we might be a wee bit foolish, to come so far from home for a church. To believe a man had seen God and God had told him to make a church in America. It had seemed like a fairy story the first time I heard it, though my mam always believed it with the sort of conviction saved for things you'd seen with your own two eyes. Even then, at eight years old, it ne'er felt like more than a tale.

But then, from the *Maid of Iowa* steaming up the Mississippi, we saw them waving at us from the pier, the Nauvoo Mormons, total strangers greeting us like friends with their handkerchiefs fluttering as they thrust them high, and I remember thinking if all these people were here because of Joseph, it must be a true church. So many people couldn't uproot their lives for something false.

If only faith were always so easy as white pocket squares in the wind.

I'm fourteen now and a Mormon. Still a maid—no leery husband for me.

Illinois wears its summer differently from Liverpool—all swamp and mosquitoes and air so thick that breathing feels like chewing. It's even hotter in the Markhams' front room than out on the street, and I feel fit to expire as I squeeze my way through the forest of petticoats and hoopskirts to where Mam is sitting on the stairs with Minnie's head in her lap like a child and not a girl of fourteen. I want to put my head there, too, don't want to be fourteen, neither. I want to sit with my mam and cry about our prophet. When we were driven out of Missouri and Ohio and New York, Brother Joseph said, "Courage," and he was the only one who could make us believe it. "God is good, and God will take care of us. God will protect us in our truth," he said, the adage that had carried Mam and me halfway 'round the world, and it had seemed true until this moment, because God did nay protect him.

Everyone is talking. "Gossiping," Mam says under her breath.

Sister Shepherd is telling the red-haired Swedish girl who only arrived last week that they whipped Brother Joseph raw before they shot him. Sister Townsend shrieks that they killed Emma, too, and I start to shudder, thinking of Sister Emma at the head of Benevolent Society meetings, her dark hair pulled back so handsome, the way I want mine to look when I'm older and Mam don't insist on schoolgirl braids and a checked bonnet each day. Minnie starts to wail again. Sister Kimball is wailing, too, sprawled on the floor with her face in her elbows. We've all become islands to ourselves, marooned in our grief.

Molly Kingston is flapping her tongue the loudest, like she always does, as if being nineteen and engaged to Emma's cousin gives her an ear the rest of us don't have. She's got tears down her cheeks, but her face is set and she's going on about when the world is gonna let us be. Where we'll go that we won't be treated like less than humans 'cause we're Mormons and follow the prophet Joseph Smith. We all might be thinking it, but she's the only one saying it.

It was Molly who once said to me at church that I could nay claim myself to know the hardships of being a follower of Joseph Smith because I hadn't been there in Kirtland, when he and Sidney Rigdon got beat bloody in the street, their skin smeared with tar before they were pelted with feathers. Mam and I weren't there in Missouri, when Governor Boggs signed the extermination order, granting the militia leave to drive out the Mormons or shoot them on sight. We weren't there for the massacres, to see our men come home bleeding or not come home at all, our families gunned down by state troops, our shop windows broken and our houses looted and burned, all because we followed Brother Joseph.

I wanted to tell Molly that maybe I hadn't been there—maybe my mam and I hadn't joined up with the Mormons in Fort Des Moines because we'd been too busy surviving the crossing from

Liverpool, too busy spending the year before that trying to convince my da to let us learn from the Latter-Day Saint missionaries, then getting turned out of the house by him when he found out Mam and my auntie had taken my two sisters and me to the river Ribble and let Heber Kimball baptize us. Maybe we hadn't been shot at by militiamen in the streets, but I'd seen my sisters breathe their last, red-faced and burning with scarlet fever, before they were wrapped like caterpillars in silk cocoons and thrown over the side of a ship. I'd watched them sink and we'd sailed on.

We had all suffered for following Joseph Smith, and now him and Hyrum both shot in Carthage. Eliza confirms it—she went to see Brother Brigham and raised a fuss until he gave her an answer.

It's like it ent real until we hear it from Eliza, ent happened when it were just Minnie shouting it on the street. But Eliza's no gossip nor a tale-teller, neither, and hearing it from her mouth feels like putting Joseph in the ground in earnest. I sit down hard on the ground. Mam starts to cry, very quietly.

Everyone wants to cry, but Eliza says we should pray instead. We all fall to our knees together, skirts blooming like daffodil cones around our waists before they settle against the boards. Mam's on one side of me; Minnie sidles up to the other side and puts her head on my shoulder. Eliza, straight across the circle from me, folds her arms and bows her head, same as Heber Kimball taught Mam and I long ago, but she keeps her eyes open when she prays.

She prays for Emma, left behind without her husband, and her babies, especially the baby she's not yet born. She prays for Joseph and Hyrum, that they're now at peace, that they didn't suffer much, that they weren't too afraid. She prays for us in Nauvoo, for the people who will be rearranging the pieces of our church now that our prophet is dead. It's a prayer for survival.

I keep my eyes open, too, staring down at the printer's ink that lines my fingernails and trying to say a prayer of my own, though the only word that seems to come to me is *why*.

Dear God, if this church is true, why don't everyone believe us and let us be? Dear God, why don't I feel you here with us now?

Dear God, why'd you let our prophet die?

I never did know Brother Joseph. Mam and I saw him ride on his big black horse in the parade with the Nauvoo legion, looking smart in his lieutenant general uniform, and sometimes I'd spot him from afar, when he preached sermons in church or pulled sticks with the men on the lawn of the Seventies Hall. The closest I got was when we saw him walking the grounds of the temple site when I were there with Mam delivering water and grits to the workers. The men liked her soda bread, and her easy smile and her freckles, but Mam were the same as Emma—she would nay take a man who had other wives.

But the plural marriage did nay matter enough to stop her believing in the rest of it, Mam said. She believed in what Brother Joseph taught—about God and Jesus and priesthood and eternity. And when we left Liverpool, I had believed she believed it, and believed that someday I might could, too, when I were grown enough, but now, kneeling on the hard floors of the boardinghouse with Eliza praying for all of us, I can't feel it. I feel propped up—on Mam's faith, on Eliza's, on all the women in this room. But all I feel is hollowed out and empty, like someone's scraped their fingernails along the inside of my heart.

And afraid, too—nary a day since we was baptized I ent been afraid. Afraid of the way the woolyback girls in America would sneer at my Scouse accent. Afraid of the stories that Mormons were dying for their faith in Missouri. Afraid I'd wish I'd stayed behind in Liverpool as soon as we reached the American coast. Afraid that we had given up kin and country for a church that might all fall apart now that our prophet was dead. As Eliza prayed, I keep waiting for the spirit of God to punch holes through that fear and let the light in, but I feel dark.

Maybe now that Joseph were ashes, he'd blow away on the wind and the Mormons would go with him.

Maybe by spring, we'd be a ghost town.

The wolf hunts began in October.

Men in Carthage met with shovels and rifles and sawed-off shotguns, and when the town constables asked what they were doing, said they was organizing a hunt for the wolves.

But it weren't wolves they hunted. It were Mormons.

It began with small things — shop windows got broken, phantom gunshots in the night, tar smeared on our windows and front doors while we slept. Men from Warsaw would ride through Nauvoo in tight packs with pistols strapped on and glinting like mirrors when the sunlight struck them.

They were trying to scare us, Eliza tells Mam and me. The night before, we'd gotten a stone thrown through our window while we slept — we'd woken to the crash, both of us in such a dead fright that Mam had herded me under the bed, and we'd lain there all night in our thin cotton nightgowns, shaking and sick and watching the torchlight pass on the street, dead certain the black-faced men would be coming for us next.

"It was just the same in Missouri," Eliza says as the three of us collect glass fragments from our bedroom floor. Me mam and Eliza pick up the big pieces, chunks worth saving, while I trail them with the straw broom, scraping up the sand into a pile along the boards. None of us has touched the rock that broke it.

Eliza steps on a shard, and it snaps under her boot heel like a breaking bone. She shies, then picks up the slivers with the tips of her fingers and lays them upon her palm. "Fear's a potent poison," she says. "And these men know it."

They would use it like a winch to try to worm us out of Illinois, same as they had in New York and Kirtland and Missouri, before Mam and I crossed the ocean. That's what Eliza says. Men were the same everywhere, she tells us. They always start by sowing fear, wanting obedience to spring up like cornstalks in long, neat rows.

I let the sparkling remnants of our window settle around my boots, and don't say that Ohio drove us out, and Missouri ended in a massacre. I don't say that we got nowhere to go from here. We were near off the edge of the map now. If we leave Illinois, there ent a corner of this country left for us to go. Nothing but wilderness ahead, and I weren't sure I had enough faith in me for that. I had already crossed an ocean for a boy prophet that were now dead. How much farther could the coattails of my mother's faith carry me?

Eliza says it's best to go on like nothing spooked us. Like the cracks aren't starting to show, like there aren't Mormon men fighting in the chapel each week about who should step up to fill Brother Joseph's stead. Mam feels the same way—so we go on like nothing were different. We go to church on Sundays. Build our temple on the hill. Tow our weeds and go to the Red Brick store, though I don't see much of Emma Smith there. Her baby were ready to pop out and Brother Brigham were giving her grief, shutting down her Benevolent Society because she says she don't want a husband that takes other wives, and he says that were what God is calling for from us.

We read our Scriptures. We pray. We ignore the torchlight on our windows and the bricks thrown at our houses and go about our lives like we're unshakable, not a temple with the foundation swept out from under us.

Brother Coulter keeps his press churning, and I go three days of the week. My da were a printer back in Liverpool, turning out books that usually weren't suitable for the eyes of his three little girls, but sometimes he'd let me help with the typeset, when it weren't too much of an education for me to be seeing. I'd set the letters in the rack, sentences spelled out backward from the hand-written drafts his authors turned in to him. "Mind those *p*'s and *q*'s, Vi," Da would say, because I mixed them up more than the *b*'s and the *d*'s. I weren't a good reader in school, because I'd been raised on letters back to front. It were Eliza who noticed this in the class-room, and it were Eliza who took me to Brother Coulter and said he might have proper work for me. Then she'd sit with me in the back of the schoolhouse when I needed it, going over letters on the slate and helping me make sense of sentences the right way 'round.

Brother Coulter were happy to have me. He hadn't had an apprentice since they left Missouri, and he didn't care I was a girl because I could spell and knew how to look at letters backward, which is more than most of the boys could do. He also said it were nice I didn't mind getting ink on my hands, so long as my mam didn't come after him for spoiling my skin. But my mam was used to it—she said it reminded her of Da.

At first my job had been to lay out the names of the dead who succumbed to malaria, and sometimes the headlines, while Brother Coulter ran the press, the ink plate clunking up and down as he shucked each sheet and replaced it with a fresh one. Then he were called by the Brethren to be printing the Book of Commandments, Joseph's last revelations, but course we hadn't known it would be the last when we started laying out the type. Now people are clamoring for it like it's a message he's sent us from beyond the grave, instructions on how to keep the church from fracturing like a beam of light through a rippled glass windowpane. Me and Brother Coulter both been laying out the type, long rows of letters the size of my pinkie nail.

It had been chapter 121 I had been spelling out when Min came flying down the street with the news he were shot. Brother Joseph had wrote it when he were in Liberty Jail back in Missouri. Where the Lord told him his suffering would be naught but a small moment if he endured it all. That his friends stood by him—though in the end, not all of them did. Sidney Rigdon and the Prophet hadn't spoken in ages when he died. James Strang were making claims about Joseph that would have felt daft but for the fact that now he weren't here for us to see his face and see the kind truth in him. Who knew what Brigham were about to do, and say it were what the Lord wanted for us. Without Joseph, who knew what God wanted anymore?

It had all seemed black-and-white as typeset back in Liverpool. Mam had been certain we'd found the truth when Heber Kimball read us from the Book of Mormon and told us about priesthood and covenants and the truth of Jesus Christ restored. It were all the things Mam said she'd never heard in the cold halls of the Church of England. And Mam had been lit up over it like the bonfires when they burn the brush fields, and standing in the heat of it had left me tanned and shiny, too, even though I was but a wee thing. You can't stand that close to an oven without coming back polished. But it weren't new now—the shine had begun to rust.

Because if it were true—all of it—why would there be fighting about who would step up now with Joseph dead? Pieces were starting to fall out of alignment, like Joseph had been a finger in a dike and now the water was starting to spill over and flood us.

Perhaps the cracks had been there before he died. Maybe now they're just splintering aloud.

The men of Illinois are hunting us from the outside.

But we are wolves, too. We are tearing up our own pack.

I'm in the print shop, picking letters out of drawers for the one hundred and thirty-second chapter, when I start to smell the smoke.

Not the normal cooking smell, or the way we catch wafts of the forge when the wind changes just right. It were proper fire, like something big and bright burning too hot. Brother Coulter's brow furrows, and he sets down the newly inked sheets he's laying out to dry. "Stay here, Vilatte," he calls to me, and I press myself against the drawers of typeset, my heart thumping even as I'm thinking it must be nothing, and how unfair it is that we're so tormented that everything gets us startled lately. Yesterday Brother Talbot's rifle backfired when he was cleaning it, and Mam pulled me into the house so quick, I nearly left my boots behind.

Brother Coulter crosses the shop and sticks his head out the window, looking up and down the street. I can hear glass shatter down the way. Men shout. Horses scream.

Someone slaps the window at my shoulder, a big, open-fisted hand on glass, and I near jump out of my skin. The letters in my hand fall to the ground with a sound like a sudden gust of rain striking a windowpane.

"Vilatte," Brother Coulter starts, but he's cut off by a scream out on the street, then Heber Kingston goes running by, the hobnails on his boots chattering against the road. "They're coming for you, Ben!" he shouts at Brother Coulter. "They're coming for the Book of Commandments!"

Right on his heels is a group of men with charcoaled faces and kerchiefs pulled up over their mouths, same as the ones who murdered the prophet. One of them pulls his foaming-mouthed horse up next to Heber and clocks him on the shoulder with his rifle. Heber drops like a stone, a long string of saliva from the horse's mouth striping his back.

Brother Coulter whips around, and we both stare at the stack of manuscript pages on the table where I'd been sitting all morning, copying out their lines. We only have some of it printed. Most is still just the handwritten pages, shifting between Emma and Hyrum and sometimes Sidney and the other scribes as they took it down from Joseph's dictation.

The last book of our prophet. The only thing left of him now.

The men charge in — there's only six, but suddenly the shop seems full of them. The tallest ones start grabbing the newly printed pages, still spicy with the smell of ink, drying on lines above their heads, and crumple them up. They overturn the press, sending paper fanning like a spreading swan's wing. The letters scatter, Brother Joseph's words jumbled into nothing. One of the men smashes his boot into them, cracking the chapter heading under his heel. Another slaps Brother Coulter across the face with the butt of his rifle. Blood sprays against the Scripture pages still hanging up to dry.

I'm not certain they've seen me yet, all pressed between the bureaus full of type. They ent seen the Book of Commandments manuscript, neither — they're fixated on the printed pages and the drama of ripping them down.

I wonder for half a moment if they'll shoot me. If saving the book would be worth it. All things die in their time and maybe there's no saving our church.

But I remember the cold shock of the water up to my waist

when I followed Heber Kimball into the river Ribble to be baptized.

I dart out from between the racks and throw myself at the desk, grabbing the muslin the pages are stacked upon and bundling them against my chest. The men are crowded around the front door, so I spring for the back, throwing my shoulder into the door to the back room with a strength that feels like it might tear it from its hinges. It opens with a crack, and I go tumbling forward, nearly tripping over my own boot laces.

"Hey!" one of the men shouts, and I feel a whistle against the back of my neck as he grabs for me, but he misses. I slam the office door behind me, though it'll hardly slow them down.

I'm out the back door, my skirts caving around my legs, and I start to tear through the scrub behind the print shop and toward the road. I hear the door slap the side of the shop as the men race after me.

Main Street is a chaos of horses and more black-faced men. They've dragged women into the road by their petticoats so their houses can be burned and tossed men into the gutters so they can step on their noses and break their fingers. The streets are muddy, though it ent water that's tamped down the dust. The city is thick with noise and soot and smoke, and I feel like I'm choking on every gasping, burning breath I take.

I hope I might lose the men in all the mess, but they're shouting after me, telling their fellows to stop the girl with the muslin-wrapped pages. One of them snatches at me from the top of his horse, but Sister Kimball steps into his path and he grabs her instead. When he tries to shake her off, she clings to his arm, trying to drag him from his horse though he must be twice her size, and stays strapped to him like a millstone. "Run, Vilatte!" she shouts, and I go whipping down Main Street, my lungs screaming.

I sprint until the road runs out beneath my feet and I'm clawing my way through the ditches that run between the cooperative fields. Dry cornstalks taller than me surround me on all sides, stripped of their ears but not yet torn up for the winter. The autumn wind, peppered with the spray from the choppy banks of the Mississippi River and kicking up mud from the marshes, spits at my face.

The stalks rip at me as I tear through them, so loud it feels like they're shouting about where I am. The men must still be chasing me, ready to kill a girl of fourteen for the words of a prophet who was her same age when he first saw God. Shoving through the corn feels like shoving through a crowd of thick-armed men, and it's slow and I'm getting tired and I can smell Nauvoo burning behind me. I can hear the broken glass, the mob sounds, the ruckus of a people driven from their home again, again, *again*.

I roll my ankle on a lump in the soil and crash to the ground, the pages bundled against me breaking my fall, though I still land hard enough that an *oof* escapes my lips. As soon as I'm still, I can hear the stalks behind me crashing as the men give chase. They're raising birds from the corn, crows cawing angrily as they tear into the sky.

I shove the pages under me and lay on my back, shivering with fear. Above me, the corn silk whispers in the wind.

I ent good at praying. Sometimes I don't listen when we say the benediction in our sacrament meetings, and I keep my eyes open and can't make myself believe the words are going all the way up to God himself, or that he's listening, or even caring. But in that moment, it feels like all I have—I can either be alone with a mob on my heels, or I can be alone with God.

Please, God, protect me, I pray—but he didn't protect Joseph Smith in Carthage. He didn't save the prophet, so why should he care for a girl in a cornfield, alone? It's a sour thought—it cankers inside me, wraps around my prayer like climbing ivy and chokes it.

I pray anyway.

After a time, I can't hear the men anymore, but that don't mean they aren't waiting. Feels like I been lying on my back for hours, breathing like drowning. The sky turns gunmetal gray with thick smoke. When he baptized us, Brother Kimball never said we'd be hated and cursed at and spit at and driven out of everywhere we lived. Though I think Mam would have gone with him anyway. Not sure if I would have.

I hear the corn start to crack again as someone tramps toward me. I scramble up, sitting on the pages, knees pulled up to my chest. *Just a small moment,* I think, and I try to be brave. I try to convince myself my faith is worth dying for, but I just ent sure it is.

Then I hear someone calling my name.

"Vilatte! VILATTE!"

"I'm here!" I scream back, because I know that voice, and a few minutes later, Eliza comes trudging through the cornstalks, parting them like a curtain on a stage. She has corn silk in her hair, scratches on her face from the dry leaves, dirt on the elbows and knees of her cotton dress, as if she fell and picked herself back up. She stops and she looks at me—sitting on the Book of Commandments.

"I'm here," I say quietly.

Eliza doesn't say anything right away. She comes and sits beside me in the dirt, and I worm the manuscript out from under me and hold it out to her. She don't take it.

"I don't know if this is true," I say.

She looks up at me. "What's true?"

"This church." It's the first time I've said it aloud to anyone.

"What makes you think it isn't true?"

"Because Joseph's dead. And everyone's fighting and men are trying to kill us and if it were right—if it were really right— wouldn't everyone else want the truth, too? Maybe we really are outlaws."

I think Eliza will give a good answer, the way she did at school when the boys would try to be cheeky and she'd shut them up with a few words in her quiet, intense teacher voice. But instead all she says is, "I don't know, Vilatte."

"Maybe none of it's true," I say. I'm crying without even realizing it, and I take a swipe at my cheek with the back of my hand. "Maybe none of it."

Eliza rips a fistful of corn silk off a stalk. "Maybe not."

"Maybe we're running and dying and suffering for things that ent true."

"Maybe."

"You're saying all the wrong things!"

She looks up at me. "What do you want me to say, Vilatte?"

"You're my teacher! Be a teacher! Tell me the right answer. Tell me I need to believe and be strong and it's real and doubt is of the devil and tell me to believe. Tell me my sisters didn't die for nothing and we didn't leave Da and Liverpool for nothing and tell me this is worth it."

"Will it help if I say all that?"

I snuffle, then rub a train of snot off with my sleeve. "Maybe. I don't know."

Eliza presses one hand flat against her lips. Her nails are worn down and dull, cracked from rubbing up against slate and permanently dry with the chalk from the schoolhouse. "You want me to tell you what I think, Vilatte?" she asks, and I nod. "I think I believe in God, and I believe God is good, and I believe Joseph was a prophet, but I believe he was a human, too. We're all of us human. You and me and Joseph and the men who are burning our city and the men who are trying to lead it. And at the end of life, I don't know what's going to turn out to be the true thing, or which church will be the right one. But I don't think it really matters."

"Then what does?" I ask.

"Finding things that give you hope, and make you want to do good things for others. And if Joseph's words do that"—she pats the Book of Commandments manuscript—"then that seems fine to me. Seems like a thing that people could need."

"What about those mobs? Why can't they just let us be?"

"I got no answer for you, Vilatte. I really don't. Don't know why some men make it their business to police what others believe."

"We should fight them."

"Didn't get us anywhere in Missouri. Just got more of our men dead."

I hang my head. Eliza sidles up to me and wraps an arm around my shoulder, and I let myself fall into her, my head against her chest so that I can hear her heartbeat through the thin cotton of her school dress. Above us, the sky burns, speckled tufts of smoke still drifting from Nauvoo.

"There are far, far better things ahead, Vilatte," she says, "than any that are behind us."

We abandon Nauvoo in February.

Everything Mam and I own is wrapped and stowed and hauled into the ferries that harbor us across the river. It all fits in two trunks. They put the oxen on the rafts with us as we ride the frigid current like corks, chunks of ice speckled with starlight floating around us so they look shot with gold like we're Argonauts afloat. The punters have to break the ice in some places, their long poles as graceful and steady as pistons.

I stand with Mam at the ferry's lip, and we watch the temple get smaller and smaller, the white walls flecked and shining with our shards of smashed china, brighter than the moon. It somehow stays a shining white, even when the fire starts to close its fist around the spire, punching through the windows and tumbling the roof.

"Go west," Brother Brigham said, so we're going west.

Emma isn't coming. Nor Sidney Rigdon, nor the Templetons or the Coulters. Some of the Kimballs are going back to Missouri. The Kingstons to New York. The last thing I heard Mol say was how much she wishes she'd never left home. Never taken up with the Mormons. We're all splitting up, drifting like chunks of ice on the Mississippi's current.

At our backs, the temple burns. At our head, the West waits. Open, wide prairie. Who knows what else.

We'll all be strangers there.

⊠ AUTHOR'S NOTE ⊠

Mormons trace their origins to a vision by their prophet Joseph Smith, in which an angel directed him to a buried book containing the religious history of an ancient people. Smith published a translation of this book as the Book of Mormon. As his followers grew, the Mormons looked for a place to set up a community of their own. They moved to and were then forcibly and often violently driven out of Kirtland, Ohio, and Jackson County, Missouri (where the governor passed an extermination order against the Mormons). Desperate for somewhere to live and worship without the fear of mob violence, the Mormons settled in Nauvoo, Illinois, in 1839.

On June 27, 1844, Joseph Smith and his brother Hyrum were murdered in prison in Carthage, Illinois. Their deaths caused a succession crisis within the Mormon Church, as well as much internal strife and division, and the weakness was taken advantage of by many anti-Mormon aggravators in the area. The Mormons were yet again driven from their city by violence, and they left Nauvoo to make the perilous trek west for the largely uninhabited Utah Territory.

Today, outside of the Mormon Church, the persecution suffered by the early members is largely unknown. Though the events in this story are fictional, the circumstances and historical context are not, and many of the characters, including Eliza Snow, were real people.

❧ 1858: Colorado River, New Mexico Territory ❧

THE MAGICIAN

ERIN BOWMAN

H ey, Rat, you got a player!" Joe called.

Ray looked up from her meal to see a mousy-haired Yankee standing beside Joe, thumbs hooked in his pockets. Moored just behind them, the *General Jesup* swayed as muddy water lapped against her hull.

Ray was not a man, nor was she a rat, but she'd arrived in Yuma Crossing around the age of eight, scavenging the shores with a mop of matted hair slung over her bony shoulders, and the name had stuck. So had the assumption that she was a boy. She'd been scrawny as a fence post then, and twice as dirty. It was easy to overlook the truth.

Now that she was fifteen or thereabouts, Ray's body was betraying her. She kept her hair short and her clothing baggy, but she'd begun wrapping her chest. The smooth state of her jaw would grow suspicious soon, too, but Ray would keep up the act as long as possible. She'd seen how women stuck out in these parts. They were full of curves and garnered attention, and they certainly didn't work as stevedores, loading and unloading steamboats' freight.

Ray set aside her can of sardines, brushed some corn bread crumbs from her lap, and signaled the Yankee. "Five hands. That's all I got time for."

Joe shouted for his buddies, and Carlos and the Bartlett twins came running to watch. Joe was the leader of the bunch, and everything Ray wanted to be as a stevedore—bigger, stronger, faster. He was charming and well-liked, too. A natural leader. He threw a friendly punch into Carlos's arm—as brown as her own—and began to debate the margin of Ray's inevitable win.

Her reputation as an unbeatable poker player had spread along the shores of the Colorado the past year, and while most of her fellow stevedores now hesitated to play her, they took pleasure in watching her whip others. Ray made it worth their while, shuffling with flair, cutting the deck one-handed, and dealing with such precision that the cards looked like blades slicing through the air. Watching Ray play was like listening to a concerto, a continued swelling of flourishes and concentration, until her opponent's mouth fell open in shocked loss come the finale.

Ray blocked out the boys' rowdy predictions and sized up the Yankee. Average build, forgettable face. His clothing wasn't threadbare enough for a copper miner, so she figured he was the owner of one of the woodyards that supplied steamers with fuel along the river. His business in Yuma Crossing didn't concern her nearly as much as his willingness to lose coins.

The man sat on the opposite side of the crate that would serve as their playing table, and Ray drew the deck she always carried from her back pocket. Pinching the stack of cards, she let them spring into her other hand, facedown. They made a satisfying, muted *thwiiiiick* as they flew through the air.

"I heard you're good," the Yankee said, watching the cards dance. "*Too* good."

If she was too good, perhaps men should stop challenging her, but it was as if the more a loss might damage their egos, the more intensely they were drawn to her table. Like moths to a flame.

"I'm all right," Ray said with a shrug.

"Then you won't mind if we use a fresh deck, I reckon?" He set a pack on the crate.

"Not at all." Ray pocketed her deck, then slit the tape on the new one. She let the cards fall into her palm and sent them springing from hand to hand, just as gracefully as with her own set.

Behind her, the boys cackled.

Ray made a few artful shuffles. Then she let the Yankee cut the deck for good measure and began the game before he could get cold feet.

Ray took the first hand easily, then let the Yankee win the next three. This was the key: to lose a small sum before winning big; to fan a man's confidence so he believed himself unbeatable.

Ray dealt the final hand. Bets were made and raised, cards traded.

"Check," she said, tapping the crate with her knuckle.

The Yankee squinted at his cards, then pushed a dollar forward. A week's pay in one bet. Combined with the rest of the pot, Ray would win back all she'd lost and then some. Her heart beat with excitement, but she made sure to keep her face as plain and emotionless as the *General Jesup*'s faded freeboard.

"What the heck," she said, feigning rashness. "I'll see ya." She counted out the coins.

"Sorry, kid." The Yankee threw down his cards, and Ray savored it a moment—his glibness and pride. Then she spread out her winning hand. Joe whistled, and Carlos slapped a knee. The Yankee swore flagrantly.

"Double or nothing," he said.

But someone was shouting from the shore. "Rat! Johnson wants a word."

Ray leaped to her feet and scooped up her winnings. When the owner of the George A. Johnson & Company requested your presence, you obliged. Besides, men could be dangerous when they'd been beaten, and Ray wasn't particularly keen on lingering around the Yankee longer than necessary.

"But I had a full house!" he went on grousing. "How'd ya beat me?"

"Just lucky, I guess."

The truth was that Ray had stacked the deck in her favor. She'd known the face value of the next dozen cards to be dealt, plus each one that had been in her opponent's hand, to boot. Some would call it cheating, but Ray figured it was only cheating if you got yourself caught. Until then, it was merely skill and sleight of hand, theatrics and misdirection.

Ray wasn't a cheat. She was a magician.

Mr. Johnson's office was little more than a hole in the wall—a tiny shanty along the edge of the river, where a string of similar shacks had been erected by the Company for storage and other business affairs. He'd done his best to make it presentable, but the once-vibrant rug on the floor was now caked with mud, and the whole place smelled musty. All the furniture was stained with water lines from a spring when the river rose beyond its banks.

"Ah, Ray," Mr. Johnson said, spotting her in the doorway. "Come in, come in."

She lowered herself into the chair opposite his desk.

"I'm assembling men for an expedition," he said, getting right to the point. "Escalating tensions with the Mormons have forced the War Department's hand, and they need to know if bringing troops into Utah by way of the Colorado is possible. Fort Yuma has ordered a detachment to accompany me for a speedy assessment of the upper river. We'll take the *General Jesup* and have twenty-five days' rations, plus a howitzer. I'm working to secure additional men now. If you're in agreement, we leave tomorrow at dawn."

Ray worked to keep the surprise from her face. Embarking on the eve of the New Year was downright foolish. The river would be low, starved from the summer heat. Sandbars would choke the passage. Ray did not take Johnson for an idiot, but Utah was more than five hundred winding miles of river north, and little more than three weeks' provisions did not seem sufficient, even for a steamer as impressive as the *General Jesup*. Besides, Ray had heard of a similar expedition, also departing on New Year's Eve.

Joe had mentioned it one mild November morning as they moved freight. "Expedition was Johnson's idea—he pushed the legislature and everything—but the Secretary of War appointed his in-law for the job."

"Lieutenant Ives," Carlos had chimed in. "His steamer is only fifty-four feet long. They tested her on the Delaware and are reassembling her out here, thinking she'll be strong enough for the Colorado."

"I heard she draws three feet of water," Joe scoffed, "leaving barely six inches of freeboard when she's loaded. Yeah, you heard me right—just *six inches* between the waterline and the deck. It's absurd!"

"Sounds like a damn wheelbarrow." Ray had laughed. "Thing's gonna sputter and struggle up every inch of the river."

Now, sitting in Johnson's office, she wondered if her boss was just as miffed that Ives's ridiculous-sounding expedition had garnered the full support of the War Department, and if his own quest to navigate the Colorado was little more than a schoolboy's battle of who could accomplish the feat first. But this was an expedition, not some steamboat race on the Mississippi. If it wasn't approached seriously, Ray wanted nothing to do with it. Hell, she didn't have the time to be involved, period. Every day she spent on that steamer was a day she wouldn't be earning coin in Yuma Crossing. And that was all that mattered these days: coin from work, and coin from cards. A ticket to San Francisco wasn't going to buy itself.

"I'll pay, of course," Mr. Johnson continued. "Fifty dollars, supplied in full as soon as we return to Fort Yuma, whether the river proves navigable or not."

Ray nearly fell from her seat. With an additional fifty dollars, she could finally leave Yuma Crossing. No more saving dime by dime. No more handing a small portion of her meager earnings to Mr. Lowry every week.

But what Mr. Johnson proposed would be no easy mission. For years, Johnson had been yammering about opening trade with the Mormons, but Ray had figured all his talk to be hot air. Above the fort, rapids made it impossible for pole skiffs to battle the currents, and sand beds and shoals on a constantly shifting riverbed had kept men like Johnson from attempting a journey even by powerful steamboat. Until now.

"Why me?" Ray asked, suddenly suspicious. "We ain't moving freight, and that's all I do for you here."

"You've worked hard for the Company, proven yourself reliable.

Without woodyards to the north, I need men to gather fuel twice daily. The boiler will need to be cleaned, provisions loaded and moved. You'll keep busy."

Ray considered Mr. Johnson. He was a serious man with a serious mustache, and he had a monopoly of business along the river. It was his steamers that brought goods from the estuary to every river settlement, and his steamers that carried ore from the mining establishments back down to Robinson's Landing to be smelted. He was a proven businessman, and if he was financing this exploration out of his own pocket, he must know what he was doing.

It wasn't a riskless wager. Steamers could run aground and sink. Boilers could explode, burning and killing crew. But the money was too good to walk away.

Ray reached out and shook Mr. Johnson's hand.

"Are you mad?" Mrs. Lowry erupted. "Three weeks on the cramped deck of a steamboat, pretending to be a boy? You'll be found out, Ray."

"You worry too much."

"And you worry too little. I'm amazed you've kept up the ruse this long."

"You're the one who encouraged it!"

Mrs. Lowry let her hands fall from her knitting. "I was trying to help you, Ray. Same as I am now. The expedition ain't worth the risk."

Ray had foreseen this argument. While walking home after work, she'd considered keeping news of the trip to herself. But then she'd pushed open the door, looked Mrs. Lowry in the eye, and the truth had come tumbling out.

Mrs. Lowry was a mess cook at Fort Yuma. Seven years earlier, she'd found Ray picking through garbage outside the kitchen, with nothing but the rags on her back and a newspaper clipping clutched in her fist. The woman had ushered Ray inside and given her a bath, surprised to find a girl beneath all the grime. "You go on letting them think you're a boy," she'd said. "Those girl bits will be our secret. Think you can pretend all right?"

Ray had not been pretending—she'd merely been trying to survive—but if being a boy could make life easier . . . Well, that sounded like magic. Ray had smiled and told Mrs. Lowry she could pretend just fine.

She swept floors and washed dishes in the fort kitchen until Mrs. Lowry's husband said Ray's help wasn't enough to offset the inconvenience of housing a child who was not theirs. Then Ray began her work as a stevedore, handing over a portion of her earnings to Mr. Lowry to cover that "inconvenience." Mrs. Lowry had since left her husband, taking Ray with her, but Mr. Lowry still knew Ray's secrets, and she still paid him a cut of her wages to guarantee his silence. If he spoke to the wrong person, Ray could lose her job or, at best, see a drastic change in her wages. Women in Yuma Crossing made less than the men, and there weren't many jobs available to begin with. Mrs. Lowry already had one of the better ones, working at the fort, and unless they were someone's wife or a painted dove at the brothels, most women in Yuma Crossing were only passing through.

"This is about San Francisco again. Isn't it?" Mrs. Lowry prodded.

Truth be told, it was always about San Francisco.

It all came back to that newspaper clipping Ray had been clutching when Mrs. Lowry found her. "Inexhaustible Gold Mines in California," the headline announced, followed by claims of an abundance of gold dust, lumps, and nuggets in the area. A brief handwritten note was scrawled in the margins:

*Ray, remember when we saw that magician performing in
New York and every card he pulled from the deck was an ace?
This will be like that, only we'll be pulling nugget after gold
nugget from our pans. Meet us in San Francisco. —LBM*

Ray hadn't been able to read or write when Mrs. Lowry took
her in, so the woman had read the message to her. Despite the
fact that Ray couldn't remember any family, she was immediately
convinced the note was from her parents. As far back as she had
memories, she'd been scavenging along the shores of the Colorado,
but perhaps before that, they'd been separated while seeking out
gold, Ray left behind in a tragic accident.

"I don't think it's addressed to you," Mrs. Lowry was always
reminding her. "I call you Ray 'cause you treasured that clipping,
that's all. It don't mean nothing."

But to Ray it meant everything. She had to believe that there
was more out there for her, that she had family waiting. That if
she went to San Francisco, she would find them. But Mrs. Lowry
maintained that Ray had been roaming the river long before the
Yankee argonauts descended on the southern trail like locusts,
and that it was far more likely Ray was a Sonoran—a Mexican,
orphaned by the war with the Americans—and that she was looking for family in places she would never find it.

Ray could see the logic in Mrs. Lowry's theory, and yet she was
unable to fully accept it. If her newspaper clipping was only a piece
of paper—something she'd happened upon as a child and picked
up by chance—what future did she have? Yuma Crossing wasn't
her home. It was a festering hellhole of insufferable heat, no better
than living on the devil's doorstep. It was just a place she was stuck.

"I'm begging you to reconsider," Mrs. Lowry said, regarding Ray sadly. "Passing as a boy for the whole expedition will be

impossible, and you make fair money working for Johnson right here. Do not gamble it away."

"I ain't gambling and I'm not gonna lose," Ray snapped. Mrs. Lowry gave her an all-knowing look, and Ray's patience sizzled. "Mark my words, I'm gonna disappear one of these days. I'm gonna vanish like magic!"

"Wouldn't that be nice," Mrs. Lowry deadpanned, "to not have to live by the rules of reality." Her tone was cheerful, but her expression sour. Ray couldn't figure if Mrs. Lowry was sad that Ray believed in such wishful thinking or disappointed that she, herself, could not.

Magic *was* real, Ray had learned. It could inspire. It could trick. It could save. It provided an escape from the dark, grueling, unfair nature of the world.

The catch was that magic demanded respect. Without believing in it, magic would get you nowhere.

So Ray had practiced and perfected and practiced more, until she trusted her fingers and felt magic flowing in her veins. *That* was when she started conning at cards. And now she'd pull one last con aboard the *General Jesup,* and then she'd disappear forever.

Ray and Mrs. Lowry ate stewed oysters, the cracking shells filling the silence between them.

"It ain't you," Ray said finally, unable to stand the quiet a moment longer. "This is just something I gotta do for myself. I gotta try to find my family, or I'll be spending my whole life wondering if maybe they're waiting for me, too. You get that, don't you, Mrs. Lowry?"

The woman patted her mouth with a napkin. "Of course, dear. And you can call me 'Ma,' you know."

It was not the first time Mrs. Lowry had suggested this. Ray was grateful for all the woman had done, and sometimes she truly did think of her as a mother, but Ray couldn't bring herself to say the word. How cruel would it be to Mrs. Lowry when Ray only planned to disappear? Still, there was a part of Ray that also worried it was cruel to withhold it.

It had been an insufferable July afternoon when Mrs. Lowry chose Ray over her husband. Ray had been in the kitchen, scrubbing burnt beans from the bottom of a cast-iron pot.

"'Course you don't care about giving me a son!" Mr. Lowry had yelled from the mess. "You got that pet rat to fawn over."

Ray froze, standing still as a statue. The couple argued so often over children that Ray was starting to suspect Mrs. Lowry was barren.

"Don't talk about Ray that way," Mrs. Lowry had countered.

"She ain't our kid. She's a bit of filth using us. Turn her out."

"No."

"Turn her out or so help me—"

"So help you what? You'll leave? Abandon us? Frankly, that might be a blessing!"

Skin struck skin, and Ray's eyes went wide. She was used to their arguments. They happened nearly every time Mr. Lowry lingered in the mess after a meal to discuss something with his wife. But he had never struck her.

"Get out," Mrs. Lowry said, so low Ray had to strain to hear.

"If I go, I ain't coming back," he threatened.

"Good! We don't need you. Go!"

A door slammed so hard, a stack of dirty dishes rattled. For a moment, the mess was eerily quiet. Then came Mrs. Lowry's crying.

That was the day they'd left to create their own home on the opposite side of the river. It was also the first day Mrs. Lowry had asked Ray to call her "Ma." Every day since, she'd failed to. Every week since, she'd given that horrible man a half-dollar for his silence and cooperation.

Now Ray dunked her sourdough bread in her tea and pulled her gaze up to meet Mrs. Lowry's. She was opposite Ray in almost every way: fair hair to dark, pale skin to brown, curves and plumpness to wiry muscle.

"It's just that I don't belong here," Ray said. "I ain't like the Yankees, but I ain't like the Sonorans, neither. I don't fit with the boys at the Company, not truly, but I also don't fit with girls. I don't fit in nowhere, and I gotta go somewhere I might."

"You fit here with me," the woman said softly.

Ray fit with Mrs. Lowry fine in this house, where there were no secrets and Ray could be herself without fear of consequence. But not in public, not if she wanted a life beyond these walls, and passing as a boy wouldn't be possible forever. What would she do when the ruse was up? What future did she have? The beds of civilization shifted in favor of men. Ray could be swept in the direction of their choosing or try to carve her own course. And by God, Ray was going to try.

Come dawn, Ray stood before the banks of the Colorado, a small bag of supplies slung over her shoulder.

The *General Jesup* was a beauty of a steamboat, capable of carrying fifty tons of freight on just thirty inches of water and making the trip from estuary to fort in a lightning-quick five days. Granted, she was nothing like the grandiose steamers that navigated the Mississippi back east. The *General Jesup* had only one deck. She was greatly exposed to the elements, little more glamorous than a flatboat. But even still, Ray felt pride looking at the side-wheeled steamer. It was no easy feat to navigate the

Colorado, and the *General Jesup* had proved her mettle countless times over. Now it was a question of if she could prove it heading north.

"You too, Rat?" a voice said.

She turned to see Joe approaching, a Colt holstered on his hip. Carlos and the Bartlett twins hurried after him, each sporting their own pieces. Mr. Johnson had said to come armed, and Ray suddenly felt foolish for the lone knife in her boot. She should have asked Joe for advice. From the day she started working for the Company, he'd always been willing to give it.

"Me too," she said.

"I didn't think rats liked water," Carlos teased.

"You forget I ain't actually a rat."

"That ain't been proven," he said, and scurried aboard the steamer, the Bartlett twins sniggering at his heels.

"Just get up there quick," Joe said, pointing at the deck, "and make 'em eat their words." Then he winked at her before following the others.

He'd been winking like that since the day they met.

She'd been eleven. Her previous employer had left the river, and Mr. Johnson had agreed to take Ray on despite the fact that much of the freight was still beyond her strength.

"You gotta lift with your legs," Joe had called to her as she struggled with a crate. He looked about fourteen or fifteen and was lean like Ray, but clearly stronger. He squatted to retrieve his own crate and stood with such seemingly little effort, Ray wondered if the case was full of feathers, not flour.

"Thanks," she'd muttered, too shy to admit she'd been given this advice ages ago and always tried to apply it.

He winked reassuringly. "No problem, Rat."

"It's Ray," she'd corrected.

His brows pitched up. Probably he'd already heard another stevedore use the nickname. "Well, just holler if you need help."

"Who do I holler for?"

"You call for me. I'm saying I'll lend you a hand."

"Yeah, I got that. I meant, what's your name?"

"Joe," he'd said, smiling brashly. "I'm Joe Henry."

How nice, she'd thought, to have two first names when she barely had the one.

Later he'd shown her a variety of tricks for surviving as a stevedore, plus introduced her to Carlos, who had skin as brown as Ray's. By the end of the day, she felt like one of the boys.

They went on calling her Rat, but Ray had decided years ago that it was a small price to pay to feel like she belonged. Besides, Joe made it all bearable. He would never imply that she actually *was* a rat, like the other stevedores sometimes did. To him, it was just a name, and that wink had become a silent encouragement, a secret handshake. *I got your back,* it said. She was lucky to have a friend like Joe Henry.

Ray squared her shoulders to the *General Jesup* and hurried aboard.

Fifteen soldiers from Fort Yuma and nearly as many civilians crowded the deck. Mr. Johnson shouted orders, anxious to set out. The boiler was loaded. Pistons fired and smoke belched from the stack. As paddles turned, muddying the Colorado, the *General Jesup* departed—not to the south, as she typically did, but to the north.

Next time Ray set foot on a boat, it would be bound for San Francisco.

She stood at the stern and watched Fort Yuma grow smaller.

✕ ✕ ✕

Besides the narrow canyon that the *General Jesup* passed through a few days after departing, the river above the fort was not all that different from the river below. It roamed and meandered through lengthy valleys, flanked by shores of mesquite and cottonwoods. Rancherías were visible on occasion; corn, bean, and melon patches peppering the banks. The rapids Mr. Johnson initially feared seemed all but nonexistent to Ray. Droves of sandbars proved just as dangerous, making navigation slow and tedious.

Besides a few of her fellow stevedores, Ray didn't know most of the men who'd signed on for the expedition, but she quickly decided the soldiers were as good as useless. They spent their days lounging on the deck, believing their responsibilities limited to security and defense only, and so Ray often found herself at the bow with Joe and Carlos, shouting out warnings of shoals as they appeared upriver. An old civilian named Paulino Weaver joined them on occasion. He knew the river from his days as a trapper, and only a Yuma chief the Yankees called Pascual seemed to know the land better. Paulino had a broad smile and spoke to Ray like she was an adult, not a child of fifteen, and she was quick to decide that she liked him quite much.

Still, Ray found herself longing for home. Even smack in the middle of a noisy stretch of establishments, neighbored by a saloon on one side and a butcher on the other, Mrs. Lowry's place had offered privacy. It had been Ray's escape from reality, the only place where she didn't have to pretend, and she hated to admit that Mrs. Lowry had been right. It was damn near impossible to keep up her con aboard the *General Jesup*.

Ray's only reprieve came twice a day—around noon and then again in the evening—when Mr. Johnson ordered the steamer moored so the crew could gather fuel. It was brutal, backbreaking work, and Ray was grateful for her thick work gloves, which protected her hands from vicious mesquite thorns and prickers. But she could relieve herself without fear, and she could think clearly in those quiet moments of solitude.

Each evening, after wood had been gathered and dinner eaten, Ray felt sharp and springy, reenergized. As bedrolls were rolled out, she'd draw her cards and put on a show of dramatic shuffles and passes. Drawn by her flair, the soldiers would wander into a game, and tempted by the pot, they'd stay. Some nights, even Joe and the stevedores would join in, perhaps out of boredom. The expedition was getting rather tedious, and the money they were slated to earn from it made a game or two against Ray worth the risk.

Regardless of her opponents, Ray always made sure to lose occasionally, but for the most part, her pockets grew heavy with winnings.

About two weeks into their journey, the *General Jesup* entered its second canyon and spent the evening moored in shadowy waters. Men stretched out in bedrolls took up most of the deck, so poker was played on land. Joe, Carlos, the Bartlett twins, Weaver, and Ray were deep in a game on the rocky shoreline, and Ray was consistently losing hands she expected to win. Joe was on such a hot streak that by the time Weaver and the twins retired for bed, Ray was nearly broke.

"You been doing awfully good tonight," she said.

"Luck," Joe replied. "Same as you on your winning streaks, I reckon."

He winked, but Ray wasn't buying it. Joe was never *this* lucky. He tried to throw players off with his theatrical expressions but always overcompensated. Any smile meant his hand was worthless. A deep frown meant his cards were solid, if not great. He was easy to read, and Ray had never lost to him unintentionally. At least not before tonight.

Carlos folded and Ray regarded her hand.

"I'm telling ya, you should fold," Joe warned. A rolled cigarette bobbed between his teeth as he gave her a dimpled smile.

It was his deal and the lantern did little to brighten their playing area, let alone make it easy for Ray to count cards. She had only the slightest guess at where the face cards sat within the deck, but her hand was too good to quit. With another king or jack, she'd have a full house. Without it, she still had a two-pair—two jacks and two kings. She met Joe's wager.

He replaced the single card she slid forward for a trade, then traded two of his own. As he dealt out their replacements, Ray caught it—how Joe drew the first card from the top of the deck but skimmed a second off the bottom. It was not a smooth sleight, nothing like how Ray could pad and stack the deck without a fumble. But in the dim lighting, with the canyon walls towering around them and Ray shrugging low inside her jacket to ward off the cold, her guard had been down.

Her hand flew out, closing over Joe's wrist. "What the hell are you doing?"

The cigarette sagged as his gaze dipped to where her dark fingers had closed over his flannel.

"I told you, Joe," Carlos muttered. "I told you you were gonna get caught. Rat's too good not to spot somebody chiseling."

"He's too good, period," Joe shot back, his eyes never leaving Ray's.

He suspected her of cheating, too. Her pulse beat wildly between her ribs. Joe held his chin high, but he always oozed confidence. The truth was in his eyes, crinkled at the corners, tense with fear. He didn't want to be revealed as a cheat any more than she did. Bad things happened to cheats—things involving fists and bullets. And they didn't know half the expedition crew. There was no way of guessing how they might react.

"How about you just surrender the pot, and we'll call it a night," she said slowly. "I won't tell the crew you been cheating, and you'll still be able to play the rest of the journey, maybe win back what I'm taking here."

"Sounds like a fair deal, Rat." He pried her fingers from his wrist. Then he leaned across the cards and coins, so close that his nose nearly touched hers. "You keep my secret," he whispered, "and I'll keep yours."

He stalked toward the steamer with Carlos, and Ray shook out her hand, flexing her fingers. She sat there on the cold rocks, shuffling the deck until her breathing steadied.

The deck of the *General Jesup* had never seemed so crowded. Joe now constantly sought Ray out to discuss the art of padding a deck or counting cards or manipulating a shuffle, and the steamer seemed to grow smaller each day.

To avoid having to relieve herself often, she drank and ate little while on the river. The weak winter sun and mild temperatures were a blessing, yet she still battled dizziness from dehydration. When the captain called for fuel, Ray went farther to gather it, relieving herself only when she felt she was truly alone. On the rare occasion that she needed to see to her business aboard the *General Jesup*, she'd take the chamber pot and disappear behind the howitzer and freight, going as fast as possible and then dumping the contents into the river just as quick, lest Joe show up in time to question why she refused to piss while standing on the lip of the steamer like a normal fellow.

On the evenings that the crew had time for cards, she refrained from dramatic shuffles or sleight of hand. Part of her wished to quit playing altogether, but that would only look more suspicious, so she settled for taking in smaller pots. All the while, Joe watched her fingers dealing and shuffling and cutting the deck. He was only looking for proof that she cheated, too, to improve his own lackluster skills, but Ray began to worry. What if he uncovered her other secret? How would the crew feel to have been cheated by a girl? How would Mr. Johnson react to learning he'd been deceived all those years?

Ray could be tossed aside, left on the banks to starve, or worse.

She shook the thought aside. Those fears might be justified if any other member of the crew discovered her secret—Carlos or the twins or one of the soldiers—but she could trust Joe. He didn't make jokes about her nickname, after all, or treat her like a rat. And for her first two years with the Company, Joe had made sure to handle her heaviest freight so she didn't appear to be falling behind.

Her thoughts drifted back to the first day they met. Ray had skipped home from the river to tell Mrs. Lowry all about her new friends, but instead of being pleased for her, the woman had put down her knitting to give Ray a stern glance.

"Joe Henry pesters the Richardson girls to no end," she'd warned. "Be wary of him, Ray, you hear me? He don't take no one's feelings to heart but his own."

At the time, Ray had dismissed this comment. She didn't expect Mrs. Lowry to understand what it was like to move freight, or to spend your whole life, day in and day out, pretending to be someone you weren't. She didn't understand the importance of Ray having a friend at work.

Now Ray wasn't so sure.

For as good a friend as Joe was, he never told the other stevedores to stop comparing her to a rat. He knew she hated it—she'd complained about it to him more than once. The boys listened to

Joe, but instead of wielding that power, he just threw around winks. Empty winks and dimpled smiles and encouragements that Ray should prove the boys wrong.

He don't take no one's feelings to heart but his own.

Maybe Joe wasn't the friend Ray thought he was.

The Mohave Canyon greeted the crew with some of the worst rapids yet, and cries to adjust the steam power were constant while the *General Jesup* battled its way up the rocky-bottomed river. When they eventually moored for the evening, rock towered around them, dwarfing the steamer.

The grueling conquest left Mr. Johnson fretful, and by the time adequate wood had been gathered for the following day and the engineer had realigned components and checked for leaking joints and cracked steam pipes, it was too late for poker. In a way, Ray was grateful.

The following days were just as exhausting, and some seventy winding miles above Mohave Canyon, the expedition found itself navigating another ravine with additional rapids waiting beyond. They were passable—no worse than what they'd crossed thus far—but Mr. Johnson and Lieutenant White had begun to argue about their thinning provisions. It was a sight to be seen, spit flying and mustaches flapping, perhaps the best bit of entertainment Ray had witnessed in weeks. In the end, they struck a compromise, agreeing that they would take a skiff through the rapids and determine their location once they had an unobstructed view of the river ahead. If the *General Jesup* was as far north as the captain suspected, the mission might be deemed a success.

After the skiff departed, Joe fanned a deck of cards in Ray's direction. "Wanna play, Rat?" He smiled, showing her those familiar dimples, but Ray shook her head. She wanted nothing less than to risk slipping up so near the end. With the help of the current, the trip home would be swift, nothing like the ascent upriver, and she couldn't wait to get out of these suffocating canyons.

Johnson returned the following day at twilight, grinning fiercely as he told them he could see a good forty miles to the north after crossing the rapids. "We are undoubtedly within seventy-five miles of the mouth of the Virgin River," he declared, "which means Utah is reachable! We've beaten the other expedition — shown that the Colorado is clearly navigable by steamer, and the Mormon settlements within reach. I say we return to Fort Yuma, triumphant!"

The claim was far from sound — Johnson hadn't actually taken the steamer all the way to the Mormons — but Ray bit her tongue, and when the *General Jesup* turned to the south, she cheered as loudly as the others.

Feigning a sickness on the return trip, Ray had an excuse to linger near the chamber pot in isolation. But fifty miles from Fort Yuma — when no one else had caught Ray's ailment — Joe seemed to figure she posed him no true risk and approached her at the bow. He leaned into Ray's shoulder, the February sun beating down on their necks, and said, for perhaps the hundredth time, "You gotta show me how you do it."

She cocked an eyebrow at him, attempting to appear cool when every muscle in her body was taut.

"Cheat all the time without getting caught," he pressed.

"I ain't a cheat," Ray said. *I'm a magician.*

"'Course you're a cheat. You've prolly been cheating as long as I've known you."

Ray's insides curled. Did he know? Had he seen or found her out somehow?

"No one wins as often as you if they ain't," he continued. "I been suspecting it for ages, and I kept quiet all this time."

His insistence had nothing to do with her being a girl, Ray realized. In his drive to learn her skills, he'd been blind to the even larger con. Ray breathed a sigh of relief.

"I reckon I should get something for that," he continued, voice light and jovial. "Like your expedition earnings. Consider it a repayment for all my losses over the years."

"Good one," Ray said, laughing.

She looked at him only to realize he wasn't joking. His brows were drawn down, and his mouth was twisted into a smirk. Only one dimple appeared.

"You can't be serious," she said.

"Oh, I'm serious as can be," Joe said coldly.

He was no longer lean like her. Over the years he'd filled out, put on muscle like extra layers of clothing. He could lift freight with ease, limbs never seeming to tire even as they bulged beneath the weight of goods. What she'd come to envy now made Ray feel small—her just fifteen and wiry, him broad-shouldered and nearing twenty. She'd be no match for Joe if he decided he truly wanted her fifty dollars. The blade in her boot felt no better than a butter knife.

"Well?" he prompted, still smirking.

Ray's gaze flicked away, settling on the muddy waters so stagnant and low that—

"Rock!" she shouted. "Rocky bottom straight ahead!"

Johnson screamed orders, and the engineer worked frantically at the valves, but the *General Jesup* was positioned midriver and running under too much steam to adequately slow or alter course.

They ran aground hard.

Propelled by the impact, Ray flew off the bow and into the shallows. Her right wrist broke her fall, and she gasped in pain, cold water filling her nose.

Coughing and sputtering, Ray rolled onto her back only to see the *General Jesup* still crawling forward, her hull tearing open with an ungodly sound. An arm came over Ray's shoulder, locked firm across the front of her chest, and yanked her away from the vessel. The steamer lurched to a stop, caught on the rocky bottom.

In three feet of water, the *General Jesup* met its match.

And so did Ray.

Because it was Joe who had pulled her to safety. Joe who still had a hand on her chest. Joe who was spinning her to face him, eyes ablaze with fury as his palms flew over her form, patting and prodding, confirming the truth.

"Joe, don't say anything," she begged. "*Please* don't tell anyone."

She'd lose her job, the expedition earnings, everything. She'd never be able to work for the Company again. And if the pain in her wrist told her anything, it would be a while before she could shuffle a deck smoothly, either.

Crew members splashed into the water, inspecting the steamer and shouting about damage.

"All this time?" Joe glowered. "For years I been helping you, and giving advice, saving your hide from underperformance, and you ain't had the decency to be honest?"

"Joe, please."

He considered it a moment, mouth in a hard, flat line. After a moment, he said, "You know what, *Rat*? It'll cost you fifty damn dollars."

The way he said the nickname made Ray's stomach shrivel with dread. She'd been wrong about everything. He might not have made jokes about her being a rat, but his silence was only complacency. He agreed, deep down, and now he'd decided their friendship meant nothing, that *she* was nothing.

The con had come crumbling down.

She had no cards up her sleeve, no way of saving the act.

It was over.

"Hey, you two all right?" someone called from the steamer.

"Well, Rat?" Joe asked, dimples flashing. "What's it gonna be?"

She still had her earnings from poker, plus everything else she'd saved up at home. If fifty dollars bought Joe's silence, well, she could make that money back. It would take ages but it was better than losing her job.

Not knowing what else to do, Ray said, "Fine. Fifty dollars."

The bastard gave the crewman a thumbs-up and left Ray standing alone in the shallows.

Mr. Johnson took a skiff to Fort Yuma and returned with a stern-wheeled steamer called the *Colorado*. Before they continued home, he had the crew build a bulkhead around his flooded *General Jesup*, which he swore he would raise and repair. Joe watched Ray like a hawk through it all, and by the time the crew moored the *Colorado* in Fort Yuma, she felt naked despite her sweat-stained clothes.

Lieutenant White marched off proudly with his soldiers, ready to send word to the War Department of their success. The rest of the crew marched into Johnson's office one by one and left with their pay.

The banknote was crisp, and Ray thumbed its edge like a card, knowing its time with her would be fleeting. She made it all the way to the alley behind Mrs. Lowry's before her shadow caught up with her. She let him brush by, his shoulder knocking into hers. Then his hands were on her arms. He shoved her against the building, pinning her there.

"Gimme my money, Rat."

She relinquished the banknote, and Joe winked. God, did she hate that wink. She hated everything about him now.

He flapped the two notes in her face, taunting her. "Watch me add to this pot."

"This ain't a game of poker, Joe."

"Oh, I think it is. See, I bet that Tom Polluck would want another whore for his establishment 'cause they don't got many youngins over there. And my wager were right. He's meeting me any minute. I'll get good money for you."

She wrestled against him. "I'm a person, not a thing you can sell."

"You're a *rat*." His fingers pinched her arms harder. "You been stealing our money, stealing an honest man's job. You're a fraud and a liar, and you're getting what you deserve. You're getting the roof you always should've been under."

He kept smiling, those dimples jeering at Ray. She didn't know how she'd ever admired Joe Henry. *He* was the rat, the louse, the swine. She squirmed against him, but her right arm was still pinned to the wall, and she needed it free. She needed to vanish.

It was time for the final act.

"Hey, Joe," Ray said coolly. "Where's your Colt?"

Finally—*finally*—he let go, dropping his head to see what his fingers could not believe. An empty holster. His gaze snapped back up, locking on the pistol in Ray's hand, now aimed at his chest. She'd lifted it off him when he'd first brushed by.

"Cheat," he snarled.

"Magician," she replied.

Using the Colt, she struck him as hard as she could. Joe Henry crumpled to the dirt. Ray gathered the hundred dollars in banknotes—his pay, along with her own—and left him in the alley, unconscious.

× × ×

Mrs. Lowry was sleeping deeply.

Ray watched the rise and fall of her chest in the feeble candle-light. She longed to say good-bye, but this was easiest. "I don't know where Ray is," the woman would be able to say tomorrow. "I weren't even aware the expedition had returned, and I haven't the slightest how Joe Henry got himself robbed."

Besides, Ray wouldn't be able to stand the begging. Mrs. Lowry would implore Ray to stay, and she couldn't, not with Joe knowing her secret. The gig was up, the show over. It was time for the curtain to fall. For so long, Ray had dreamed of leaving, and now that the moment was here, she was startled by how much it hurt.

Ray knew she might never find her family. Quite likely, the only family she had was right here in Yuma Crossing. But she was tired of pretending, and here along the river, she was a mystery even to herself. She was a boy and she was a girl. She was mother-less and she was someone's child. She was a soul wanting to belong and a soul desperate to escape. If she left, she could become more than these labels. In San Francisco, she could find who she was.

By the light of the flickering candle, Ray unfolded the news-paper clipping, crossed out words, and wrote new ones until the note read:

> ~~Ray~~ Ma, remember when ~~we saw that magician performing in New York and every card he pulled from the deck was an ace~~ I said I was going to disappear? This will be like that, only ~~we'll be pulling nugget after gold nugget from our pans~~ I'll probably miss you. Meet ~~us~~ me in San Francisco (if you want). —~~LBM~~ Ray

She placed the clipping on Mrs. Lowry's nightstand, along

with one of the fifty-dollar notes. Then she gathered her few possessions, packed a small rucksack, and crept for the Colorado.

The river was inky black. The current tugged south.

She stepped onto a skiff and, with the moon as her only audience, the magician disappeared.

⚉ AUTHOR'S NOTE ⚉

I have written two novels set in the Southwest during the second half of the nineteenth century, and both focus on revenge and justice—quintessential themes of the Western genre. With "The Magician," I wanted to tell a different type of Western story, one about identity, family, and uncertainty; about finding your way in a world that is rapidly changing.

While Ray and her fellow stevedores are fictional, the expedition they participate in is not. The George A. Johnson & Company was an influential steamer business in New Mexico Territory's history, and many of the details of Ray's trip—from embarking on New Year's Eve and trying to beat the War Department's official survey of the river, to running aground and sinking just fifty miles shy of their return home—are true. In researching Ray's story, I pored over literature on steamboats and scoured maps of the Colorado River, one of which was created from Lieutenant Ives's survey. It noted where his expedition made camp and illustrated quite clearly how grueling—and slow—an ascent of the river was in 1858. But as a result of the initial expeditions, the Colorado soon became a major shipping line for goods, bringing modern conveniences to mining towns along the river and to inland settlements much faster than by wagon alone. In the following years and decades, the area in which Ray's story is set was redrawn as Arizona Territory, and the arrival of trains made shipments even speedier. If anything was constant during this time in history, it was that *nothing* was constant. Which is perhaps why Ray relied so heavily on magic. Cards, she could control.

LADY FIREBRAND

MEGAN SHEPHERD

The dining room of Drexel Hall was everything one would expect in a grand plantation home: miles of floral wallpaper, a cherry dining table set for twelve, a chandelier threatening to buckle under its own opulence. Rose Blake, exiled to the farthest end of the table—suitable only for visiting relatives—eyed the chandelier, secretly willing it to fall. Anything to end Aunt Edith's latest tirade.

"It's positively *uncivilized,*" Edith drawled from the better-lit end of the table. The primary victim of her attention was an officer who'd been recently stationed at Fort Sumter. A handsome young officer, Rose couldn't help but note, tall and graceful as a mountain lion, with blue eyes and chestnut hair pushing the limit of regulation length.

"I haven't had fabric from France in two years because of that dreadful Union blockade," her aunt continued. "Tell me, Captain

Austin, what material am I to use when Stella outgrows her dresses? The curtains?"

She motioned to Rose's eleven-year-old cousin, Stella, who was wearing a worn yellow frock and staring at the handsome officer with big moony eyes. Stella was so tiny that there was no danger of her outgrowing anything anytime soon, especially not with the war reducing Drexel's usual feasts to meager rations and wormy cabbage and granting all their ribs new prominence.

Captain Austin didn't answer immediately, which secretly pleased Rose. There was nothing worse than a man who spoke the first thought in his head. He dabbed his mouth with his napkin, which had once been expensive but was now unraveling, fading into disrepair like everything else at the planation. No wonder Aunt Edith kept the lanterns set low.

"We must all make sacrifices in a time of war," he said at last.

"But surely not for dresses," Edith huffed, patting her rouged cheeks, more like a spoiled girl than a woman of thirty-six.

Rose held her tongue against the ugly words that flooded her mouth. People were dying, and all her aunt thought of was next month's ball with the soldiers at Fort Sumter. Rose stabbed the sharp tines of her fork into a pea.

A young male slave dressed in ill-fitting livery waited by the servants' entrance to clear the second course. His reddish-brown jaw was clenched, his folded hands tensing every time Aunt Edith complained about a triviality. Rose glanced over her shoulder to catch Pauline's eye, wondering what her friend thought of it all. Pauline was seated far out of sight in the corner by the buffet table, her mahogany hair tidily braided and her homespun lavender dress freshly pressed. As far as Rose's aunt and uncle knew, Pauline was her free colored maid, whom Rose insisted always be close by in case she needed her. Pauline met Rose's gaze, her pretty honey-brown face wearing a carefully blank expression. *An excellent actress,* Rose thought. Acting skills would be required of both of them if they were to accomplish what they'd come to Charleston to do.

Rose's uncle, Cornelius, leaned forward to speak with Mr. Fillion, the owner of the neighboring Mayfair Plantation. Rose strained to catch what they might be conspiring about. *Union frigate just off the coast . . . Crates with blue crests . . .*

Edith signaled for the slave in livery to refill her wine. "Captain Austin, you must tell your commander that we are suffering more than our fair share. That Union blockade is strangling us. We can't get our cotton to buyers in London. Which means we can't get the supplies we need from their agents in Nassau. And now even the blockade runners are too frightened to attempt a voyage because of that masked renegade."

Captain Austin sat straighter. "What masked renegade?"

Edith clapped her hands together. "Ah, you haven't heard! Why, Charleston has its own vigilante. A Northern sympathizer. He goes by the name of—"

"Lord Firebrand!" Stella cried in delight.

Edith *tsk*ed. "Yes. A provocative alias, isn't it? He's made it his mission to destroy the last three cotton shipments from Drexel and Mayfair. They say he makes explosives from black powder. He always strikes just after sundown." Edith dropped her voice. "Rumors are he's an Englishman who's come to America and taken up the Northern cause."

"He dresses all in black and wears gloves and a mask to disguise his face," Stella added, "because he's a real, famous lord, and he doesn't want to be recognized!"

"If he is indeed a rogue Englishman," Edith continued, "then he's terribly misinformed. The British, like the Northerners, don't understand the realities of plantation life. They only read sensationalist slander in the newspapers. It's a regrettable truth that some mistreat their slaves, but *we* don't. Why, our slaves are like family to us."

The young slave in livery shifted uncomfortably while pouring her wine, his jaw clenching tighter. Rose curled her fingers around the hilt of her butter knife, wishing she could stab it into something—or someone. Across from her, Captain Austin's gaze shifted to the young man, and for a moment, her hopes lifted. His sinewy hands were squeezed around his butter knife, too. Just because he was a Confederate soldier didn't mean *he* personally condoned slavery. Any reasonable person wouldn't. . . .

He gave a tight smile. "Family. Exactly."

Edith beamed, and Rose stabbed her dinner roll. She glanced toward Pauline, whose blank expression had slipped, showing weary eyes and a hard set to her mouth. Pauline nodded toward the window. Nearly sundown.

They needed to get out of there.

"What do you think, Miss Rose?" Captain Austin said. "You must have a strong opinion on the relationship between slave and master."

Rose nearly dropped her knife. *"Me?"*

"Your uncle told me your father is a clergyman," he explained. "In my experience, the clergy always has a strong opinion, regardless of the subject at hand. And I believe Scripture can be particularly difficult to interpret when it comes to matters of slavery."

She eyed him closely, trying to see past his devilishly calm smile. What else had her uncle told him? It was Cornelius's secret shame that his brother, Rose's father, had been linked to abolitionists decades ago. And living in Boston, a sinful Northern city where free people of color mixed with whites, made Rose and her father pariahs as far as their Charleston family was concerned. But as she watched, Captain Austin's expression remained open and the slightest bit bored. He was just making conversation.

John 3:18, she wanted to tell him. *Let us love not in word or talk but in deed and in truth.*

Captain Austin was still looking at her expectantly, so Rose forced a giggle. "I only know what dear Uncle Cornelius tells me about such matters. I find the war so unsettling to discuss. Though"—she leaned forward and gave an impish grin—"if I'm honest, I've always fancied dashing rebels. In literature, that is. The only character more romantic is a young man in uniform." She waved her butter knife suggestively in the direction of his epaulettes, and he went very red for a man who must be used to female attention.

Aunt Edith tittered. "Forgive her, Captain. She's young, and men are so scarce these days. All the Fillion boys are serving in the military, isn't that so? It's practically a nunnery around here. Except for you, dear."

Uncle Cornelius grunted as he wiped a napkin over his red nose.

"And you can hardly blame the poor girl," Edith continued. "Living in Boston, surrounded by all those hotheaded abolition-ist fools. When she wrote asking to stay with us for the summer, we felt it was our duty to bring her to the South, where life is still civilized." She took a long drink from her chipped wineglass. "Of course, the neighbors were shocked we'd let a Northerner in our home, even our own niece. But how could we have said no? After *all she's been through,* the poor thing."

She looked pointedly at Rose's lap.

Rose felt her stomach twist. The last thing she wanted was their pity—though it had its uses. But this time her aunt had gone too far.

"If you'll excuse me," she said tightly, "I've lost my appetite."

She gripped the round wooden rims of her wheelchair, rolling herself away from the table.

Captain Austin stared at her.

She felt her face warm. Well, let him stare. Charleston was full of wounded soldiers — surely he'd seen a wheelchair before. If he hadn't noticed that her seat wasn't the same as the others at the dining table, then that was his own lapse in observation.

Pauline was behind her in an instant, the soft smell of her lavender soap comforting to Rose as she took the wheelchair's handles and helped guide Rose out of the dining room and into the hall. When Rose had first shown up at Drexel Hall with Pauline, Aunt Edith and Uncle Cornelius had refused to have Pauline under their roof. They worried that a free colored woman's presence might incite their slaves to revolt. But Rose had mustered tears and pointed to her legs and insisted that she needed Pauline, who had been specially trained to help those in wheelchairs. They'd given in eventually. Tears always did the job.

The *tick-tick-tick* of the mantel clock followed them down the long hallways, past her uncle's locked library, to the first-floor parlor that Aunt Edith had made up as a bedroom for her.

Pauline closed the door, pressed her ear to the crack, then turned and let out a frustrated sigh. "Lord Jesus, slaves are like kin? I could have strangled them." She paced around the room. "You did a good job throwing off that captain's questions. His face was red as a beet."

Rose fanned her own still-warm face. "It was a rather nice face to look at, wasn't it?"

Pauline tossed a pillow at her. "Rose, he's a Confederate!"

Rose ducked the pillow. "I didn't say I approved of his politics. I don't like cigars, either, but that doesn't mean they can't come in a pretty package."

"Oh, never mind him." Pauline knelt to drag the carpetbag out from under Rose's bed. "He won't be a problem as long as we run this mission while they're still at supper. We have enough black powder, don't we?"

"Half a pound, in the last stall in the stables." The military had conscripted all but one of her relatives' horses, making the nearly empty stables the perfect place to hide their supplies. Rose wheeled herself to her dressing table, trying to put the attractive enemy officer out of her mind. She opened the drawer and sorted through the glass bottles for a small vial that she'd hidden among her beauty tonics. She held it up to the light. Nitroglycerin— exceedingly hard to come by. They'd stolen it from the assistant to an Italian chemist who'd been invited by the Boston Society of Natural History to give a public lecture. One flirtatious wink from Rose and the apprentice had bounded after her into the coatroom, while Pauline rifled through the collection of rare chemicals he was supposed to be guarding.

Pauline opened the carpetbag and took out a man's shirt and pair of breeches that they had stolen from neighbors' clotheslines. She started to unbutton her dress. "Did you hear what your aunt said about Lord Firebrand being a real English lord? Did you start those rumors?"

Rose picked innocently at her fingernails. "I might have sent an anonymous note to the newspaper. We had to have *some* reason for why he covers his entire face and body." She wrapped the vial of nitroglycerin in a handkerchief, thinking back over Uncle Cornelius and Mr. Fillion's dinner conversation. "Mayfair Plantation is disguising its cotton shipment as war rations bound for the hospital. The boxes are marked with a blue crest. Try to blow them up with black powder first. Use the nitroglycerin only if you must—we're running low."

Pauline pulled the man's shirt over her head, then tucked it into the black breeches and pulled on gloves. She reached for the vial.

Rose handed it to her, then grasped Pauline's other hand and squeezed tightly. "Be careful, Pauline."

Since coming to Drexel Hall, Pauline had risked her life four times to commit acts of sabotage, sneaking out under the cover of night, finding the cotton shipments, and laying the explosives that Rose had prepared. Each time, Rose had stayed home with her dreaded family, praying for Pauline's safety. That Pauline wouldn't be harmed by the explosions. That she wouldn't be attacked by a stranger or raped on the five-mile walk to Charleston. And of course, Rose's greatest fear, for which she prayed especially hard: that Pauline wouldn't be caught by soldiers. A free colored woman in possession of dangerous chemicals, committing criminal acts . . . It made Rose sick to think of what could happen. They wouldn't just arrest Pauline. She could be sold into slavery. There could even be a noose. And Rose wouldn't be able to help her.

She squeezed her useless knees. "You shouldn't have to do this on your own."

Pauline gave Rose a hug. "I know the risk," she whispered, though her voice was shaking. "Don't worry. Lord Firebrand will never be caught."

The first time Rose met Pauline had been in a graveyard when they were seven years old. Rose's father had told her that they were going to a church outside Boston for a secret meeting with colored pastors, and it had sounded like an adventure. But the men's droning talk of abolition wasn't nearly as interesting as the butterflies outside. She wandered through the cemetery, chasing them, vaguely aware of the honey-brown girl her same age on the other side of the cemetery, the daughter of one of the colored preachers,

Reverend Jacobs, a man born free and educated by Quakers. The other girl's long braids swung as she also chased the butterflies. But Rose was white and Pauline was colored, and they were too shy to speak to each other until a trio of rowdy farm boys scared a rabbit into the cemetery, beating it with sticks. Rose had gasped. Pauline had jumped up. Their eyes had met and the two of them had rushed at the boys, screaming and wailing like ghosts, startling them so that the rabbit got away. Rose and Pauline had been friends ever since.

Now, two weeks after the interminable dinner with Captain Austin, Rose sat on Drexel Hall's wide back porch, her wheelchair settled amid the row of empty white rocking chairs, watching a rabbit munch on Aunt Edith's rosebushes. Tall white columns extended the length of the porch, creating a haven away from the bustle of the slave quarters on the other side of the house. From here she couldn't see the cotton fields, half of which had been torn up and replanted with potatoes and peas, being worked by most of the plantation's forty slaves. But she could *hear* them. Sharp, distant yells from the white overseer, cracks of his whip, a child crying until the whip snapped again. She'd peeked out her window night after night to see the slaves trudging back to their cabins clutching sore backs, clad in sweat-soaked dresses and pants, some still bleeding from the lashes. That was plantation life: tradition masking something uglier. If Rose had her way, it would have ended long ago.

Before she came to Drexel Hall, she had only met her aunt and uncle once. They'd come to visit her father's church in Boston when she was just a little girl. Her uncle's whiskers had been black then, but his voice had been just as booming. He'd made Drexel Hall sound like something out of a fairy tale: cotton like small wisps of clouds, the salty breeze from the coast, monstrous alligators stalking the swamps. Rose had dreamed of coming to Drexel. But now that she was here, it turned her stomach. It was beautiful, yes, but no fairy tale.

Pauline came onto the porch with a picnic basket. "Your family went to Mayfair Plantation for the afternoon; your aunt told May in the kitchen that you'd rather stay here and that she should make you lunch. I, ah, slipped something in there for you." She opened the basket to show that beneath the sandwiches were crisp bundles of money. Rose glanced around the porch. Even with her family gone, there were still the slaves and the overseers, but fortunately she and Pauline were alone.

"Goodness! All this from your mission last night?" Rose whispered. The previous evening, Pauline, dressed as Lord Firebrand, had held up a stagecoach carrying Confederate funds.

Pauline nodded. "Enough, don't you think?"

"I'll say." For the past two months, Rose had been anonymously paying off the occasional guard or soldier to look the other way, and the Charleston newspapers to spread the rumor about the masked vigilante. "With this much money, Lord Firebrand could even—"

The rosebushes suddenly rustled and a round face popped out of the leaves with even rounder eyes. Rose's red-cheeked little cousin, Stella. "Did you say Lord Firebrand?"

"Stella!" Rose gasped, slamming the basket closed. "Shouldn't . . . shouldn't you be at Mayfair?"

"Lord Jesus!" Pauline grabbed the basket, breathing hard.

Stella scrambled up onto the porch and pointed to the basket. "Where'd your colored girl get all that money, Rose? Did she steal it?"

"Hush!" Rose cried. Heat was spreading up her neck. What had Stella heard? Who would she tell? *Blast!* She glanced at Pauline, who met her gaze and then quickly disappeared into the house. Stella tried to follow her inside, but Rose grabbed the girl. "Stella, wait. Let's play a game!"

"But she's a thief!"

The screen door slammed. Pauline was probably hiding the money, and, Rose hoped, hiding herself, too. Rose's hands were shaking. She had to think fast. Pauline was in enough danger already; Rose *had* to keep her cousin quiet. She heard the rattle of wheels and, with an increasing sense of dread, looked up to see a Confederate army carriage bouncing along the oak-lined path beyond the gardens.

"She didn't steal it," Rose said in a rush. "It's . . . mine. Brought with me from Boston."

Stella scrunched up her face. "Do you really know Lord Firebrand?" Her eyes suddenly went wide. "Are you secretly in love with him? Is the money so you can run away together?"

The carriage stopped on the far side of the house. A man's deep voice spoke with the house slaves. Her pulse thundered. A Confederate soldier here, *now,* and her cousin blabbing enough to cause them all sorts of trouble!

"It's true," Rose said quickly. "I am passionately in love with the dashing Lord Firebrand. We are going to elope. But it's a secret. You mustn't tell anyone."

Footsteps sounded on the porch.

Rose shook Stella, whispering low. "Our secret, right?"

Captain Austin appeared at the far end of the porch, smiling. "Good day, Miss Rose. Miss Stella." He paused. "Am I interrupting something?"

Rose's fingers dug into Stella's arms. She gave Stella a long look, and Stella nodded.

"We were just playing a game!" Stella said, a little too loud. Then she giggled and scampered off.

Rose slumped back into her chair in relief.

Captain Austin, oblivious, motioned to the empty rocking chair beside her. "May I join you, Miss Rose?"

She nodded, barely hearing him, blood still throbbing in her ears.

"What . . . what brings you back to Drexel, Captain?" she asked, trying to keep the shaking from her voice.

He held up a book. "Returning a volume your uncle lent me when I was here for dinner." Something on the ground caught his eye, and he reached down and removed a piece of straw from the spokes of her wheelchair. "You've been in the stables?"

"Yes. I, ah, I like to visit my uncle's horse. I used to be fond of riding." She squeezed her knees hard, but as always, felt nothing. She swallowed a bitter pang, thinking of the accident: her mare Hurricane spooked by a snake, the fall that broke her spine. She drew a deep breath. "You can leave the book with me. I'm afraid the family's gone to Mayfair."

For a few moments, he said nothing, only rocked slowly. And then he cleared his throat. "In fact, it was you I wished to speak to, Miss Rose."

Her pulse still hadn't slowed from nearly getting caught; now it thumped even harder. Had he heard Stella yelling about Lord Firebrand? Or was this some sort of declaration of affection? Goodness, he was nice to look at, but the last thing on her mind now was romance.

"At our dinner," he continued in a quiet voice, "you mentioned you attended Prestley School for Girls in Boston. Later that night, I remembered that I had a friend who went there. Belle Stafford.

She's in Wilmington now. I wrote her and got her response this morning. She said she knew you. That you were brilliant at chemistry. You even blew up a tree stump one summer." He paused, and Rose squeezed her armrests. Why was this captain so interested in her schooling? And in *explosions*? "And then I ran into an officer who had spent some years in Boston and asked about your family. He said your father was rumored to be involved with abolitionists in the eighteen thirties. That he might even have been responsible for an explosion last year in Virginia that took out an important tactical bridge for the Confederacy."

Alarm shot through Rose. But she'd gotten Stella under control and she could manage this captain, too. "That's . . . that's ridiculous!" She tried for a laugh. "He's a man of God, not of explosives."

"Is he?" *He* wasn't laughing.

Rose's face drained of blood. "What exactly are you saying, Captain?"

Captain Austin took a piece of paper out of his pocket. "I found this in the stables. It's the label for a container of black powder. Someone had hidden it in the straw." He toyed with the piece of straw that had been caught in her wheels.

Rose gripped the chair's armrests, feeling dizzy. How could she warn Pauline? What could they do if the captain arrested them? Bash him over the head and flee? They wouldn't get far, not in her chair. Perhaps she could force some tears and beg his mercy. It had worked before, with a Confederate spy in Boston who had caught her riffling through his letters. She'd sobbed and claimed she fancied him and she'd only been reading the letters to see if he had a sweetheart, and he'd let her go.

She leaned in, trying to hide how her heart was walloping. "It almost sounds like you're trying to suggest that *I* am that masked rebel, which is ridiculous. Lord Firebrand *walks*."

His gaze fell to her knees. "You must have a partner. If I had to guess, I'd say your maid is the one in the black costume, and you're the one preparing the explosives and sending anonymous letters to the newspapers. Together, the two of you are Lord Firebrand."

She sucked in a quick breath, masking panic with indignation. "Have you gone mad?"

He rubbed his chin. "Deny it all you like, Miss Blake, but I know it's true. And I know how dangerous it is for you, and especially for your associate. She'd be in far more trouble than you if you two were caught. A well-heeled, pretty white victim of a tragic accident might escape the hangman's noose. But not a colored girl."

Rose was quiet. She didn't quite know what to make of Captain Austin. Once she and Pauline had grown up and become more interested in abolition than butterflies, they had joined their fathers' clandestine organization. They had helped to arrange hiding places for escaped slaves from the South and seduced secrets out of suspected Confederate spies. But then Hurricane had stumbled. There had been weeks in the hospital, months of recovery, the crushing disappointment of never being able to walk again. Or spy.

It's over, she had said to her father. *I'm useless to our cause now.*

Her father had shaken his head. *You don't need to walk to make a difference for the Union.*

At Pauline's urging, Rose had agreed to start up their work again. She'd missed it—using her talents for something she believed in. It had taken a while to figure out how they could continue their work with Rose in a wheelchair, but then she'd gotten a condolence letter from Aunt Edith and Uncle Cornelius, who were rumored to have ties to the blockade runners. Pauline had suggested she write her aunt to ask for a convalescence at their plantation, and thus Lord Firebrand was born.

Now Rose drew herself up to her full height in the chair. "Good luck convincing anyone of your theory. You'll look mad, arresting a girl in a wheelchair."

"I haven't come to arrest you, Miss Blake." Captain Austin dropped his voice. "Don't you understand? I've come to hire you."

She blinked. "What did you say?"

He scanned the porch, the garden, the rosebushes. "I work for General McClellan. My brother enlisted for the Union, and I wanted to enlist, too, but General McClellan said my services would be more valuable as a secret operative. I made a show of breaking with my family so I could enlist for the Confederacy. I've been trying to uncover the identity of Lord Firebrand for some time now. That's why I pulled strings to have myself sent to Fort Sumter."

"You're a Union spy?" she asked, suspicious it might be a trap.

"And *you* are Lord Firebrand." A smile stretched across his face. "Or perhaps I should say Lady Firebrand."

"Show me proof, then," she demanded.

"What more proof do you need other than the fact that I haven't arrested you?" His eyes danced. "I'm very impressed, you know. You and Pauline must have suspected that everyone would underestimate you."

She settled back in her chair, eyeing him with cautious curiosity. "But not you."

"No, Miss Blake. Not me. And not General McClellan, either. If you and your associate would be willing to help us, we have a mission for Lord Firebrand. It could change the course of the war. We just lost the Battle of Winchester — that's thousands of Union men captured or killed. General Lee is getting more aggressive. We need you now more than ever."

She paused. What would Pauline make of this? If the Confederacy won, Pauline would likely be enslaved — or worse.

Rose flinched, thinking of the plantation slaves with their crusty, oozing cuts from the overseer's whip, and of Mr. Fillion's leer as he ogled the brown women who worked in the house.

Pauline had every reason to want to see the South defeated. She would think it worth the risk.

Rose leaned close to the captain. "Tell me what you want us to do."

Captain Austin—Henry—came to Drexel Hall often over the next few weeks under a variety of pretenses: a forgotten cap, a book to lend Uncle Cornelius, updates on the war. At every visit, he and Rose snuck away to meet in the stables while Pauline kept watch—keeping a particularly close eye on Stella.

It was maps that General McClellan was after. Specifically, maps of the sea routes that blockade runners were using to sneak between the Union frigates stationed around the port of Charleston. Through his spy network, the general had learned that Uncle Cornelius, a former sea captain, was the one charting the routes—and that blockade runners were planning a massive smuggling operation: ten thousand Enfield rifles, a million cartridges, and four hundred barrels of gunpowder. All to be delivered on the first of August. Rose and Pauline's mission was simple: locate the maps, copy them, and turn them over to Henry so that Union forces could confiscate the weaponry for themselves.

There was just one problem: they couldn't find the maps.

Rose spent days pretending to read a book while she listened in on her uncle's conversations. Pauline spoke to the carriage driver to learn where Cornelius went and who he met with. At night they ransacked the guest bedrooms, the bookcases, even the pantry.

Nothing.

"The maps *must* be in the library," Pauline concluded. "It's the only place we haven't been able to search. He disappears in there for hours on end, and Mr. Fillion's usually with him." She tapped on Rose's dresser and raised an eyebrow. "Nitroglycerin would break the lock."

"Yes, and also make enough noise to rouse the dead. We used the last of it, anyway. But maybe there's something else . . ." Rose rifled through the vials in her drawer. "Ah!" She held up a bottle of aqua fortis. "Henry gave me this in case Lord Firebrand needed it for one of his missions; Fort Sumter has quite a chemical arsenal. In the right conditions, it will silently eat away at a brass lock."

"And in the wrong conditions?"

Rose scrutinized the bottle, thinking back on the public science lectures she'd attended in Boston, throwing her friends off by claiming she only went because she fancied the museum's handsome young ticket-taker. "It's dangerous if mixed with organic compounds, like turpentine." She mimicked an explosion with her hands. "But I don't think they used turpentine on the door. It isn't varnished."

"What about the lock, though? Your uncle will see that it's been broken."

"There's nothing to be done for it," Rose said. "We'll just have to hope he assumes it was a common thief or an army deserter, after hidden valuables."

"I hope you're right," Pauline said. "The first of August is in two days. If we don't have the maps when Henry comes tomorrow, the Confederates will get all those weapons."

Rose nodded. "Tonight, then."

Since Aunt Edith had given Rose a ground-floor bedroom on account of the wheelchair, it was much easier to sneak around without worrying about squeaky stairs or having to enlist someone to carry Rose from upper floors. Once they were certain the household was asleep, Pauline pushed Rose quietly down the hallway.

Pauline held a candle while Rose measured five milligrams of aqua fortis into a glass eyedropper and applied it to the lock. An acrid smell filled the hall, along with a faint fizzing sound. Rose waved her hand in front of the door, trying to dispel the fumes. Worries cycled through her mind as she counted to one hundred, giving the metal time to cool. She kept glancing at the stairs, making sure Stella wasn't eavesdropping again. But even so, she felt good. It was thrilling, directly helping the Union cause again.

"Hold the candle a little closer." She leaned as far forward as she could in her chair, peering into the lock. The exterior portion was completely melted, and most of the tumblers, too. She twisted the handle cautiously open. "It worked!"

"Bravo!" Pauline squeezed Rose's shoulder and pushed her inside. They searched the library quickly, Pauline checking the upper shelves while Rose took care of the lower ones. Opening books, shaking pages, pulling open drawers, sorting through cabinets.

"Nothing!" Pauline whispered.

Outside, the first light of dawn broke on the horizon.

Frustrated, Rose gripped her chair's wheels and rolled backward, but misjudged the slope of the floor and rolled right into the umbrella stand. She cringed, expecting a crash that would wake her relatives, but it landed on the rug with only a soft thud. She let out a breath.

Pauline knelt to straighten it. "Rose, look!"

Amid the canes and umbrellas were a handful of long paper rolls. Pauline untied one and they gasped at the same time.

Maps.

"Quick!" Rose whispered, wheeling herself to the desk. "Get some paper. We'll make copies."

They worked under the light of the single candle, Rose tracing the nautical lines, Pauline filling in the place-names in her small, precise handwriting. Dawn continued to rise outside. Something *thunk*ed in the kitchen.

Pauline straightened. "That must be May, making breakfast. I think we can trust her—I've overheard her and the scullery maid talking about sneaking food to a man who runs a safe house at the docks. But the family will be up soon."

"Almost done . . ." Rose said, tracing the last route. "There. Finished!"

Pauline rolled up the maps and shoved them back in the umbrella stand. Rose shuffled the papers on her uncle's desk and pocketed his silver paperweight, hoping that would convince him that the broken lock was caused by a thief.

Footsteps sounded over their head. Someone upstairs was awake. Pauline pushed Rose down the hall to her bedroom and closed the door just as someone came stomping down the stairs. Breathless, they looked at each other in satisfaction.

"Lord Firebrand strikes again." Rose grinned.

Pauline grabbed a handful of hairpins from Rose's vanity table and crouched at the foot of the wheelchair. "I'll pin the maps to your petticoats, like we used to do in Boston."

Because of the wheelchair, Rose couldn't wear the same bell-shaped hoopskirts as most Southern belles; she wore a modified corset and thick padded underskirts. Pauline lifted Rose's dress—a soft pink cotton that, like everything else at Drexel, had been fine once but was now worn around the edges—and experimented with securing the maps to the copious folds of Rose's petticoats.

"There," she said, smoothing Rose's skirts over the maps. "You can't tell. Though you won't be able reach them yourself, which means Henry's going to have to root around beneath your skirts to free them."

Rose patted the ruffles of her skirt. "Goodness. Well. We must all suffer in times of war, right? I suppose if an attractive young captain must root around in my skirts for the sake of a Northern victory, then I simply must allow it."

Pauline gave her a pinch on the arm. "You always were a shameless flirt. Some things never change."

All that morning, Rose waited anxiously on the front porch for a glimpse of Henry's carriage. Pauline did the wash and the mending, a chore she loathed. Rose wished she could spare her that much, but she had no choice if they wanted to avoid suspicion that Pauline was anything but Rose's maid. Rose wore a blanket over her lap despite the early-summer heat, to further disguise the rustle of papers hidden in her petticoats. Her cheeks warmed at the thought of Henry crouched in front of her, lifting her cotton dress, fingers sliding among the silk petticoats. For the past few weeks, she'd come to enjoy his visits more and more. The last time she'd seen him, he had let his fingers rest too long on her wrist, his lips close to hers as they had whispered plans. Would he ever kiss her?

Her thoughts darkened as she realized that, while unpinning the maps, he would see how thin her legs had become from lack of use. Would he be repulsed? No. He was the kind of man who would find every part of her beautiful. She started to imagine writing a letter to her father. *Papa, I've met the most wonderful man. . . .*

Noon came, and Henry still hadn't arrived.

Rose pretended to read her Bible, her gaze darting anxiously to the road every few moments, but the only person who came was the post boy. Shortly after the clock chimed one, Stella came charging out the door like some wild creature, tears streaming down her face.

"Stella!" Rose called, alarmed.

But the girl ran through the live oaks, wailing.

The front door opened again and Aunt Edith rushed out. "Child, come back here!"

"What happened?" Rose asked.

Edith shook her head. "You know how she's always hiding? Well, a moment ago a letter arrived from Fort Sumter, saying Captain Austin was arrested as a Union spy. Stella overheard your uncle and me discussing it." She patted her rouged cheeks off-handedly. "Hard to believe. Such a polite young man. *Most* impressive jawline."

Blood roared in Rose's ears, and her heart started to pound. Surely she hadn't heard right. "Captain . . . Captain Austin?" Her voice sounded strangely distant.

Aunt Edith gave her a sideways look. "Don't tell me you fancied him, too. Oh, of course you did—what girl wouldn't? Well, he's being held in the Old City Jail until his trial. Cornelius was suspicious of him; he was a bit too rehearsed. Too careful in his words. And Stella had seen him acting oddly."

Rose listened in a stunned silence, terror snaking up her back. She closed her eyes. *Stella couldn't have told about the money, about Pauline's mission. She couldn't . . .*

"Stella told us she'd seen Captain Austin sneaking around the house, testing out a door on the first floor. It must have been the library, because this morning Cornelius discovered the lock had been broken and a valuable paperweight was missing. It must have been Captain Austin. Cornelius wrote to the general immediately." Her voice dropped, heavy with lurid excitement. "*He's* Lord Firebrand, don't you see? He was likely trying to rob us to gain money for the Union."

Rose felt the air catch in her throat. She couldn't breathe.

She had stolen that paperweight, not Henry. And the room

Stella had seen Henry trying to enter secretly—had it been her own bedroom, perhaps, instead of the library? Had he been intending to find her, to talk in private? About the mission—or to finally share that kiss?

Aunt Edith turned and called back into the house. "May, we'll have two fewer places for lunch. Stella's run away, and Captain Austin certainly won't be joining us!"

Rose rolled up and down the hallways, calling Pauline's name. She found her in the wash yard, hanging up dripping sheets in the sun. As she managed to choke out the story, Pauline's eyes went wide and she reached down to clutch Rose's hands.

"Shhh." Pauline nodded toward the four slaves at the well, only ten yards away. They were older women, their sleeves pushed back over brown skin further darkened by sun, their faces shining with sweat as they struggled to haul up buckets of water by hand, since the military had taken the pump handle for its metal.

"Not here." Pauline pushed Rose's chair through the gardens to the empty stables.

"It's because of me," Rose gasped. "Pauline, I can't abide it! Henry isn't Lord Firebrand—*we* are!"

"The last thing he'd want is for us to give up. He was going to take the maps to a contact in Milford, right? At the inn by the river bend? We'll go there ourselves."

"How?" Rose whispered. "I'm in a wheelchair, and you can't walk to Milford alone in broad daylight. We can't trust that your papers will keep you safe." She glanced at the sun, still high. "If we could wait until night, you could go under cover of darkness in the Lord Firebrand costume."

"It would be too late." Pauline paced the length of the barn, looking at the big old draft horse in the next stall, the only one that hadn't been conscripted. "We have to go now. Do this together, like we used to."

"That's impossible." Rose followed Pauline's gaze to the horse. "We can't steal a carriage. We'd be found out immediately."

"Not a carriage. Just the horse. We'll be back in half an hour. Your family's napping; we won't be missed."

"But you don't know how to ride a horse, and I . . ." She clutched her knees. Bitterness rose again in her throat.

"Do you remember the military parade in Boston last January?" Excitement brimmed in Pauline's voice. "There was a soldier whose legs had been amputated; he rode in a special saddle that kept him upright. He must have figured out how to modify it."

"But we don't have a saddle like that. Nor anyone who could make one."

"We don't need it. Not if we both ride. I'll sit in back and hold us on, and you take the reins and command the horse, and tell me how to signal him with my heels. You won't need use of your legs."

Rose's lips parted, ready to insist it was madness, but she paused.

Ride a horse again, after the accident?

Could it be possible?

She pressed her hands against her legs, kneading them beneath her skirt. Pauline's plan sounded dangerous—Pauline could fall, or Rose could fall again. Would she hurt herself even more?

She swallowed down her fear and thought of praying with her father by the light of a candle. *And he made from one man every nation of mankind to live on all the face of the earth.* It was Acts 17:26, the verse that always reminded her that all people were created in God's image and all deserved justice.

She took a deep breath. "I suppose it could work if I tell you how to signal him with your legs. He's an old horse—that's why the army left him. There's no danger of him bolting and throwing us off."

Pauline squeezed her shoulder. "We need May's help. Hold on." Pauline disappeared to the house and soon returned with the cook. At six feet tall, May stood even-eyed with most of the men of Drexel Hall. When they explained to her what they intended to do, May shook her head.

"Miss Rose riding a horse, when she can't walk? Are you girls crazy?"

"It's for a good reason, though we can't tell you why." Rose added slyly, "If it works, it will hurt my aunt and uncle's pride."

May clapped her hands together. "Up you go, then."

Rose gripped the base of the horse's mane in one hand and the back of the saddle in the other, and with Pauline and May lifting her, she was able to pull herself up so that her stomach rested on the saddle. Then Pauline helped her move one leg around the horse's back, so that she was straddling it and could sit upright. Pauline arranged her legs in place, setting her boots into the stirrups. As soon as May had returned to the kitchen and they were alone again, Pauline lifted Rose's skirt and refastened some of the maps that had come loose from the petticoat ruffles.

As Pauline worked, Rose knit her fingers between strands of the draft horse's mane, feeling as though she were moving in a dream. She'd forgotten the earthy smell of a horse and the feel of its hair beneath her palms, like coarse velvet. Something tugged in her chest. Whenever she had ridden Hurricane, she'd felt like the wind itself, free and unyielding.

Pauline stepped on a wooden crate and climbed up behind her, sliding her hands firmly around Rose's middle, squeezing her legs around the horse to keep them steady.

"You're sure about this?" Rose asked.

Pauline nodded. "Are you?"

Rose took a deep breath. Right after the accident, her mind had gone to a dark place, defeated and frustrated. It had been her father's belief in her that had pulled her out of it, and the lessons she found in the Bible, reminding her that she couldn't sit by and benefit from an unjust system. She'd tried so hard not to let Pauline down after the accident. To prove that she was still useful, that she recognized the risks Pauline was taking, and that she would always help where she could. Now, Pauline's presence gave her all the strength she needed. Ever since that first day in the graveyard, saving the rabbit by chasing off those boys, they'd taken courage from each other.

"I'm ready." She picked up the reins. "Squeeze your heels into his side."

She felt a jolt as Pauline signaled the horse, and, with a snort, it took a step forward.

Rose grinned. She and Pauline were a team again. She'd been so afraid after the accident that her missions were over, and that if anything went wrong for Pauline, she wouldn't be able to protect her. But now she started to see a future where the two of them could work side by side to help the Union. Tears started running down her face.

"Pauline—" she started, but couldn't finish. She wanted to tell Pauline how much this meant to her. The horse, their mission, and most of all, Pauline herself. Pauline and she, they were more than coconspirators. They were more than Lord Firebrand. They'd be there for each other in hard times and in good times, no matter the danger, always trusting in each other's strong heart.

By the time they reached Milford, Rose's spirits were soaring. The horse had obeyed their every command, almost as though he had sensed the importance of their mission. They spotted the inn as soon as they crossed the bridge, and guided the horse into a copse of maple trees tucked by the riverbank.

"Give them this note and the silver paperweight," Rose said, "or they might not believe you."

Rose handed Pauline the silver paperweight from her uncle's library and a note she'd written while Pauline had fetched May. Pauline slid off the back of the horse and, after making certain no one was watching, ran around back. It was only a few moments before she came out with an elderly couple with pale but kind faces, the husband leaning on a cane, the wife with thinning white hair twisted in a knot.

The woman's forehead knit together as she looked between the note in her hand and Rose atop the horse, half hidden in the maple branches. She glanced at the road in the distance. "Your maid says Lord Firebrand sent you?" she asked in a low voice.

Rose nodded.

The elderly couple exchanged a cryptic look, and the man cleared his throat. "You've wasted your time. We've no association with such a criminal."

"Of course not," Rose said. "But if you *did*, or if you knew someone who did, we have a message on his behalf. A certain military captain has been arrested, but we've brought the package he was supposed to deliver."

The old man looked keenly around the trees, as though expecting the Confederate army to burst out from behind the bushes. "This isn't some game you girls are playing?"

"It's no game," Rose promised. Her heart was pounding; she was risking just as much as the innkeepers. Pauline was risking far more.

Pauline lifted the top layer of Rose's skirt, revealing the maps hidden in Rose's petticoats. The innkeeper's eyes went wide as he unfastened one of the maps and unrolled it, eyes tracing the nautical courses. "Nancy, look!"

The wife rested a hand on his shoulder, beaming. Quickly, she and Pauline unfastened the rest of the maps. Then the woman ran into the stable to fetch an old feed bag, which they stuffed the maps into. From high on the horse, Rose kept an eye on the nearby road.

"You'll get them to General McClellan?" Rose asked.

"We will," the man said. "By tomorrow, that Confederate shipment will be captured. Do me a favor and thank Lord Firebrand for his work. A wonder, that man is." He lowered his voice. "Is he truly a British lord?"

Rose and Pauline exchanged a look.

"Ah . . . he certainly is," said Pauline.

The man chuckled to himself and carried the maps into the inn, but his wife lingered. She stroked the horse's flank. "I have a feeling that the true thanks might be due elsewhere. After all, it isn't an English lord I see before me now, nor a Union spy. It's two girls." She smiled kindly. "Whoever Lord Firebrand is, he's fortunate to have you on his team. I daresay if I was in trouble, I'd turn to the two of you before any English rogues."

She winked, glanced at the road, and hurried back inside.

They rode back to Drexel Hall in triumph and slipped into the stables. May helped Rose ease carefully off of the horse and into the wicker-lined seat of her chair.

"So what do we do now?" Pauline asked as soon as May was gone.

Rose leaned forward to stroke the horse. She couldn't stop thinking about the young man who had trusted the two of them, the young man with such delectable eyes and an even more attractive spirit. Was he worth one more risk?

She gave Pauline a sly smile. "How do you think Lord Firebrand would feel about a prison break?"

Pauline cocked her head. "I thought we were out of nitro-glycerin."

"I'm still in correspondence with that Italian chemist's apprentice. He's coming back to America next month for another round of lectures. . . ."

Pauline's eyes lit up. "In that case, I pity the prison guards holding Henry. I think Lord Firebrand just found his new mission."

❈ AUTHOR'S NOTE ❈

Though the masked rebel known as Lord Firebrand is fictional, female spies during the Civil War were a matter of fact. Most notable was the Union spy and founder of the Underground Railroad, Harriet Tubman, as well as Union spy Elizabeth Van Lew and Confederate spies Antonia Ford and Belle Boyd. These women — especially if they were young, attractive, or of high society — used their position to gain valuable information from male officers, which they then might pass along to their connections by hiding notes in their elaborate hairstyles or hoopskirts.

I love writing about brave girls who are often underestimated, like Rose and Pauline. I hope you like reading about them, too. And I hope you feel inspired by these women who fought for what they believed in, not on the battlefield but in the daily choices they made to risk their lives to build a better world.

Special thanks to Dhonielle Clayton, Anna Henshaw, Daniel Pierce, Beth Revis, and Ryan Graudin for their thoughtful notes and expertise.

STEP RIGHT UP

JESSICA SPOTSWOOD

I step onto the ridge of the roof of the First Presbyterian and open my parasol.

Well, it isn't exactly *my* parasol; I thieved it from my sister, Pearl. She carries a painted blue silk parasol all summer long so the sun won't darken her skin—which is dumb as bricks, if you ask me, 'cause Tulsa is Indian Territory, half Creek and half Cherokee. Most of our neighbors got Indian blood and brown skin; it's nothing to be ashamed of. But Pearl's a priss. Always worried people might talk. That's only one of the ways we're different, Pearl and me.

I just about live for making people talk.

Right now, down there on the southeast corner of Fourth and Boston, there's a whole crowd hollering up at me. They started gathering when I pushed open the shutters on the bell tower, and the crowd kept on growing as I stepped onto the ledge, flung myself onto the sharply pitched roof, and climbed up to the ridge.

"What the heck are you doing, Ruby?" Fred yells.

Fred's got no imagination at all. What does he *think* I'm doing? I'm certainly not about to jump to my death. I swear, I don't know what Louise sees in him.

I can hear her down there, too. Louise Whitehill and I have been best friends since we were little, and I can just picture her, her dark eyes squinched up, hiding her face against Fred's chest, scared to watch for fear I'm going to fall and break my fool neck.

I take a tentative step forward. The church isn't *that* tall. Not compared to the fancy Opera House or that new high school they're building. But it's tall enough that walking it makes my heart race and my head spin a little. It's taller than our porch roof and a sight taller than the rail fence behind the schoolhouse. It will be the tallest thing I've ever walked.

I take a deep breath. Miss Etta wouldn't be scared. She'd be flashing that pretty red-lipped smile of hers. Last summer when Archer Brothers was in town, she crossed the high wire and didn't wobble once. Did a perfect pirouette in the middle. I remember how the whole crowd watched, hushed, and held their breath, and then exploded in furious applause when she finished.

If she can do that, surely I can do *this*.

I take another step. Then another. Below me, my crowd hushes. By now somebody's probably run to get Momma. And Uncle Jack. My skin shivers at that thought, but I daren't look down. I've got to keep my eyes locked on the other end of the ridge. Above it, the sky is a stormy blue-gray just the color of Miss Etta's eyes. To the east, storm clouds are gathering.

A breeze flutters the hem of my second-best blue dress and tugs at the parasol. It's probably making my hair go all askew, even after I sat so patient and let Pearl do those pretty braids around the crown of my head. She smiled all secretive and proud while she did it, and I know she thought I was finally taking an interest in some boy. But no boy can make me feel like this.

I take another step. I hear the rattle of wagon wheels, the *clip-clop* of hooves, the thud of my own heartbeat. The crowd's quiet, but I can feel their eyes on me. All those eyes. It feels *magnificent*.

Up here, I am strong and brave and beautiful. Up here, no one can touch me.

I am almost there. Just a few more steps. I imagine the applause when I reach the end. I imagine how tomorrow morning I'll go down and meet the circus train at the depot and tell Miss Etta. She'll be so proud. Proud enough to agree to my proposition, maybe.

The wind blows a little harder. Too hard. It catches the parasol and lifts it, and, distracted, I hold on when I should let go. I lean too far and lose my balance. My right foot slips off the ridge, and I fall.

I let go of the parasol and grab for the ridge with both hands, but I miss and start sliding down the roof, feetfirst, on my belly. Flailing, my fingernails clawing against the shingles, boots scrambling for purchase, I bump and skid down toward the drainpipe.

The crowd is shouting, panicked. Louise screams. The sliding seems to last forever, scraping up my palms and snagging my skirt. Finally, toward the bottom of the roof, I catch myself. I hang there, my breath coming fast. My shoulder throbs.

After a minute, I scuttle sideways like a crab, inching back toward the bell tower. When I get there, I rise to my feet, unsteady, both arms out for balance. I climb back to the window ledge and crawl inside, bloody and defeated. Not so untouchable after all, I guess.

In the privacy of the bell tower, I take a slow inventory. My shoulder hurts like heck from how I caught myself, and my palms are all scratched up and bleeding. My skirt's got two big jagged tears, and there's another one in my right sleeve. My straight-as-a-pin hair has fallen out of Pearl's pretty braids and hangs in clumps around my face. I'm pretty sure there's a bruise already rising on my hip and a brush burn on my forearm. At least my petticoats stayed down; I don't think I could bear the indignity of having shown everybody my knickers, too.

Still, no point hiding in here. Louise is sure to come find me sooner or later. And accidents are part of the business, Miss Etta says. Long as you get back up, there's no shame in it.

There's a smattering of applause when I walk out. Not nearly so much as there would've been if I hadn't fallen, but enough that I smile and drop a curtsy for the crowd.

Louise rushes up and hugs me fierce. She's wearing her new pink hat with the flowers on it, but beneath it her brown cheeks are wet with tears and her full pink lips are trembling. Lord, she's pretty. The prettiest girl in town if you ask me, with her glossy black hair and high cheekbones and big brown eyes.

"You could have *died*!" she shrieks.

"Well, I didn't. I'm right here," I say, a little bit thrilled at the reminder she still cares. She's been awful preoccupied with Fred ever since he gave her that ring.

"That was pretty brave," Fred says. "For a girl."

"I'd like to see *you* try it," I retort.

Louise clings to him. "Don't you dare."

I turn away. Louise used to cling to me almost like that. She'd look up at me with a smile like I hung the stars in the sky, and I'd daydream about leaning down and kissing her. Then she took up with Fred, and I realized she only wanted to kiss boys.

While they canoodle, my eyes dart nervously through the crowd. There he is. Uncle Jack, storming toward me just like a big angry bull. Momma trails behind him, her shoulders hunched, making herself as small as possible.

Louise extracts herself from Fred and grabs my hand. "You all right?" she asks. "That looked like it hurt."

I raise my chin. "Nothing but my pride."

She shakes her head, the flowers in her ridiculous hat bobbing, as she examines me with gentle fingers. "You're a mess. Lord, look at your palms. You're bleeding!"

I barely get a chance to enjoy the attention before Uncle Jack is on me.

"What were you thinking, making a spectacle of yourself like that?" He grabs my arm roughly, and I try to pull away but can't. "Ruby Porter, are you wearing rouge? What do you think you are, an actress? A prostitute?"

"A *performer,*" I correct him. Maybe the rouge was too much. I ordered it from a catalog because I couldn't exactly buy some from Uncle Jack's store. But I know Miss Etta wears it when she performs. Lipstick, too. It makes her lips look as red as fall apples.

"You see all these people gawping at you? At your momma and me?" Uncle Jack roars, and Louise and Fred beat a hasty retreat. Louise has bandaged me up often enough to know what his temper's like.

"You're lucky you didn't kill yourself, Ruby! You could have broken your neck." Momma jumps between us, patting my arms, her brown eyes full of worry. Like she hasn't seen me broken before. Like most of my bruises haven't come from the man at her side. Like all her tears and *sorrys* are worth a damn.

Pearl sashays up behind them, torn blue silk and splintered steel ribs in her hands. "You stole my parasol! Ruby, someone could have thought that was *me* up there!"

I look at her—not a molasses-colored curl out of place, not a speck of dust on her—and let out an unladylike snort. "Not likely."

"Oh, you think this is *funny?*" Uncle Jack's big hands fist at his sides, and Pearl shrinks back. "What about you, Pearl? *You* think this is funny? We got us a pair of comedians here?"

Pearl fidgets with her skirt, avoiding my eyes. "I think it's scandalous, is what it is," she says primly.

My shoulders slump. Fact is, nobody in this town is going to stick up for me anymore. It was one thing when I was five, or eight, or eleven, or maybe even thirteen. But I'm seventeen now, and even Louise thinks it's time for me to find a nice boy and settle down.

That's why I've got to get away. Soon, before I stop wanting things altogether. If I ever get that hangdog, faded look Momma's got, like every bit of spark in her has gone out—well, then Uncle Jack will have won, and I just cannot bear that.

Back home, he backhands me so hard, it sends me tumbling clear across my bedroom. My head knocks into the armoire, hard, and I see stars. Blood trickles down my forehead, warm and wet, but I wipe it away and scramble up. *Long as you get back up, there's no shame in it.* Miss Etta was talking about falling, not being knocked down, but it's sort of become my personal motto.

Uncle Jack doesn't like it. He'd rather I cower on the floor and cry.

He hits me again, with a closed fist this time, right in the stomach. It knocks me breathless, and I fall to my knees.

Stupid, I think, wiping away the tears pooling in my eyes, determined that he won't see them. It is stupid, not brave, to keep getting up. To keep defying him. I should be an obedient, butter-wouldn't-melt-in-her-mouth little priss like Pearl—or I should at least do a better job of *pretending*. I think of Momma's words on the walk home. *You're seventeen now, Ruby, and you need to consider your reputation. What will people think?*

Folks thought I was marvelous, up there on the church roof. I know they did. For a minute, they forgot I was scrappy little Ruby Porter, and I was a star.

Do you see Louise acting like that? Men don't want a girl who sasses them and tries to walk fences. They want a girl who's pretty and sweet and doesn't make any trouble. They want a girl who acts like a girl.

But Momma's never seen Miss Etta. She's more than just *pretty*. She's the most beautiful woman in the world, *and* the bravest. She doesn't bow down to anybody.

Uncle Jack stands in the doorway, his breath coming fast, his face flushed beneath his reddish-brown whiskers. "You have a roof over your head and food to eat because of *me*, Ruby Porter. Because of my charity. I could've tossed you and your momma and your sister out on your ears when Ma died, but I didn't. And this is how you repay me? Embarrassing me like that in front of the whole town?" Spittle flies from his mouth. "You might not care about our good name, but the rest of us do. If you can't act respectable, then you won't leave this house."

"What are you going to do, lock me up?" I heave myself onto the bed and brace myself for another hit.

He doesn't hit me. He just smiles, real slow, and it is downright creepy how pleased he looks with himself. "That's exactly what I'm going to do. You won't leave this house. You won't leave this *room*. Long as I see fit. Long as it takes for you to get it through your thick skull how to behave like a lady."

He slams the door shut. A key turns in the lock.

I sit there, blood dripping down my cheek, my head and arm throbbing. He locked me in. He's never locked me in before.

"But—but Archer Brothers comes tomorrow," I say softly, sure he can't hear.

He knows. He knows it's the day of the year I love more than anything—more than Christmas or my birthday. That's why he's doing this.

The Archer Brothers Circus has been coming to Tulsa every July since I was five and Pearl was three. That first time, Daddy took Pearl and me to town to see them. We drank lemonade and ate roasted peanuts and laughed at the clowns and watched, wide-eyed at the elephants and the lions and the human pretzel and the albino girl and the armless lady and the snake charmer and the acrobats and the bareback riders and the jugglers and most especially the wire-walker. Pearl loved the bareback riders best, but for me, it's always been the wire-walkers. That afternoon, Daddy taught me how to walk our rail fence out at the ranch.

The next day, Daddy and the circus were both gone.

That's when Momma sold all our cattle to the Gillespies and moved us into town. A woman with two little girls can't manage a ranch by herself—or at least Momma can't. And all her folks were back east in Baltimore. That's how we came to live in town with Uncle Jack, Daddy's half-brother. It wasn't so bad before Granny died, but after that—it's like I turned into a lightning rod, and Uncle Jack's the lightning. I used to think, least he's hitting me and not Pearl. But lately—well. Lately, I want to hit back, only I'm a good foot shorter and about a hundred pounds lighter, and I don't think that'd go so well for me.

Granny said our daddy was a dreamer, that he had a restless

spirit and a wandering heart. Uncle Jack says any man who runs off and leaves his family like that ain't worth remembering. But lately, I've been worrying maybe I have my daddy's heart, 'cause all I can think about is running away.

Next morning, just as I'm getting so antsy I can't stand it, there's a soft knock at my door. "Ruby?"

It's Pearl.

"He and Momma went to the store. Took the key with him. I'm sorry." Uncle Jack runs Porter's Grocery, and today it'll be hopping. Town'll be swarmed with oilmen and cattlemen and their families come in to see the circus. The store will close for the parade, but before and after, Momma and Uncle Jack will be there.

It hits me like a punch: I'm going to miss the parade. I never miss the parade. Most years I'm down at the depot to watch the circus train arrive, too. They'll be wondering where I was. What good is Pearl's "sorry" now?

"Four elephants, same as last year. Talked to Harvey and Miss Jo. They send their regards. Said they'll keep an eye out for you at the parade."

I crawl off the bed and gawp at the closed door. Pearl went down to the depot? Prissy Pearl? Usually I've got to drag her with me to the matinee.

"Saw Miss Lula, too. She asked after her little chickadee. I reckon that's you."

Miss Lula is the snake charmer, really Mrs. Lula Antonelli. Her husband, Alberto, is one of the Flying Antonellis.

"How's Stella May?" I ask.

"She's gone," Pearl says, and my heart drops. Stella May is— was, I guess—Archer Brothers' albino girl. At first I was real shy of her and the other sideshow freaks. I'm ashamed to say it, but the first time we met, I was afraid of her pale skin and white hair and nearsighted pink eyes. But I was only six, that first year I went without Daddy. After the matinee crowd cleared out, I snuck into the backyard, where the circus performers played cards and sewed up rips in their costumes and practiced their acts. They weren't supposed to talk to towners—it "ruins the mystique," Miss Jo says, and it's dangerous for kids to be running around back there besides—but they couldn't resist little me: blond-braided, fierce-eyed, looking for my daddy. I'd convinced myself he'd run off with the circus and was there somewhere, as a roustabout, maybe, or behind a clown's greasepaint.

Daddy wasn't there, but they let Pearl and me stay anyhow. And we've gone back every year since.

Pearl hears me sniffle. "Wait—no! She's not dead! She got picked up by Cole Brothers."

"Oh." I'm glad Stella May is still alive and well, but . . . "I can't believe she left. She's been there forever." A dozen years at least.

That's one of the things I love about the circus. It welcomes all kinds. It doesn't matter whether you're rich or poor, young or old, fat or thin, black or white or Indian, long as you have a talent of some sort. Long as you can make people stare and clap, you're family. I guess they have their squabbles and spats, but mostly they stick up for one another.

Maybe joining them would give me a do-over where family's concerned.

"Did you—did you see Miss Etta?" I practically hold my breath while I wait for Pearl's answer. The Bible says we mustn't worship false idols, but Miss Etta makes that real hard. I want to be just like her someday: brave and magnificent and kind, too. Last year she let me walk the low wire she claimed she strung up for practice—but she doesn't need practice on a low wire; I know it was just for me—and she taught me how to do a pirouette.

"Yep. She says hello and she'll see you after the matinee. I didn't say anything about you being locked up. Didn't think you'd want her to know," Pearl whispers. "I told them you were feeling poorly. Had a headache."

I groan. Like a headache would keep me away! They'll know better. Know something's wrong.

Won't they? Or will they think I'm growing up and turning respectable on them?

Still, it took guts for Pearl to go down to the depot by herself. "Thank you," I say through the door.

Pearl clears her throat and then slides something beneath the door. It's a small, brightly colored rectangle of paper.

My ticket. The advance team came through town a few weeks ago with dozens of posters, and I asked for a particular one for Porter's Grocery: a big colored illustration of Miss Etta up on the high wire with her parasol. Giant letters advertise her "death-defying feat of balance." We got two free tickets for displaying it in the front window.

"How am I supposed to use this?" I ask. "I can't break the door down."

"Well, it's a good thing you ain't scared of heights, then." I can hear a smile in Pearl's voice. "Go look out the window."

I scowl. "I ain't scared of heights, but I can't fly, Pearl." Uncle Jack's a bully, but he isn't stupid. There's no trellis, no drainpipes, no tree near enough my bedroom window. The porch roof is clear on the opposite side of the house. I can't see any way out, not unless I want to jump down two stories onto the hard, sunbaked summer ground. It never did rain last night, despite those storm clouds.

"Just go look."

I walk to the window and look out and, somehow, there's a ladder. A real tall wooden one, like somebody would use to paint houses or do work on a roof. In fact, this ladder looks sort of famil- iar. Like maybe—like maybe it's one from the construction site over at the new high school. How on earth did it get through town and beneath my bedroom window?

"Pearl!" I press myself back against the door. "Did you *steal* that ladder?"

"I certainly did not." But she laughs.

"How did it get here, then?" I ask. "'Cause it ain't Christmas and it sure wasn't Santa."

"Well . . . I maybe encouraged Frankie Kneeland, and Louise maybe encouraged Fred to borrow it. There's no construction going on today anyhow on account of everybody going to the circus. That's a waste of a good ladder, if you ask me."

Oh, my Lord. My little sister encouraged her new beau to steal a ladder for me!

"*Thank you.*" My voice is fervent as a prayer. I could hug her right now.

"Just—be careful, all right? The boys are downstairs. I'll send them out to hold it in a minute. And, Ruby?"

I'm already whirling around the room, hastily rebraiding my hair so it doesn't show the cut on my forehead, fastening the buttons on my boots, shoving Momma's pearl ear bobs through my ears. "Yes?"

"Uncle Jack'll be watching the parade in front of the store. Steer clear of him, all right? Try not to draw attention to your- self for once. He hears you're out and he'll come looking for you and . . ." Her voice wavers. We both know what'll happen if he catches me. He'll beat me within an inch of my life.

"I'm not scared of him."

"Maybe you should be," she suggests. "Please be careful, Roo. Just this once. For me."

She hasn't called me Roo for years. Not since we were little.

"All right," I say, and she promises to send the boys out to hold the ladder.

I finish braiding my hair and buttoning my boots, and I put the ticket in my pocket. I add the old photograph of Daddy and Momma and Pearl and me from the summer he left. I stole it from Momma years ago, and she's never asked for it back.

I gaze at myself in the looking glass over our armoire. I've got Momma's dark-blond hair, but Daddy's dark eyes and high cheekbones and lean figure. Momma says I take after him in other ways, too. *You can be real charming when you want, Ruby Leigh. Just like your daddy.* I'm not exactly pretty, but I don't need pretty where I'm going. I just need brave. I just need to get back up when I fall.

I watch the parade from down in front of Farmer's National Bank with Louise and Fred. It's down the block from Porter's Grocery, so if I lean around Fred and stand on my tiptoes, I can keep an eye on Uncle Jack. He and Momma and Pearl—and Frankie Kneeland—got a prime spot right out in front of the store. They're playing like they're a happy little family. Must be easier without me, since I don't give a lick what the neighbors think. But Uncle Jack has aspirations. Wants to be more than a shopkeeper someday, he says.

I watch their act from afar: Momma in her high-necked navy day dress and Uncle Jack in his second-best suit, smirking and glad-handing anybody who gets close enough. Pearl wears a pink pin-striped dress, her hair in two dark braids, squealing in pretend fright as the dancing bears pass by. Her playing scared gives Frankie an excuse to squeeze her, even in front of Momma.

To the other folks lining the street, the parade's a spectacle.

Miss Jo taught me that spectacle's real important in the circus. The whole point is to put on a good show, after all, and give the towners a holiday. We're supposed to watch the parade of beautiful girls and human miracles and terrifying animals and be amazed, so we'll spend our hard-earned money on tickets—and then we'll spend a little extra to get into the sideshow, or get some treats from the candy butchers, or buy a souvenir picture of one of the freaks. We're supposed to see them as wondrous figures, larger than life.

To me, it feels like a reunion with old friends. And a reminder of what can be, if I've got the grit to make it happen.

Uncle Jack and Momma, Pearl, the girls at school and at church—they've called me a lot of things, but a coward ain't one.

The beautiful painted wagons are passing by. Some of them are cages with menagerie animals inside. Pearl throws herself at Frankie when the lions go by, and I roll my eyes. We both know that the zebras and camels are meaner.

Miss Jo's girls come next, riding high-stepping, shining white horses. For all that Uncle Jack goes on about the immorality of the circus, I bet he's eyeing the girls' legs, exposed to the knees in their short flared skirts.

I spot Harvey in his white greasepaint and high-collared costume. He spots me, too, and does a pratfall, landing right on his rump, to the laughter of the crowd. He sits there for a minute, pouting, till another clown pretends to kick him. Then he jumps up and does a somersault. When he lands, he grins and salutes me. I wave at him till people start to look in my direction, and then I duck back down into the crowd. I promised Pearl that I wouldn't draw attention, but it's harder than I thought.

So I don't wave when I see Miss Lula in her wagon, holding her big boa constrictor up for the crowd to see. Louise clings to Fred, and I crane around them and see Pearl clinging to Frankie.

Truth be told, I don't love Edgar, either. He winds around Miss Lula's waist, his yellow a stark contrast against her ruffled, low-cut violet dress. Miss Lula has the kind of curves I'll never have, the kind men will pay a pretty penny to see. I joked once with Fred that I'd have to rely on my legs, seeing as how I don't have a nice bosom like Louise, and he blushed bright red all the way to his ears and Louise had to remind me I shouldn't talk about bosoms with him.

Miss Lula spots me even though I'm not waving and winks at me, her dark eyes winged with kohl. Circus performers are meant to look exotic, like they're braver and more mysterious than regular folks. That's part of the illusion.

The Antonellis come next, turning cartwheels and somersaults and climbing on one another's shoulders till they've built a human pyramid. The children around us *ooh* and *aah*. Some of the boys jump into the street and turn cartwheels of their own, ignoring the dust and dirt that cake their hands and faces, and I wish for a second I were a boy. I can turn a better cartwheel than any of them.

But wishing I were a boy doesn't last long because here come the elephants, and riding them are the biggest stars of the Archer Brothers Circus. Miss Jo waves like a queen from the howdah on Junior's back. And after her comes Miss Etta, pretty as can be in her ruffled pink dress and brown curls. She's carrying her pink parasol like a fine lady, like Pearl afraid of damaging her skin in the hot Tulsa sun. But it's the same parasol she uses as she dances and pirouettes across the high wire.

I want to be like her. I want it so badly, it's become a permanent dull ache, somewhere behind my ribs, gnawing at me night and day.

I look back at my family, and for a minute I think Momma

sees me. Will she tell Uncle Jack? I crouch down behind Fred and Louise, my heart hammering, and I know I can't keep on like this.

One way or another, my life changes today.

Between the parade and the matinee, I go with Louise to her house. She's got seven little brothers and sisters, and with all the kids running around and hollering, her momma hardly takes any notice of us. There's leftover roast pork and fresh-baked bread with thick slabs of butter and icy glasses of milk. Mrs. Whitehill jokes about needing to fatten me up 'cause I'm so skinny and boys like girls with some meat on them. I laugh and then almost cry, thinking of how many times I've eaten here to escape Uncle Jack's temper and Momma's thin-lipped disapproval and Pearl's silence.

"You're leaving, aren't you," Louise says later, the two of us alone in the room she shares with her sisters.

"If they'll have me. If I stay, I think he'll kill me." I push my braid out of the way to show her the cut on my head.

Louise grabs my chin with pinching fingers and stares at me, her dark eyes real solemn. I remember how she was the first one to clap the first time I walked the rail fence behind the school. We shared a desk every day after that. She always stuck up for me when the other girls were mean.

"I'll miss you, Ruby," she says, tears in her eyes.

I'll miss her, too. More than she knows. But it's a big world and there are other girls out there, and maybe I'll find one who might want to kiss me back.

"Be happy," I say. "Fred ain't so bad."

She blushes and grins at me. "He's all right."

× × ×

After lunch I head down to the big field where the circus is set up. I get there before the menagerie tent is even open, so I wait for Pearl outside the big top. There are a couple hundred people milling around already, everybody in their finery, exchanging news. The Atlantic and Pacific Railroad ran an excursion train from nearby towns this morning, and today's *Indian Republic* newspaper blared headlines about the circus coming. It's better than a church picnic for gossip about who's courting and who's feuding and whose farm is losing money.

Part of me is scared Uncle Jack will show up instead of Pearl. He could have gone home for lunch and found my room empty. Momma could have told him she saw me at the parade. If I wasn't where he left me, it wouldn't take him two seconds to figure out where I'd be.

I breathe a sigh of relief when I see Pearl. She wouldn't have come unless she thought it was safe, unless Uncle Jack was still at the store. Pearl puts herself first, always. I figure it's time for me to do the same.

I pull her into the long shadow of the big top. "I need to tell you something."

This is the hardest part. I'll miss Louise, but I know she'll be all right, and I'm tired of pining while she's happy with Fred. Pearl—well. What if Uncle Jack turns his fists on her once I'm gone? She stood up for me today. She schemed and stole for me, and if Uncle Jack had caught her—well, it means something that she risked that for me. How do I tell her that I'm running off, just like our daddy did?

"You're not coming back home." Pearl smiles her big, buck-toothed smile. "I knew before I went and stole that ladder. Once you got free, you couldn't go back."

"I'm sorry," I say. I remember how Bobby Billington made fun of her teeth and called her a rabbit, and how I punched him and got sent home from school for it. How many times I've sassed Uncle Jack when he was in a mood to make sure he'd hit me and not Pearl. How can I leave my little sister behind?

She shrugs. "You looked after me the whole time we were growing up. It's time for me to look after myself now. Least till Frankie and I can get married."

"Get married!" I echo, surprised that she's thinking of that already, and she giggles.

"We all got our own plans, Roo. Marrying Frankie might not be as grand as running off to join the circus, but he makes me laugh. Once he finishes school, he'll have a job working in his daddy's drugstore. He'll take good care of me. And he's a real good kisser."

I blush and Pearl giggles again. Maybe she ain't such a priss after all.

We dart inside the sideshow tent the moment it opens and hurry to Miss Lula's stage. She winks and holds Edgar up in my direction. "You want to hold him, missy? Don't be scared—step right up!"

Much as I want to prove her wrong, I shudder back like she knew I would, and she wheezes with laughter. If there's anything at the circus I'm still afraid of, it's Edgar. I know he's already well fed and sleepy, so he won't actually squeeze her to death, but I never have liked snakes.

Next we pop into the menagerie tent, where Pearl wrinkles her nose at the rank smell of manure. We steer well clear of the black-and-white-striped zebras, swishing their tails lazily to keep the flies off. Harvey told us that they bite, and the tawny camels from the Arabian Desert will spit at people if they get mad. The bears and lions are all off getting ready for the show, but people crowd around the elephants' pen to watch them shuffle and stomp, clouds of dust rising with every step. They are real majestic, but their eyes always look sort of sad.

Then the ringmaster, Cal, in his black suit and black top hat, starts calling people in with his big deep voice. "Step right up!" he hollers from the entrance of the big top, and people throng toward the opening. "Step right up!"

There's nothing else on earth like it.

I watch, rapt, clapping till my hands hurt. Part of me is sad, knowing this might be the last time I ever watch the circus with Pearl. After today—if it all goes well—I'll never be a spectator again. But for today, part of me still feels like that little wide-eyed five-year-old girl, bouncing in her seat, hooting with laughter as the clowns perform between acts, chewing salty roasted peanuts and washing them down with sweet, tart pink lemonade from the candy butchers, surrounded by the smells of grass and sawdust and sweat.

The audience giggles at the dogs that leap through rings and do other funny tricks, then roars with laughter at the bears that walk on two legs and play catch. We all gasp as Evangeline stands in a cage surrounded by sleek powerful lions, a whip in her hand. It's not as dangerous as people think—I happen to know that whip's just for effect—but it's not easy, either. Beneath her lacy yellow dress, her arms and legs are covered with thick white scars.

After the animal acts comes the aerial ballet. The Antonellis fly from one trapeze to another, leaping through the air so graceful, I half believe they'd keep soaring even without the bars.

Pearl leans forward when the equestrians ride in on their high-stepping white horses. They're still her favorite after all these years.

When Miss Jo stands on her horse's back, then does a somersault, I can't help but grip my skirt nervously in my fist. She looks as dainty as Pearl. One time her horse shied and threw her, and she got trampled by its hooves and broke her ribs. Another time she busted her arm. But she always gets back up.

We watch the jugglers and the acrobats on their rings, but I'm eager for the lights to dim on the two side rings and Miss Etta to take the center stage. Even the parade of elephants, walking on their hind legs, can't hold a candle to Miss Etta.

She's last, like the star she is. I hold my breath while she climbs up to the high wire. She looks impossibly tiny up there. If she falls—

Well, that doesn't bear thinking about. The circus is dangerous. The artists are always trying to better their acts, do something more impossible and wondrous, something to make our jaws drop and our hands sore from clapping.

The crowd hushes as Miss Etta begins a pirouette, then releases a noisy breath when she's facing front again. She keeps moving, always, and when she's only got a third of the way to go, she does a few dance steps, as though she's waltzing with an imaginary partner. The crowd roars and I flush, their approval and excitement coursing through me like it was me up there.

After—after Miss Etta has climbed back down to earth, after the Roman chariot races on the hippodrome track—we wait for the crowd to disperse some.

"The bareback riders are still my favorites," Pearl admits, as if I don't know.

"They were good this year." There was a new rider—a tall, graceful girl with dark curls and long, shapely legs beneath her short red skirt. She didn't look much older than me.

"What're you thinking about?" Pearl elbows me. "You're blushing!"

"Nothing!" I say quickly. "Come on, let's go."

Pearl and I climb over the ropes and get waved past the NO ADMITTANCE signs into the yard.

"Ruby, honey!" Miss Jo cries, catching me by the shoulders and hugging me tight. She smells faintly of lavender water. "There you are. We missed you this morning. Pearl here said you weren't feeling well?"

"You were amazing," I say, evading the question as she hugs Pearl. Miss Jo just laughs and pulls off the long black Cleopatra wig she wore for the chariot races.

"Isn't she, though?" Harvey already scrubbed off his greasepaint and took off his high-collared, ruffled clown costume. Now he's just a bald man in his shirtsleeves and suspenders and trousers.

"That our Ruby?" Miss Lula smothers me in another hug. "You look so pretty, sugar. How come you ain't married yet?"

"What's that I hear? My protégée's not getting married?" Miss Etta strolls out of the dressing tent. She's shed her ruffled pink gown for a simple ivory dress, but she's still wearing her red lipstick.

"Never," I say stoutly, my heart singing. She called me her protégée!

"Oh, sugar, don't say never. You never know when you might meet an Italian acrobat who'll sweep you right off your feet," Miss Lula says, and sure enough, Alberto scoops her up into his arms. She's taller and broader than him, but he dances a few light steps before he puts her down, leaves a loud kiss on her cheek, and wanders off.

"I'll leave the marrying to Pearl," I say, and they cluck over her like a bunch of mother hens, asking about her beau while she giggles and tosses her hair.

I don't get stage fright, never have, but I'm nervous now. I've never been good at asking permission for things, but I need their help. If I go to the manager with the support of the circus's best performers behind me, he might just take a chance on me.

"What's wrong, sugar? You look like you're about to faint, and you're not the fainting type," Miss Lula says finally, squinting at me.

"Tonight—" The words strangle in my throat, and I cough. "Tonight, when the circus train leaves, I want to be on it. I want to join Archer Brothers."

I don't know what kind of reaction I expected, but it's not this—a terrible silence, and then an explosion of questions.

"You want to run away from home?" Harvey asks, thumbs hooked under his suspenders. There's a stray swipe of white greasepaint by one of his ears. "What about your family?"

Miss Etta gives a tiny shake of her head, chestnut curls bobbing. "You're not ready for the high wire yet."

"I can learn." My voice comes out high, desperate. It doesn't sound like me. "I just need a chance."

"What about your family?" Harvey asks again. "What about your sister, here?"

"She's got to go." Pearl's voice is firm. "Uncle Jack—he and Ruby are like oil and water. They don't mix. He hits her."

"Just her? What about you?" Harvey asks.

Pearl shrugs. "I got my own plans. And I can bide my time."

They're silent again. They've never seen the bruises. Those usually come *after* the circus leaves town.

"No." My voice is stronger now, even as I'm searching for the right words. I need to say this right. "I'm not just running away from Uncle Jack. It never has been about running away. It's about running *toward*. This—" I throw my arms wide, encompassing the backyard and the big top and the menagerie tent and the sideshow tent. "It's some kind of magic. That feeling, when they all watch and hold their breath and then clap"—I turn to Harvey—"or laugh—or, Miss Lula, when you and Edgar make 'em squirm—there's nothing else like it. And I just feel like—like my whole life here would be wasted. If I got married and had babies and never walked the church roof again, maybe I could go on living, but it'd be some pale ghost version of me."

I feel the sudden, horrible urge to cry. My throat knots and my eyes fill with tears. Pearl takes my hand. For a moment, there's just silence.

"You walked the church roof?" Miss Etta asks. "Which one?"

"First Presbyterian. But the wind caught my parasol and I fell. I was almost across, though."

She laughs and it sounds like church bells ringing. Like hope.

"I'd better keep teaching you," she says. "Or you're going to get yourself killed."

Really? I launch myself at her, hugging her so tight she makes a little choking noise.

"We'll have to find something else for you to do in the meantime. A low-wire act, maybe. You ever ride a bicycle?" Miss Jo asks, and I nod.

"I can teach her how to do some tricks," Harvey says. I've seen him ride a bicycle in his act, swerving all over the place, being chased by a yappy little terrier.

"You'll have to work hard. Alberto and his brothers, they've been training since they were children," Miss Lula says.

"I'm not afraid of hard work," I promise.

Miss Lula smirks and pets Edgar, who's lying like a mink stole around her shoulders. "Only snakes, huh?"

There is a commotion back by the ropes and the NO ADMIT-TANCE sign. Some drunk trying to get in and look at the elephants, maybe. We all turn to look.

It's not a drunk; it's Uncle Jack shoving his way past two clowns. The town sheriff is following him.

My stomach sinks. Am I being arrested for running away?

I can't be. *This* is my family. This strange group of people of all shapes and sizes and abilities, *this* is the family I chose for myself when I was just a little girl.

I glance toward Pearl, but she's done some magic of her own and melted into the crowd. Out of the corner of my eye, I catch the flap of the mess tent swinging shut.

"Ruby Leigh Porter, what in blazes are you doing here?" Uncle Jack lunges for me, but Harvey steps between us. "Get out of my way. That girl is a thief and a runaway. I've brought the sheriff here to arrest her."

"A thief?" Harvey looks at me.

"She stole those pearl earrings she's got on," Sheriff Moore says. "They belong to her momma."

I pull them out of my ears and hand them to the sheriff. "Here. Take them."

"Well, there. That's settled now. You her father?" Harvey asks Uncle Jack. He knows better; he's making a point. "This your father, Ruby?"

I raise my chin. "No."

"I'm her uncle. My brother—half-brother—ran off. Always had his head in the clouds, that one, always thought he was better'n everybody else, and she takes after him. I been raising this girl since she was five years old, so I think I got as much authority as any father. I'm taking her home. Come with me now, Ruby. Don't make a fuss."

"I *will* make a fuss," I say. "I will make the biggest fuss you ever saw. You'll have to drag me back through town, kicking and screaming. You know I'll do it."

"She's my niece. My *property*," Uncle Jack says, turning to the sheriff. "Arrest her!"

"For what?" Sheriff Moore says. "She ain't broken any laws. She gave the earrings back, and Marianne didn't want her arrested for that in the first place. This seems like a family matter, not a law matter."

"Maybe you should let us take her off your hands," Harvey says. "Seeing as how she's so much trouble for you."

"I will be," I vow. "I'll be so much trouble, you'll never get to be mayor."

I can tell that hits him hard. His chances are far better without me around. "You'll regret this, Ruby. Leaving your family? What kind of girl does a thing like that?"

"*Our* girl," Miss Etta says, flashing him a smile. Alberto saunters over, flanked by his brothers. They're short but stocky, and real strong. "And we take care of our own here, so don't you even think about coming back tonight to bother her."

Like most bullies, Uncle Jack backs down when confronted by somebody his own size.

"Yeah. Leave, and don't come back!" I add.

Miss Jo wraps an arm around me. "You won this round, honey," she whispers. "Best be quiet now."

"Let's go, Jack," Sheriff Moore says, and they walk back toward the big top, the Flying Antonellis shadowing them as far as the rope.

"I'm staying," I say dumbly. "I'm really staying?"

"You really are." Miss Etta grins, and Miss Lula cackles.

"Step right up! Step right up! See the amazing Ruby Leigh

Porter, modern woman, riding a bicycle!" Harvey calls, grinning. "We'll have to get you some of them bloomers."

"Harvey! Don't talk to the girl about her undergarments on her first day," Miss Jo says.

"I ain't easily shocked," I promise them.

"'Course you're not. You're one of us now, sugar," Miss Lula says.

I laugh. *Bloomers.* Next year when Pearl comes to see me, she'll have a conniption.

I can hardly wait.

⬧ AUTHOR'S NOTE ⬧

I have always been fascinated by families — both those we are born into and those we create. As a teen, I found a second family in theater, which — like the circus — tends to accept those who are outsiders and outcasts in need of refuge.

The circus is problematic. It has been exploitative to some of its performers, particularly those in the sideshows, and its animal practices have not been without cruelty. But as I read about the golden age of the American circus, particularly the women who became famous worldwide for their feats of daring, I was fascinated by the microcosm of circus life, so separate from the traditional mores of the day. And I was curious about exactly what kind of girl might run away to join the circus.

For further reading, I recommend *Wild, Weird, and Wonderful: The American Circus 1901–1927: As Seen by F. W. Glasier, Photographer,* by Mark Sloan, and *The Circus, 1870s–1950s,* edited by Noel Daniel.

Special thanks to Gwenda Bond for her notes on the circus, and to Lindsay Smith for her notes on early Tulsa.

GLAMOUR

ANNA-MARIE MCLEMORE

The first time Grace saw the cover of *Photoplay*, she knew. It had been Clara Kimball Young on the front, pink roses and sage-green leaves crowning her braided hair. Her eyes looked out, glinting but bored, like she knew everyone in the world loved her, but she barely cared.

Every issue Grace could save the twenty-five cents for, every cover girl staring out from the front, just made her more certain. Lila Lee carrying a basket of lilacs, the wind swirling her hair and the blue ribbons on her cream dress. Constance Talmadge holding a strand of peach pearls, two parakeets fluttering above her. Katherine MacDonald gazing off the page, her painted blue eyes catching the candlelight.

What Grace wanted was to be one of those girls, pin-curled and dripping with ribbons. What she wanted was to be a star.

That was before she'd gotten cast as one. Star No. 7—she didn't get a name in this picture—out of twenty stars in all, in *A Night in the Heavens*. The director wasn't even trying to pretend it wasn't a flat-out copy of *Le Voyage dans la Lune*. He had such ideas about being the new Georges Méliès, he even thought he could get the studio to pay for coloring the film, thousands of frames painted by hand.

Grace and the other star girls were little more than living, sparkling set decoration, a backdrop for the lead actress. Costumers pinned and basting-stitched them into dresses that shimmered with copper beads, glittering and heavy as new pennies.

Grace's Hollywood wasn't quite the chandelier-lit parties of the magazine pages. Not yet. Hers was more cold-water flat and five-cent Hershey bar dinners. She was a long way off from the starlets who sprinkled themselves with Guerlain perfume every morning. Grace had saved for months for two tiny bottles of l'Heure Bleue, one for her and one for her mother. She'd tried it out at Macy's, and that scent, the swirl of jasmine and heavy vanilla, was the smell of Hollywood.

Even this early in the morning, Grace's breasts ached. When she got her first part, the other girls had shown her how to flatten them down so the strands of beads on her costume would drop straight. That was one of Grace's first lessons about Hollywood. Lines ruled over curves, so she'd have to straighten hers out.

A scene painter walked by, carrying a white moon. The crisp, sharp smell of the paint reminded Grace of her father and brother coating the almond trees.

Up close like this, the moon looked no more real than a child's crayon drawing. But by now Grace knew that so much of what was dazzling on film looked a little bit off in real life, the way things looked in dreams. The chandeliers were made of cut paper.

Blossoms on trees were the same kind of tissue that came in dress boxes. Mansions and pillars that seemed like honest-to-God brick and marble were plywood painted *trompe l'oeil,* which as far as Grace knew was French for fake.

Before that moon got its second coat of paint, Grace and Star No. 12 had tried, laughing, to lift it. Drunk on a flask Star No. 12 kept tucked into her garter, they'd been aiming to get it up to the overhead grid. It'd be a riot, everyone coming in the next day and seeing that crescent over their heads, stuck in the grid above the pulleys and cables. Thank goodness the same flask that gave them the bright idea left them too sloppy to carry it out. They both would've been replaced faster than the click of a clapperboard.

The quicker that scene painter went, the more Grace noticed his gait, like the off-kilter rhythm of rain dripping off a roof. He had a limp. The middle of the inner crescent sat against the boy's shoulder, his fingers splayed over the outer edge. Grace couldn't see his face or hair. But the shape of him clawed at her. His hands, his walk. He was short, the same height as a boy she'd kissed a few months ago. In trousers, suspenders, and cuffed-up sleeves, he seemed fourteen or fifteen instead of the eighteen or nineteen he probably was.

He set down the moon. Its shadow slid off him, giving her a clear view of his face.

The face of the boy she knew.

No. The word rang in Grace so loud, she kept her lips together to be sure she didn't say it.

No. Sawyer could not be here.

Grace had gone out for this part to avoid him. She'd heard he'd been hired onto some picture about Cleopatra.

His back was to Grace, so Grace turned her back to him,

hoping he wouldn't see her. Maybe she could hide out in the dressing room. Maybe she could avoid him for the whole picture.

Or maybe she was being ridiculous, and he wouldn't even
remember her.

That last thought left a bitter taste on her tongue, like the bite
of orange pith.

The crew hurried all twenty star girls into their flying har-
nesses. They clipped them in, checking the lobster clasps as Evelyn
Farwell swept onto the set. Her curls haloed her like whirls of
lemon meringue, and she'd painted her lips the deep red of
Valentine's Day roses. She had the straight lines of a magazine
girl. No curves that needed flattening.

"Evelyn Farwell," the head costumer snapped.

The woman's voice came so shrill the gaffer almost dropped a
Fresnel lantern. The metal barn doors flanking the light rattled.

"You take that color off this instant," the costumer said.

"It keeps my lips from disappearing," Evelyn said.

"I don't care," the costumer called across the set. "Wash it off.
You look like a Mexican."

The words cut into Grace like the leather straps of the harness.

She gritted her teeth into a smile as flying cables hoisted each
star girl up. She fanned out her arms, shifting her weight so the
strands of copper beads would glimmer on film.

Evelyn Farwell, her cupid's bow now brightened with a
Bourjois pink, her straight hips in her velvet-covered harness, rode
the crescent moon into the air. Her dress flowed out behind her,
smooth as a Brandy Alexander. So many glass beads had been
sewn in that Grace could see Evelyn tensing to keep the train
from pulling her backward.

Grace was a single star in a constellation of silver and copper
dresses.

Less than that. She was something so terrible Evelyn Farwell couldn't even wear a lip color that suggested it.

Grace blotted off her camera makeup. The blue greasepaint rimming her eyes. The sweeps of lavender powder contouring her cheeks and brow bone. The yellow lipstick that made her look sick but came out soft on black-and-white film; everyone but the lead girl had to wear it.

By now, the other girls had skittered off for the holiday. The nice ones asked was she going home; the chatty ones wanted to know where home was. Grace always said Bakersfield. Her hometown, a few miles outside, was small enough that she never named it. There were only so many families in Almendro, and they all knew one another.

Grace sat alone in the dressing room, lights clicking off outside.

Those *Photoplay* covers had promised the things Hollywood held, waiting in the shadows of the blue hills. The sureness that she could become a girl with a smile as light as a spritz of perfume. A girl with laughter ready on her lips. And the ease of knowing she was wanted, and that being wanted let her belong not just somewhere but anywhere.

It promised more than that Grace could become someone beautiful.

It promised that she could become someone who could take a full breath in this world.

She slumped forward, elbows on the dressing table. Her forehead settled on the backs of her wrists.

You look like a Mexican.

She should have understood that the girl she'd been born was worth no more in this town than the tin canister holding a film reel. The words shouldn't have landed this hard. By now, she should have been used to them.

The snickers from the cameramen. *You ever go down to Tijuana? Those girls down there*—then, always, a whistle of wonder—*they're ready whenever you are.*

The chatter in the dressing room. *Did I get too much sun over the weekend? I'm starting to look like a wetback.*

An investor bringing his fur-coated wife to the set on their way to Café Montmartre. A lament from her. *I want plums—don't you all keep any fruit around this godforsaken place?* His laugh before he said, *Darling, if it's plums you want, I'll hire a dozen Mexicans to go out right now and pick you some.*

To them, Grace and her family would have been nothing but these words, these names. The cameramen did not have to fear being beaten and arrested if they lost their way at night and wandered too close to strangers' farms. The talcum-pale girls in the dressing room mirrors had never been barred from town shops or turned away from doctors. The producers' sons had never endured what her brother had, strangers assuming he was not a soldier but a criminal, that he had lost half his leg not in the war but by robbing a bank or stealing a horse.

Grace sobbed onto the backs of her hands, the hard, gasping breaths alternating between sounding soaked and parched. Her fist hit the dressing table. She didn't realize she was doing it until the pain rattled her wrist.

Every day, it was harder to stay Grace Moran. Every evening, she collapsed into bed, wrung out with the effort of draining the color from herself. When she let herself give into what she was, it rushed back into her so fast it felt liquid. It was a pond flooding her bed, and she had to tip her head back to keep enough of her face above water.

The color glamour was borrowed magic, an heirloom her great-grandmother had handed down like a wedding quilt. But Bisabuela had warned her that the longer she kept it up, the more it would exhaust her. It would be worse than wearing shoes that pinched or a necklace with a clasp that bit the back of her neck.

She'd almost let the glamour slip that night with Sawyer. Both of them had gotten drunk on brick wine the crew had smuggled from Amador County. Without even changing out of her costume corset and petticoat, Grace had taken hold of Sawyer's suspenders and tugged him into the lead actress's green room. The woman was literal about it: green damask settee, green brocade fainting couch, green drapes framing the mirror. Bits of her producer boyfriend's tobacco were ground into the green tufted rugs, filling the air with a smell like liquor and vanilla.

By then the lead actress was off to her wrap parties, so Grace pulled Sawyer down onto that fainting couch, his fingers following the laces of her corset.

When Sawyer had set his mouth against her neck, she'd felt the glamour giving. Her focus, her will, flinched enough to weaken that inherited magic.

Grace had shoved Sawyer off her and run out of the green room. She hadn't even glanced back, not wanting to see whatever pained look, whatever wondering, showed on his face.

She'd never let him close enough to smell her perfume again. She couldn't afford to. One kiss, one blush or grazing of fingers that caught her off-guard, and Grace Moran might vanish like a curl of smoke off a cigarette.

The glamour was hollowing her out. Her one hope was the cascarones, and the rumor about wishes made on an Easter full moon. If the cascarones granted her this wish, she could become a girl who belonged in *Photoplay*, laughing and lovely. The knowledge that the world would make room for her would feel so thick and soft she could revel in it as though it were a fine coat.

"Are you okay?" Sawyer's voice broke through the quiet in the dressing room.

Grace startled, sitting up.

Before she could look for Sawyer, the mirror in front of her caught her, stilled her. It showed a girl Grace knew but had never seen in this glass, in this dressing room.

In place of Grace Moran's fair pin curls, a color between dark blond and very light brown, there were Graciela Morena's brown-black waves, full and unbrushed. Instead of Grace's cream complexion, her skin was tan as the shells of the almonds her family grew. Where a minute ago there had been eyes blue as the ocean off the pier, a pair as brown as magnolia bark blinked back.

Grace touched her face. Graciela mimicked the gesture.

Out of the corner of her eye, farther down the mirror, she found Sawyer's reflection. And he was staring.

Everything she'd been afraid he'd see when she was kissing him. Everything she worried would show when his breath fell against her neck. This mirror showed it all, how badly she'd let the color glamour slip.

She met his eyes in the glass. "Get out."

His reflection stayed, blinking at her, as if this mirrored boy did not know how to make the real Sawyer do anything.

"Get out," she said, yelling now.

This time he flinched. He left the dressing room fast enough that even as she watched Graciela Morena in the mirror, she caught his limp.

Grace slowed and steadied her breathing until the color

glamour settled back over her. It bleached her hair. It lightened her skin. It spun the brown of her eyes back to the shimmering blue of the whole Pacific Ocean.

She drove Graciela Morena and all her shades of brown out of her.

Grace caught up with Sawyer halfway across the studio lot. She had to play nice now. She could not be wild-eyed and worried.

"Look," she said, but any next words turned to a breath.

He gave a slow nod. "Sawyer."

His smile, both sad and resigned, prickled. He really thought she hadn't remembered his name?

"I know it doesn't roll off the tongue quite like 'the kid with the gimp leg,'" he said, "but at least it's shorter."

She felt the flush rise to her cheeks, a flush that would show more in the cream of Grace's skin than the brown of Graciela's. She'd never called him that, but it wasn't as though she'd never heard it around the lot. That first picture they were on together, rumor was he'd managed to get himself hired by a director whose brother had lost his left arm in the war. But that didn't stop the director from looking the other way when the grips mimicked Sawyer's walk.

"For what it's worth"—Sawyer slid his hands into his pockets—"I think you're better the way you were."

She wanted to tell him no one but the painted moon and backdrops cared what he thought, that he didn't know from nothing.

Sawyer shrugged his good-bye and kept on across the set.

She wished her next impulse had to do with being kind. She wished it had to do with anything except getting on the good side of a boy who had seen Graciela Morena.

A boy she'd already been cruel to three pictures and all those months ago.

"Sawyer," she said.

He turned around.

"You have somewhere to go this weekend?" she asked.

"Pobrecito." Her mother took Sawyer's face in her hands.

Sawyer hadn't even put down his bag, or Grace's, which he'd insisted on carrying. He looked a little worried. Grace wished she could tell him the pity in her mother's face had nothing to do with his limp. To her mother, Sawyer's presence here meant he either had no family or that he couldn't see them for Easter, and this, not his walk, was worth her sympathy.

Grace took the suitcases while her mother was talking at him. He was too distracted to notice.

Graciela. She was with her family, and she was Graciela now. She had let the color glamour fall. For this weekend, she was cotton dresses and almond blossoms, not beaded gowns and pressed powder. She could let her breasts loose instead of flattening them.

Being Graciela Morena took so much less work than making herself look like Grace Moran. Without the effort weighing her down, the suitcases felt light as baby chicks.

Her mother swept Sawyer outside into the almond orchard, saying they would go find Graciela's father.

Graciela left her suitcase in her old bedroom, the bed covered with Bisabuela's rose-embroidered wedding quilt, and Sawyer's in the room at the end of the hall. She hadn't bothered packing clothes. Graciela Morena's soft cotton skirts were all waiting for her, in the room she'd told her parents they could clear and rent out. But they hadn't.

Instead she'd stuffed her suitcase full of candy bars that were easy to find in Los Angeles but that her family had to go to Bakersfield to get. Mounds for her mother, Heath bars for her father. And in the inner pockets, money they would never accept. She would have to slip it into the coffee can when they weren't looking.

One day Graciela wanted to be a big enough star to buy her mother a pair of the two-tone Chanel heels all the girls on set went mad over. She wanted to buy her family one of the new refrigerators, so her father didn't have to worry about whether the iceman would come out this far.

She wanted to get Miguel to doctors who could help him stop having dreams that he had all the parts of himself he'd had before the war.

A life as Grace Moran promised more than a little place carved out in this world that loved fair-haired, sea-eyed girls. It promised the things she could give her family that they could not give themselves.

"Hermana," her brother's voice called from a half-open door.

She dashed into the room so fast, she almost slipped on the tile. She threw her arms around her brother. "You're here!"

"Where'd you think I'd be?" he asked, ruffling her hair.

"Married with a hundred babies." She pulled back to look at him. "That girl is in love with you."

"Well." Miguel gestured at his face and body. "Can you blame her?"

Graciela punched his shoulder and went back across the hall.

"If you keep her waiting"—Graciela called from the open door, digging through her suitcase—"I'll strangle you with your Easter Sunday necktie."

Miguel's shadow crossed the sun cast through the linen curtains. "You'd attack a man who doesn't have two legs to run away?"

The fact that Miguel could joke meant he was healing in places she could not see. He had fewer nightmares, Mamá had written her. He went out walking with the crutch instead of shutting himself up in his room, no sky but his ceiling.

"I'd smother a man in his sleep with his own pillow if he broke that girl's heart," Graciela said.

When Miguel had come off the bus with his trouser pant pinned under where his leg now ended, Dolores hadn't flinched. She'd thrown herself onto him like he was strong enough for all of her, her wide hips and eager hands and her mouth that had no shame kissing him in full daylight. That was good for both Dolores and Graciela, because if she'd left him, Graciela would've gone after her with her father's Winchester.

Graciela handed Miguel a Butterfinger bar and threw a dozen more onto his bed.

He ripped open the orange-and-blue package. "I had to save up for a good ring for her." He bit into the bar. "Viejo Garcia'll be done sizing it tomorrow, and if you don't think it's perfect, I'll eat this wrapper."

Miguel sat on his bed, holding the candy bar in one hand and parting the curtains with the other. "You taking in strays now?"

"He couldn't go home for Easter," Graciela said. "So I invited him here."

"Why?"

"Because I'm a kind and generous person."

Miguel started laughing.

Graciela nodded at the candy bars on his bed. "Keep laughing, and I'll crush those to dust."

"Then I'll eat them over toast." Miguel's hand dropped the curtain, and the panel fell back into place. "If he's here, he must already know about you, right?"

Graciela gave a slow, wincing nod.

"Did you tell him?" Miguel asked.

Graciela studied a band of light on the floor. "He saw me."

Miguel whistled softly. "What are you gonna do?"

"Get him drunk and see if Bruja Licha can make him forget," Graciela said, wanting to hear her brother laugh again. "Wanna help?"

"For you, you know I would." Miguel clucked his tongue. "But it's Easter. The Lord frowns on drunkenness during la Semana Santa."

La Semana Santa. For a minute, she'd forgotten it was Holy Week. In two days, she would fold all her hopes into the glitter of a cascarón.

"Easter's a full moon." She leaned against the door frame. "I'm gonna make my wish."

Miguel's smile fell away. "Graciela," he said, with the sad look he had when he'd told her that la llorona was not some fairy whistling on the wind but the spirit of a grieving mother. "It's just a story."

Graciela pushed herself off the door frame. "Not to me."

She kicked out of her shoes and walked barefoot, the sound of her mother's laughter pulling her down the hall.

She stopped in the doorway to the kitchen.

Sawyer stood at the sink, washing his hands. The afternoon sun came in from the orchard, filling the sink, and water left the fine hairs on the back of his wrists glistening.

"And we'll teach you all about the cascarones," her mother told him. "It's a full moon, and Easter, so if you're lucky, they can grant you wishes."

A ribbon of worry snaked down the back of Graciela's neck.

She loved her family's generous laughter, how they invited strangers to their table for tamales at Christmas and chiles en nogada in the fall. The warmth of masa and the dark sugar of pomegranates was the smell of their kindness.

But the cascarones, the story about making a wish when the full moon fell on Easter, this was her family's magic. And her mother was telling their secrets to a boy who knew Graciela's. She was giving this boy more power over Graciela, when he already had too much.

For a minute, Graciela wondered if this was a good thing, him warming to her family. One more reason for him not to turn on her. But watching him here, this boy from the world of *trompe l'oeil* sets, reminded her of all she'd bartered off. She'd kissed him once and then shoved him away, holding her own glamour closer than she held him or even her own family.

Sawyer stood as a reminder of all the cruelty she had to fold into herself to keep Grace Moran.

When she helped her mother with the cooking, Graciela was so distracted, she nicked her thumb slicing potatoes. Throughout dinner, she watched this boy, her mother's mole rojo bitter on her tongue. She gave thanks that her father and Miguel were so loud and laughing, with their stories about winning fine watches off rich men playing cards, that Sawyer didn't notice.

After they had cleaned up from dinner, after her father had shown Sawyer the new chickens Miguel had bought, ones who made blue and green eggs, that anger and fear still wove through her.

She had invited Sawyer here because she thought if she was nice to him, he wouldn't squeal on her, tell the director she was really some wetback in a witch's costume.

She hadn't realized how odd it would feel to see this boy among everything she'd tried to hide. This world of her mother's mole and so many white-blossoming trees only her father could count them all. As far from the blond and blue shape of Grace Moran as the stars were from the earth.

After everyone else had gone to bed, she waited outside his door. She waited until she heard the sounds of him changing. The soft, blunt landing of his shoes on the floorboards. The click of buttons as he threw a shirt over the back of the wooden chair.

She wanted him to know, just for a second, what she had felt. To feel that seen, laid bare.

This was who she was. Not Grace Moran, poised and polite. She was Graciela Morena, dark-haired and brown-skinned like her family, but as vindictive as her family was generous.

Before her mother's voice could wedge its way in, urging her to show kindness to boys who could not go home to their families on Easter weekend, Graciela opened the door.

Sawyer froze, the glow from a lamp lighting half of him. It warmed the shade of his dark hair. It flashed off his eyes so they looked like the sun through a marble.

He was not naked. She was a little disappointed. Not because she had wanted to startle him, she realized. Because she wanted to know what he was like under his clothes, what she had missed the chance to learn when she threw him off her in the green room.

But as the room's wood smell rushed at her, relief filled her. She did not want to be the girl she was in this moment. A girl who forced her way into this boy's room just to catch him off-guard. The fact that she knew what it was like, that feeling of being seen when she didn't want to, gave her less of a right to do this, not more.

Sawyer had his shoes off, but pants and socks on. He'd cast aside his collared shirt for a loose sweater, one so pilled and worn soft, he'd probably relegated it to an extra layer on cool nights. At the cuffs and collar, the cotton of a long-sleeve undershirt showed.

On the chair, next to his collared shirt, Sawyer had thrown a few wide ribbons of cloth and a thick swathe of all-cotton elastic.

She thought of his leg. He walked in a way that made him seem so used to himself that she'd always thought whatever happened had been a long time ago. Now she wondered if he'd been injured in a way he had to keep wrapping and tending to.

"Are you hurt?" she asked.

"No," he said. A resigned laugh opened inside the word.

"If you are, we can get you help," she said. She could put on Grace Moran's colors, her best dress, and a coat of lipstick, and charm some doctor into seeing this boy.

"I'm not hurt," he said. "But you're afraid."

Graciela tried to keep herself straight and tall, a star girl in a flying harness. "No, I'm not."

"If you weren't, you wouldn't have invited me here," he said.

"That's not true," she said, the lie dull on her tongue.

He held up a hand, a gesture that said he wouldn't believe any arguments, but that it was okay, he didn't blame her. "You're afraid I'll tell everyone something you don't want them to know."

He came forward, edging farther into the lamp's light. At first it felt like a threat, a way of commanding the space between them. But his stance was more assurance than threat. He was neither scared nor trying to scare her.

She wouldn't have caught it if he hadn't let her, if he hadn't moved this slowly and stood where she could see him. But when he stepped into the light, the lamp showed the shape and shadows of him. What was under the sweater and shirt he would sleep in.

"I'm not gonna tell your secrets, Graciela," he said.

Her name, her real name, in his voice, brushed the back of her neck like feathers.

"I know what it means to have things you want to make sure stay yours," he said. "I would never tell what wasn't mine to tell. I need you to know that."

In that moment, Graciela was one of her family's almond trees, and understanding landed on her like finches.

If Grace had reached for Sawyer's belt when she was kissing him on that brocade fainting couch, he would have stopped her. He would not have let her unbuckle his belt and get her hand inside his trousers. He would not have let her find the shape of him with her fingers, no more than she would have chosen to let him see her with her glamour fallen away.

"I'm sorry," Graciela said, the words as deep and true as confessing a sin. She was sorry for walking in on him. For pushing him away months ago. For thinking he was a boy who could never understand the fear and the loneliness of having truths no one else could know.

Her favorite tree was waiting for her, the stars above sharp as the glitter in a cascarón. The magnolia's thick boughs formed a bowl she and Miguel had crouched in on summer nights, and now she sat with her back against the cool bark.

"Grace," Sawyer called to her across the rows of flowering almonds. The fluffy branches shifted in the night breeze.

She slid down from the tree.

How awful she'd been to wait outside that door. How thoughtless to see him bear the taunts of the other men on set and still assume he did not know what it was to be out of place.

How petty to want vengeance against this boy for doing nothing but seeing her as she was.

He stopped at the tree's base, again wearing his collared shirt. She'd thought walking out of the room was the polite thing. Now she cringed with how he'd had to get dressed again to come outside and find her. His shirt had been buttoned one off. His suspenders hung down against his thighs.

"So that's it?" he asked. "Stalemate?" No worry in his voice. Just a question.

Graciela put a little of her weight down on the soft dirt, and then all of it. She brushed the magnolia bark dust off her hands, feeling the shame of how she'd acted. She'd walked in on him, and in the face of her doing this, he'd offered her even more of himself than he had months ago. Then she'd walked out on him.

A question swirled around her feet like dust.

"Is that what happened to your leg?" she asked.

She'd always thought it was polio. If he hadn't been so young, she would've thought he'd been in the war like her brother.

"What are you talking about?" Sawyer asked.

"Did you make a bad bargain with some bruja?" She'd heard of that, women who pretended to be curanderas but who instead dealt in the trade of souls and hearts. She might have promised she could help him live as a man and not told him her price, that it would cost him the easy use of his leg.

Sawyer's laugh was small and sad. "You want to know what happened to my leg?"

"Was it because someone found out?" she asked, her shoulders tight against the thought of it.

"No." Again came that pained laugh. "I lived like this"— Sawyer looked down at his shirt and suspenders—"like I am, even before I came out to California. My mother"—now his smile was soft—"she's never fought me on it." Sawyer lowered his eyes. "She's always been good to everybody. She even took in a boarder no one else would rent to. He'd served for most of the war and he wasn't right, not after the things he'd seen. But he was nice to me. Called me 'son' and always wanted to give me advice about women."

Beneath the nectar of almond blossoms and magnolia, the wind brought the bitter scent of almond bark.

"But on one of his bad days, he didn't recognize me," Sawyer said. "He thought I was someone else. Later he said I looked just like some kid in his division. He thought of me dying like that, I guess, and he wanted to save me. He wanted to make sure they could never call me up. So he did. He made sure of it."

A well of protectiveness rose up in Graciela. Not because Sawyer belonged to her; he didn't. But because there was already so little sense in how Miguel had lost his leg, and there was even less in this, how the war had done this to Sawyer even after it was over.

"He did that to you?" she asked.

Sawyer shifted his weight, heels scuffing the dirt. "He'd, uh, he'd helped out the medics over there, during the war." He swallowed, hard. "So he knew which muscles to get at."

Graciela tasted iron on the wind, Sawyer's memory so strong it chilled the air.

"My mother got him to some people who could maybe help him," Sawyer said.

"Help him?" Graciela asked. "She forgave him?"

"What good would it do to be mad at him?" Sawyer shook his head. "The whole history of the world, it's kings and generals deciding where everybody goes. Not guys like him."

Sawyer looked down at his thighs, noticing the suspenders.

"The whole town was talking about it." He pulled the straps onto his shoulders. "I couldn't get away from it. So my mother let me go out to California."

Graciela pressed her palm against her stomach. She tried to stop imagining it. The hands of a man who considered wrecking a boy's leg a kind of mercy, a way to save him from the things he'd seen. A town's gossip driving the boy from his own home.

Sawyer looked down at his shirt, like that suggestion of what was underneath might be visible now. It wasn't. He'd layered it over, bound it down as well as when he came to set.

"That day in the dressing room," she said.

The back of her throat felt tight, knowing that if she said it, he would understand. Of course he would. This boy given a girl's name when he was born. This boy hurt in a way meant to ensure he would never go to war. This boy whose walk made the grips on set laugh at him even when — especially when — he could hear them.

But the explanations turned to ashes on her tongue.

"I just want to be a star," she said. "It's all I've wanted since I was a little girl."

"And you want to do it by pretending you don't have this family, and you're not from this place." He looked down the rows of almond trees, bowing their petaled branches. "I get it."

"If everyone knows what I am, do you know what kind of roles I'll get?" Graciela asked. "With what I look like? Maybe none. If I'm lucky, a girl in some whorehouse scene, or if I'm really lucky, a dancing girl in a Western saloon. Over and over until I'm too old and they throw me away."

"Why do you want to work for people who would ever think about throwing you away?" Sawyer asked.

Graciela took in the magnolia's perfume. It wasn't the powder and violets of l'Heure Bleue, but it gave the air the smell of lemon cream.

She had never said the truth out loud. Not to her mother,

who would've told that costumer to drop dead. Not to Miguel, who always said the girls in *Photoplay* looked like they'd been left out too long and bleached in the sun. Not to her father, who had blessed her leaving Almendro, but whose heart would crack like ceramic if he knew why.

She had told no one why she wanted to become Grace Moran: because the world left so little room for Graciela Morena.

"You heard my mother talking," she said. "The full moon's on Easter this year. I know my wish. You can make one too. Your leg, maybe." Graciela had already tried talking Miguel into the same thing, but she doubted he believed enough to try. "Maybe it could be fixed."

Sawyer shook his head. "I'm not broken. This is who I am. Everything that's happened to me, it's who I am."

"So there's nothing you want?" she asked.

He came toward her, so slowly he did not limp. "I didn't say that."

He slid his hand onto the back of her neck and kissed her. He tasted like the honey and first-harvest apricots they'd eaten after dinner. Amber sugar. Fireweed. It made her bite his lower lip just hard enough that the sound he made could have been either pain or him asking her to do it again.

For a second, that taste faded away, leaving behind the bitter tang of brick wine. For a second they were back on that brocade fainting couch, and she was flinching under the feeling that one more kiss would break down the girl she'd given everything to be.

But this was not some borrowed green room. This was the night air threading through her family's almond trees. She was not laced into some costume corset, a petticoat rough against her legs. She wore a dress made by her mother, the skirt smooth as poured cream.

This was not some set where she had to stuff herself into a girl called Grace Moran.

There was as much room for Sawyer and Graciela as the whole shimmering sky.

She wanted to be both here and in that green room, so she could do something other than what she'd done. Pull him against her instead of shoving him off. Letting him tangle his hands in her hair instead of wishing her hair was cream-rinse blond and fine as a doll's bangs.

Graciela knew more of Sawyer than she had in that green room. Now she wanted to touch him between his legs like she'd touched herself between her legs. She wanted his hands over her like his fingers had splayed over that white moon. She wanted to lick the little flecks of paint off his neck.

But they were not alone. Grace was there, hovering among the stars, reminding her that this was a boy who knew the distance between Grace Moran and Graciela Morena.

Graciela pulled away.

Sawyer stilled, lips parted. Then he pressed them together, nodding like he understood.

He took his hands off her.

She hadn't meant it like that. It had nothing to do with his limp, or what was under his clothes. It was that he knew she was two different girls, one blue and blond and another in shades of brown.

"Sawyer," she said.

But he was already walking away.

She stayed. Running after him seemed like rubbing in the fact that she had two good legs to catch him.

✕ ✕ ✕

At breakfast, they did not speak. And later that day, there was no chance to.

Her father and Miguel were painting the almond tree trunks. All the farmers were saying this summer would be the hottest in years; the white paint would seal the wood from the scorch of the sun. When Sawyer offered his help, they handed him an extra brush.

Graciela spent the day at the kitchen table with her mother and aunts, hollowing out eggs. Washing and drying the fragile shells. Filling them with glass glitter and sealing them up. The eggs they'd poured out would go into empanadas and capirotada, the bread pudding they ate during Lent but that her mother made with chocolate for Easter Sunday.

She tried to laugh when they laughed, to shriek at their gossip, to tease Dolores about how many babies she and Miguel would have. But Graciela was choking on the hard knot of everything she wanted.

To become the girl on the moon.

To kiss the boy who had painted it.

To disappear into the pale colors of Grace Moran and every promise she held.

To keep her family and never miss a Pascua with them.

All of it wrung her out so much that after dinner she was a starling scared out of a tree. She was running through her father's fields, her skirt filling with night air. The almond rows opened up in front of her, branches so thick with blossoms, they looked like a hundred thousand sticks of rock candy.

She wanted to run fast enough down these rows that she would break from the earth. She wanted to spin out into the sky and turn to constellations. She wanted to become a shimmering thing children would make wishes on, instead of a girl whose own unmade wish blazed inside her.

It was Holy Saturday, the moment of la Semana Santa she hated most. It was not Good Friday, the day of grief they all knew so well. It was not the Sunday of glorious resurrection. This was el Sábado Santo, the in-between day, and it stretched in front of her, a Holy Saturday as long as her whole life.

Miguel had warned her that if she made her wish at the Easter full moon, it might not work. But it might. She might become Grace Moran, and she would never again look like a Morena. She would not have her mother's hair and her father's eyes.

But if she didn't make that wish, she would never be the girl in the moon.

The price of getting everything she wanted would be every-thing she was.

She slowed, breathing hard. Almond blossoms clung to her hair and stuck to her damp forehead. Their perfume mixed with the sharp smell of drying paint.

The color glamour was wearing her out. It had never been meant to be used this way, to become someone else. It had always been so a Morena daughter could go places too dangerous for a brown-skinned girl. It had been to buy medicine or seeds, candles or wedding rings, things that some doctors and merchants would not sell to families who looked like the Morenas.

But she had used it to pretend this was not her family. She had traded being her mother and father's one daughter to be one of twenty identical stars.

A hand rested on her back.

"Hey," Sawyer said.

Graciela turned.

The wind was sticking petals to him too. They caught in his hair, and Graciela couldn't tell which flicks of white were blossoms and which were paint.

"Come with me, okay?" he asked.

He led her down the rows, and they came out from under the flowering branches.

Graciela stopped, a breath rising out of her, spinning into a gasp.

Sawyer hadn't just painted the almond trees.

He'd painted the dark trunk of her magnolia.

But not all of it.

"I wanted to paint enough of it so it'd be okay out here, when it gets hot," Sawyer said. "But not so much that it didn't look like your tree anymore."

On the widest stretches of bark, and up into the boughs, he'd painted patches of white, just where the sun would hit hardest. Where the heat might weaken or split the bark. If she took a few steps one way, the white broke into ribbons. A few steps the other way, and the patches almost vanished, like a trick of the light, the moon's glow on the boughs.

"I know sometimes you've gotta wear colors that aren't yours," Sawyer said. "But if you wear too much of somebody else's colors, there's none of you left."

Graciela looked at him. The way he licked his lower lip seemed more like a nervous gesture than a sign he wanted to kiss her. But she wanted to know in what measures he was recklessness and fear, hesitation and certainty, and where he'd gotten his faith that he was worth more than what other people decided. She wanted to know what all those things tasted like on his tongue.

"Wait here," she said.

Graciela snuck back inside, stealing cascarones from the dark kitchen. She and her mother and aunts had made so many, no one would miss a few.

She brought them outside and asked Sawyer to help her get them up into the magnolia tree. She did not ask if his leg would stop him, and when she did not ask this, his face lit up like stars. It made her wonder about all the things he had been denied because someone else assumed he could not do them.

They climbed the boughs, handing the delicate eggs back and forth.

Tomorrow, at the moment of the Easter full moon, her family would be out here. Laughing. Celebrating the ring Miguel had slid onto Dolores's fourth finger. Breaking cascarones over one another's heads until they were all covered in glitter.

There were so many things to wish for.

Children for her brother and Dolores, and the health to run after them even if Miguel needed a crutch to do it.

Years for their mother and father to watch over the orchard they'd built, and to see their children make their own homes.

Safe nights for sons and daughters whose lives were shades of brown more beautiful than they knew.

Full breaths for boys who walked with crutches, or limps, or with the fear of anyone else deciding who they were.

For this boy climbing the magnolia with her to know his eyes were the brown-gold of the water in her father's irrigation ditches, and that to her this was a color more beautiful than any blue.

There were so many wishes she wanted more than to erase the girl her mother and father had made her.

Graciela and Sawyer settled in the magnolia's boughs, the almost-full moon above them. They broke cascarones over each other, the grain of glitter on their skin and between their lips.

They gave themselves to el Sábado Santo, this in-between night, letting the wind carry the glass glitter to anyone who needed the shimmer and hope of wishes yet to be made.

❈ AUTHOR'S NOTE ❈

In the imagination of many Americans, Golden Age Hollywood was a time of elegant gowns, cigar-smoking tuxedoed men, and starlets posing in soft focus. But Hollywood was a place of as much racism, homophobia, transphobia, and ableism as the real world in which the studio lots existed.

Though not all Latinas of the silver screen guarded their identities as closely as Graciela, some of the most successful Latina actors of the Golden Age gave themselves stage names rather than using the birth names that signaled their heritage.

When it came to representation of LGBTQ identity, portrayals were overwhelmingly reduced to stereotype and sensationalism, played for laughs or shock value. Like depictions of characters of color, depictions of queer and transgender characters mark some of the most offensive and damaging moments in Hollywood history.

Sawyer could expect his disability to be the subject of jokes that would go unchecked on a Hollywood lot, if he was hired at all. Ableism was no less rampant in the 1920s, even after hundreds of thousands of men had returned from World War I with physical injuries or psychological damage that resulted in long-term disabilities. Veterans like Miguel faced a society that ridiculed them and turned them away from jobs, even as Hollywood profited off portraying their experiences.

This story is my wish to give Graciela, a daughter of Mexican-American farmers, and Sawyer, a transgender boy living with a disability, the space that history would have tried to deny them. And it's a wish to give them room for their own magic, from the sparkle of a Hollywood set to the glitter inside a cascarón.

Many thank-yous to Kayla Whaley, Tehlor Kay Mejia, Mackenzi Lee, and the transgender boy I'm lucky to call my husband, for their notes that enriched and deepened this story.

I chose to write magical realism not only because it's where my stories most often live, but because it's an important part of the history and heritage I come from as a Latina woman. In the midst of oppression, seeing the magical even through the tragic, the unjust, the heartbreaking, is a way of survival, for people, for communities, for cultures. Our spirits depend on not overlooking that which might be dismissed or ignored. I write magical realism not only because I'm a queer Latina woman, but because the world is more brutal than so many are willing to see, and more beautiful than they imagine.

BETTER FOR ALL THE WORLD

MARIEKE NIJKAMP

We have the same first name. We are almost of an age. We hail from the same county. We have a lot in common, Carrie Buck and I. More than anyone might think.

It isn't obvious at first. She doesn't look a bit like me. She carries herself with purpose and dignity. Her black hair is cropped short, while my brown hair falls over my shoulders. Her dress is plain and worn, while mine is soft and new. She is called feeble-minded, while I'm considered difficult. But we are alike.

And no one can know.

"The sole effect of the operation is to prevent procreation by rendering the patient sterile. In short, it is a eugenical measure and nothing more." The attorney's voice fills the chamber, and I gently rock back and forth to the cadence of his words.

It's relatively empty up in the visitors' gallery. Perhaps because of the weather: after a hot spell, the April weather has turned and the afternoon is looking dreadful. Perhaps because this case is too sensitive for most. After all, sterilization procedures are hardly subjects for proper conversation. Mother would have apoplexy if she saw me here. The only talk we've had of reproduction was when she told me she expected me to find a husband back home and start a family.

"It would be better for all, Carrie," she told me on that occasion and countless others, "if you would keep your head down. This is what the world expects of us, not your grandiose ideas of education and a career. Stick to a boy who will tolerate you and the pretense of a normal life."

But I don't want the pretense of a normal life. I want an education. I want a career. And she can't stop me. For all that she tried and tried, she can't stop me.

I'm here.

When I arrived in Washington, Aunt Elizabeth asked me why I wanted to pursue a career in law when only a handful of law schools even accept women. There are a thousand reasons, and I can name them all. The world's expectations were not made to fit me. The laws and structure calm me. In the practice of law, no one minds an inquisitive and obsessive mind. But as I listen to Carrie Buck's attorney argue against a doctor who called his client *a genetic threat to society*, I cling to the most important reason of all: it matters. What these attorneys and judges do, the cases they argue and decide, the cause they serve, it *matters*.

And I want to be a part of it.

"Excuse me?"

The young man sitting in front of me turns, and it's only then that I realize I've spoken out loud.

"I'm sorry. I didn't mean . . ." My cheeks grow warm. Someone shushes us, and I wish I could melt into these seats, but they're stiff and unyielding.

The boy in front of me smiles. "It's your first time?"

Two rows ahead, an elderly man turns to both of us with a scowl so ferocious, even Mother would be impressed.

I nod, quite unwilling to say anything more.

The boy's smile widens to a grin, and I'm terrified he'll continue speaking, but he merely winks at me and returns his focus to the court proceedings down below. The elderly man continues to stare. I shift and try to avoid his glance. I bounce my foot against the seat in front of me, but it does nothing to distract me.

My heartbeat picks up and my skin crawls. I'm used to stares and scrutiny—I got enough of that back home—but if he stares long enough, he'll see I'm different. Different, different, cold, uncaring.

I *can't*—

I rock back and forth until I settle into the familiar sense of repetition, and I remember how to breathe again. In front of the court, the plaintiff's attorney continues to talk. His voice drones on, warm and assured, pleasant even. It reminds me of Grandfather, who believed in Aunt Elizabeth's dreams and who believed in mine. That helps, too.

I focus on the attorney's arguments. The Fourteenth Amendment and bodily integrity, and the state's intention "to rid itself of those citizens deemed undesirable according to its standards."

We have a lot in common, Carrie Buck and I.

The oral arguments take hours, and I drink in every single moment. The elderly man up and left after Attorney Whitehead's statements, but the young man in front of me is still there. When the Court rises, we do, too, and he turns to me. He holds a legal pad scribbled full of notes. Is he a law student? He appears to be a year or two older than I am, which makes it both possible and enviable, and I cannot deny a stab of impatience.

He catches me staring and moves forward. Before I can stop myself, I take a step back, bumping into the seat behind me. He doesn't move forward again, but he doesn't turn away either.

"I wish to apologize for imposing upon you earlier. It was horribly impolite, and I promise you my manners are usually better than this . . . although my father might disagree." He scratches his temple. In demeanor, he is all too like my younger brother, caught in a wrongdoing. But in appearance, he is nothing at all like our family. His suit is tailored and speaks of society.

He bows slightly. His dark hair flops around his eyes. "Alexander Holmes, at your service, Miss . . ."

A flutter of panic teases me.

"Allen. Carrie Allen." I wonder if I should curtsy or reach out my hand to him. Aunt Elizabeth has been educating me on the rules of etiquette, but I'm not yet comfortable enough with them to know how to respond to this — to a boy who talks to a girl without an introduction. I don't know how to deal with it when someone doesn't follow the rules.

And Alexander Holmes doesn't. His bright smile is back, uncharacteristically bold for these dark and dignified surroundings. He smiles freely. "Delighted to know you, Miss Allen."

He walks around the row of seats and waits for me at the end of my row. "May I walk you out? It's not often I have the pleasure of meeting other legalese enthusiasts." He colors slightly. "And certainly no one like you."

I've never heard anyone say that like it's a good thing. "You are quite unlike anyone I've met in Washington so far," I tell him.

He offers me his arm, but I keep my hands close to my sides and squeeze past him into the aisle. I am uncomfortable being touched. He seems unfazed.

"You're from out of town?" He does not wait for my answer but instead falls into step with me. "Then what brings you to these arguments? Or, more specifically, to this hearing?"

I reach for the closest truth. "Fortunate timing."

"For both of us, then." He holds the door open for me, and we walk out of the hallway, into the rotunda, where we pass underneath the magnificent dome. Aides and lawyers are walking around and talking, and it's as if we're leaving behind the sanctity of a church for the overwhelming chaos of politics. Voices everywhere, and I cannot drown them out.

I shrug into my coat and curl my fingers around the small, round pebble in my pocket. It's cool and comforting, but the energy I took from the quiet courtroom is already draining from me and I shrink toward the walls.

Alexander Holmes glances at me, and his brown eyes crinkle. "Come, I'll show you a quieter route. It's overwhelming, isn't it? Don't worry—you'll fit in soon enough."

I want to believe him. At home, I could not walk around town without eyes on me, without stares and whispers. *Cold, uncaring Carrie. She thinks she's better than us. Her poor mother, she's at wit's end. Best to send the girl away.*

I hoped I would be able to breathe here. To get lost amid history. To become who I want to be.

I just don't know if I will be enough.

After dreaming of it for so long, observing this Court case both fills me up and wears me down. I'm bone tired and my mind won't stop going over every single detail of the case and of the entire past week—not just what I saw, but how I acted. Did I say the right thing? Did I say it at the right time? Did I act normal enough? Were people staring? Did I draw attention to myself? I may be able to shrug into a guise, but I've never learned to fit in; it's always been pretense.

I'm curled up in a large leather chair in Aunt Elizabeth's office reading about the history of law when the door opens and closes.

"Come with me to tea this afternoon," Aunt Elizabeth says. She stops in front of my chair. She wears a deep-green day dress and holds her coat in one hand. She looks resplendent, and I am momentarily disoriented. Today is Saturday. We didn't make any plans for today. Today is *Saturday*. We didn't make *any* plans for today.

She continues, "It'll be a chance to meet an old friend of mine, with whom, I believe, you may have a lot in common."

I close my book with more force than I usually would, to try to snap myself out of the repetition. But my hands tremble.

"Today is— We didn't make any plans—" I breathe in sharply. I don't want to betray the panic building inside me, but my voice quivers. I escaped small-town expectations when Aunt Elizabeth invited me here, and she accepts my oddities with more grace than most everyone back home. She supports my right to choose my own path. She allows me to carve out my own space. But I know it is sufferance. Mother made that very clear. We live in a world that measures people according to standards of desirability and undesirability. And I am undesirable.

"Carrie, I know you have your heart set on a legal career, and in this day and age, it's not just about knowing the law; it's about knowing the right people. Grace Hays Riley is the dean of the

Washington College of Law. An introduction to her will be an asset to you once you apply there for your baccalaureate."

"Yes, Aunt Elizabeth," I say. "Except . . ." Today is Saturday. We didn't make any plans for today. I wring my hands so tightly, my knuckles crack, but it doesn't help.

"Carrie?"

I can't find the right words. The chair becomes uncomfortable and Aunt Elizabeth is too close and my head hurts and *we didn't make any plans for today.*

"Carrie, look at me." Aunt Elizabeth crouches down in front of me. Mother would have forced me to meet her eye, but to my shock, Aunt Elizabeth places her hand on the chair's armrest, careful not to touch me, and she allows me to stare at the fabric of her dress instead.

"We didn't make any plans for today, did we?"

I shake my head, the words threatening to stumble out of my mouth again.

Aunt Elizabeth shifts. "Are you tired?"

"Yes."

"Would you rather stay in?"

I nod.

After a moment, she nods, too, and her dress billows around her. "On the condition that we do go out next weekend. You can't only divide your time between the Court and our house. People will . . ." She sighs.

"People will talk," I finish for her. "They always do."

Mother would tell me to mind them.

"They ought to know better," Aunt Elizabeth murmurs, and I feel a rush of gratitude toward her, not just for accepting my no, but for directing her anger at *other people* instead.

"Do we have an agreement, Carrie?"

I sit back in the chair. My shoulders ache. I don't want it to be this hard. "Yes, ma'am."

She pulls up another chair and folds her coat over the backrest. She sits down next to me, and I glance up just in time to see her smooth a frown. "Will you tell me about the arguments? I do not know a great deal about this particular Supreme Court case, but I trust you can fill me in on the right details."

I don't tell her about Alexander. I call him Alexander in my mind. I don't tell her, because I don't know what he means yet. He was kind to me, but it may just be good manners. Etiquette.

Still.

It's not etiquette when Alexander appears on Sunday after church and *asks me out for a walk*. Aunt Elizabeth frowns at me, a deeper frown than yesterday, tinged not with the disapproval I expect but with questions she doesn't ask.

Alexander and I walk in silence at first. He leads me toward the National Mall, where my eyes stray toward the Washington Monument and then toward the Capitol. I cannot look away. The buildings—their meanings—they transcend us.

"Have you been here before?" Alexander asks.

Aunt Elizabeth showed me around extensively when I first got here, but back then, the sound of construction on the Arlington Memorial Bridge drove out all sense of peace. Today the Potomac is quiet; the ships and dredging work have ground to a halt.

"How did you find me?" I counter instead. It's not an answer, but I want to know.

Alexander leads me past the newly dedicated Lincoln Memorial. Its gleaming white columns remind me of the Capitol Building. It makes me wonder if this memorial will still stand fierce and tall in a century and a half and beyond.

"I try to keep abreast of everything that happens in this city's society," he says. And again he reminds me of my brother, who also makes up the most outrageous lies, and who has more charm than sense.

It's so familiar, I know exactly how to deal with it: I snort.

"It's true," he protests. "Or rather, I'd like it to be. In effect, it only holds true for those members of society who attend Father's socials. It just so happens that one of them heard that Miss Elizabeth Allen, infamous bachelorette and erstwhile writer for *The Suffragist*, took in a stray."

I smile. It's been so long that I didn't think I would remember how. "Mr. Holmes, did you find me by heeding gossip?"

"That sounds far more ugly than being 'well informed,' don't you think?" Alexander puts his hands in his pockets. He walks me to West Potomac Park, where the paths are covered in faded and trampled pink flowers. It's a little too late for cherry blossoms.

There are more trees than people. And he may not know it, but I appreciate that.

"The thing is, Miss Allen, I'm usually the youngest in the visitors' gallery by a mile, and I'm usually the only legalese enthusiast. You intrigued me."

"Are you a law student?"

"I start Georgetown in the fall. One might say it's a family trait. I would disappoint Father if I didn't make judge somewhere, although I'd much rather argue cases."

"I'd much rather argue cases, too," I say, softly. Too softly, perhaps. I curl my fingers around the pebble in my pocket and clear my throat. "I hope to enroll at Washington College of Law in a year."

Alexander cleans a bench for me to sit. "Madame Justice Allen." He inclines his head.

"Clerical support somewhere, more likely," I say.

"Don't sell yourself short, Miss Allen."

I'm not. It's a step up from not-believing, and I know how to be realistic. Most law firms don't take well to female lawyers, and even a single case exhausts me. Besides, Aunt Elizabeth was right about my lack of connections. I do not have the family name to make a place for myself in society, and I would likely flounder even if I did. I will have to stand on merit alone, and I merit little.

Alexander produces a paper bag filled with taffy and offers me one. I want to decline, because I hate the texture, but I don't want to be impolite. I pick out the smallest piece and unwrap it as slowly as I can.

"So if you're not a student yet, why do you go to the arguments?" I ask.

Alexander picks a larger piece of taffy, as if he doesn't notice the sticky sweet chewiness and the way the taffy wraps around your gums. I can't ignore it for even a moment, but he seems to appreciate the candy.

"To learn from the best, of course," he says. "And it interests me to see which cases are brought to the Court. What did you think of Friday's arguments? Why would anyone wish to take a case like that to a court—and to the Supreme Court, no less?"

"Doctors trying to sterilize a young girl for no apparent reason? Why *wouldn't* anyone take that case to the Supreme Court?"

"Because it might be seen as inappropriate?"

"To discuss a matter of law?"

He cocks his head. "Miss Buck is feebleminded. Her doctor prescribed sterilization to avoid further . . . What did they call it? Socially inadequate offspring. It wouldn't have any effects on her general health. It's not a question for the law; it's a matter of medical integrity."

"No." I grow cold all over. "It's not just medical integrity, Mr. Holmes. It's bodily autonomy. She is a person. She has a *right* to decide for herself whether or not she wants to have children, like all of us. That's personal choice, and by denying her that, her doctors made it a matter of law." I tap my foot, and I can't stop. I don't know if any of this is appropriate, but I cannot stop. These are the questions I wanted to hear at the court case, and I need to share them with him. "She has a right to due process like all of us, does she not?"

He stares at me for a moment. He opens his mouth and closes it. Something shifts behind his eyes, but I don't know what it means.

Then he ups and walks away, and I'm left sitting there, on a bench in the park. Alone. And the convincing words I pride myself on, all the points I want to argue, flee me, too.

I do not return to Aunt Elizabeth's home until hours later, chilled to the bone. She keeps me with an elderly tutor for the next couple of days. According to her, there's more in this world than the law, and she wants me to study literature and mathematics in the comfort of her house. I quote Hobbes at her—that without laws to govern us, there would be "no knowledge of the face of the earth; no account of time; no arts; no letters; no society." It does not convince her, but the relative quiet and safety calms me.

It's Wednesday before I find my way back to the Capitol, ready to hear more arguments. From up close, the grandeur of the building still overwhelms me. This Capitol was built to weather ages, and it's a stone-carved reminder that anything is possible.

Atop the steps, I'm greeted by a surprising presence: Alexander.

He stands—or rather, paces. He wears a long coat and leather gloves, yet he still looks cold. It's almost May, but it feels like winter. When he sees me, he smiles. His whole face lights up. "Miss Allen."

I hesitate. "Mr. Holmes. Were you waiting for me?"

"I hoped I'd find you here."

"That seems like a gamble." He's only seen me here once; he can hardly draw conclusions from that. For all he knows, I only meant to observe those arguments and nothing more.

"Were you here the last two days, too?" I ask.

He looks down a little. "I wished to explain my sudden departure on Sunday."

"It was rather unexpected."

"It was, and I apologize."

I reach for the pebble in my pocket and roll it between my fingers. Back and forth. Back and forth.

Alexander clears his throat. "When I told you law was a family trait, I wasn't joking. My grandfather sits on the bench."

Oh. "Oliver Wendell Holmes Jr.," I say. I wonder why that didn't come to me sooner.

"Associate Justice of the Supreme Court of the United States."

"That must be . . ."

"Intimidating? I've never known any different, though you can imagine the family gathering, I'm sure. We all want to live up to his legacy."

Not knowing what else to do, I wrap my arms around my waist and walk into the Capitol, and he falls into step with me. I don't quite see (or want to see) how his grandfather could have caused Alexander's sudden departure on Sunday. When I say as much, he takes my hand and draws me to a quiet corner. I pull back my hand.

"I don't just go to the arguments to hear the attorneys. I go to see if I can anticipate the Court's rulings or explain them afterward, especially in those cases where Grandfather wrote the opinions. That's what I meant when I said I wanted to learn from the best. *He* is the best."

I cannot meet his eyes, but I wait to see what comes next.

"And you . . . you challenged that. You challenge everything he taught me. You probably don't even do it on purpose, but you come to me with arguments that I haven't considered—that I *should* have considered. You see connections as easily as he does, and you make me want to listen to your side of the story." He flushes. "I want to. I *can't*."

I hesitate. "Thank you?"

"You're different, Miss Allen. And you leave me uncertain."

I flinch.

Alexander winces. "I'm sorry, Miss Allen."

"So am I." Though I do not know if I can honestly blame him. I *am* different. I know the weight of expectations and of family.

And it's not just that. I know the weight of society. Carrie Buck's case is clear-cut to many. It is to Dr. Priddy, who first suggested sterilizing Carrie Buck. To Dr. Bell, who took up the case. *A genetic threat to society.* Alexander may not have come right out and said it, but why should it not be clear-cut to him?

The thought nags, but at the same time, I don't want to walk into this building alone. Alexander made me smile. We share the same dream. He did what no one has ever done before: he waited for me.

"I know the answer now. I believe in public welfare," he starts, apparently ready to revisit our argument.

I raise my hand to cut him off, and I swallow hard. I am used to pushing away my discomfort. "What's on the roster for you today, Mr. Holmes? Will you join me in hearing arguments on why gains from illicit traffic in liquor are subject to the income tax?"

✕ ✕ ✕

That afternoon, it's illicit traffic in liquor. The next day, we listen to arguments about forest fires. As the attorney drones on and on, Alexander slumps in his seat and mutters, "Just get to the burning point." It surprises a laugh out of me, and I have to start coughing to mask it. I can't remember the last time I laughed out loud. But once Alexander realizes wordplay amuses me endlessly, he makes it his mission to come up with the most hopeless of puns.

Even with a mind for structure, it is far more natural than I anticipated to fall into a rhythm with Alexander. We meet each other at the Capitol's steps every morning and sit in on the day's arguments. It becomes easier — though not easy — to walk through the crowded hallways. We discuss the cases we hear, we compare notes, and we battle our respective positions. More often than not, we disagree, although rarely as radically as in the case of Carrie Buck. He brings it up again. He's convinced he's right. He tries to convince me. "Society should be warded against lesser —" "She isn't as human —" "You don't understand —"

It becomes harder — though not impossible — to cut him off instead of arguing. It's simpler that way.

Because he makes me laugh out loud. And this may be friendship. Masked and cordoned off by the knowledge of who we truly are, but friendship nonetheless.

I don't usually forget, but it's only when the weekend arrives that I suddenly remember the promise I made to Aunt Elizabeth. A social function. Meeting with the dean of the Washington College of Law.

I can't do it. I'm raw and exhausted from too many days of trying to become who I want to be and being who I'm not. And I've only been at court three days this week, to observe, nothing more. I can't do it. I can't do it.

"Why are you so hesitant, Carrie?" Aunt Elizabeth tentatively places her hand on mine. I know she expects me to either pull away or smile at her. I do neither of those things, but it takes all my focus to keep my hand on the desk in front of me.

I would never answer this question if Mother asked it, but if home is a place to let one's guard down, Aunt Elizabeth is working hard to build me a home here.

I tap my foot against the leg of my chair. I owe her an answer, even if I don't quite know what it is. "People look at me and think I'm different. Maybe not at first—just like no one thinks Carrie Buck is different just from meeting her. But we cannot hide forever. I understand the rule of law. I do not understand the rules of society. I do not understand how to fit in, even when I'm trying my hardest to learn."

I expect Aunt Elizabeth to agree, but instead she counters, "You are new to the city, Carrie. When I first arrived here, I didn't feel like I belonged, either. It's magnificent, but it's overwhelming. You have to give yourself time; you've come so far already."

That isn't it, though. I should fit in. I should keep my head down. But I can't do it. "I have so far still to go. And I can only pretend to be someone else for so long."

"You shouldn't have to pretend," she says. "You have a mind for arguments. It may not work the same way as mine, but why shouldn't that be an asset? You could be a magnificent legal strategist."

I sway back and forth. My foot stills. I could belong here. "It frightens me."

Aunt Elizabeth sits back. "Are you afraid they won't accept you? I can't imagine they won't. You have so much potential."

That's hardly a good counterargument. We are in Aunt Elizabeth's office, surrounded by books and copies of *The Suffragist*.

Surrounded by the thoughts and opinions of a great number of people who all had great minds and great potential—but they were all able to find their place in the world. A great mind and potential is not enough.

"Or"—she breathes in deeply—"are you afraid that they will accept you and you'll not be enough?"

I still, my eyes fixed on the wooden paneling on the walls.

No. Yes. I don't know how to admit to that.

"Do you think I'll send you back home?"

I don't know how to admit to that, either.

"I would never," she says softly.

I stay silent, because I don't want to argue it.

Worry edges around her voice. "This had better not be about that Holmes boy. Is it? What did he say to you?"

"Nothing, he—he could be a friend," I say, and I wait for her to tell me his company is too good for me—or mine not good enough for him.

She doesn't. Instead she keeps her voice neutral. "What makes you say that?"

"He listens to me." I never had a friend before. "He respects my opinions." At least the ones we talk about.

"And it feels good to be heard?"

"Yes, ma'am."

"You deserve to be heard," Aunt Elizabeth says. "You deserve to be seen. You deserve to be respected." She said these same words to me when she collected me off the train. "Does he respect you?"

"He respects who he thinks I am."

She doesn't respond to that for the longest time, and an uncomfortable silence settles around us. Then she squeezes my hand and lets go.

"I still want you to meet with Dean Grace Hays Riley. We'll have tea together. But we'll set the appointment when you ask for it. Agreed?"

"Yes, ma'am." I get to my feet, grab a book from her shelves, and curl up around it, while Aunt Elizabeth sits down at her desk.

"Respect yourself, Carrie," she says. "Respect, and perhaps, one day, even love yourself. It's the most radical decision you can make."

Ten days after those first arguments, ten days after meeting Alexander Holmes, he stands outside the Capitol again. Waiting for me. He rocks back and forth on the balls of his feet, but in his case, I think it's excitement rather than a way to soothe an overly active mind.

"Good morning, Mr. Holmes."

He nearly pounces on me when I walk up the steps. "Miss Allen. I've seen the slip decision. I want you to read it."

The world stops turning, for just a moment. There's no question which case he's referring to, and there's no question he's excited. It makes me ill at ease. The words are on the tip of my tongue: *Alexan— Mr. Holmes, you can't convince me, please do not try. I don't want you to convince me.*

But I want the ruling. I've wanted this ruling for weeks. Months. Years. Even if he's happy. Even if this is the worst-case scenario. I want to know.

So I let him drag me to his grandfather's office while I push my pebble deep into the palm of my hand. The pain doesn't calm me the way repetition does, but it centers me. As a result, when Alexander pulls me into the empty office and shows me the writ, the words make sense.

I wish they didn't.

I read aloud:

"In view of the general declarations of the legislature and the specific findings of the Court, obviously we cannot say as matter of law that the grounds do not exist, and, if they exist, they justify the result. We have seen more than once that the public welfare may call upon the best citizens for their lives. It would be strange if it could not call upon those who already sap the strength of the State for these lesser sacrifices, often not felt to be such by those concerned, in order to prevent our being swamped with incompetence. It is better for all the world if, instead of waiting to execute degenerate offspring for crime or to let them starve for their imbecility, society can prevent those who are manifestly unfit from continuing their kind."

I try to catch my breath, but I still feel like I'm choking. My eyes glance over a sentence in the next paragraph: "Three generations of imbeciles are enough."

I can't read on. I can hardly think. I can only stare at the writ in my hands, the cruel words.

"I know we stood on opposite sides, but I wanted you to know Grandfather cared about public welfare when he wrote this."

I stare at the words before me, and I can't find my voice.

"It's the same principle that sustains compulsory vaccination. This is a matter of public health, too. Do we not, as a society, want to banish undesirable elements? It's not that Grandfather—and I—don't think she should have rights. But there's the greater good to consider, too."

The words sound familiar. It takes me a moment to realize they're akin to what I heard during oral arguments. *This is the state's intention to rid itself of those citizens deemed undesirable according to its standards.* Only, it hadn't been the doctor's side. "That's what Whitehead said. *In defense* of Carrie Buck."

Alexander shakes his head. "Even Carrie Buck's lawyer knew that this was an impossible case. He knew we must weigh the autonomy of the few against the protection of the many."

I place the writ on the table in front of me. I keep trying to breathe, but I feel light-headed. I need something to calm me. I need something to calm my mind. Then Alexander steps forward to support me. It's only a split second—his hand underneath my elbow—but I jump back. *"Don't* touch me."

Instead of moving back, he takes another step forward. "Miss Allen—*Carrie,* I didn't mean to upset you. I wanted you to know the utmost care went into this decision, and eight judges agreed."

I turn away. It's the smallest mercy that one of them dissented. Eight judges agreed Carrie Buck's rights didn't matter. Eight judges agreed that she wasn't enough.

"Come, let me take you to lunch. It's the end of the term. We heard the arguments. We'll read more decisions and opinions. We live to study the law another day."

Except, out of all the arguments we heard and all the cases we argued, there wasn't another one like this for me. It was never just about one girl's right to reproduce. I told Aunt Elizabeth I loved that Alexander made me feel like he valued my opinions. But this. This matters to me. And he doesn't see it.

"Remember when you asked me why I came to this particular case?" I say softly, and Alexander stops shuffling papers at the desk.

"Fortunate timing, you said. I happened to agree with that. It was most fortunate, in that it allowed us to meet."

He smiles. He hasn't a care in the world. And right there and then I hate him for it. "Truth is, Mr. Holmes, I lied."

He stills. The room grows dead silent.

"Carrie Buck's case . . . I've followed it since it was in the Circuit Court at Amherst County. My county, as a matter of fact. We've never met. She's from Charlottesville and my family lives in Schuyler. We've never even crossed paths. But we have a lot in common, Carrie Buck and I. And I wanted to believe she had a chance."

"It's better for all—"

It's better if you keep your head down. It's better if you leave to stay at your aunt's. It's better if you hold your tongue. It's better if you forget your dreams.

"If what? If we start deciding who's good enough? Who matters enough to deserve rights and sovereignty?"

"She is feebleminded."

"She is human," I say flatly. "Eugenics has nothing to do with the public welfare."

Alexander sits down in one of the high-back leather chairs. He rakes his fingers through his hair. "You said you and Carrie Buck have a lot in common."

We do. I want to tell him that I know too well what it feels like to be lesser, to be constantly judged and found wanting. That after seventeen years, it still seems to me as if the rest of the world knows rules that I was never taught. That sometimes my mind snags on words, phrases, repetitions. That I can pretend, but it's all I can do.

But maybe that's not entirely true. This city overwhelms me with its busyness and noise, but for the first time, I want to shout back.

I breathe in sharply. "We have more in common than you may think. Feebleminded? By whose standards?" I take a step forward, and all the words that have floated just out of reach snap into place, fueled by rage and despair and everything I've ever wanted to do and be and reach for. "Carrie Buck is a girl like me. Despite everyone telling her that she didn't matter, she came here to fight for her choices. She has the *inalienable* right to do so. But instead of recognizing that, we assign value to her, to each other, to ourselves. We tell her she isn't competent enough. She isn't fit enough. She isn't *equal* enough. Do you know what would be better for all the world? If instead of fighting to limit her rights—our constitutional rights, our fundamentally *human* rights—we fought to embrace them and strengthen them. If we limit equality, we can never be truly equal."

I am trembling all over, and I am *relieved*.

Alexander has paled. He trembles, too.

"You really should be a lawyer, Miss Allen." He extends his hand, but he doesn't acknowledge my words. "Come, let me apologize and take you to lunch. I know a quaint little place close by that I'm sure you would appreciate. The weather's turned again. We could walk the Mall and talk, perhaps."

I regard his outstretched hand. His words are stuck in my head. *You really should be a lawyer, Miss Allen.*

I really should be a lawyer.

When I said I wanted to believe Carrie Buck had a chance, I wanted to believe *I* had a chance.

I keep my hands to my side. "It was a pleasure to meet you, Mr. Holmes, and a greater pleasure still to spar with you. And I *will* be a lawyer one day."

Before he can respond, I turn away. I walk out of the room, and through the hallway, underneath the proud dome, where the sandstone walls rise high and golden light filters through. I hold my head high.

When it's better for all the world that we are not to be given chances, the only option we have left—the only option *I* have left—is to grab them instead. To fight for them, even if it means courting probable failure.

I hope Aunt Elizabeth will be at her office. I want to reschedule that tea. Perhaps she can introduce me to the dean after all—though I will do this on my own merits. I want to do this on my own merits, no matter how much time it takes. I curl my fingers around the pebble in my pocket. I'll carve out my own space.

I believe I may be starting to understand what Aunt Elizabeth meant. Given time, I could grow to love myself. And in a world where we are considered undesirable elements, Carrie and I, perhaps that is the most radical act of all.

❈ AUTHOR'S NOTE ❈

In the first half of the twentieth century, most states adopted sterilization laws. Based on Laughlin's Model Eugenical Sterilization Law, these laws focused on intellectually and developmentally disabled people and mentally ill people but also included physically disabled people, d/Deaf and blind people, and people considered "dependent (orphans, ne'er-do-wells, the homeless)."

Carrie Buck was one of the first recommended for sterilization under the Virginia Sterilization Act of 1924. Her case became a trial case to test its constitutionality.

When Carrie Buck became pregnant from rape, her foster family petitioned to have her committed to the Virginia State Colony for Epileptics and Feeble-Minded for showing hereditary traits of social inadequacy. After losing the case, in part due to her attorney's not putting up a defense, Carrie Buck was sterilized. Under the guise of a routine surgery, her half-sister was also sterilized; she only found out many years later.

Diagnoses were commonly wielded as weapons. This was true for Carrie Buck, who was not "feeble-minded," but was deemed undesirable/inconvenient.

In the name of eugenics, over sixty thousand people were forcibly sterilized. Among and alongside disabled people, women of color were disproportionately targeted. *Buck v. Bell* has never been explicitly overturned.

Further reading on this subject: Paul Lombardo's *Three Generations, No Imbeciles* (about Carrie Buck's case) and Angela Davis's *Women, Race and Class* (specifically: "Racism, Birth Control and Reproductive Rights").

WHEN THE MOONLIGHT ISN'T ENOUGH

DHONIELLE CLAYTON

Before the war, moonlight used to taste like sugar and butter and fresh cream. Mama would fold in the ingredients until it fluffed up like meringue. She'd even sprinkle it with cinnamon. But now she's only got sprigs of mint, a few basil leaves, or a stem or two of rosemary from her kitchen garden, and sometimes the soil won't even give her that. Still, she's always made sure I've never tasted it raw. Pure. Straight from the sky. It's too bitter and sharp.

The water around my ankles is still cold for late spring. Oak Bluffs hasn't warmed yet. It always feels like Massachusetts—especially Martha's Vineyard—is the last place on Earth to grab heat and let it press down into the water and into the land. We've been here five years, and it feels like it's colder and colder every year.

Standing in the small lake behind our house, I grip the two canning jars and wait. It seems like I'm always waiting these days.

For Molly to come over.

For the moon.

For another spring cotillion.

For something, anything, to happen.

The feeling rises up like a tide ready to flood my insides, drown my heart, choke my voice, and swallow me whole.

I watch the sky. It looks different now. Maybe gunpowder gets trapped in clouds and these have drifted across the Atlantic from the battlefields. Maybe it's just me—and my eyes have changed and I can't see the same things anymore.

The clouds break to let out the moon. It's fat and slightly blushing with a halo. Mama will be happy. This is one of her favorite types of full moons.

The rays hit the water's surface. They climb over the cool ripples step-by-step as if called to my legs.

I let the beams kiss my skin, make the light brown glow like fireflies, before I dip the jar into the water. The liquid does not enter. Instead, the moonlight itself folds into the glass receptacle, attracted to the blood coating its inner walls. Mama's blood tonight. Mine tomorrow. Daddy's the next night. We take turns with the bleeding.

The light thickens like sweet pudding.

I fill both jars, then stand there as if the great glowing orb could tell me something. When will the war end? Will we have to move again? Will I ever get to see the world on my own? Is this how my life will always be?

I wait for the moon to leave words etched onto the water or spread letters through the clouds or send down messages in the beams.

But it gives me nothing but its light.

"Emma, get in here right now. Been out too long. It'll spoil without a covering." Mama's voice carries from the back of the house to the lake. It can always find me, especially when I'm thinking of something she wouldn't approve of.

"Coming!" I holler back.

"You want to wake the whole world?" she snaps when I walk in the house. She stares down at me like I'm a little girl again and too loud during a church service.

"You yelled first," I mumble.

"What did you say?" she asks.

"Nothing, ma'am." My cheeks burn with heat, and a wish bubbles up inside my chest: a desire to be free of her and on my own for a little while.

She stands in the doorway, her hair spilling over with pin curls that poke out from under her scarf. Her freckles cover her light-brown cheeks like chips in a cookie. Not that there is much chocolate with the rations these days.

I hand her the glass jars. She lifts them up and sucks her teeth. "You could've caught more than two jars' worth. We've got to keep the stores full. Always."

"I will tomorrow. It was sluggish tonight," I lie.

"Seems more like you are." She eyes me. "You've been walking around here dragging your tail these past couple of weeks, and I'll have no more of it."

"I don't—" I start to speak, then swallow the words. I want to tell her that I'm tired of always doing things her way, that I haven't been a child for a very long time and I'm tired of being treated like one.

"Go to your room. I'll wake you when it's ready." She shoos me upstairs.

I slam my bedroom door and ignore Mama's shout of displeasure.

✕   ✕   ✕

Mama jostles me out of bed before dawn. The house smells like fresh biscuits and bacon and honey. The moon fades into a pale-blue sky as the sun starts to poke its head above the horizon.

Mama has the candles lit in the kitchen and at the table. She doesn't like to waste electricity when the sun's about to come up and do its duty. Daddy reads the paper, using a thick candle bearded with drippings as a paperweight. The headlines almost scream in thick black ink:

MacARTHUR IN AUSTRALIA AS ALLIED COMMANDER; MOVE HAILED AS FORESHADOWING TURN OF TIDE

THIRD NATIONAL ARMY DRAFT BEGINS IN CAPITAL

NAZIS CLOSE PORTS OF NORTH NORWAY

BILL FOR WOMEN'S AUXILIARY CORPS OF 150,000 PASSED BY THE HOUSE

I slide into the seat beside him. "'Morning, Daddy."

"'Morning, butterbean."

I stare at the pictures of General MacArthur's men and ships. I toy with a question. It rolls around on my tongue and teases my vocal chords. I've always been able to talk to him. Mama says he's got a listening spirit, and it was one of the reasons she married him.

Daddy looks up from the paper. A crease mars his forehead like the wrinkles in a raisin, and his left eyebrow hitches up. "What is it? I can see something knocking around in there."

"You think the Nazis will make it over here?" I ask.

"They could."

A deep shudder ripples through me. Every day the radio hosts warn listeners about the presence of German U-boats off the eastern coast, and how if the Nazis came here, they'd tear America up just like they were doing in Europe.

"Then, why are we staying this time?"

Daddy scratches his beard. "I'm getting tired of moving, butter-bean, and this has been my favorite place of all the ones we've lived." He pats my hand. "Also, I don't really think this war will reach us."

"But if it did, what would we do?"

"What we have always done."

"Leave," I say, and grit my teeth.

"Yes. Find a faraway corner to hide in."

"But what if the Nazis spread to all the states? What if they find out about us? What would happen?" My heart knocks against my rib cage, each thundering beat anticipating his answer.

"We'd make sure we weren't found. Cross the border into Canada again or go back down into Mexico. You know what's at stake if anyone figured out what we can do." He takes a deep breath. "They'd lock us up in their hospitals. They'd poke us with their needles and measure our skulls and take our blood. They'd study us like the animals they already think we are."

"Would you join if you could? To help keep us safe from the Nazis?" I ask in a whisper.

"Join what?"

I point at the picture on the front page. His lips purse, and he doesn't look up.

"You already know the answer to that question, and you know I don't like to talk just to hear myself. It wastes the good Lord's air."

"But this time we stayed!"

"We don't get involved. We're not patriots," he says. During the

Civil War, we left New Orleans for a small village in Mexico, and when America entered the first Great War, we headed north out of New York City to Canada. When the wars ended, we came back.

He continues to read the paper. The silence thickens between us as I try to gather the courage to ask him another question. The word *patriot* reverberates like a ghost floating through the room, setting my nerves on edge.

The ration coupons sit on the kitchen counter like paper-thin reminders that the world is starving. The radio reports the body count each day and reminds us how perilous life is for our soldiers in Europe and the Pacific. The two white boys who used to bring the papers into Oak Bluffs enlisted and died. Now the newspapers warn that Japan could invade from the west and Germans from the east if we don't fight back.

I've never seen any of this before. Mama and Daddy always took me far away, where all of these things were legend and myth. War never felt real before.

Now it's everywhere. On the tips of people's tongues. In every newspaper. On every radio program. Part of every passing conversation.

I've dreamed about it since the attack on Pearl Harbor, since President Roosevelt declared war. In my dreams, the war comes like a great storm, a blizzard of dust with angry spirals and sizzling lightning and thick gunpowder clouds that rage in the sky and cast a suffocating darkness over the world. It feels like the hand of the Devil sweeping over us with his fingers gathering into a fist, ready to squeeze us all. I wake up soaked from head to foot.

Daddy glances up. "What is it?"

"Don't you want to help? Use your medical—?"

"Help?" He thumps the newspaper.

I stuff my mouth with a piece of biscuit. Its folds are fluffy like what I think a cloud might be like, if I could catch it like I catch moonlight.

"War is not a fairy tale, butterbean. Men die." His wire-rimmed glasses slide down the bridge of his thick nose. "I'm much too old to entertain heroics, especially for a country that doesn't care about people who look like you or me."

"I know. But—"

"But what?"

"We never do anything. We just move."

Mama overhears me and fumbles with a plate stacked high with biscuits. They tumble along the table, leaving tiny buttery fingerprints on the tablecloth. "Best be dropping the topic." Mama resets the pyramid of warm biscuits and hands out milky glasses of moonlight.

"But you're a nurse, Mama. And, Daddy, you're a doctor. Don't you feel like you should help this time?" After the first Great War ended, we moved to the capital, where Daddy and Mama studied at Howard University and worked in the colored hospital there. I thought it might be the place we finally stayed—Mama seemed happier and even let herself have friends—but people started asking questions after they both served ten years at the hospital without a single change in their outward appearance.

Mama's hazel eyes narrow. "I *was* a nurse, and your father didn't study medicine as some kind of duty to others. We did it so we could always take care of ourselves, so we'd never have to go and ask for medical attention. Now, let's move on. You're gonna make me fly off the handle, and the Lord doesn't like ugly, especially this close to Sunday."

"Let's remember we're blessed. We're alive. We will be here forever. We have the moonlight." Daddy lets his eyes linger on mine before turning to Mama.

The McGees mind their own business.

The McGees hold on to their own breaths, Mama says.

The McGees only worry about the moonlight.

I already know this. It's settled deep in my bones and tissues and soul. We lived through slavery, and we survived. We moved north after Emancipation, and we survived. We kept our heads down and mouths shut, and made our way out of no way.

The moonlight always provided.

Mama raises her glass. We all follow, just like we always do. I tip the rim to my lips and let the liquid tease my mouth. I wonder how quickly I'd age if I didn't drink it. Would my body shrivel within a month? Would my bones start counting the days and weeks and months and years like everyone else's? Would I feel even more empty than I already do?

It goes down like flames every time. A hot surge that travels through my throat like a snake and curls into my belly like a fire in the hearth. Daddy says it's worse than Scottish whiskey, but I've never had more than a sip of champagne. Mama says it burns because it's pushing into our bones, keeping us alive no matter what. She says it's a gift from the Lord. I've had it once a month since I turned sixteen on December 12, 1768, on Honey Alley Plantation outside of Jackson, Mississippi.

I'm 191 years old. But I have always been sixteen.

"This one is too puffy, I think." Molly prances through her bedroom, twirling in her cotillion dress. Her willowy arms are the color of the honey caramels Mama used to make and give as gifts when we lived in Philadelphia. The dress *is* too puffy; Molly looks like she belongs on top of a wedding cake.

I mostly look out of her little window. All the houses line up like gingerbread ones in a fairy tale with primrose-pink and lemon-yellow and robin's-egg-blue piping, and flower boxes spilling over with spring blooms. Rocking chairs creak on tiny porches that reach like poked-out lips onto Clinton Street. Mrs. Brooke tends to her victory garden. Mr. Jordan hobbles along with the help of his granddaughter, Sadie. The church ladies pass by in their pillbox hats and white-gloved hands with big smiles swallowing their brown faces. The *click-clack* of their heeled shoes creates a melody. You can hear everything so clearly now. The gasoline ration means most people are walking these days.

Molly jostles my shoulder. "I said, what does your dress look like?"

I want to tell her I have a closet full of dresses. This is my twenty-seventh cotillion, though it's my first in Oak Bluffs. The cotillion dresses I've worn in the past zip through my head like the turning of a film reel. I loved the champagne empire-waist gown I wore after Daddy bought our freedom from Master McGee at Honey Alley in 1809 and we joined the free colored society of New Orleans. Also, the blush-pink bustle one I wore in 1880 while in Atlanta. And the cream chiffon one with the trumpet-shaped bottom in 1902, when we lived in Chicago. Or the flapper-style one I swapped for the one Mama picked when we were in Harlem in 1922.

But I can't tell Molly any of that. We've known each other for three years now, and I know everything about her, and she barely knows anything about me. I should feel lucky Mama let me have a friend this time around. I haven't had one since 1938 — right before we moved here — when it didn't go so well in Boston. Mama let her guard down a little with the Brooks family, and little Lilly May found the moonlight. We had to spin so many lies to explain that Mama made us leave immediately.

"Do you ever wonder about what's going on over there?" I ask.

Molly frowns. "Over where?"

"In Europe. You've seen the papers, right? Heard the radio?"

"I'd much rather talk about your cotillion dress. Did you get it yet? July's coming quick." She rubs her hands over the bodice. Tiny pearls catch the light.

"It's only the end of May," I remind her, then take out the newspaper I borrowed from Daddy's desk and spread it over her floor. The headlines talk of war, increased rations, an East Coast blackout, men dying, U-boats spotted in the Atlantic, and the Nazis.

Molly smooths a loose curl from my bun. "You think George will be a good dancer? Caroline says his feet don't work and his hands get all wet when he's nervous, and I should've picked Brandon. We haven't even practiced. I don't want to look like a fool." She prattles on and on. "Will you go with Raymond Finley?"

I scoff. "He hasn't asked."

"Well, George says it's 'cause he can't figure out if you actually like him."

I'm not supposed to like anyone. I'm not supposed to let anyone close.

I shrug. "Maybe I won't go."

"Won't go?" Her nose crinkles with disgust.

"It's not like it's my own wedding."

"It's the first big thing that ever happens to a girl. Your wedding will be second," she says.

I won't ever get married. I'll always be with Mama and Daddy. The thought hits me in the chest. I'd always just accepted that. But now, the desire to do something, anything else burns inside me like a hot coal.

"I heard Miss Claudine say we might not have any dessert to serve at the ball this year. Can you believe it? There's not enough butter or chocolate to make a big enough cake to feed fifty people."

"Is that so?" My mind drifts off.

"Also, my mother thinks I should wear my hair out. I don't think we'll have enough bobby pins for a full updo. She's not willing to buy me some under the counter. She thinks they're cracking down and that colored folks who get caught will be treated harsher."

"We'll have to deal with worse if the war comes here."

"To Oak Bluffs?" She laughs. "Never. Nothing ever comes here except people on vacation." She turns back to the mirror. "Why are you so worried?"

I can't find an answer. It all feels wispy and out of touch and half formed. I close my eyes and see the storm from my dream — a roaring black mass of death. The headlines, the radio news reports, the rations, the looks on people's faces swirl inside the chaos. Maybe this is why Mama and Daddy usually leave. So we won't have to *see* it, anticipate it, worry about it. So that we could always just come back after things were okay again.

"I just am" is all I can muster.

"Well, my mama says there's no use in worrying yourself sick about things you can't change. I'm going to busy myself with the cotillion and George. Mama thinks he might ask me to marry him after we graduate." Molly tries on another dress while prattling on about getting married. "This one's my sister's old cotillion gown from five years ago. You think it's out of fashion?" She sighs with disappointment. "I hope no one remembers it. The rations have made it impossible for me to get another one made. You know I like more than one option. I'm not keen on either of these." A deep flush blooms beneath her pale cheeks. Even in selfish anger, she's one of the most beautiful girls I've ever seen. Mama calls her "Red Molly" and says her bones must be red on the inside 'cause her skin's so light and pale and yellowy instead of deep brown.

"Emma." She squints. "What do you think?"

The tulle blooms around her waist like a lovely upside-down church bell, and the sweetheart neckline shows off her perfect collarbone. The lace is like intricate frosting.

"That one is delicate. Very pretty."

She beams, flashing a perfect set of white teeth. "Maybe I should go with this one, then. Even though my sister wore it." She dances around the room, lifting her legs and swishing around while pretending to do the jitterbug. "Dance with me."

"No," I grumble.

"Yes." She reaches out her hands.

I groan but let her drag me up off the floor. She turns me in circles, then pulls me in for a slow dance. Her skin smells of lavender. She hums a popular song from the radio. We bob left and right, then left again.

"What do you think will happen?" I whisper into her shoulder.

"We'll dance and sneak champa—"

"No, in the war."

"I don't know." She pivots me around, then catches me again. "Don't you think about it? Pearl Harbor?"

"No."

"Why not?" I pull back and stare into her hazel eyes. We could be sisters in the winter, when the sun doesn't color my skin so deeply and Mama pulls the frizz out of my hair with her pomades.

"I have other things on my mind, as should you." Molly places a hand to my forehead. "Are you ill? What's wrong with you?"

I break out of her grip and walk to the door. She calls after me, but I don't stop.

I let Raymond Finley put his tongue in my mouth even though I shouldn't. I let him unpin my hair so it falls down my back in frizzy waves. I let him whisper in my ear about his plans to give me his grandmother's ring when I turn eighteen like him. He was the first boy I met when we moved to Oak Bluffs. He tried to kiss me on the old fishing pier, but I didn't let him until a month ago.

I sink into this fantasy and pretend until my lips are swollen and I'm out of breath from kissing him. I've only kissed five boys in over a hundred years, and it always feels like the very first time every time.

We're in the large oak behind his house. Our legs dangle from its sturdy boughs, and its thick green leaves hide us from any prying eyes.

"I'm going away," he says, leaning back to stare into my eyes. He's the color of a smudge of peanut butter and has the smallest gap between his front teeth that makes him look clever.

I'd always thought I'd be the one leaving him.

"I mean, I'm planning to," he says. "So I will miss being your cotillion date."

"You haven't asked me," I say. "Where are you going?"

His eyes dart all around. "You can't tell anyone what I'm about to tell you." He takes my hand, and I nod. "I'm enlisting."

His words are a firework exploding between us.

"I filled out the paperwork and I'll ship out soon."

"They're going to let you fight?" My hands go all fluttery, and he grabs them to hold them still. My stomach pinches and I think about what it might be like to go to Europe or the Pacific or wherever they're planning to ship him out to. I wonder what he'll see.

"In one of the colored units." He kisses me again with a smile. "Will you write to me?"

A searing hot wave of jealousy shoots through me.

"Will you?" he presses.

"Of course."

"I want to fly a plane." His smile grows so big it almost

swallows his face. It makes me think of what he must've looked like as a little boy.

"What if I told you I wanted to go, too?"

A small chuckle escapes his mouth. I clench my teeth and slide away from him. "War is no place for girls or women." He reaches for me to bring me closer again.

"Why is that?" I snap.

He twirls my hair around his fingers. "It's a place where men fight and win, or fight and die." He sounds like Daddy.

"And you want to go there?"

"I want to do something to help us, to help our people."

His words pluck the same feeling straight out of me.

"But why?" I ask, and sound like Mama. I wonder why Raymond and I both want to go and fight but neither Mama nor Daddy wants to.

He takes a piece of paper from his pocket and unfolds it to show me a torn-out article from the *Pittsburgh Courier*, a black newspaper Daddy often reads. He points at the headline:

DEMOCRACY: VICTORY AT HOME, VICTORY ABROAD

"We can change things here if we fight overseas. We can also fight for our rights."

"I want to be part of something, too," I say, not sure exactly what that might be. Maybe helping other colored people or maybe the war effort. Maybe both. The confusion tangles into a knot in my stomach.

He traces his finger along my nose and mouth. "I'm making a memory of you."

"You'll come back," I say, knowing that I most likely won't be here when he does because Mama and Daddy might pack us up again.

"Will you wait for me?"

I kiss him long and hard, knowing this is our last kiss. I try to take in every scent of him, every flavor of his mouth, every part of his touch.

I want to be him. I want to be able to enlist. I want to see the world. I want to do something that matters instead of always hiding.

Martha's Vineyard is shaped like a very old turtle and her babies. That's how Mama described it to me when we first moved. With Oak Bluffs at the peak of the shell, and Aquinnah and Chilmark at the tail, and Edgartown at the head. The turtle's babies float above her — the Elizabeth Islands across the sound.

Mama and Daddy love it here. The colored community is quiet and small, mostly tending to their own affairs. No one has noticed that the McGee family hasn't aged. The white folks aren't the mean kind who spit or call you names or give you dirty looks. They're the "all right" kind, Mama says. The kind we can live beside without any trouble.

Out of all the places we've lived, the Vineyard is the most beautiful — and the most boring.

"I don't think I've ever been anyplace I wanted to stay until we got here, butterbean," Daddy says as we drive to the post office in Vineyard Haven. The one in Oaks Bluff closed last year. He parks the car across from the filling station, where a little white boy throws a rubber ball into a wire-fenced crate for the metal-scrap drive.

"Come, let's be quick, Emma. Before Mama finds out we took the car." Daddy leads me forward. "She'll give me an earful about wasting the gas."

The bell chimes when we walk into the post office. Some white people let their eyes linger on us for a few seconds too long before setting brown paper–wrapped parcels on counters or joining us in the line to buy twenty-five-cent war stamps. We're the only black people in here.

Daddy's tall frame curves like a question mark over the postal counter. A man behind us reads the newspaper. I crane to see the headlines:

AMERICAN CASUALTIES CONTINUE TO GROW IN THE PACIFIC

ALLIES SMASH BACK AT JAPAN

SIX AMERICANS KILLED ON BRITISH SHIP

Worries seep out of everybody but Daddy. It's in the way they purse their lips and knit their hands or fuss with their briefcases or purses. We're all holding our breath and waiting for the world to fall out from under us.

Cheers draw everyone to the post-office windows. Youngish white boys dressed in army uniforms jump into cars. The small crowd claps. The boys' cheeks flush pink as they flash us their perfect teeth. I think of Raymond. How the olive green of his uniform will make his skin glow. How he'll earn medals of honor to decorate the lapel with because he's smart.

A little girl sets her elbows on the window ledge. "I wanna be like them, Mommy. I wanna wear a hat like that."

The mother draws the little girl's attention to a wall poster. "This lady has a hat on, too, Wendy."

It's a pretty white lady in a green army hat. Buttons shine on her lapels like fallen stars. The caption reads:

You Are Needed Now. Join the Army Nurse Corps.
Apply at Your Red Cross Recruiting Center.

I take a step closer. My heart thuds in my chest as if it's grown fingers of blood and tissue, ready to latch on, grip something other than all it's ever known.

"I heard them saying in Edgartown that there're still men trapped in the ships at Pearl," our neighbor Montgomery says to Daddy. They're playing bid whist and sipping amber liquid from two glittering tumblers. Mama's packing up a meal for Montgomery. She feeds him on occasion since his wife died last year. Daddy says Montgomery's not a man who pays attention to details, so he's easy enough to have around without our secret slipping out.

I linger near the parlor door. The radio crackles in the background, reporting the latest news.

"Let us not worry ourselves with such sad talk," Mama says.

"Them Nazis might show up here. I went and got me some blackout curtains, and I'm going to set up my own bunker." Montgomery rubs the salt-and-pepper whiskers across his cheeks and chin before setting down a card on the table. "Then what we gonna do?"

"No use in—" Mama calls from the kitchen.

"There's black soldiers headed there, too," Montgomery adds.

Mama joins them in the parlor with a skillet of golden corn bread and a jar of fresh honey.

"They're not going to let us fight. Really fight," Daddy says, flicking a card from his hand. "Even if more of us wanted to. They'll make us stay in the kitchen or mop up the blood of white folks."

"You'd think they'd want to send us over there to die, and be rid of us." Montgomery reaches for a slice of the warm corn bread. "The colored newspapers been telling our boys to sign up. That we can fight for our rights abroad and at home."

My heart squeezes. My hands flutter, and I clutch them tight.

"The Finley boy enlisted," Montgomery reports.

Mama starts a worried hum and rocks back and forth on her heels. I hold my breath.

Daddy drops his head. "Now, why would they let him go on and do that?"

"He didn't give them a choice," Montgomery says.

"He up and left?" Mama asks, horrified.

"Sure did."

My heart beats so loud, I'm certain they can hear it.

"His mama cried and cried. He said he wanted to fight for his country."

"His country? *This* country?" Daddy slams his cards down on the table. "Who sold him that lie? That this has ever been or ever will be *his* country is the greatest lie ever told. When has this country cared about colored folks? Maybe when they were selling them on the auction block and needed them to pick cotton? But we're nothing but flies in the milk here. That's the way it's always been and how it's always going to be. Finley's a damn fool. His father is probably grumbling around in his grave."

"We shouldn't get mixed up in this. White folks' wars always get the rest of us in trouble," Mama says with fear crackling in her voice. She told me that before she met Daddy, she'd been taken by a British soldier, and that she had to resort to means she wouldn't tell me to get away. Daddy told me the sight of soldiers kick up bad memories for her.

I want to feel like Mama and Daddy. I want to *not* want to do something. I want to be like an untethered balloon, floating. I want to fight the urge swirling in the pit of my belly. I want to do things like we always have.

But I understand Raymond Finley.

His kiss still warms my mouth.

I remember the people clapping and the pride of the soldiers Daddy and I saw at the post office. I remember the way the little girl looked at them. I remember the poster.

I understand wanting to belong somewhere, wanting to be part of something, wanting to do something—anything—to make things a little better for all of us.

I lean farther into the parlor as Montgomery starts to whisper.

Mama's eyes find me in the doorway. She strides over.

I should step back.

I should scamper up to my room.

I should apologize.

Her teeth are clenched. "This is grown folks' business." Mama closes the door right in my face.

I put a hand on the door. My palm burns with the desire to shove it back open. I've been alive longer than Montgomery. I've earned the right to have an opinion.

But I can't muster the courage to push.

The next afternoon I tell Mama I'm heading to Molly's but ride my bike to Vineyard Haven and find the Junior Red Cross in the Brickman Building. I pace up and down the street. A few white onlookers stare, and a blush settles into my cheeks. There aren't as many people who look like me outside of Oak Bluffs. My stomach flutters.

I should go back home.

I should go to Molly's.

I should remember the years and years when I was content with just doing what Mama and Daddy asked me to do.

I take a deep breath, walk up the long staircase, and ease open the door. The bright-red cross blazes on it, almost alive with warning.

All the white women freeze over their worktables. Bundles of white gauze sit like small pillows in front of them.

"Can I help you with something, miss? Are you lost?" one of them says. She hitches a blond eyebrow up at me.

"I—I wanted . . . Are you taking more volunteers?" I squeak out.

An older woman wearing a nun's habit approaches. "Yes, of course. Many hands make the Lord's work lighter."

The room's so quiet, you could hear a mouse tiptoe. She leads me to a corner table, and we settle across from one another.

"I'm Mother Powell."

"Emma," I whisper. "Emma McGee."

"And where are you from?"

"Oak Bluffs."

"Of course. How did you hear we were in need of help?"

"I saw a poster about the Red Cross."

She nods. "Very well, then. Wash your hands in that bowl." She points to a water basin. "Must keep them clean. Then use this here." She places a square template in front of me. "Fold in on all four sides."

"What are these?" I whisper.

"Medical bandages for the soldiers."

The conversation in the room picks up as I fade into the background like a vase on a stand. The other girls discuss boys they fancy and the music on the radio and what might happen to the world if Hitler succeeds.

Hours pass. Girls and young women drift in and out. I fall into a rhythm. The simple folding action fills a hole I didn't know existed. The ache of needing to do something, anything of meaning besides collecting moonlight. The bundle of bandages becomes a mountain.

"We're closing for the day, dearie," the nun says.

I gaze up and realize I'm the only one left.

"Thank you for volunteering." She transfers the bundles to boxes. "You are most industrious. You have a good touch."

I walk toward the door. Her desk has a pile of Army Nurse Corps forms. My fingers float over the pages, feeling buzzy and light.

"Will you come back? We could use more hands. Always," Mother Powell says.

I reach for the doorknob and fight the smile tickling my lips.

"Yes," I reply.

I swipe an application before slipping out. I press it to my heart.

"Maybe we should leave again." Mama's voice carries up the stairwell, where I'm hiding and listening.

I should still be asleep. I should be waiting for her to wake me for our early-morning breakfast and moonlight. She caught the rays tonight as I watched her from my bedroom window.

"I like this place," Daddy replies.

"This war could be worse than the others. What happened at Pearl Harbor was bad. And even though it feels far away, maybe it isn't. Maybe it's coming and will show up on our doorstep before we've even gotten the chance to plan. I won't live with soldiers around ever again."

The scent of bacon finds me. My stomach gurgles. I hold it so it won't give my hiding spot away.

"Where would we go, Matilda? We've found a good place here. It's a sleepy community. One that avoids suspicion. We know how to get through the worst of it."

"Maybe Toronto? Or Montreal?" Mama frets. "Or back to Mexico, even."

"I'm tired of running. Packing and moving. Then unpacking and trying to settle back in somewhere new." Daddy's paper crackles. The candle burns out. "Light me another, please."

"Malcolm, maybe—" Mama says.

The hiss of the match echoes.

"I'll think about it. If the Nazis or the Japanese make it to our shores, then we must go. I won't allow what happened to you before to happen again. I promised you that many years ago." He reaches for Mama's hand. "I do what I say I'm going to do."

"I know," she replies.

"We're safe when we're together. We're better when we've thought things through together." He kisses her hand. "Go on and finish breakfast. The bacon's burning."

Mama's cast-iron skillet makes a bang. "Emma's walking around fussin' about the war. You seen her?"

"She'll be all right."

"You always say that," she says. "It doesn't feel like it this time. She's changing."

I hold my breath.

"She's been our little girl for almost two hundred years. Surely she'll remain that way for two hundred more," Daddy says.

"I don't want to be your little girl anymore," I whisper under my breath, then clasp my hand over my mouth.

"She's got an itch that I'm not sure I can scratch out of her."

"Well, we're going to have to," he says. "We have to just focus on the moonlight."

It takes me an entire month to gather all the documents needed to join the Army Nurse Corps and sign up for training. I steal

Mama's nursing license and graduation certificate from her nursing school out of a tin she keeps in the bottom of her desk. We have the same name—Matilda Emma McGee—even though everyone calls me Emma. I change the dates to last year—no one will believe I was old enough to graduate nursing school almost twenty years ago. Then I forge Daddy's handwriting to write a note about my good health, and write a letter from Molly testifying to my moral and professional excellence.

I try to quiet all the troublesome worries in my head: *Emma, you don't know anything about medicine. Emma, you aren't a nurse. Emma, you could hurt someone. Emma, Mama would be so upset and say this is unethical.*

"I will pay attention to every bit of training. I will not take any risks with anyone's life. I will ask to be assigned simple tasks," I tell myself.

I use my best pen to fill out one of the numerous birth certificate forms Daddy has stockpiled in his office. I will my hands to stop shaking. I write in a new birthday—December 12, 1921. I'll be twenty-two years old. That seems like a good age. One that implies trust and responsibility. One that fits within the requirements: twenty-one to forty years old. One that I can pass for.

I pack a small satchel with just the necessities—clean underwear, a few dresses, toiletries, the only two stockings I have left after a year of rations. I leave room for the moonlight jars.

Mama peeks her head into my room. "Come help me pluck the string beans for supper."

I pull one of my pillows over all the forms. "I promised Molly I'd help her pick out a dress for the cotillion."

"And when might you be picking your own?"

"I don't think I want to do it this year."

"You don't think?" Her mouth purses.

"Yes, ma'am. I thought maybe I could not have a debut."

"Everyone has one. You know this."

"I've had so many. Maybe we can do something diff—"

"Different?" she says.

I nod.

"What's all this different talk?" She steps farther into the room.

I shrug. I want to tell her I'm tired of being sixteen. I'm tired of going through the same rituals and milestones every year. I want something new. But she lifts her eyebrows and purses her lips. "It's nothing. I'll pick my cotillion dress tomorrow, Mama. I promise."

She eyes me, then smiles. "Whichever one you choose will be beautiful. You always look lovely in them." A sadness creeps into me, and I wish I could tell her the truth and make her understand.

I take out the cotillion dress I wore in 1934. We'd returned to New Orleans, and I loved being back in the city, especially to ride their new trolleys. I'd been escorted by Christophe Laurent, and he'd left tiny grease stains all over the waist of the dress from all the food he ate that night. Mama liked him. If I were a girl who could get married, she'd have picked him for me.

I leave the dress on the bed with a note for Mama that I think I want to alter this one since the war rations will make it near impossible to buy another of equal value and beauty. I bet she can do something about the grease stains and alter it so it doesn't look nearly a decade out of fashion. But I don't plan to be around for the cotillion.

I ride my bike into Vineyard Haven with all the documents tucked into the front wicker basket. A new summer breeze pulls some of my hair from its bun. The stickiness of late June has now settled over the island. The sound of bleating frogs and chirping crickets mixes with the few cars still moving across the Vineyard roads and risking their gasoline ration.

The Junior Red Cross has fewer volunteers today. Fewer people to stare at me and wonder what a colored girl is doing outside of Oak Bluffs.

Mother Powell nods at me and motions to a table with a bowl of water. I wash my hands and start to work on bundling the bandages. She smiles at me. The monotony of the work usually makes me forget how many hours have passed, but today I can't help stealing glances at the parcel of paperwork I've brought. It almost has its own heartbeat.

If I turn it in, the process starts. I will have to leave Mama and Daddy and take a ferry to mainland Massachusetts and then a bus to Fort Devens. I'll be trained to be a war nurse and then shipped off to Great Britain.

In 191 years, I've never been away from them. I don't know what it would be like not to see them every day, not to have Mama mix up the moonlight, not to hear Daddy's voice.

I close my eyes and imagine my future: me in a nurse's uniform, sitting on a ship headed across the sea, tending to men like Raymond. Then Daddy's warm smile and Mama's hurt eyes erase the picture.

My stomach knots.

A hand touches my shoulder and I jump. My eyes snap open.

"You all right, child?" Mother Powell gazes down at me.

"Yes." I hand her the parcel before I lose my courage. "I want to help in the war effort."

"Is that so?"

"Yes." I rest my hands on all the paperwork. "I want to join the Nurse Corps."

"You're a nurse?"

"I am," I lie, and tell her a few old nursing stories Mama used to tell me after coming home from the hospital when we lived in Washington, D.C.

"The Vineyard ferry's leaving tomorrow around sunrise. Some girls headed up to Fort Devens will be on it. If you want to go, show up there."

The moon is high by the time I get back home. I park my bike in the garage beside Daddy's car and try to slip through the door into the mess room.

The light flickers on. Mama stands in the doorway, arm jammed to her hip and a scowl across her face. "And just where have you been?" she barks.

"At Molly's."

"How about you try again with the truth?"

"I . . ." My stomach bubbles up like it might come out.

"Clare called me about whether you would want to have a lady do your makeup before the cotillion. She was going to set it up for you and Molly. She told me you hadn't been by today."

I nibble my bottom lip. A dozen more lies flicker through my mind. None settle. None feel good enough to withstand Mama's interrogation.

"We don't lie to each other." Tears brim in her eyes, and she's shaking mad with upset.

I sigh. "I went to volunteer."

"Where? And for what?"

"The war effort. Women are folding bandages and putting together care packages at the Junior Red Cross in Vineyard Haven."

Her fists ball. "You're to stay out of it, you hear me?"

The light bulb goes out, and we're bathed in darkness. Only the moonlight illuminates the cobblestone driveway.

"Did you hear me, Matilda Emma McGee?"

"Yes, ma'am." Guilt and anger tangle inside me. I've never defied her before.

I climb down into the cellar with an oil lamp. I hold my breath as my feet seem to hit every creak in the wooden ladder. It's as if my own feet want to give me away and wake up Mama or Daddy. A menagerie of moonlight illuminates the room like hundreds of fireflies sprinkled across a dark cornfield. The glow awakens inside the glass cages as it senses my presence. Shelves upon shelves of mason jars cover each wall, full of surging moonlight. At least three years' worth.

When I was little, Mama would only stockpile a month at a time to keep it fresh. There'd always be one or two jars in the pantry or the icebox if she wanted it cool. The moon would provide forever. Now she doesn't seem so sure.

I swipe four jars. Enough for one person for four months.

Outside, I gaze up at the house and the moon.

"I'm sorry, Mama and Daddy," I say below their bedroom window, hoping and wishing that the message will somehow find them in their dreams.

⚘ AUTHOR'S NOTE ⚘

I like history with a teaspoon of magic. I need it to counteract the pain and bitterness, making history more palatable for me as a black American. As a child learning about the horrible atrocities faced by my people, I realized quickly that this country—and history itself—was not kind to us.

I was inspired by one of my favorite books as a child:

Virginia Hamilton's *The People Could Fly*. It is a collection of black American folktales full of wonder wrapped into our historical experience. As a young reader, I loved falling into those stories about strong people who could perform otherworldly feats in the face of chattel slavery, the system of white supremacy, and institutional racism.

"When the Moonlight Isn't Enough" seeks to grapple with something that bothers me: How can one be a patriot of a country that hates you? How can one participate in the protection of a place that doesn't seek to protect you? How can one love and hate a country simultaneously? I set the story in Martha's Vineyard because I'm fascinated with black communities that — against all odds and in the face of white terrorism — succeeded and built their own prosperous havens. My wonderful friend Allie Jane Bruce took me to Martha's Vineyard last summer, and I fell in love with the island and its interesting black history. I knew that I wanted to explore this subculture of black folks who have lived, worked, and vacationed there for decades.

I was drawn to 1940s America partly due to music, mostly due to the fashion from the era, but also because it is one of the time periods (along with the 1950s) that many white Americans are most nostalgic about as a golden age of America, a time when America was "great." My grandparents were nine and ten years old during World War II America; their childhood was marked by the war and its aftermath. There are very few stories about what nonwhite people endured at this time, and I wanted to explore that.

Last, I'm obsessed with the moon and its light. I hope readers can catch some of their own.

THE BELLE OF THE BALL

SARVENAZ TASH

Mr. Pendergrass didn't stand a chance.

As soon as we walked in and Sandra glimpsed the substitute teacher's precisely trimmed mustache, she turned to me with a mischievous grin. She'd had it in for him ever since two weeks ago, when it had become abundantly clear that he wasn't going to call on a girl for an answer, even if that girl was confidently punching the air, indicating that she knew every single one.

I snuck a second glance at the teacher's rigid back as he wrote his name in neat block letters on the chalkboard. Judging by the handful of times he'd subbed for our class, he wasn't the type to take a joke.

But I could see Sandra was ready and waiting for her lines.

He was doing the roll call now, looking stern any time he said one of the boys' names, like he maybe expected *them* to try something. He seemed to have no such expectation for any of the girls.

All we got was a smile dripping with condescension and, occasionally, a "Nice to see you again, dear."

That sealed the deal for me.

What could I say? I got an inexplicable thrill from defying expectations. I actually, physically felt it on the back of my neck, a tingle that bubbled its way to the tips of my fingers and toes, like soda pop fizzing over.

If my mother knew about it, she would call it "unbecoming."

But I lived for it.

I scribbled out the scene on a piece of paper and casually dropped it on the floor next to me. I heard the scrape of Sandra's chair right as Mr. Pendergrass got to my name.

"Rosemary Sweeney," the teacher droned.

"Present," I said in a calm, clear voice, belying my nervous anticipation for "Sandra Tanner" and "Bobby Weaver"—which would signal the end of roll call and the start of our scene.

Bobby had just announced he was present when I saw Sandra's hand waving in the air. I leaned back just a smidge, ready to enjoy the show.

At first, Mr. Pendergrass simply pretended he didn't see Sandra at all. "Mrs. Morris has written a note that you were to have started act 5 in *Macbeth* by today," he said. But my best friend would not be deterred by something as trivial as being blatantly ignored. She waved her hand, slowly at first, and then as emphatically as a Dodgers pennant on game day, until it was obvious that every single person in the class—except for Mr. Pendergrass—was staring at her. I could even see some of them smiling in anticipation of whatever antics "Sandra" had come up with this time.

Finally, in the middle of tonelessly recapping some of the statistics of Shakespeare's play (first performed in 1606, often called "the Scottish play"), Mr. Pendergrass addressed Sandra without looking up from his book. "You, miss, can go to the powder room after class."

"And leave my nose unpowdered all that time? How barbaric," Sandra quipped. "But, no, that's not why I'm raising my hand, Mr. Pendergrass."

He looked up at her, irritated. "Well, what it is, then? The lecture hasn't started yet, so I can't imagine you have some pressing academic question."

"Oh, but I do. It has to do with Lady Macbeth," Sandra said with a polite smile.

"Lady Macbeth?" Mr. Pendergrass asked, clearly still suspicious.

"Yes. Act 5, scene 1 is her big scene, isn't it? Some would say her most famous scene."

Mr. Pendergrass frowned but looked down at his book, skimming over the pages in front of him.

"Yes, I suppose that is likely true." He said it like it was costing him something to admit she was right.

"'Yet here's a spot.'" I recognized Sandra's Ethel Barrymore voice immediately as she quoted the text.

"Ye-e-e-s," Mr. Pendergrass said slowly. "Now, class, let's talk about . . ."

But Sandra was now out of her seat, staring off at a space in the distance and moving slowly toward the front of the class like a guilt-ridden sleepwalker. "'Out, damned spot! Out, I say!'" she whispered furiously.

Mr. Pendergrass practically jumped back in alarm. "Excuse me, Miss . . ." He looked frantically down at his roll call, clearly trying to remember Sandra's name.

"'One: two; why, then, 'tis time to do it.'" Sandra continued to walk slowly and regally to the front of the class. I saw more than one classmate fighting back a smile, including Tomás Chavez, whose reactions I noticed more than most. "'Hell is murky!'" Sandra suddenly screamed as she turned around and stared at a point above everyone's heads, before making her voice soft once more. "'Yet who would have thought the old man to have had so much blood in him?'" At this point, she turned her head slowly and gave what could only be described as a chilling stare at Mr. Pendergrass.

"That's why I always rely on the cleaning power of Tide!" With a snap of her head, she was facing the class again and had suddenly adopted a cheerful midwestern drawl along with a Pepsodent smile. "Tide gets clothes cleaner than any soap! And we are so lucky to have this wonderful product as sponsors of the Macbeth family. It's on your shelves at the grocer's. And if it's not there, ask him to put it there!" She placed her hand on the hip of her belted skirt and froze in place.

Most of my classmates had already burst out laughing, instantly recognizing the riff on the laundry detergent commercials that Red Skelton did almost every week as part of his shows. I laughed along with everyone else and allowed myself another covert glance at Tomás, whose lips were parted in a grin that made me feel things.

Like, for one of the first times that I could remember, disappointment that nobody besides Sandra knew I had anything to do with the class disruption.

I watched Mr. Pendergrass's mustache wiggle up and down in anger, looking incongruously like Groucho Marx's eyebrows, as he told Sandra to immediately pack up her things and take herself to the principal's office. I didn't want to get in trouble, wasn't brave enough like she was, and yet . . .

And yet, maybe I wanted the credit for coming up with the bit in the first place. Maybe I wanted one of those laughs to be directed at me. Maybe, most of all, I wanted to finally have the discussion with my mother. The "Why, Rosemary?" and the "How ill-mannered, Rosemary!" and, most hopeful of all, the "You are clearly not cut out to be presented as a deb, Rosemary, and will obviously be an embarrassment to me and our family, so we can just forget that whole thing."

But a much more realistic part of me knew that, barring some sort of tragic bus accident, my mother would not let me out of this stupid debutante ball even if she had to drag me there in chains. It was too important to her. In fact, I'm sure she'd pictured my coming-out party as soon as the doctor had informed her that she'd just had a baby girl.

After school, as I waited for the light at the crosswalk to change, I eyed the bus driving past me. Then I remembered that it was Monday. *I Love Lucy* was on. Maiming myself could wait.

Mrs. Lucy Ricardo's impending shenanigans were the only thing that propelled me to our block of crowded brownstones, through our front gate, up our stoop, and through our apartment's door.

Because Mondays also meant something else.

"Hurry up now, Rosemary," Mother said as she came out of our parlor to greet me, nearly bumping into the seventeenth-century baroque side table that was one of the only pieces of her inheritance that she'd managed to salvage. It was huge and ungainly, especially for the small sitting room, and I'd never quite figured out why she had chosen to keep that piece out of all of them. But maybe nobody wanted to buy it. "Didn't Mrs. Fenton insist she would drop you from the class if you were late one more time?"

If only that were more than an empty threat, I'd figure out a way to inspire a massive subway strike.

I hated cotillion classes with Mrs. Fenton, a woman who glided like a swan, chirped like a sparrow, and seemed determined to live her life like she was some sort of a decorative bird instead of a grown person. Worst of all, my mother paid her to try to teach me to do the same. I wasn't sure what would happen if I didn't tap into my inner hummingbird during the waltz or peck elegantly at my salad with the correct fork, but judging by the severity of Mrs. Fenton's reaction, I'd guess something on the scale of Pompeii.

"Would that be such a bad—" I started.

"Not today, Rosemary. You've made your views on this dance quite clear, and so have I. Let's spare both of us the irritation, and, please, just get to your class. We both know you are going to anyway." Mother pointed a finger out the door.

Frankly, she was right. I *did* always do what she asked eventually, no matter how I felt about it. The sense of familial duty that was hammered into me from an early age, coupled with my mother's formidable personality, were too intimidating to overcome—especially in combination.

I turned around and marched back out onto the street, taking my frustration out on a stray baseball that one of the Powell boys next door must've forgotten. I kicked it all the way to the entrance of the subway that would lead me from Brooklyn into Manhattan, where all the other debutantes naturally lived and, so, where Mrs. Fenton could make a living waxing poetic about cutlery.

The cotillion classes took place in the basement of a church downtown. There were eight of us "lucky" eighteen-year-olds, forced to partner up to learn the waltz and fox-trot and some other dance, which, honestly, felt exactly the same as the other ones. Either way, I danced it just as clumsily, as pointed out to me frequently by Mrs. Fenton in a "ladylike" voice, which apparently meant speaking in whispering singsong. After all, far be it for a *lady* to speak in any tone in which she might actually be heard.

As always, I left the church in a foul mood, my breath visibly indignant in the brisk early-March air. I made the trek back home, reclaimed the baseball that was still by the subway station, and kicked it right back to the Powells' front yard. As I was depositing it back under their azalea bush, I heard Mr. Powell's voice wafting from his kitchen window.

"Women just aren't funny." The words rammed into me like a freight train. "Bob Hope is funny. Jerry Lewis is funny. Laurel and Hardy, Charlie Chaplin, the Marx Brothers. You know why there isn't a Marx sister? No one wants to see a woman make a fool of herself like that."

He said it like he was announcing the weather or reading a newspaper headline—like it was a foregone conclusion, a boring but irrefutable fact.

It was his matter-of-fact tone, more than anything, that made me stop in my tracks. Because Mr. Powell was a professional and had actually written for some of the very people he'd just mentioned. Sure, it was hard to reconcile some of those famous, raucous bits with the serious man next door, but they had indeed bloomed from his mind.

So how could he say that? How could he *believe* it? Women weren't funny? Of course they were. What about Rosalind Russell? *What about Lucy?* I wanted to yell right through the window.

"Lucy who?"

I blinked. Had I said that out loud?

I turned around slowly, and there was Tomás, looking at me from the stoop. The Powells lived below his family. Lucky them. My family lived underneath the Midnight Bowling and Shotput League of America, Brooklyn Chapter.

Ever since Tomás had moved here back in October, I'd been

trying to get this kid with his beautiful, lilting accent to speak to me, and this was how he finally did it: calling me out for talking to myself in the middle of his front yard.

"Ball," I responded. "Lucille Ball." Well, I was going with it. I'd waited all this time to have a conversation with him, and I wasn't about to miss the opportunity.

"Oh," he said. Then, after an interminable pause: "Like on television?"

I broke out into a big grin. For a second, I thought he might not have known who Lucy was and that definitely would have tarnished his appeal. But now, standing in front of me with his slightly too-long dark hair and that tiny smile that was more in his eyes than his lips, he remained a perfectly suitable leading man. "She's sort of my hero."

"You want to be Lucille Ball?" he asked.

"No," I responded. "I want to be Madelyn Pugh."

Tomás looked at me blankly. Obviously, he wouldn't know who that was. *Come on, Rosemary. The boy is dreamy, but he isn't perfect!*

"She's one of the writers for *I Love Lucy*," I explained.

Pugh's name had gleamed out at me from the very first time I saw the show's credits roll, like an oracle predicting my future. If someone named Madelyn could write for the funniest show to ever exist, then why couldn't someone named Rosemary?

A full smile spread across Tomás's face. "Like how you write for Sandra?"

My mouth gaped. "You know about that?" Sandra had long worn the crown for class clown, but all this time, I'd thought my role in it had been the best-kept secret at school.

"I've been watching you," Tomás responded with a sheepish grin. "I saw what you wrote. And then a few minutes later, Sandra said it . . ." He tapered off. "Why aren't you the one to say it?"

It was my turn to shrug. "I'm more of a behind-the-scenes kind of girl. I love Lucy but ..."

"You want to be a Madelyn?"

I gave a small laugh. "Exactly. So do you watch the show?"

He started to play with one of the early-blooming azaleas on Mrs. Powell's bush, looking a little embarrassed. "I've seen an episode at a friend's house. But we don't have a television."

"We only got ours last year," I said quickly, hoping he wouldn't feel ashamed. Honestly, most people on our block had only gotten a set recently. "Did you like it? The episode you saw?"

"I did. It was very funny." He paused. "You don't usually see a guy who looks like me on television."

It took me a moment to realize he meant Desi Arnaz. And another to realize that he was completely right. I couldn't think of another Latin man on TV.

"I like Desi, too. He's a great straight man to Lucy."

"She is very funny," he agreed. "So is the woman who writes her lines."

"*I* think so." I lowered my voice. "Apparently, *he* doesn't." I gestured toward the ground floor of his building.

"Mr. Powell?"

I nodded as his voice came through the window again. "I'll just have to convince George that the show doesn't need 'a female touch,'" he said. His son Gary had been boasting all over school about the great gig Mr. Powell had finally landed—a new NBC television show. Rumor had it that the Powells had fallen on some hard times due to the Hollywood blacklist—hence their move to our working-class neighborhood.

"It can get on just fine with me, Eli, and Peter. Fifteen years of being a powerhouse team ... all our credits ..." Mr. Powell grumbled. "Auditioning female writers. Ridiculous!"

I rolled my eyes at Tomás, who seemed frustrated on my behalf. "He's the one being ridiculous," Tomás exclaimed. "He should read some of your bits from school!"

I snorted. "If only."

Tomás let go of the flower he was pinching, and the delicate stem snapped right off the bush. We both watched it flutter and land amid the frost-covered grass. Then he looked up at me again, brushing his dark hair off his forehead, before shoving his hands deep in his pockets. "I'm sorry, but I have to go. I'm supposed to watch my brothers for Mama."

"Okay," I said.

"Okay." It looked like he might say something more, but then he turned around and walked into the house.

Drat. If I could've scripted that, maybe it wouldn't have been so anticlimactic. Or maybe, at least, I could have said something funnier for him to remember me by. Like something about how Mr. Powell tuning out women's voices was self-preservation after having to hear his wife sing "I've Got a Lovely Bunch of Coconuts" every time she did the washing up. Assuming the Powells' ceiling was just as thin as the walls between our two buildings, surely Tomás would've gotten the reference. I could've gotten a laugh.

Instead, I absentmindedly picked up the purple flower from the otherwise spotless lawn and took it with me inside my own building.

All night, Tomás's words stuck with me. What if Mr. Powell could read my work? He had said something about auditioning female writers, hadn't he? How did that work?

I mulled it over during my walk to school, which was prime daydreaming time anyway: thinking up jokes or stunts to file away for possible future use. I wasn't used to being interrupted, so it took a while for me to realize someone was calling my name.

When I finally turned around, Tomás quickened his pace to catch up to me. "Mind if I walk with you to school?"

"Of course not." For a moment, I wasn't sure if I was still in daydream mode after all.

He fell into step beside me. "So what did you think, then? Of last night's episode?"

I glanced curiously at him. "Of Lucy?"

He nodded.

I grinned. "It was spectacular, of course," I gushed. Strangely enough, on last night's episode of *I Love Lucy*, Lucy had accidentally eavesdropped on her neighbors' conversation, too, only in her case she thought she heard them plotting her own murder. "There was a scene with Lucy on the phone to a police officer . . ."

"Where she said she pretended to be a chair?" he finished.

"Yes!" I replied. "Hey! I thought you didn't have a television."

"I don't. I asked Gary if I could watch theirs last night." Tomás grinned, and I could tell whatever he was about to say was why he had flagged me down this morning. "You will be happy to know I caught Mr. Powell laughing at least twice."

My heart soared. Good ol' Lucy. Still . . . "Only twice?"

"I know. For a man who writes comedies, his sense of humor seems . . ." He gestured with his hands, obviously looking for the right word.

"Nonexistent?" I attempted. "Six feet under? The size of a peapod . . . from a dollhouse kitchen set?"

Tomás laughed. "Yes. Definitely one of those."

"So tragically true," I said as I hoisted my bag higher on my shoulder. Tomás made like he was about to offer to carry my books, but I immediately thought of something much more important.

"Did he say anything more about auditioning female writers for his show?"

Tomás shook his head, moving his hand away from my bag. "I could maybe find out? Are you thinking you might audition?"

It would sound silly to say yes. After all, I didn't know how to write a real script. Or how to get Mr. Powell to read one from an eighteen-year-old girl he knew best from snooping in his front yard and, one time, accidentally crashing a tricycle into his wife's prized azaleas. (All right, so maybe it wasn't quite an accident. Maybe it was an attempt — a successful attempt, I might add — to get my younger brother Jacob to laugh at the sight of me on his bike after some older boys had chased him away from their baseball game.)

But I smiled. And said yes anyway. I'd already told Tomás more about who I really was and what I really wanted than practically anybody, except Sandra. Why stop now?

"Let me see what I can find out," he promised as we neared the school. And I suddenly felt much lighter than if he really had carried my books.

LUCY'S LIVING ROOM

LUCY is vacuuming. ETHEL walks in.

ETHEL
Lucy, did you hear about

Did you hear about . . . what? A carnival? A circus? A discount at the beauty parlor?

I had been agonizing about that line for an hour. It was also the only line I had written.

Tomás had come back with the intelligence that the scripts—the ones by other female writers—were being sent through the mail for Mr. Powell to evaluate. I'd seized my opportunity and borrowed one of the many manila envelopes I'd seen the postman drop off at Mr. Powell's mailbox. It was the only way I could think of to see an example of a real, live script. After I hastily copied it out and returned the original, I pored over it. It was *fascinating*. I watched and listened to all of the comedy that I could, but I'd never seen the jokes laid out like this before. This one was a sample sketch for *The Red Skelton Show,* which made me think I should write a sample episode of the show that *I* knew and loved best.

But I needed further research. So on Monday, when *Lucy* came on, I decided I'd try my hand at being a scribe.

When the show first started airing last year, it was only Jacob and me who really watched, with Father reading his newspaper and Mother flitting in and out as she cleaned up. But as the season progressed, I noticed that the living-room mantel seemed to suddenly need extra dustings on Monday and that, more often than not, my father would only think to turn the page of his newspaper during a commercial. Though I was elated by this revelation, I knew better than to bring attention to it. It wouldn't take much for Mother to denounce the show as vulgar or low class, especially if she knew that I saw it as more than a weekly diversion and more like a potential career path.

But I certainly wasn't able to go unnoticed that night when the four of us were gathered around our television set. Mother, Father, and Jacob all watched me agape as I wore out two and a half pencils trying to transcribe Lucy's and Ethel's every word.

"Rosemary, may I ask what on earth you think you're doing?" Mother finally asked as a piece of paper flew from under my graphite-covered hands and nearly hit the ceiling before fluttering slowly and dramatically to the ground.

I didn't want to answer her, afraid that I would miss the next line if I did.

"Rose . . ."

But better a few lines than the whole thing, so I thought quickly. "Oh, it's an assignment. A transcription assignment. For my journalism class."

"I see," Mother said after a pause. "I didn't know you were taking a journalism class."

But then, thankfully, she left well enough alone. By the end of the episode, my fingers had the posture of Quasimodo and the living room looked like it had been feted by a ticker-tape parade, but I thought I might have a good idea of how the show was constructed.

Although now, staring at the blank page in front of me, it dawned on me that it was quite hard to come up with a whole new scenario and then . . . make it funny.

I stared up at the piece of paper I had pinned above my small desk.

> *"Women aren't funny."*
> —James Powell

That lit the appropriate fire.

I placed my pencil emphatically back to the end of Ethel's line, closed my eyes, and plucked the first word that came to my mind.

Carousel. "Did you hear about the new carousel in the park?"

I wrote it out slowly, realization dawning that a walk in the park might help me air out my ideas. Or, better yet, maybe I could go over to Sandra's. I'd already told her all about my harebrained scheme to submit a script to Mr. Powell, and she'd loved the idea. She'd always been my collaborator anyway, bringing my work and ideas to life with her perfect delivery. Maybe that was what I needed: a sounding board.

I got up from my desk like a woman possessed, marched out of my room, and went to grab my coat from the hall closet.

"Rosemary," my mother called from the dining room. I quickly pulled on my coat and had my hand on the doorknob when she appeared, the click of her heels alerting me too late to her presence.

"I need to get back to the tailor about your fitting."

Drat. Sometimes, I could swear that woman was a hawk in a previous life: swift, silent, attuned to when its prey, aka her daughter, was at her most vulnerable. Though to be fair, my head was in the clouds often enough that I usually wasn't in any position to fend her off.

"We should go tomorrow . . . Rosemary, what on earth?" she exclaimed as she looked me over, her beautiful face pursing into that look I knew all too well and her hand now on the hip of her immaculate yellow-and-white-striped dress. "What is this about now? *Please* don't tell me you're thinking of setting up another . . . play." She said the word *play* the way she would say the word *rodent*. I already knew how she felt about my attempt at staging an impromptu show with Sandra in Prospect Park last summer. Though, honestly, that lake was just begging for an Ophelia by way of Mae West routine.

But I had no idea what she was so upset about now. There was really nothing wrong with my shoes, or skirt, or . . . oh.

Apparently, in my haste, I'd grabbed the first bit of greenish fabric that I saw in the hall closet. Which was not my woolen pea-coat, but my father's jacket. My father's army jacket, with gold, red, and blue emblems on the pocket, brass buttons on the lapels, and sleeves that came down about a foot past my fingertips.

Well, now, that was . . . funny, actually. I wondered how Sandra would have reacted if she saw me in it—it might have led to a good bit. Perhaps some other time, I thought, as I took the coat off and hung it back in the closet before turning to face Mother.

"I made the dinner reservation at the St. Regis. Would you ring up Julian to let him know?" she asked.

I sighed. Of course she would want to talk about the ball, something I hadn't given a thought to in hours because I'd been preoccupied with more pressing matters, like what sort of trouble a redheaded housewife could get up to.

"Yes, but . . . what if we skip dinner?" It wasn't just that I didn't want to spend extra hours with Mother and Father and Julian, my escort and the dull son of one of my mother's childhood friends, whom I'd only met a handful of times and spoken even fewer words to. The restaurant at the St. Regis Hotel was also far too pricey. I took a closer look at my mom's dress and realized the white was slightly dingy from too many washings. The last thing we needed was to spend more money we didn't have. Especially on something as trivial as a pre-dance dinner.

"Rosemary!" Mother exclaimed. "Dinner before a cotillion is tradition."

"But what if . . . I don't know. We could have dinner at home. Two of the girls from cotillion class are doing that."

It was true. Annie's and Josie's families were each throwing a small dinner party in their honor at their respective homes. But I saw my mother looking uncomfortably at our narrow entryway and that lone fancy end table, and I knew she wouldn't want anyone coming here.

"We could just pretend we did," I said quickly, putting my hand on her arm and looking her in the eye. "No one would have to know we didn't have a real dinner party."

For a moment, when she looked back, I knew we understood

each other perfectly, the unspoken dialogue between us a current that was pinging back messages in the same language. But then she looked away, and the cable line snapped.

"Don't be silly, Rosemary. It'll be a lovely dinner. Mrs. Chambers has simply raved about the salmon, and your father has been looking forward to it for weeks. Would you please just ring up Julian to let him know?" The bright smile was back on her face, now that she was assured of my compliance.

I nodded, watching her swish back into our tiny parlor. I didn't know how accurate Mrs. Chambers's feelings about the fish were, but I knew for a fact that my father hadn't looked forward to much since he had worn that army jacket himself.

For all her poise, sometimes my mother seemed to me a woman huddled over the tatters of things that had long disappeared: a stately childhood home; a maiden name that vaguely stirred up ideas of grandeur for people of a certain age; a boy she loved who, for all intents and purposes, never came back from the war at all.

It was like she couldn't bring herself to accept that she lived in this apartment building in Brooklyn with the Powells, and the Chavezes, and everyone else on this block—not the slightest bit of difference between us.

But me, I had always lived here. And I'd never once wanted the Park Avenue address.

At least not by marrying into it.

It was one tedious phone conversation and half an hour later that I made it out of the house. By then, any flits of writing inspiration seemed to have left me completely. I was going to go over to Sandra's anyway; I needed a pep talk.

As soon as I walked down my stoop, I was met by a wave and a big smile from someone else—someone who had apparently been waiting for me to appear. Tomás jogged up to me. I could feel my cheeks lifting to match his.

"How has it been going? The writing?" he asked, and my face fell. "Oh. Not good?"

I shook my head. "I seem to be stuck. I just can't think of a good setup. I had Ethel ask Lucy if she's heard about the new carousel in the park and then . . . I have no idea what happens next."

"Oh," Tomás said, his eyebrows furrowed.

"Can you think of anything?" I asked hopefully. Sometimes Sandra would throw out random ideas, and one of them would catch, blooming joyously into something unexpected as it filtered its way through my mind.

"Umm," Tomás stammered. "So they go to the carousel. And they ride it. And they get dizzy . . . and maybe one of them gets sick?"

Clearly this was not one of those times. I smiled politely. "Maybe."

"Oooh, or how about they go to the carousel. And then they argue because they both want to ride the same animal. Maybe the . . . giraffe!" he exclaimed, laughing, as if that were clearly a punch line.

I had to laugh, too, at his enthusiasm. "A giraffe, huh?"

He nodded.

"It's an idea," I said noncommittally, not wanting to hurt his feelings.

He looked at me shrewdly. "I'm not helping, am I?"

"Not really, but you're making me smile. And that's more than has happened all day."

"I will take that." His dark-brown eyes looked into mine and, in the quiet that ensued, I knew what was supposed to happen next.

Every movie I'd ever seen and daydream I'd ever had about this very moment told me.

But he hesitated; I could tell he was wondering if he should.

I thought of my mother, who was inside the house, only a few feet away. She might look out the parlor window. What she would think if she saw me kissing the boy next door—who didn't have a name or a fortune? Who didn't even have the right color skin?

And then I thought about what *I* wanted.

I closed the gap between us and let my lips meet his.

My mother didn't see us. I could tell because she didn't come running out in a fit and proclaim her plan to ship me off to a Swiss finishing school.

Sandra seemed a little disappointed that the Alps weren't in my immediate future. "Just how great would it have been if she *had* seen you, Rosemary? It could've been your chance. Your big moment to give her a piece of your mind." Sandra had just put the needle on the Doris Day record when I'd told her what happened. She hadn't harped on the fact that I'd kissed an extremely handsome boy, but, rather, that I had done it where Mother might have seen.

Sandra had wanted me to stand up to Mother for years. She'd even offered to act as my stand-in. Playing the role of Rosemary and reciting the lines I'd write, she would tell Mother to "put a sock in it," as she so gleefully put it. I admit, I was twistedly curious to see what Mother's reaction to that might be . . . though in a fly-on-the-wall, purely scientific sense. The actual thought of being on the receiving end of Mother's reaction made me repeatedly swallow like a nervous contestant in an amateur fire-eating contest.

"I just need to get through this dance," I told Sandra. "And then, maybe, Mother . . ."

Sandra raised her eyebrows at me.

"Okay. Definitely. I will tell her."

My plan after high school was not to marry some Rockefeller and settle down on the Upper East Side like Mother wanted. It was to move to Los Angeles with Sandra and try to make it as a writer in Hollywood while she got her acting career going. I'd even looked up some screen-writing programs there, particularly at the University of Southern California.

"And besides," I continued, "today wasn't about defying Mother. I just . . . wanted to kiss him."

Sandra smiled at that. "Well, all right, then. Good for you. And how was the kiss? Did it live up to expectations?" She came over and flopped down on her bed next to me.

I grinned. "I wouldn't mind going back for seconds."

Objectively speaking, the girl in the mirror looked pretty good. It was the dress, mainly. The silvery white taffeta did something to my pale skin, made it glow and even look a bit tanned as opposed to the tinge of gray that tended to settle in after a long New York winter. The appliqué beaded flowers on the full skirt, in a smoky shade of blue, caught the light and glinted at unexpected moments. And the corset kept everything in its proper place as long as I was supposed to resemble a certain antiquated timepiece made of glass and sand (which Mrs. Fenton had assured me I was). But I couldn't breathe, the scratchy fabric made my skin feel like it was being stung by a thousand tiny bees, and keeping my balance in the strappy silver high heels meant scrunching my toes in a way that made them turn purple.

Mother did not care one jot about any of these complaints. "You look lovely, Rosie," she whispered when she saw me. "You know, the night I came back from my deb ball, I didn't sleep a wink." Her voice was far away. "I couldn't stop thinking about dancing with your father. I was doing all the steps in my bed the whole night."

The night hadn't even happened yet, but I knew I wouldn't feel any of those things. I couldn't dance very well as it was, never mind in those shoes. I was going to spend the whole time trying to keep the curtsies and salad forks straight in my head. And the only boy I'd want to dance with certainly wouldn't be there.

I felt a pang when Mother grazed my shoulder and breathed out the word "lovely" one more time. It was easy to feel frustrated with her, angry at her, for not understanding me at all. For not looking at *me*, the person I was instead of who she wanted me to be. But at the same time, I was the one who kept my true self hidden, who followed her every instruction with meek protests, who let Sandra say the lines I wrote, who kissed the boy I wanted to kiss but hoped Mother hadn't seen.

In that moment, looking at her face in the mirror, the glass was showing me a side of us I wouldn't have been able to reach on my own. Maybe she really thought becoming a society wife was what would make me happy because I had let this fantasy of the girl in the mirror go on for too long. Maybe if I was the one writing the lines, it was time for me to speak them, too.

The girl in the mirror placed her hand over her mother's and made a silent vow to herself.

I would go to this ball for her. I would do my best to be the polite well-bred girl she had taught me to be. But then I would leave that girl at the dance, shedding the snakeskin that had never fit my coils. And I would breathe . . . in every sense of the word, I thought, as I envisioned breaking the boning in my corset with Jacob's baseball bat first thing tomorrow.

$$\times \quad \times \quad \times$$

My mother had the cab drop us off in front of Tiffany's. Ostensibly, it was because she wanted to start off the evening by gazing at the famed window displays. She'd always said they put her in the right frame of mind: peaceful, elegant, and just a little bit detached from the vulgarities of real life. But I knew that she didn't want anyone to see us pulling up in a regular old yellow taxicab instead of an elegant town car. And even that taxi had required careful saving up.

Mother sighed in contentment as soon as we glimpsed Julian Dupont waiting for us in front of the St. Regis. A bland smile was already punctuating his classically handsome face. His sandy-blond hair was parted neatly, with just the right amount of pomade to keep it in place. His tails grazed below the knees just as they were supposed to, and his white bow tie was perfectly centered. It was hard to imagine that anyone in Julian's carefully curated life had ever looked at him and felt the inexplicable revulsion that was oozing out of my pores. But I was surprised it didn't stain my dress.

He said and did nothing that veered one iota from that rehearsed exterior. He was a perfect gentleman at dinner, steering the conversation from the weather to the meal and back to the weather again. He made two feeble jokes, which received raucous laughter from Mother, polite chortles from Father, and very strained smiles from me, after Mother kicked me under the table. It was undoubtedly the most painful when he was trying to be funny.

For just a moment, the conversation steered toward baseball, and I thought I saw a hint of something that might resemble passion, or a personality, or simply a sign that he wasn't a Macy's mannequin brought to life. But a minute later, we were back to what a chilly March it had been, and I was left wondering whether I had willed that spark out of sheer boredom.

I winced when the bill came and I glimpsed the

twenty-five-dollar tab. It seemed a ridiculous price to pay just to be seen.

After we left, Mother and Father let us walk ahead of them over to the Park Lane Hotel, obviously hoping for some sparkling conversation to take place between Julian and me. A couple I had seen at dinner was walking ahead of us, clearly headed to the cotillion, too. She was radiant in white, a matching fur shrug contrasting with her sleek black hair. He was tall and wearing a tuxedo, and they were walking arm in arm. Together, they looked like they might have stepped out of a black-and-white Ginger Rogers and Fred Astaire movie.

"So what do you think?" I turned to Julian conspiratorially as the pair floated down Fifth Avenue. "Are they Russian spies? Or automatons?" I nodded toward the couple, whom I had decided to christen Natasha and Bot Wonder.

"Sorry?" Julian looked at me blankly.

I pointed to them. "They're too perfect, right? So either they were sent here by the Ruskies," I said in a bad Eastern European accent, "to infiltrate New York City as American teenagers, but their only frame of reference was the movies, so they look like they just stepped out of one. Or they are, in fact, robots and we have a lot more to worry about than a silly little war with Russia."

Julian's expression did not change, except for maybe a slight tinge of confusion that snuck onto his perfect mask of a face. I waited a beat before I felt I had to explain. "It's just a game, a joke," I said, which of course ruined the very nature of either.

"Oh," Julian replied, and, after a moment, bestowed a small smile upon me.

The rest of the night was almost too boring to mention. We arrived at the ball; I was announced; I curtsied; I danced (poorly). Then we were entertained by a pair of professional dancers who glided across the floor, further driving home just how badly I had failed in my attempt to do the same.

But just then, the most glorious, wonderful thing happened.

The girl dancer wore a dainty little mask over her face, pale pink rhinestones framing her large blue eyes. I suppose in the story of their dance, they were supposed to be at a masquerade ball. And that's when I was struck with an idea. A *funny* idea. An idea I thought I could easily turn into an *I Love Lucy* episode.

What if Lucy went to a masquerade ball because she heard there was going to be a television talent scout there, and she wanted to get Ricky booked on a TV show? Only, of course, there would be a case of mistaken identity, and the person Lucy was try-ing to woo would actually be a masked thief, there to steal from all the finely bejeweled ladies at the ball. Lucy would inadvertently spend the entire ball thwarting him. She would be a masked hero! I could almost imagine the orchestra playing a version of *The Lone Ranger* theme song, a wink to the audience.

My mind churned. I wished I had a pen and paper. I looked ruefully at all the tiny and dainty purses my fellow debs had brought and knew I'd be hard-pressed to find one here. I took to staring off into space instead, trying to commit to memory all the one-liners and sight gags that were suddenly whizzing around in my brain. Julian had to ask me to dance three times before I heard him. I only said yes because saying no would've required extra conversation that my brain simply had no room for, and also because I caught my mother's frown and remembered my unspo-ken promise to her. I owed her one last glimpse at the daughter she wished she had.

Finally, finally, the clock was ticking midnight and the cotil-lion was over. I felt like a reverse Cinderella, itching to get back to my own clothes and—most important—my own desk, where beautiful white sheets of paper and a glorious ballpoint pen were awaiting me.

Mother and Father had left a little earlier, Mother no doubt hoping for a spontaneous—though, of course, appropriate—romantic moment to erupt between Julian and me if only we were left alone for a bit.

But I hardly remembered how I said a final good-bye to him—certain and entirely unconcerned that I would never see him again—or how he hailed me a cab. All I knew was that, finally, I was sitting in the back of a warm taxi and furiously thinking by the lights of the Manhattan skyline.

I was dropped off at the end of my block, where I promptly took off my shoes; even though I only had a few yards left to walk, I wasn't going to spend one more minute in them. Then I started to actually skip toward my brownstone.

"You look happy," a soft voice said.

I smiled before I even saw him. "I am, Tomás."

He stood up from his stoop, where he was rolling around an old baseball. Now I knew the reason for all those stray ones under Mrs. Powell's shrubbery.

"Have a good time at the dance?" he asked.

"Yes, actually," I said, pausing for dramatic effect. "Because I figured out what I'm going to write for Mr. Powell."

He smiled and walked down his steps toward me. "That's wonderful. Can I read it?"

"When it's finished," I agreed.

"Thank you. You look . . . beautiful," he added after a small hesitation.

I looked up at him, my eyes questioning.

"It's just . . ." He paused again. "I just like the way you normally look even better." He looked away, clearly uncertain whether he had said the right thing.

I smiled. "Me too."

There was probably more to be said on a beautiful moonlit spring night, standing in front of a boy I liked in a ball gown and bare feet. But there was something more important that I simply had to do right then, before the jumbled words in my head had a chance to escape into the abyss.

"I have to go. To write," I told Tomás.

He nodded and stepped out of my way, and that one gesture was probably the most romantic thing he could've done. I let my arm graze his as I walked past.

I was in luck. Though my mother had obviously intended to wait up for me, she had succumbed to sleep on the couch. I tiptoed past and went to my room. Without even taking off the gown or the corset, I sat down and I wrote.

The next afternoon, I sat on our sofa in the parlor, a manila envelope in my lap, my legs crossed at the knees, waiting quietly.

"What on earth are you doing sitting around in the dark, Rosemary?" Mother asked as she walked in and drew up the blinds. She was humming a little, obviously in a good mood.

It was too bad I was about to spoil that.

"Waiting for you." I stood up and faced her. We were squared off, our wide skirts touching.

"Oh?" She looked surprised but kind of pleased. I again felt a pang—regret mixed with a dollop of fear—at having to yank her out of this haze of security. It wouldn't be easy to disappoint her, even if I knew that it was my fundamental self that she wished she could change, the part of me that was set in stone. But after eighteen years, it was time for me to tell her the truth. It was past time.

"I want you to read something." I stuck out the envelope so that it was only inches from her face.

She looked down at it, puzzled. "Mail for Mr. Powell?" she asked, reading the address I had carefully written on the envelope.

"It was intended to be," I said. "But now it's for you. Or, at least, I want you to read it first. Before I give it to Mr. Powell."

She looked up at me, and I could see the crease already starting to form between her brows. "Rosemary, what . . . ?"

"It's a script." I interrupted her in a calm, measured voice, just the way I had rehearsed it. "I wrote it. Mr. Powell is audition-ing female writers for his show, and I wrote a sample script of *I Love Lucy*."

Mother stared at me doubtfully and then broke into a small laugh. "You're pretending to be a writer now? That's a pretty silly trick to play on our neighbor."

"I'm not pretending. I *am* a writer. Look." I shook the envelope in front of her again. "I wrote *this*."

She laughed again but made no move to take the envelope. "Rosemary, I appreciate that you're a bit of a daydreamer, but Mr. Powell is a professional and I'm sure he doesn't have time for—"

"It doesn't matter," I said, interrupting her again. "He'll read it. And maybe he'll think it's funny. Maybe he won't. But the thing is, I *know* I'm funny. And I know I'm a writer. I know it because I've been doing it for years in school and in my head." Just a hint of emotion got into my voice, but I stifled it. My mother respected poise over all, and she was going to get it this time, when what I had to say mattered most. "I may be a daydreamer. But if I am, it's in the best way. It's in the way that lets me imagine better things than what's placed in front of me. It's in the way that makes me go after those things, no matter what or who stands in my way."

We were the same height now, my mother and I, and I looked evenly into her pale-blue eyes. It was like she was frozen in place. Even the breeze from the window didn't deign to ruffle her skirt.

I knew my cue to exit. I'd always had excellent dramatic timing.

"I would appreciate it if you read this," I said to her, then, quieter: "I think it's good. I'm going to drop it off at Mr. Powell's tomorrow."

I placed the envelope on her oversized side table, and then I turned on my heels and walked out.

In my mind's eye, my mother was picking up the envelope and looking at it. Maybe in a few minutes, she would open it and start poring through the pages inside.

But I didn't look back to check.

Instead, I thought about how it was perhaps a little too chilly to be outside without a coat, but I didn't care. The brisk air felt good against that spot on the back of my neck that had just started to tingle.

✖ AUTHOR'S NOTE ✖

Rosemary and I are alike in a lot of ways.

I, too, love Lucy. It's hard not to admire a woman who was one of the funniest, most indelible comedians to have ever lived and whose antics can make us laugh more than sixty years later. But besides that, Lucille Ball was a trailblazing businesswoman. She was the first woman to head up a major production company, where she was responsible for shepherding multiple groundbreaking shows, including *Mission: Impossible* and *Star*

Trek. She fought to have Desi Arnaz as her on-screen husband in *I Love Lucy* when the network was skeptical of it because he wasn't white. Best of all, she was a woman who didn't care how foolish she looked if it served her comedy.

Also like Rosemary, I've always watched the credits roll on movies and TV shows, and I've always looked out for the female names. Even from an early age, I think I was hoping I could see myself reflected in those credits—though it took a while for me to realize I wanted my own name up there.

And although I had a great, life-altering, and positive experience when I attended film school, my time there was also permeated with lines like "Women just aren't funny." In all honesty, it's not really an opinion that belongs firmly to the past, though I wish it did. For every Tina Fey and Amy Schumer and Mindy Kaling, there are just so many more male comedians and writers being given opportunities.

But the way I'm most like Rosemary is that I, too, get an inexplicable thrill from defying expectations. Don't you?

LAND OF THE SWEET, HOME OF THE BRAVE

STACEY LEE

I *should be Miss Sugar Maiden because sugar is in my blood.*
Pops borrowed his boss's 1944 Chevy pickup to drive me to the audition. It's a real skuzzbucket, with a grill that looks like someone busted out of jail. I wish we had taken the bus. Every few moments, we jerk back and forth like an old couple constantly on the verge of nodding off.

Pops glances at me. His gray eyes dance like silver fish in a dark pond. "That's a good hairdo on you," he grunts. "You look like Elizabeth Taylor."

I sigh with mock irritation, nervously pulling at the curls Mom ironed in place. "Well, that is a bummer, because I was going for Marilyn Monroe."

He winces. "You're going to send your old man to an early grave. Haven't I been good to you, Lana?"

"I still haven't received my pony."

"It's in the mail. Express." Pops's cheeks bunch, though we've rolled out that Pony Express routine at least a hundred times.

The car hits a pothole and we bounce. My ukulele squeaks inside its scuffed case, and I transfer it to my lap. It's my most important treasure, an heirloom from my maternal grandmother, Oba, who passed it on to me in her final moments.

Pops jerks his head to the instrument. "You ready?"

"As spaghetti," I say firmly, though a minnow jumps in my belly.

What was I thinking, signing up for this audition? I remember the day only one month ago when Mom stuck the flyer my face. "Read."

> *Seeking girls (age 14–19) to be our 1955 Miss Sugar Maiden!*
> *Cash award, $500, plus trip to New York City! Be prepared*
> *to state why you should be on the box of Sugar Maiden,*
> *America's favorite sugar brand. Must possess grace, talent,*
> *and a good face.*

Mom knocked my arm with her swollen knuckles before I could even snort my derision. "You should do it," she said. "You got one out of three!"

As much as I wondered if she was serious, I also couldn't help wondering which of the three targets she thought I had hit. Mom often complains that I walk with the gait of someone with a grudge against the earth, so it couldn't be grace. As far as talents, I can play the ukulele, as long as you like the key of C major. But probably it was my face, the quality I have the least control over. I'm the spitting image of Oba with the exception of our skin. The cane fields of Maui had browned hers like a potato.

"You could go to Berkeley," Mom said brightly. UC Berkeley

had accepted my cousin, but she had declined after adding up the high cost of books, room, and board.

"Sugar doesn't come in yellow." I folded the paper into fourths. If I did by some miracle win, the first thing I would do is take Mom on vacation. She needs one, especially her eyes. Turns out bone charcoal—the ground-up skeletons of cows used to bleach sugar—irritates the eyes with repeated exposure. After several years of complaints, Sugar Maiden had finally switched Mom from Processing to Quality Control, which stopped the constant itching, but she still iced her swollen eyes every night.

It would be bittersweet, using Sugar Maiden's money to give Mom the break she deserved.

Anyway, maybe it was time for a nonwhite on the box. Sugar Maiden's product comes direct from Hawaii, born of the sweat of thousands of islanders—Japanese, Chinese, Portuguese, Korean, and Filipinos—yet the girls on the boxes have always been as snowy as its contents.

"Look! A moose!" Pops elbows me back to the bumpy reality of the Eastshore Highway, using one of his favorite tricks. There has never been a moose sighting in the history of Oakland, California.

I sigh. "I was just wishing Mom could take today off." She works six days a week and jokes that she's seen so many sugar cubes, you could roll her eyes as dice.

"Count your blessings. If she were here, she might wolf whistle."

I crack a tiny smile. Oba taught Mom that useful skill before she could read. It's easy to get lost among the sugarcane stalks.

The July day is liquefying the Max Factor Crème Puff in Twilight Blush I swept over my face. Mom spent a whole $1.25 on it after I announced that I would try to win the contest. The packaging promised that the powder would give me a sheer, smooth radiance, but it feels like I've rubbed on Crisco. I roll open the window, and the breeze off the San Francisco Bay blows the last of my curls away.

We don't often make the trek into Oakland from our strip of land in Crockett. When we do, my neck goes stiff from gawking at the windows of Capwell's Department Store, or scouting out a sky-blue Austin-Healey—the best color. But today worries clutch at me, and the city sweeps by in a blur. This is a very bad idea. Yellow sugar never makes it past inspection; it routinely gets tossed down the sewer even though it tastes the same as white. Public humiliation is not worth five hundred dollars.

The Paramount Theatre perches like an exotic bird on a wire of everyday pigeons. Its vertical sign bisects twin mosaics of a man and a woman that soar at least a hundred feet. My heart quickens when I read the marquee: WELCOME MISS SUGAR MAIDEN CONTESTANTS!

Cars line up in front of the theater, pausing while a man in a red waistcoat helps the occupants out of their vehicles. Girls float from their carriages like springtime lilies, most sporting Christian Dior's "New Look," with ballerina hems, cinched waistlines, jeweled collars, and fitted cardigans.

My own garb suddenly strikes me as garish and silly. When Mom offered to make me a dress using the bark cloth Oba had brought with her from Hawaii, I thought it was a boss of an idea. Though the thick cotton with its bold patterns is traditionally used in home decoration—this piece was supposed to be our curtains— the fabric might help me stand out. Why didn't I realize I needed as much help standing out as a jelly roll on an anthill? I wipe my sweaty palms on the ridiculous fabric.

Pops throws the gears into park, and our princely vehicle gasps, probably uttering its last breath. Pops takes in my death grip on the ukulele and my tight smile. "I hear there's a place around the corner that sells pineapple sundaes," he tosses out. "We could . . ."

He's giving me an exit? Any reservations I felt fly out the window. *I should be the next Miss Sugar Maiden because my family deserves this. Because only the truly brave can work a curtain with hibiscuses on it.* "Pineapple gives me pimples."

The valet squints through my half-opened window but makes no move to unlatch the door. I heave it open myself, almost swiping him in the soft parts. He glares at me.

I crane my head back through the window, noticing for the first time how skinny Pops's legs look on the pedals, like a kid trying to play an organ. His socks are two different colors, but at least his shoes are shiny. A cobbler's shoes should always be shiny.

I groan. "Fine. We can get a malted milk afterward, but *you're* paying."

Pops winks. "I'll be there as soon as I can find a parking space." The truck pitches forward.

I enter the theater cradling my ukulele case the way a diver clutches his last tank of air. Lana Lau, there's no going back now.

The lobby looks even grander than I imagined, with scarlet carpets and marble columns threaded with silver. A line of topless maidens whose skirts look surprisingly Polynesian spans the walls. If Sugar Maiden doesn't want me here, maybe *they'll* have me.

Dozens of people cluster around the entrance, staring at a glowing pile of gold crystals backlit by a wall of jade light. It looks like something from outer space. I imagine it as a lonely meteorite, hurling through the cosmos with the rest of the unidentified flying objects until landing in this precise spot. Now it has found its life's purpose casting its weird green light into its viewers' darkest thoughts.

Is it possible to know one's life's purpose at sixteen? When Oba was sixteen, she was already pregnant with Mom. Keeping Mom alive must have been her life's purpose. One thing's for sure — Lana Lau has greater aspirations than to be Miss Sugar Maiden. Maybe I'll be a lawyer, stopping big companies from bulldozing the little people, or maybe I'll start my own company of little people.

"Are you Lana Luau?" trills a woman clutching a clipboard. A tag with the name "Billie Lovejoy" is pinned over her heart. I marvel at the way her peach suit perfectly matches her pin-curled hair and sets off her ivory skin. Now, this is a woman who knows how to apply her Max Factor Crème Puff.

"Y-yes, I mean, it's actually 'Lau.'" I hand her the confirmation slip I kept in my pocket.

"You're just as cute as a button. Look at those round cheeks, and those Cupid's bow lips." She cups one of my cheeks with her perfumed hand. "Just like a doll's."

I produce a queasy smile. Mom would've growled at the comparison to such a passive object. Oba's smile had never wavered even after years in the hot fields, not even after her Portuguese husband left her, pregnant, to fend for herself. My smile — Oba's smile — is hardly a Cupid's bow. More like a scythe, curved, and glinting with iron.

"I'm Miss Lovejoy, your two o'clock monitor. They audition ten girls an hour, which means you'll have six minutes to introduce yourself and show us your talent." She bats her mascaraed lashes at my uke case. "How darling. What is it?"

"It's a ukulele."

She scratches her pen on her clipboard. "Oo-koo-lay-lee. Well, we are just dee-lye-ted to have an ethnic element this year. I love oriental anything."

I shift around in my flats, the soles of which my sweat has glued to my feet.

"No costume changes needed, right?"

"Right."

"You're our last performer, number ten. Please follow the signs to the ladies' lounge. I will get you when we're ready."

"Thank you."

She beams again, then marches toward a cluster of girls. I pad through the carpet to a gilded staircase, conscious of eyes following me.

"Orientals," as whites love to call us, are not a rarity here in California, but people prefer to see us in our own neighborhoods, as if we were all buttons that should be boxed by color. That means Chinese—and Filipinos—in Chinatown. Japanese—well, people prefer not to see us at all. If we'd lived here on the Pacific coast instead of in Hawaii during the Second World War, we'd have been caged up—Mom for the crime of being "half-Jap," and my Chinese pops for the more foolish crime of marrying her.

I pass under a heavy velvet curtain into the ladies' lounge, where it is clear that a thousand roses died in vain, their fragrance overwhelmed by the stench of body odor and Chesterfield cigarettes. The room features dove-gray walls and a domed ceiling from which a giant orchid of a chandelier blooms. Girls lounge about in various stages of repose. Some look fresh and prim, as if they've just been planted, while others stretch out on upholstered sofas like wilted blades of grass.

When the girls notice me, it's as if some invisible conductor has lifted his wand, cutting off the symphony. After everyone has gotten a good look—even the wooden puppet on the arm of a milky-faced girl—the voices resume, whispers punctuated by snickers.

A tall brunette cranes her long neck in my direction, frowning.

She is exactly what Audrey Hepburn might've looked like after an accident with a wall—doe-ish brown eyes cresting a squashed-in nose and chin. Beside her, a petite blonde trims her nails with manicure scissors. The blonde resembles Doris Day, with freckles and white-blond locks cut above her ears. I would bet a half-dollar that she'll be singing "Secret Love" for her talent.

Doris Day levels her cornflower-blue eyes with mine, sizing me up, cutting me down. Just like her beanstalk of a buddy, a disagreeable expression sours her good looks.

Doris drops the scissors into a smart-looking clutch with gold tassels. Fluffing up her hair, she sashays over, lemon skirts swishing. Audrey slouches after her. Bad posture for Audrey and high heels on Doris put them about the same height as me—five foot three. Height seems to be one of the few ways in which being average gives you an edge. The short will ruin their feet for it, just as the too-tall will offer up their spines.

When Doris reaches me, she jams a fist into her hip and her eyes drift like blue-jay feathers down to my sling-back flats, which I considered a practical, if not boring, choice. "Looks like someone got lost on her way to the tiki bar." Her bottom lip sticks out more than the top so that in profile, her mouth resembles a miniature boxing glove.

Audrey sniggers, fingers twisting at a ring. "Trader Vic's is just down the street. I hear they'll take anyone."

I clap a hand to my cheek. "I must have taken a wrong turn at Stabby City. But it looks like I found a couple of piña co-bimbos right here." The best defense is to hop on the fence and throw tomatoes, Pops always said. When you're a duck in a chicken world, you learn to peck with a little in-your-face humor, which tells people not to mess with you. Of course, it doesn't always work.

From behind my two new friends, the girl with the puppet

laughs. At least her puppet laughs, a replica of its animator with the same nutmeg hair parted down the middle. They're even wearing the same white dress with blue flowers.

A flush stains Doris's neck. "They'll never choose you to be Miss Sugar Maiden, and you know why?"

"Something tells me I'm about to find out," I say cheerfully.

"Because no one will buy sugar if your face is on the box. They want to see something sweet, not"—she hitches her shoulders—"jungle."

Audrey adds in a nasally voice, "It's like how Ivory Snow detergent has a baby on the box. Babies are sweet and pure, just like the soap."

I clasp my hands together and rock forward. "Oh, I think I understand. It's like how your face would go well on a bottle of cod liver oil."

Audrey's trap falls open, flattening her nostrils.

"And how yours would go well on a box of rat poison," I tell Doris so she doesn't feel excluded.

Doris's cheek twitches, and I'm reminded of the tiny crack in Oba's old teapot. No one thought much about that crack, until one day the pot just shattered. Glass remembers past wrongs, said Oba, and maybe it's the same way with people. But then again, teapots don't go around insulting people for sport. In my mouth's history of wisecracking, I've only been called to the mat once, in fifth grade when a kid called me a chinkie-winkie, and I told him it must be exhausting to fit his entire vocabulary into one sentence. He clocked me with his three-ring binder even though the principal was standing right there, which goes to show how stupid he was.

To my surprise, Doris polishes up a smile, one that shows a smear of red on her teeth. It's either her lipstick or she bit the head off a mouse. Audrey notices and, with a meaningful glance, discreetly gestures to her own teeth. The buddy system works its magic. Doris takes out a compact, into which she bares her teeth, then erases the wayward stain in one quick motion. "I'm sorry. We seem to have gotten off on the wrong foot. This is Penny Pimsley, and I'm Martha Roth." Martha's eyes cut to mine. "You are?"

I grudgingly hand it over, wondering at the abrupt shift in temperature. "Lana."

"As in Turner." She snaps shut her compact. "How scandalous."

The sexy starlet Lana Turner has been called the baddest beauty to ever grace the screen—she's on husband number four—but for me, Lana is short for Lanakila, meaning victorious. Mom named me that after I put her through eighteen hours of labor.

Martha turns her mischievous eyes to my ukulele. "You playing that little thing for your talent?"

"Yes," I say guardedly, preferring outward hostility to this faux friendliness.

"I'm singing." She pats her friend's arm. "And Penny's dancing. Well, if you consider 'tap' dancing."

Penny's cheeks pinken, and she lowers her eyes to her patent-leather tap shoes. I'm about to ask what the chickens else you would consider it, but then I wonder why I'm even in this conversation.

Before I can leave to find better company—myself—Miss Lovejoy's peach-hued figure sweeps through the curtained entrance. "Ladies, ladies! Remember to place the items you will require on the cart." She lifts a hand toward a two-tiered rolling tray on which several objects have already been placed. I spot an accordion, a top hat and cane, a pennywhistle, and a bongo drum. "An attendant will bring your item to you when it is your turn to deliver your act. I'll fetch you in fifteen—please be in ready form."

"I need to powder my nose. Good luck, *Lana*." The way Martha drops my name triggers a warning, the same feeling you get when you step on something that you know is a wad of gum. You keep walking, hoping you were wrong but, inevitably, you're not.

Martha and Penny disappear through another set of curtains that I presume leads to the sinks and toilets. Slowly, I exhale, only now realizing how tightly I've been holding myself. Oba always said to take it as a compliment when someone treats you like dung, because it means you're destined to make the world grow into a beautiful place.

I remove Oba's ukulele from the case and store the case by a rack sagging under the weight of too many purses and coats. All the chairs are full, so I huddle by the least occupied wall and tune my instrument.

Oba gave her uke to me the day she died. "You should have this, since your mudda has a wooden ear," she said in her soft Japanese accent. Then she went into her bedroom and closed the door the way she did before she took a nap. When I went to wake her, her skin was clammy.

As instructed, I carefully set Oba's uke on the pushcart, suddenly reluctant to part with it — the only friendly face in this room. But feeling the eyes of the other girls searing into my back, I release the wood. Then I feign interest in a glass etching of a nude sitting backward on a prancing goat.

"That could not have been comfortable," squeaks a voice like a rusted hinge. It's the girl with the puppet — though again, it's the puppet speaking.

"For the girl or the goat?" I ask.

The puppet laughs, but the girl's mouth barely budges. How does she do that?

"I meant those girls, Martha and Penny. Word is, Sugar

Maiden's looking for someone 'different' this year. They can't stand it, well, mostly Martha. She goes to my school, and she's stuck-up."

"I'm Lana."

"I'm Maude." The puppet points to the girl. "And she's Judy. Who taught you to be so funny?"

I've never been asked that before. "My pops. He was an embalmer." It's what brought him to Hawaii from his native California. There was a shortage of embalmers in the navy. After returning to the mainland after the war, someone offered him a job as a shoe cobbler, which he took because, unlike bodies, shoes still had their soles. "If you couldn't find your funny bone, you didn't stand a chance. He liked to say embalmers were more than a couple of working stiffs."

The puppet laughs, and for the first time, I catch movement from Judy's shell-pink lips.

"Do you always talk for Judy?" I ask Maude.

The puppet takes a good look at Judy's round face, pushes her wooden hands into Judy's pert nose, then pulls at the girl's ears. "If I don't, she stammers. She's been this way since she was seven."

"I see," I say, even though I'm not sure I do.

Judy closes her fist and the puppet crosses her arms in front of her chest. "I hope that's not a problem for you" comes Maude's voice, even squeakier than before.

"Of course not." We all need people to lean on, even if they are made from wood and cloth.

Both Maude and Judy tilt their faces to one side. "Are you Japanese or Chinese?"

I brace myself. "A little of both. I hope that's not a problem for *you*."

"Of course not."

All three of us smile, though now I'm not sure who I should

be looking at. I marvel at how sometimes it only takes one kind person (or puppet) to run the squeegee across one's sullied outlook. "What I really want to know is, who gets to be on the sugar box if you win?"

The puppet turns her painted-on brown eyes to Judy. "People say she has the better bones. It's not a fair comparison, since I don't actually have bones."

A flash of peach sends a nervous thrill to my heart. "Ladies, it's time," Miss Lovejoy announces in her chirpy voice.

We are marched up a ramp in a rustle of silk and satin and the catch and release of held breaths. Penny, as the first contestant, trails just behind Miss Lovejoy. Separated now from Martha (number nine), Penny isn't slouching anymore. With her shoulders back and her slender neck held aloft, it's clear she's here to win—a fact that improves my opinion of her. Martha strides before me, placing each foot down with the confidence of a man laying down aces.

Once backstage, we park ourselves on a line of wooden chairs, with Penny closest to the wings and me closest to a costume of a rhinoceros in a tutu. Maybe I should put that on and break up some of the tension here. Anticipation hangs in the air like the knotted and frayed ends of the stage ropes. The scent of turpentine and musty curtains tickles my nose, goading me to sneeze.

Then Miss Lovejoy, the only one allowed in the wings, sweeps her arms at Penny, meaning, *Go!* The girl's dance shoes *pa-tat! pa-tat!*, and she disappears from view.

PENNY: *My name is Penny Pimsley, and I'm eighteen. I should be Miss Sugar Maiden because I'm sweet as vanilla Coke.*

MAN: *Where are you from, Miss Pimsley?*

PENNY: *San Francisco. It may be foggy, but I am told that I bring sunshine wherever I go.*

Appreciative chuckles from the audience.

WOMAN: *Where do you see yourself in ten years?*

PENNY: *I've always wanted to travel to Spain. I'd love to travel anywhere, actually.*

MAN: *Thank you, Miss Pimsley. Please proceed.*

There's the sound of men's shoes walking onstage from the other direction, probably bringing Penny her cane and hat. Then a piano starts playing "You Are My Sunshine," and Penny begins tapping.

All seems to be proceeding as expected, until the sound of a cane clattering to the ground interrupts the flow of the taps. The audience gasps, but the piano keeps up the melody.

Beside me, a smirk lights Martha's face. Some friend. The mistake might've cost Penny the crown, a thought that should cheer me but doesn't.

Martha catches me watching her, and her eyes sharpen. Penny picks up her routine, and Martha withdraws her daggers, more concerned now with flicking lint off her skirt. There's a deliberateness to her movements, as if milking each moment for maximum value.

The other acts follow. I suddenly hate the number ten, which forces me to endure a barrage of unnatural peppiness, bootlicking, and admittedly good talent. The bongo drummer makes even me tap my toes.

When number eight, Maude/Judy, sallies forth into the spotlight, my fingers tingle with nervousness for her.

MAUDE: *Judy should be Miss Sugar Maiden because like sugar, she is wholesome and children love her. Also, she sits nicely at a table.*

An amused chuckle follows.

MAN: *What is your favorite dessert?*

MAUDE: *Marshmallows.*

MAN: *All right, Judy, er, Maude. What will you be doing for us today?*

MAUDE: *I will be reciting a poem called "The Climb."*

She clears her throat.

> *"A man filled his wheelbarrow*
> *With his every worldly thing.*
> *'I'm off to climb the mountain*
> *And live there like a king.'*
>
> *The way was always up,*
> *No downs did he encounter,*
> *But on and on he toiled,*
> *For soon he hoped he'd mount her.*
>
> *His favorite book bounced out*
> *And tumbled down the slope,*
> *But he wouldn't stop to catch it—*
> *At least it wasn't his soap.*
>
> *A flash of gray came at him,*
> *A wolf with eyes of yellow.*
> *It bit his leg and ripped it off;*
> *Still onward marched our fellow.*
>
> *His burden eased as more fell off,*
> *His fedora and his rope.*
> *A grizzly took his arm for lunch;*
> *A blackbird pinched his soap.*

At last he hopped the final step,
Half the man as when he started,
But seeing just how far he'd climbed
Made our chap lighthearted.

'All those things I carried up,
I didn't need them after all.
They even took my arm and leg,
But I'm still standing tall.
Yes, I'm still standing tall.'"

A robust applause fills the theater.

I can't help wondering why Judy chose that poem. What was her treasure, and how hard was her climb? And what about Martha, beside me, with her streak of ruthlessness and her boxer's glove of a mouth?

I glance at the row of now-empty chairs. Ten girls an hour for eight hours makes eighty in total. Eighty wheelbarrows being pushed up our own personal mountains.

Finally, it's Martha's turn. She gives me a glittery smile before gliding away.

MARTHA: *I'm Martha Roth, I'm seventeen, and I should be Miss Sugar Maiden because it is simply my destiny.*

Laughter, followed by applause.

MAN: *I like your confidence. Tell us about your favorite hobbies.*

MARTHA: *I love gardening. My apricot tulips took first place at the county fair last July. Also, I play a mean game of tennis. I bet I could beat you.*

MAN (teasing): *I would love to see you try.*

She certainly has *his* vote. The piano starts up, and Martha begins "Secret Love," which surprises no one. Regrettably, despite my fervent prayers, her singing voice doesn't sound like a bullfrog dying of dysentery.

I twist wrinkles into my dress, then press them back out with my sweaty fingers. Martha's voice, a lighter version of Doris Day's, grates my nerves. I tune her out and imagine Oba playing the song I will play, her face lost in a memory as she strums the chords. She used to sing it to the baby daughter strapped to her back—my mother—as she hacked at the cane.

> *My love is like the cane fields,*
> *Every day, there to meet me,*
> *Hips a-swaying,*
> *Chatting gaily in my ear.*
> *Sugar on her breath.*

When the audience claps and cheers, I pretend it's for me. Miss Lovejoy gives me the signal. I fix Oba's iron smile on my face and step into the light.

There's a wide expanse of black where the audience should be, a darkness thick with whispers that sound more surprised than welcoming. I shrink inside my curtain dress, wondering if my talent could be to disappear inside it. Did they whisper for the others? I didn't notice.

"My name is Lana Lau, and I'm sixteen." I cringe at how shaky my voice sounds.

"Yeah!" cries a man, along with the squeak of a chair. "Yeah! That's my girl!" Pops.

I give a small wave in his direction, imploring him to sit down. Then I inhale deeply, scattering the moths that flutter in the pit of my stomach. "I should be Miss Sugar Maiden because"—why? I can't remember. Something about being sweet? No, that's someone else. People like me can't afford to be sweet.

Though I can't see Pops, I know his heart reaches for me.

I can do this for him. For Mom. For Oba. "I should be Miss Sugar Maiden because Oba, my Japanese grandmother"—I can almost hear all the eyebrows raising—"she worked in the sugar fields for most of her life. Even as a woman, she cut and stripped the cane and burned the stalks when the harvest was done." The more I project, the more the stage amplifies my voice, giving it a heft and ring. "Each crystal bears her fingerprint."

No one moves, and I wonder if I should somehow signal that I have finished speaking. "And that is why I would make a great Miss Sugar Maiden."

"Miss Lau, you're pretty enough, but it wasn't so long ago that we were fighting a war against your country. You think an American serviceman or his wife will buy sugar with a Jap face on it?"

A fire roars to life in my belly. I can't see the speaker, but I imagine he is slovenly, with a face full of grape-size moles. Where are the easy questions the other girls had, about my hobbies and such? But I keep my smile tightly screwed on. "My father would buy it. He served in the navy for six years. And if you did not think my Japanese mother was American enough, you wouldn't have hired her to make sure your sugar meets industry standards. Mom wanted to be here today, but she decided that her job should take priority."

More murmurs travel through the audience, but I continue, keeping my tone light, though my knees tremble. "If you're looking for an American face, a face with a family history of loyalty to your brand, you need look no further." I spread my arms like a grand dame of the American theater.

The theater goes quiet, and suddenly the darkness feels brittle, as if the whole thing could shatter apart with the flick of a finger. But then someone begins to clap—Pops—and a polite applause rises to meet his. It sounds like summer rain.

A woman says, "Let's move on to your talent. Robert, bring out the girl's instrument."

A young man in a red attendant's uniform hurries to meet me, my ukulele in his hands. He shakes his head, hazel eyes wide with confusion. "I'm sorry, miss," he whispers, handing me the wood, "that's how I found it."

All four strings hang limply, severed in the middle. How?

I can hardly breathe. The strings can be replaced later, but the prank feels like an injury against Oba herself. Tears begin to collect in my eyes, but I refuse to release them. Who could've done this?

The manicure scissors. Martha and her spiteful, flicking fingers, telling me that I am lint she can neatly flick away. If ever I thought the devil had two horns and a pitchfork, I was wrong. The devil has flaxen hair and high heels, and she wields her wheelbarrow like a steamroller in her quest to conquer the mountain.

The woman announcer clears her throat. "Er, is everything okay, Miss Lau?"

"Yes." *Keep swimming, keep moving, and you can be the king of the ocean just like the sharks,* Oba says in my ear. I affix her unwavering smile on my lips and hold out my instrument by the neck. "I *knew* I shouldn't have washed my guitar in hot water."

A few people laugh. I hand my damaged ukulele back to the attendant, who ferries it away.

Now what?

"More jokes!" yells Pops.

I cough, highly doubtful that Sugar Maiden is looking for a comedian to represent America's sugar. Then again, telling a few jokes surely beats my current impersonation of a curtain. I'd rather be pelted by tomatoes than go down without a fight. Martha is probably in the audience, counting down to victory.

I say a prayer, then raise my chin. "Did you hear about the peanuts walking late at night?"

"No," a man throws back.

"One was a-salted."

No one reacts for a moment. But then someone giggles, someone with a voice like a rusted hinge. It's Maude, maybe even Judy. My cheeks flush in pleasure that she stayed. Her laugh oils the way for others.

"But that's nothing compared to the fight at the aquarium," I continue, my voice coming stronger. I shake my head in mock sadness. "Two fish got battered."

More laughter rolls out, and a few jokes later, I'm rewarded by cheers and shouts for more.

I bask in the glow of the audience's approval, approval lit by a father's love. Fifty miles away, Mother is wolf whistling. On a cloud even farther, Oba blows me a kiss. Suddenly I don't care so much about winning this particular contest. Battle has been waged in this theater, and Lana Lau is still standing tall.

❈ AUTHOR'S NOTE ❈

The first time I went to Hawaii, I was struck by how strange it felt to be among so many Asian Americans. It was the closest I'd ever come to feeling like part of the "majority." It may come as a surprise to some that the sugar industry was responsible for the Pan-Asian traditions of our fiftieth state. As California's Gold Rush expanded settlement of the West Coast, demand for agriculture from Hawaii surged. Miners found that it was cheaper to import things from Hawaii than across the American interior. Faced with a limited workforce, the sugar plantations, tightly controlled by missionary families, began importing Chinese, Korean, Japanese, and Filipino laborers to meet this increased demand. These plantation owners played a large role in the U.S.-backed overthrow of the Hawaiian monarchy, for which President Bill Clinton issued a formal apology in 1993.

During World War II, when President Franklin D. Roosevelt issued Executive Order 9066, authorizing the removal of "enemy aliens" from the West, those Japanese in Hawaii got off relatively "easy" compared to their mainland counterparts. Of the 157,000 Japanese living in Hawaii—one-third of Hawaii's population—less than 2,000 were put in camps, compared to 100,000 of the 126,000 interned on the mainland. Why? Economics. Interning one-third of Hawaii's population would have been disastrous for the economy.

As President Clinton stated in his apology letter sent to Japanese Americans interned during World War II, "In retrospect, we understand that the nation's actions were rooted deeply in racial prejudice, wartime hysteria, and a lack of political leadership. We must learn from the past and dedicate ourselves as a nation to renewing the spirit of equality and our love of freedom. Together, we can guarantee a future with liberty and justice for all."

THE BIRTH OF SUSI GO-GO

MEG MEDINA

I.

Susana and Martha stopped at the corner on their way home.

"Your turn," Martha said. She untucked her blouse and handed over a tattered copy of *Rosemary's Baby*, the cover sweaty from being stashed in her waistband since lunch. "You've got a week. Then it goes to Mina."

Susana slid the book deep inside her bag. The girls in their civics class had been sharing it, though it gave them nightmares. The Sisters at Christ the King School had banned it, which was all the more reason to read it.

They started along again, arms linked, even though it made them look like old ladies instead of sophomores. Susana didn't mind. At least Martha never teased about Susana's faint accent. (*Shicken,* some girls mimicked.) She never asked unanswerable questions, either, like *How do you say shithead in Spanish?*

They had gone halfway up the block when Martha slowed and squinted at a point in the distance. "Is that his car?" she asked. She was so stubborn about wearing glasses. Susana always had to tell her what was written on the blackboard.

"Yes," Susana said. "It's Tommy."

"He's early." Martha's new boyfriend sat at the wheel of his yellow Mustang, the engine idling. The girls could hear the rumble from here.

"We're going to Flushing Meadow to skate," Martha said. "You could come along."

Susana unlinked her arm and adjusted her book bag. "Not today," she said, and smiled as best she could manage. "Too much biology homework."

But they both knew it wouldn't be today or any day in the near future. Susana's parents had strict ideas about things, especially American boys.

When they reached the car, Martha hopped in and offered Tommy a peck on the cheek. Then she took Susana's hand and squeezed it. "Call me tonight when you get to the good part."

Susana waved as the engine roared and they pulled away.

Skating? she thought. Knowing Martha, definitely not.

II.

She sat reading on the closed toilet lid that night, while her parents entertained guests in their living room. The bathroom was the only place no one would come looking for her, asking her to join them.

This time it was a man named Gustavo, who had dark circles under his eyes. He'd come this morning to rent the studio apartment next door, only to be told that it had already been taken. Now, at ten o'clock at night, he'd come back to see her father for advice.

New arrivals from Cuba like Gustavo always made Susana nervous. They usually came to ask her father about jobs at the office building where he cleaned, but their mouths overflowed with stories of wives stranded on the island or in Spain, with tales of having been cheated by bosses, with despair. Their problems seemed too big and tangled for anyone to fix.

She got to the end of her chapter and put her ear to the door before opening it a crack. The smell of Gustavo's cigarette smoke was overpowering.

"I'm not particular, you understand," he was saying as he rose from his folding chair. "Un trabajo cualquiera, hermano, so long as it pays. I have my girls to think about."

"Of course," her father said, letting him out. "I'll do what I can."

Susana slipped quietly into her room to get ready for bed, listening as he chained the front door.

A book can bring bad dreams, but memories are more efficient enemies. Soldiers know this. Children of war. And Susana.

Mami has cooked with the shutters closed all day.
Her hair smells of orange and garlic,
and sweat fills the creases behind her knees.
"This is a secret, just for our family.
Don't tell anyone.
Promise me, angelito.
Do you understand?"
Mami has asked her many times.
Then a knock at the door turns her family into statues.
Papi is the first to break the stone and get to his feet.
Someone hurries her toward her room at the back of
the house.

Through the cracked door, she watches Mami slide their oily
*   pork secret*
into their laundry hamper, burying the contraband with dirty
*   clothes.*
Then Papi unlatches the wrought-iron gate with a loud
*   squeak*
and Fela's voice floats back.
She is the lady next door who used to give us cookies,
the one Mami calls the Spy.

III.

"Remember Lázaro, who sold ice cream back in Sagua?" her mother asked.

Susana shifted a bit in the kitchen chair. Outside, a looping jingle was blaring from the speakers of the ice-cream truck that was still making its rounds, though it was already autumn. It made it hard to concentrate on her homework. Math had never been her favorite.

"The tall one?" Susana was always carefully vague in answering questions like this. Otherwise she could get stuck in one of her mother's long stories of the past. They hadn't lived in Cuba since Susana was four, but Iris still talked about neighbors and specific streets as if it had all been yesterday instead of twelve years ago.

"Sí, claro." Iris turned from the stove where she was frying bananas. "He sold coconut ice cream. You were crazy for it and always begged Abuelo to buy you some. Lázaro had a lazy eye. Remember?"

"That's right," Susana mumbled.

Iris smiled, satisfied. She lowered the flame and speared the sliced plátanos with her cooking fork. "Si Dios quiere, when your grandparents finally get here, we'll buy them all the ice cream they want."

"Yes." Susana closed her book a little harder than she intended, thinking of Carmen at school, who now shared a twin bed with her aunt, who had arrived that July.

She went to the window and watched the kids outside clamoring for Bomb Pops. The truth was that when her grandparents finally arrived, Susana's life would be upended, much like Carmen's. Iris had it all planned, in fact. Susana would sleep near the stove in the kitchen's eat-in alcove, a curtain strung up for privacy. Susana wouldn't be able to sneeze without someone knowing.

Unless.

Rumors were circulating that President Nixon might soon suspend the Vuelos de la Libertad, which had been ferrying refugees to the States for seven years. Her mother had cried bitterly a week earlier when she'd heard about the precariousness of the Freedom Flights. "Then what happens?" she'd wailed. "Our family will never see each other again!"

It was a terrible thing to want. Heartless and selfish. Susana knew this. And yet, it was her only hope.

Susana didn't like to remember Cuba, not Lázaro or ice cream or her grandparents or anything else that her mother mourned. What was the point? They were living here now. The break from their country had already knit together inside her, misshapen like unset bone, but done.

IV.

The newly elected leadership of el Club Cubano of Queens was waiting to enjoy finger sandwiches in the Riveros' living room when the intercom buzzed. Martha was downstairs.

"We're going to Rockaway to swim," she said when Susana pressed Talk. "The water's still warm. Come on!" It was September, but summer hadn't released its heavy grip. Even with the fans blasting, Susana's blouse was sticking to her skin. In this heat, she wanted to be anywhere but inside the plaster walls of their apartment in Corona. She decided to take a chance.

She released the button and found her mother in the kitchen.

"Can I go to the beach with Martha, Mamá? It's just for a little while. And it's so hot."

Iris clicked her tongue. "Niña! And what am I going to do with all these ladies by myself?" She had just been installed as the president of the club, and this was her first official meeting. There were events to plan, finances to go over, and the Woolworth's reimbursements to finalize.

"*Please*," Susana said.

Iris gave her an exasperated look and tossed down her dishrag. Then she peered out the window at the street below where Tommy was parked behind a rented moving van. Susana's stomach squeezed as she stood behind her mother. Iris had a long list of qualities for young people that she had dragged with her across the ocean. Decent girls, for example, should wear polished shoes and avoid torn jeans, which made them look like hippies. Susana had tried to explain that patches (KEEP ON TRUCKIN' or even a peace sign) were just a fashion here, not character flaws. Even the nicest girls at school had jean jackets covered with patches that they melted on with irons. But Iris was firm.

Glancing down at Tommy, Susana knew it was hopeless. He wore mirrored sunglasses and smoked as he waited. A disaster.

"With *that* sinvergüenza? De eso nada," Iris said. "Your father would kill me. Now, help me with these trays."

Susana walked back to the intercom, hating herself almost as much as her mother. "Can't today. See you Monday." She didn't wait for a reply. A moment later, the roar of the car came from below.

With a cold look over her shoulder, her mother uncovered the perfect tower of deviled ham sandwiches and headed out to the living room.

"¿Un bocadito?" Susana held out the tray for the club officers as her mother looked on in sickening approval. *They're too salty,* Susana thought with satisfaction. Not that anyone would complain about her mother's recipe. After all, everyone knew they were lucky not to be like their relatives back home, where there wasn't a ham sandwich to be had, with or without a ration card.

The ladies were gathered on the plastic-covered sofa, thick legs crossed at the ankles. In no time they were chatting about towns Susana didn't know and families she'd never met who had scattered as far as Canada, those poor frozen souls. The women smelled of Aqua Net as Susana leaned in to offer seconds, their hair sprayed expertly into more or less the same bouffant as her mother's, acquired at Julia's House of Beauty for three dollars on Fridays.

"Susana, you have gotten so beautiful," Blanca said. "Just like your mother." The new treasurer was a round-faced woman with large brown eyes. "My Enrique tells me you are the number one student in science class this year. Is that true?" She plucked a particularly fluffy triangle from the tray and sank her dentures into the bread.

Susana's cheeks flushed. The smell of ham and the heat were making her dizzy, so she glued her eyes to the colonial scene on the platter's edges. The blue-and-white images were like something from her fourth-grade American history textbooks. (*North* American history, her father liked to correct.) Ladies in big hoop-skirts, holding parasols.

"Mi amor, habla," her mother coaxed. "She's so shy, Blanca. I'm sorry." She gave Susana a pained look and motioned her toward the other ladies, still waiting.

"I just like biology, I guess," Susana replied glumly. (A lie.) "It's not very hard."

"Maybe you'll be a nurse, then," Frida said, surveying the tray Susana offered. She had worked in a pediatric ward in Havana, but English had been her undoing and kept her from passing her exams here. At her age, Frida claimed, a new language was practically insurmountable. For now she worked at Flushing Hospital in the cafeteria, telling the Dominican cooks racy jokes. She served as secretary for the club, too, and her typed directory almost never had errors.

"Or even a doctor," Iris added. "Hoy día . . ." She twirled her wrist as if flicking off a concern and then lowered her voice, a habit from when her husband was home. "No one has to wear an apron anymore, you know."

The ladies nodded and laughed.

A doctor? Susana bit her tongue as she kept circulating. God forbid! She did have good grades, but she had absolutely no interest in medicine. She found the smell of alcohol unnerving, and even paper cuts made her queasy.

"Médico, enfermera . . . it doesn't matter. She'll be something wonderful, and she'll make enough money to take care of you when you're old," Blanca said brightly.

Susana glanced at the clock. Was it stuck?

"You know," Blanca continued, "I have a handsome nephew who is thinking of studying law one day." She arched her brow coyly at Susana. "Te lo voy a presentar . . ."

Susana's tray lurched to the right, and a few sandwiches tumbled into Frida's lap.

"Careful!" said Iris, steadying it.

"Sorry," Susana mumbled. Her mother's friends had begun making alarming personal offers like this lately, hoping for una muchacha fina! Someone they could talk to without a Spanish-English dictionary in their pocket. Their clean-cut sons came to the club dances twice a year to sit with their families, sweating in their polyester blend shirts. But they seemed as dull to Susana as the sandwiches on the platter—and left her just as thirsty, too.

Susana had dark longings for another kind of boyfriend altogether, someone American and a little indecent, if possible. Maybe she'd take up with a boy who had thick sideburns or even long hair. (How her mother gossiped about boys with melenas!) She wanted someone like one of stars of *The Mod Squad*, a show her mother had despised after she'd learned the backstory of the young detectives on the show: A drug addict. A criminal. A runaway. "¡Qué barbaridad!" she'd said. "Delinquents! Even worse than the Beatles!"

It boiled down to this: Susana didn't want to be the good Cuban girl the ladies imagined for their sons. She had been raised right here in Corona. She'd grown up on *Romper Room*, not *Olga y Tony*.

Iris dabbed her upper lip with a napkin and took the tray from Susana's sweaty hands to keep it safe. It was her nicest one, bought after months of saving green stamps at the A&P.

"You're flushed, Susana. Let's open more windows, mi vida," she said. "Lift the ones in your bedroom to get a cross breeze." She turned to the ladies. "Remember those delicious breezes back home?"

Relief washed over Susana as she left them behind and retreated to the back room. She threw open one of the windows and sat at the edge of her carefully made bed. For now, this space was still hers, right down to the Twiggy poster her mother didn't like ("¡Ay qué flaca! Es puro hueso!"), and the transistor radio that her father had won in the holiday grab bag last year at work.

She lay back and stared at the cracks in the ceiling as the ladies' voices lifted and fell in the other room. The quilted satin spread that her mother had given her for her fifteenth birthday felt luxurious beneath her, but the plastic doll that sat wide-eyed against her pillows had to go. Iris had brought it home from work last week.

"Remember the doll collection Abuela had for you in Cuba?" she had asked, fluffing the toy's skirt as she placed it on the bed. "The pretty ones with the porcelain faces?" Then, quietly: "Who knows where they ended up?"

Maybe with a little girl who actually likes dolls, Susana had wanted to say. But she knew it wasn't the dolls Iris was really wondering about. It was all their belongings. The milicianos had taken meticulous inventory of their home's contents when they had applied for exit visas. Nothing was theirs after that. Dolls, curtains, beds, rocking chairs, spoons. It was all to become property of la revolución.

Susana kicked the doll to the floor and closed her heavy eyes in the heat. It wasn't long before she was dreaming.

v.

Papi's friend Luis, who has hairy knuckles,
zigzags through traffic.
The capital is hours away, so they have had to leave quickly,
her favorite playerita still drying on the line.
Rushed good-byes, tears, and now
a hard suitcase bangs against Susana's knees in the backseat.
Later she thinks about her dress, stiff and bleached in the sun,
as she lies wedged between Mami and Papi in a stranger's bed.

Luis sleeps outside in the car.

"What if someone shoots him out there?" Mami whispers to
    Papi.

But he doesn't reply.

Susana woke with a start in the quiet apartment. The bed-spread beneath her was damp with sweat, and the sky outside was darkening. Had she slept all afternoon?

She crossed the room to open the second window. They almost never opened this one due to the building rules, which Iris followed to the letter. (You never knew who was watching you.) Nothing was permitted on the fire escape. No plants or grocery carts or drying laundry, even if your apartment had small closets.

Certainly no people.

But that was precisely what Susana found when she finally cracked the dried paint and opened the sash with a shotgun bang.

A blond woman not much older than Susana stood on the other end of the escape way, right outside the window of the apartment next door. She turned at the sound and smiled.

"Hello."

A shocked giggle rose to Susana's lips as it always did when she was nervous—a habit she had tried for years to break, especially at funerals. Her eyes flitted below, in case the super was lurking.

The girl's paisley minidress ballooned in the breeze, but if she was concerned about the old men in the courtyard looking up her dress (as they certainly were), she didn't show it.

Then Susana's eyes fell on the girl's white patent-leather boots. They reached all the way up over her knees and seemed to glitter in the waning sunlight.

"This heat's a bitch, but I love them," said the girl, as if reading Susana's mind.

Susana couldn't speak. Her mind raced for something to say, but her natural shyness thickened her tongue.

"Are you the new neighbor?" she finally managed to ask.

"Just got here today." She tucked a long strand of hair behind her ear and grinned.

"Susana!" Iris's voice startled her from the other side of her bedroom door. "Are you feeling better? What was that noise?"

"I take it that's you? Susana?" said the girl.

Iris knocked louder and opened the door. "You were feverish, so I let you sleep."

Susana dropped her curtains over the window just in time as her mother stepped into the room. She climbed back into bed, her heart racing, as Iris handed her two aspirins and poured the chamomile tea. She drank down the lukewarm brew, annoyed; she hadn't had a chance to even ask the girl's name.

VI.

All that week, Susana found herself checking the windows as she did her homework, but she didn't see the girl in the boots again. Finally, on Friday, as she was waiting on the stoop for the postman, she realized he might be able to help satisfy her curiosity.

"It's a real roaster out here," he said as he pushed his cart inside the vestibule. He wore shorts, dark knee socks, and a pith helmet to guard against the sun. His face was shiny with perspiration. "Hope it breaks soon."

Susana followed him inside. "Anything for us today?" She stood as close to his pushcart as she dared so that she could get a good look at the letters. It wasn't that unusual for Susana—or any of the Riveros—to be eager to see what had arrived. Over the years, the mail carriers had seen her mother rip open onionskin envelopes right there in the lobby.

"I don't see any airmail today, Miss Rivero," the mailman said gently. "Sorry." He turned his master key and pulled open the brass plate covering all the mail slots.

Susana shrugged. "Next time, then."

But she watched carefully as he sorted the letters into the right spaces. Was she becoming a North American version of Fela the Spy? It was a troubling thought, but at least she wasn't searching for contraband food or taking bribes to keep quiet about it.

Just then came a stroke of good luck: the mailman finally deposited a letter for the tenant next door. It was addressed to Linda Turner.

Aware that she was reading over his shoulder, he held out a stack of the Riveros' bills and frowned. "*These* are for you," he said pointedly.

Susana blushed as she accepted them. "Thanks."

She climbed up the stairs, satisfied. Now at least she had a name for her next-door neighbor.

Linda. She rolled the name on her tongue in Spanish, dragging out the *e* to say the word. Leen-dah. How wonderful, she thought, to have a name like Pretty.

A week later, even better information came her way. Susana was home for Columbus Day while her parents worked. She was on the way to the cellar, a basket of her father's undershirts perched on her hip, when she heard footsteps from below. Linda Turner was climbing up the steps with a bearded guy in tow. Susana nearly swooned when they came into full view. The visitor was shaggy and handsome, and he held Linda's hand. Susana pressed herself against the wall as they edged past.

"Hey, kid," Linda said, pausing. "Susi, right?"

"Hello," Susana replied softly, not correcting her. She coughed to mask her nervous giggle as the couple climbed past her. She didn't move until she heard Linda's door click shut behind them.

Susana loaded the dirty shirts into the machine, her imagination filling with ideas about the couple's risqué romance somewhere above.

She pushed the button marked Hot. Some girls, she decided, had all the luck.

VII.

"Where are her parents, even an aunt or a cousin?" Iris asked. Susana and her parents were standing at the cash register at Wilkins. They were opening a layaway account for a vibrating recliner Iris had seen in the display window.

Word about Linda Turner had spread through the building in the usual way: at the bus stop, on the stoop, in the laundry room. Iris wasn't too pleased about this type of girl-next-door. She didn't call her Linda. She called her esa — that one. Esa was a rule-breaker in every way. She was inconsiderate for leaving her things in the dryer after her time was up. Their shared fire escape was now cluttered with plants. What if there was a fire? They'd all burn to death thanks to that selfish girl! And more ominously, the smell of incense wafted in the hall outside her door. It was a known fact, Iris said, that drug addicts tried to mask the smell of marijuana with incense.

Susana felt annoyed on Linda's behalf. "She's just a college student, Mamá. She carries books all the time. Haven't you noticed?" It was true. Susana had spied Linda waiting for the bus at the corner stop, a book bag slung over her shoulder.

"College students," her father muttered darkly as he signed the layaway form.

Susana fell silent as the old grievance filled the space. The university where her father had once been a beloved professor had been shuttered to stop student activists, among them Iris's younger brother, Eduardo.

But when the campus reopened under Fidel a few years later, the purge of antirevolutionaries was under way and her father found himself out of favor.

"What kind of worm turns his back on his country?" Eduardo demanded when he found out that Iris and her husband had applied for exit visas.

It wasn't long after that the once "esteemed Dr. Rivero" was relieved of his post.

Whenever Susana's father told the story, he called the incident an ax that had cleaved their family in half.

"She's harmless," Susana insisted.

But Iris was still spitting tacks. "But indecent! Living alone and inviting men to see you at all hours? And those boots . . . ¿Viste? She looks like a . . ."

Susana's cheeks blazed as her mother's voice trailed off into unspoken accusation. She adored Linda's boots, their shine, the color, the way they made the girl look so carefree. Susana had even window-shopped downtown, hoping to find a pair exactly like them in one of the shoe stores. There was something almost magical about those boots that her mother would never understand. Maybe they were enchanted, Susana thought, although she was sure Iris would say *cursed,* like the tannis root from *Rosemary's Baby.*

And yet.

Susana locked her bathroom door the next day and stood before the full-length mirror. Still in her school uniform, she rolled down the waistband of her plaid skirt. With two fistfuls of her father's minty shaving cream, she covered her legs, just over her knees. If she squinted, they looked like boots. She stood on her toes, pursed her lips, and jutted out her hip like . . . a go-go dancer. If only her hair were blond, she could look like Linda or even better: like Goldie Hawn from that show *Laugh-In* on TV.

It was thrilling to look so untethered from her parents' judgments and fears, so scandalous and, well, American. So far from revolutions, and family axes, la lucha y el desespero.

"I'm out of shaving cream again," her father complained at dinner. Now he would have to use the Ivory soap, which gave him neck rashes. "I think they're cheating and not filling the cans up at the factory."

Susana pushed her rice and beans around the plate to cover the ladies in their hoopskirts. *Susi,* she thought, her calves still tingling. *Susi Go-Go.*

VIII.

The big news didn't come in a letter. Instead, a pimply courier delivered it by telegram on a quiet Wednesday afternoon.

Susana was busy doing her homework in the living room while her mother plodded through her English lessons aloud. She had been reading the practice dialogue from the book.

How do you do? It is a pleasure to meet you, Sylvia.

The pleasure is all mine.

Susana's father answered the door and rushed in a few seconds later, waving the note from Western Union. "Iris! They were assigned a flight! They'll arrive at JFK on Friday!"

"Who?" Susana asked.

"¡Tus abuelos!"

"¿Qué dices?" Iris shot out of her seat and ran to him. "*This* Friday? How can that be?"

"That's what it says. Look!"

Iris pored over the telegram and then pressed it to her chest, thanking Dios y la Virgen for the news.

Susana tried to will herself to be happy. Her own flesh-and-blood grandparents would finally be able to reunite with them after all this time. They'd be a family, and the holidays would include grandparents at the head of the table, the way they should.

But the walls of the kitchen still felt as if they were closing around her, and weariness and shame crept up her spine. There would be more late-night pencil-and-paper budgets worked out at the kitchen table. Their only television would be tuned to el canal en español instead of her favorite shows in English. She'd be called on to translate at social services, at the doctor's office, at the check-out line of the supermarket. And, of course, these strangers would expect the little girl she had been, the one who loved coconut ice cream and dolls.

"Pobrecita," her mother said when she saw the lost look on Susana's face. "You've been overwhelmed with emotion." She gave her daughter a squeeze and then ran off to the phone to see about buying Frida's old twin bed for the kitchen.

IX.

Shoes that click and pinch her toes
as she is hurried through the crowded airport.
Mami's hand sweats in hers as the man in the hat rechecks
their papers.
He motions and then
picks through Mami's teased hair, feels along the hem of
Susana's dress
until she shrinks behind her father in shame.

Later, she peers out the tiny window, listening to the noisy
propellers as
cotton clouds swallow their plane.

Susana tossed and twisted in her sheets for hours that night before she finally sat up in bed.

Down the hall, her father was snoring, as he always did after he drank. Her parents had toasted the good news of their family's impending arrival with friends from el Club Cubano. They'd come home laughing, any worries numbed by rum and their eyes glassy with hope.

Susana slipped out of bed and went to the window to see if the night air might clear away the dream. Why wouldn't dreams leave her in peace? Why did they chase her into the past, alone and defenseless against memory? She pulled up the sash and leaned out the window to take a deep breath. The temperature had finally started to drop, and a chilly gust of air moved the curtains like spirits all around her.

That's when she saw them.

Linda's white go-go boots were on the other side of the fire escape, near the potted plants, drooping lifelessly to one side.

Susana had no right to them. They weren't hers. But she suddenly craved those boots more than anything she had ever wanted in her life. Before she could stop herself, she stepped onto the fire escape. Shaking, she forced herself not to look down at the street, four dizzying stories below. She crawled slowly across the metal expanse. *What am I doing?* she wondered. She despised heights. In all the years her family had lived here, she had never dared to venture out her window.

When she reached Linda's window, she peered inside like a burglar to make sure she wouldn't be seen. There was no sign of her neighbor, and the bathroom door was closed. Susana lingered, taking in the studio. A television was tuned to a late show. A small dining table sat in one corner, and a large unmade bed was pushed up against the wall. Clothes were piled on the floor, some still in boxes.

Susana pressed herself down until she was almost on her belly and crawled the rest of the way to the boots. When she reached them, she pulled them close, sniffing at the scent of leather and something like alcohol. Against her cheek, they were as soft as she had imagined. She slipped them over her bare feet carefully, pulling them on like a pair of silk stockings that hugged her calves. When she was done, she stretched out her legs to admire them, wiggling her toes against the unfamiliar ruts of a stranger's feet. She stood up slowly and looked down at herself. There, in the middle of the night, hair loose and wearing only her baby-doll pajamas, she felt dangerous and strong, like someone else entirely.

"You look like Wonder Woman," a voice said from behind her.

Susana whipped around, startled, and nearly lost her balance. To her horror, Linda stood at her window, smoking and regarding her in amusement.

Susana's tongue became a brick; her face burned. She grabbed the edge of the fire escape to steady herself.

"I'm sorry. I was just—"

"Stealing my boots." Linda gripped her cigarette between her teeth and swung her legs—pale, unshaved—over the ledge to reach the fire escape.

Would a girl like Linda get angry? Susana wondered. *Shove me to the pavement below?* She laced her fingers tightly around the metal banister just in case.

She must have looked horrified, because Linda suddenly rolled her eyes. "Be cool," she said. Then she took a deep breath of the night air and leaned against the building. "I broke a heel and glued it back, just so you know. They're out here to dry."

Susana glanced down at her feet. The left boot had a light yellow line of goop at the seam. The funny smell, she realized, was like Duco cement from a model building kit.

Linda took a long drag and flicked the ashes down below. "So what brings you to my patio in the middle of the night?"

Susana struggled to loosen her tongue. "I couldn't sleep."

"Oh. An insomniac." Linda squinted one eye as she took another drag. "Maybe you're feeling guilty. Are you a night thief or something?"

Susana's heart raced. She felt so foolish. "No. I've never stolen anything."

Linda arched her brow, waiting. "Really?"

Susana sat back down and stared at the incriminating evidence on her feet. What had she been thinking?

"I'm sorry. I'm not myself," she began. But the words dried up on her lips. The truth was that she had no idea what being herself actually meant. "It's that . . . my relatives are coming," she finally whispered.

Linda frowned. "That won't hold up in court, miss," she said. "A family visit doesn't make it cool to take a five-finger discount on my boots, if you know what I mean."

"I wasn't stealing them," Susana mumbled. "I was trying them on—that's all. And it's *not* just a family visit. They're coming from Cuba. To live."

Linda's eyebrows shot up. "Cuba?" she said brightly. "It must be beautiful there."

Susana fell silent; in truth, she didn't know. All she had were Iris's stories and those awful scraps of memories.

"And El Che was *gorgeous*," Linda added. "So sad about him.

Damn CIA murderers. They're killing all the heroes." She shook her head and took another deep drag.

Susana flinched at the mention of the guerrillero's name. It wasn't allowed to be spoken in their apartment. He'd been executed in Bolivia a few years earlier; that much she knew. But these days, his face was on posters in even the most unlikely places. Iris had been recently stopped cold in front of a record shop window on Main Street, staring at a velvet interpretation of El Che in horror. He'd been Fidel's handsome number-one man, the soldier who had led the firing squads of Batista's old sympathizers. That's all Susana knew. But what if her parents weren't telling her every-thing? Was he a hero or a villain? Who got to decide the truth?

Disoriented, she began again. "They're finally getting out. They weren't allowed to leave. But now we'll all live together."

Linda shrugged. "I take it you don't dig them?"

Susana's thoughts jumbled into a thicker knot. Did you get to dislike your family—even if you didn't remember them? Even if they had been trying to reach you for years? "I'm not sure," she confessed. "It's been twelve years since I've seen them."

"Twelve?" Linda repeated. Then she smiled. "I've got a few relatives I wouldn't mind losing for twelve years."

Susana regarded her quietly. Linda Turner, the American girl. Linda, whose name meant pretty. Linda of the peace-sign earrings. Linda, who went to college in stylish boots and had good-looking boyfriends following her every move. Everything was easy and happy for Linda. She was older by at least three years, but sud-denly it was Susana who felt as if she had lived an entire lifetime more than her neighbor. How was that possible?

"Twelve years," Susana said again. "They'll need my room now, and we'll take care of them. Everything will be different."

An ambulance raced down the street, flashing lights but no

siren, like a silent scream. Linda finished her smoke quietly. "Well, I've got an early class tomorrow," she said, her blue eyes resting on the boots.

Susana started to pull them off, but Linda held up her hand. "Keep them," she said, shrugging. "The glue won't hold for long, anyway." She held up two fingers. "Peace."

Then, nimble as a cat, she slipped back inside.

Susana stayed on the fire escape for a long while after the light in Linda's apartment went out. She watched the night world go by beneath her as she sat thinking. One thing was clear: these boots were fashion to Linda, nothing more. A girl like Linda could give them away without a look back. Nothing would change for her if she discarded them.

But what if you were a different sort of girl? Susana wondered. What if you wanted all that breezy happiness but already knew the sting of having the most important things taken?

x.

That Friday, Susana waited in the kitchen for her grandparents' arrival from the airport. She had barely slept the night before, so her mother had allowed her to stay home from school. She had, however, left clear instructions.

Susana had made ham sandwiches and wrapped them as her mother had asked. She had dusted the apartment, put clean sheets on her grandparents' bed and on the cot that was now pushed up near the kitchen window. There was fresh fruit on the kitchen table to welcome them. The coffee pot was loaded with Café Bustelo.

The last thing her mother had asked was that she look nice. "Ponte linda," she'd said. Get pretty.

When the cab pulled up to the curb, Susana was ready.

She watched as her father paid the cabbie and then pulled the single suitcase from the trunk. The elderly couple that stepped out from the backseat wore gray coats that looked too heavy. But at the sight of them, Susana's heart squeezed into a fist. She could hear her patent-leather shoes clicking against the shiny airport floor. She could feel the heat of someone whispering in her ear: *Quiet, now, mi amor, until Fela leaves.* She could smell lilac water caught in the fabric of her drying sundress.

The intercom buzzed a few seconds later. Susana's hands trembled as she pressed the button that let her family into the lobby. Then she checked herself in the full-length mirror one last time. First impressions, as her mother always said, were the most important.

She opened the apartment door and paused at the top of the landing, listening. There was no sign of Linda next door, just the faint scent of incense.

The sound of footsteps grew louder until her relatives rounded the corner of the staircase and came into view one floor below. Her grandparents looked around the gloomy hallway in uncertainty.

"We're one more flight up," Iris said, out of breath, pointing up the stairs. "This way."

That's when her eyes fell on Susana. She frowned, and her mouth dropped open.

But before Iris could scold her, Susana swallowed hard and climbed down the steps. She was dressed in a miniskirt and V-neck sweater, both borrowed from Martha. And on her feet were the recently shined white patent-leather boots, glue and all.

"Susana," her mother began in a sharp tone. "What's this?"

She glanced down at her boots and smiled. "You said ponte linda, and I did."

With that, she walked directly to her grandparents. "Soy Susi," she began. But then, all she could do was search their faces.

Her grandfather bit his lip as he regarded her with watery eyes. When he pulled her close, she was surprised by the earthy scent that was at once familiar, like palms and tobacco, like an old wooden swing that she suddenly recalled without the slightest prompt from her mother.

Then her abuela nestled in for her turn. The embrace was long and sweet, and Susana felt something open gently inside herself, a small crack that seeped drops of all that had been missed and erased. They stood together for a long while.

If her grandmother was surprised by what Susi was wearing, she didn't say so. Instead, when she finally pulled away, she took Susi's face in her freckled hands and gazed at her. They were Iris's eyes and Susana's, too.

"I would have recognized you anywhere, mi vida," Abuela whispered. "How I've waited to see you again, Susi."

And with that, Susi took their hands and led them on the steep and uncertain climb for home.

☒ AUTHOR'S NOTE ☒

Fidel Castro (1926–2016) was the leader of Cuba from 1959 until 2008. He took power with widespread support of Cuban citizens in response to a coup by his predecessor, President Fulgencio Batista. Fairly quickly, however, he allied himself with the Soviet Union and communist doctrine. Over the course of his almost fifty years in power, he remained a defiant neighbor of the United States and a critic of what he felt were its imperialist policies. Worldwide, he is both revered as a revolutionary hero and reviled as a ruthless dictator.

Over the course of Fidel Castro's leadership, more than 1.5 million Cuban citizens would eventually leave the island nation. Whether via the early Freedom Flights initiated by President Lyndon Johnson or by taking to the ocean in handmade rafts, many sought to flee from the difficult economic conditions that unfolded and from the strict political and social controls imposed.

"The Birth of Susi Go-Go" looks at the realities of Cuba's exile community as its children began to merge into American culture in the late 1960s and early 1970s. For Americans, those years are remembered for social change, free love, and the important fight for civil rights. But how did those social movements look to refugees who had only recently fled a communist ideology?

Susana's struggle to embrace her life as a "normal" American teen while coming to terms with personal loss is an experience that I think the newly arrived will recognize. How do we reconcile competing accounts of history when we're caught in between? How do we respect our parents and still find our own way among new friends who neither know nor understand what we have experienced to get here?

TAKE ME WITH U

SARA FARIZAN

I used to have a life, until a war ripped me away from it.

My little cousin Amir and I sat on the steps of our apartment building as we ate ice-cream cones and watched people walk their dogs. I still found that strange. We had stray dogs in Tehran, but hardly anyone ever claimed ownership and no one picked up their feces.

I was not used to the humid August heat, either. Tehran could get blistering hot, but it was never *wet* the way Boston was. I had only been here a month, and I missed walking to school with my girlfriends. I missed the fruit trees at my grandfather's house. I missed Friday nights when the family would get together and go to a restaurant for dinner.

I had just started to get used to the new rules in Iran—not that I was enthusiastic about them—but in America, all those rules went out the window. Things I was trying to get used to now: not having to wear a head scarf when I left the house, my aunt and uncle fighting about money, and the homesickness that I couldn't escape, even in my dreams.

Amir and I watched the cars drive by, blasting music from their radios. I recognized a song from one of my favorite shows, *Solid Gold*. Most of my days in America had consisted of watching copious amounts of television and trying to expand my English vocabulary while looking after Amir. I loved *Solid Gold*. The men and women dancing to the sounds of the latest hits felt so . . . outlandish. I mean, who wore leotards like that in real life? Back home, pop music was a very private experience. After the Islamic Revolution, I was only able to get bootleg recordings, and it was even more difficult to find new music from the West. If you wanted to dance to a new record, you had to stay inside and hope the police would not break up a private party. I wore out my contraband ABBA tape back in Iran.

Now I couldn't listen to "Waterloo" without feeling a pang of homesickness. I told myself that was okay, because ABBA was passé and for children anyway. The singers featured on *Solid Gold*, like Irene Cara, were the sound of now. ABBA was no Irene Cara. Irene Cara could *sing*!

As the car drove away, I began to sing, continuing even after it was out of earshot. I didn't know all the words to "Time After Time," but I remembered the chorus and made up some noises to fill in for the words I didn't know.

"Hey!" A young Asian woman with short hair stuck her head out of her apartment window. "You've got a decent set of pipes!" I didn't understand what she meant, exactly, but she was smiling, so I took that as a sign that I wasn't disturbing her.

"She doesn't speak English so good," Amir shouted back, and

I flushed. "And we're not supposed to talk to strangers! Are you a stranger?"

The young woman shouted again, and then disappeared from the window.

"What did she say?" I asked Amir in Farsi. His face was splashed with chocolate from his cone, and he was looking more and more like a Monchhichi doll the longer his hair grew out.

"She told us to hang tight. That means she wants us to wait here." His Farsi was tinged with a slightly American accent.

"Why?" I asked him. He shrugged. He was more concerned with licking dribbling chocolate from the side of his hand. How stupid was I to have to rely on a He-Man enthusiast to be my translator?

The woman met us on the steps wearing neon-yellow shorts, a blue tank top with a picture of a blond woman singing on it, and a guitar strapped to her back. Her cropped black hair had a purple streak in it, and the toenails on her bare feet were painted black. I thought I was looking at someone from outer space.

She blinked at me a few times and said something in English. I looked at Amir desperately to help translate.

"She says you look like Apple Own Ya," Amir said, wiping his hands on his shorts. I was going to have to wash those, the little devil. But he was my little devil and I loved him. How humiliating was it that my only friend in the United States was my six-year-old cousin?

The way the young woman looked at me, I wondered if I had some ice cream on my face too. What was an "Apple Own Ya"?

"Sorry! Where are my manners? I shouldn't stare at you like that. My name's Mai! I live upstairs on the fourth floor." The young woman stuck out her hand in that very confident American way I'd seen on TV.

"I am Soheila. Hello. It is very to be nice meeting you," I said, self-conscious of my accent. Amir laughed at me a little. But Mai beamed, so I guess I introduced myself well enough.

"Do you go to college around here?"

"No . . . I am not a student." I didn't know how to explain my situation.

"She's here because of the war," Amir interjected. That I understood well enough. "War's bad. Except in the movies. Then it's fun."

"Oh. Where's um . . . sorry . . . where's the war?" Mai asked.

My uncle had warned me not to advertise where I was from. Back when he was a college student during the U.S. embassy hostage crisis in the late '70s, he was beat up by some American students.

But I wasn't ever going to be ashamed of where I came from, no matter who was in charge of the government. "I'm from Iran," I said with pride.

"Oh, bitchin'! Right on. You must have seen some crazy shit, huh?" Mai asked.

"'Shit'? What is 'shit'?" I asked in English, which made both Amir and Mai laugh.

"It's a bad word that means poop! *Poop!*" Amir shouted joyously in Farsi. Now I knew a new word in English. This was progress.

"Listen, do you guys live here? Do you want to come visit my apartment? I'm not a weirdo or anything—I promise." Mai crossed her heart with her index finger. I didn't know what that gesture meant—or what "weirdo" meant.

"Do you have ice cream?" Amir asked.

"Lots of ice cream. Brigham's ice cream, too. The best kind," Mai said.

"You play the guitar?" I asked.

"Oh! Yeah. I go to Berklee College of Music." Mai swung the guitar around to her front and began to play a familiar tune.

Since I had come to Boston, I had been having the same nightmare: my mother and father were alone in their basement, hiding from Saddam's missile strikes. My mother yelled for me. I tried to run to her, but I couldn't move. Then I woke up sweating, my heart thumping so loudly, I hoped it wouldn't wake Amir in the bed next to mine.

The only thing that calmed me down was the acoustic guitar music coming from the apartment above my uncle's. I didn't know who played such gorgeous music, but I had vowed that if I ever met him, I would thank him. Now I had met the mysterious musician—Mai! I felt stupid for assuming the guitar player was a man. I just didn't know many women guitar players. There had been women pop singers before the Revolution, but I hadn't seen a woman play the guitar before in person.

I absolutely loved it.

Amir always jumped up whenever he heard his father sing from down the hallway, alerting us (and perhaps the whole building) that he had returned from his garage space. Mostly Uncle Khosro would sing a lot of off-key disco like the Bee Gees. He forgot many of the words and made up his own lyrics depending on his mood.

He was still singing loudly as I opened the apartment door for him. He held our dinner in his greasy hands: a bucket of Kentucky Fried Chicken and a two-liter bottle of Pepsi.

"Hello, my beautiful family! Tonight we feast because of a great military man named Colonel Sanders," Uncle Khosro exclaimed in Farsi. I took the soda and chicken from him so he could scoop up Amir and hang him upside down.

"Khosro, don't do that! All the blood will rush to his head!" Aunt Fariba hissed. She never greeted her husband with the enthusiasm Amir did. I got the impression that when Aunt Fariba came here in 1975, she thought she was marrying a man who would give her a fancy American lifestyle: expensive cars, large homes — the way the people on *Dallas* lived. Khosro was a good man, but he was not Bobby Ewing (portrayed by the incredibly handsome Patrick Duffy). To be fair, Fariba was no Pamela Ewing. I think it had dawned on her that she never would be.

My family back home came from means, but my uncle had a much different life than he would have had if he had stayed in Tehran. He hadn't exactly been truthful about the life he was living when he spoke to my mother on the phone. Uncle Khosro had told my mother that he lived in a "luxurious condo" and had "an incredible job." The condo was actually an apartment on Gainsborough Street in a run-down building full of low-income tenants, including many college students. His incredible job was as a mechanic at a BMW car dealership instead of working for my grandfather in the import-export business. But I didn't tell my mom the reality of my uncle's situation during our weekly phone conversations. I felt it wasn't my truth to tell.

"But he's enjoying it so much!" Uncle Khosro was hanging Amir upside down, swinging him from side to side. The little Monchhichi screamed with glee. I had a pang of longing for my own father. The way Uncle Khosro looked at his son reminded me of how my father and I used to play when I was little.

God, I missed him.

"Keep it down or you'll disturb her," Aunt Fariba warned in Farsi.

Like clockwork, Mrs. Abney, the across-the-hall neighbor, opened her door to see what all the fuss was about. Whenever she decided to make eye contact, she looked at us as though we were insects who had infested her home.

"Hello, Mrs. Abney! It is so nice to see you!" Uncle Khosro called through the open door to the stone-faced widow. She was wearing her house shoes and an oversize floral print dress, and I thought she looked very much like the woman in the Wendy's commercials who complained that there was not enough meat in the hamburger. Uncle Khosro was too nice to her. I was all for respecting one's elders, but not when they were prejudiced assholes.

Mrs. Abney had pinned a yellow ribbon on her apartment door. My uncle told me it had been a symbol of hopeful return for the American hostages during the Iranian hostage crisis in 1979. The hostages had been returned in 1981, but Mrs. Abney's yellow ribbon went up in 1982 when Uncle Khosro and his family moved in. The gesture was not lost on him, but he still felt that with kindness, he could win over Mrs. Abney. I was pretty sure he could reach Mister Rogers's level of kindness and still not make much progress with her.

"You're too loud," Mrs. Abney said. "Some people are trying to live in peace. You people might not know anything about that, but Sunday is the Lord's day. It's a time of respite and prayer."

I didn't know what "respite" meant, but I knew she wanted us to shut up.

"You are so right, Mrs. Abney! Would you like to have dinner with us? We can enjoy this nice day together?" Uncle Khosro said, one hand clutching Amir's legs and the other hand over his heart, bowing slightly to the elderly woman. "We are having the Original Recipe! They do chicken right! Please, you would make us so happy if you joined us."

"I've got my own food. Just keep it down," Mrs. Abney said before she slammed the door.

Uncle Khosro flipped Amir in his arms so he could kiss his cheeks. "Always remember to be nice to lonely people, okay?" Khosro told his son as he carried him into the kitchen.

I had noticed that Mrs. Abney never had any visitors, too. Was there no one to check on her, no one who cared for her? Didn't everyone have someone to care about them, even if it was strictly out of guilt and obligation? That was the Persian way. Guilt always made the heart grow fonder.

We sat down at the table to eat our fried feast, but I didn't have much appetite. Colonel Sanders's cheerful face was a poor substitute for my mother's cooking. I missed her loobiya polo, long-grain basmati rice with tomato, lamb, and string beans that smelled of turmeric and cinnamon. She always told me I should learn how to cook my favorite dishes, but I never took her up on it. Now I wished I had paid attention.

The TV was on during dinner. There was a commercial for Ronald Reagan's reelection. It seemed like everything could be sold over the television here, even politicians.

"How was everyone's day?" Uncle Khosro asked us cheerfully.

"Soheila and I made a friend today," Amir said.

"Oh?" Aunt Fariba said in a disapproving tone.

"Yeah! She had purple hair!" Amir bit into a chicken leg while Fariba shot her husband an alarmed look.

"Um, how did you meet this person?" Uncle Khosro asked me diplomatically. I explained that Mai lived upstairs and was very nice. My aunt and uncle looked at each other for a moment before Uncle Khosro addressed me again. "Soheila, while you are here, your aunt and I are responsible for you, and while we are sure your friend is nice . . ."

"American girls are trouble," Aunt Fariba said. "They're into sex and drugs. We want you to be careful." I wondered how she knew, since I didn't see her with any Americans. Most of her friends were Iranian immigrants like her.

"I . . . She seemed very kind. And she can play the guitar so beautifully!" I tried to defend my potential friend. I was desperate to talk about something other than Orko and She-Ra. Amir and I had exhausted the topic of Orko, the hooded wizard with the tinny voice, and how he was the absolute worst.

"Maybe you could have her meet us?" Uncle Khosro asked. He was asking his wife more than he was asking me. From her sour expression, Aunt Fariba wasn't sold on the idea.

So, on the days when Aunt Fariba went to work, Amir and I snuck upstairs to Mai's apartment and listened to music. All the music I didn't know I had been missing. Mai had magazines filled with photographs of musicians, young and old. There used to be magazines like this in Iran when I was younger, but that had all changed after the Revolution — and then before we had time to adjust to all the changes, the war began.

I spent *hours* poring over all the cover art on Mai's albums. The three of us danced to beats so good, they couldn't have been created by humans. It was a huge change of pace from studying all the time for my college entrance exams. I was worried that I would be behind when I went back to Tehran, but for the time being it was nice to take a break.

My bedroom back home was tidy, pristine. Mai's was messy: sheet music was strewn on the floor, her bed was never made, and her closet was full of raggedy shirts that she had cut up. Her walls were plastered with posters of rock stars that I didn't recognize. I learned their names like they were holy leaders: Pat Benatar, Men at Work, the Clash, Talking Heads, and someone with huge eyes who I only knew was a man from his mustache.

"It's so funny you keep looking at that photo of Prince." Mai was lying on her bed while Amir and I sat on the floor. "Since you look just like Apollonia, and she falls in love with him in the movie and all."

"What?" I understood what Mai had said. I just didn't know what the hell she was talking about.

"You know, in *Purple Rain*," Mai said.

"What is 'Purple Rain'?"

"WHAT?" Mai screamed. Amir jumped up and began crying. "Shhh. I'm sorry, little man. I didn't mean to scare you. You want a Jell-O pudding pop?"

Amir wiped his eyes and nodded, and Mai went to the kitchen. She had stocked her freezer with all of Amir's favorites. She seemed to be able to buy anything she wanted, and she had a big television and a state-of-the-art record player, so I assumed she came from a wealthy family. She lived alone, which I couldn't understand. I wondered if she ever got lonely. I would probably live with my parents until I married.

I thought it would be gauche to tell Mai that I came from money, too, which is how I was able to come to the U.S. My mom had offered to send money to my aunt and uncle for taking me in, but Uncle Khosro wouldn't hear of it. That was another point of contention between him and his wife. I knew Aunt Fariba didn't want me there. She never said it outright, but I was a burden to them. She was polite to me, but I felt like she assessed every piece of food I put on my plate and how much time I spent in the shower. I was draining their resources — or at least that's how she made me feel.

"Here you go, He-Man." Mai passed Amir the pudding pop before turning to me and pulling an album from her record collection. "We're going to listen to this all afternoon, and then I'm taking you to the movies. As soon as possible." Mai carefully slid the vinyl album out of its shiny cardboard sheath. She gently handed the album cover to me and then flitted to the record player.

Every song was a masterpiece, a story, and a world unto its own. I didn't even understand all the lyrics and I still felt that way! The energy of "When Doves Cry" floored me. The drama of "Let's Go Crazy" made my whole body tingle. My favorite song, "The Beautiful Ones," made me ache for someone I hadn't met yet. I didn't know exactly what Prince was saying in that song, but I felt the pain and anguish just the same. It was an album chock-full of the emotion and expression that I needed. This man from a place called Minnesota, his music made me feel *alive* instead of just existing.

I was nervous that my aunt and uncle wouldn't let me go see *Purple Rain* with Mai. I *had* to see this movie after listening to the album all week. But Aunt Fariba, as hip as she thought she was, wouldn't be pleased with Mai's look. My aunt and uncle weren't a religious or conservative household—my parents were far more traditional—but Fariba was very quick to make snap judgments based on people's appearance. When she came home from the hair salon, she would tell story after story about all the women who came in and what they looked like before and after. "She came in looking like a walking dead person and left the salon looking like a walking dead person," or "She looked like she was on drugs. You know, one of those party girls," or "I'm sure she was a prostitute. I mean, the way she moved and her skirt was so short," and so on.

Initially, it made me self-conscious about my own appearance, until I thought about Fariba's own look. She wore far too much makeup. Her hair was crispy from Aqua Net hairspray. Her bangs were teased to the point where it looked like a giant claw was

protruding from her forehead, doing its best to clutch you, welcoming you into her realm of misery.

I checked myself in my room's mirror while Amir watched me.
I wore a simple black shirt, nothing too revealing, and blue jeans
with black ballet flats. My hair was up in a high ponytail. I had
a little pink blush on my cheeks, but not enough to give Fariba
or Khosro the idea that I was up to something. Fariba wore lots
of makeup, but she was married, so that made it okay for some
reason, which I thought was ridiculous. I never understood why
adults always thought girls with too much makeup on were up to
something. No one ever asked boys with too much bulge in their
jeans if they were up to something. Double standards for men and
women seemed to be international.

"How do I look?" I asked Amir in Farsi. "Am I bitchin'?"
I asked in English. I was picking up words like "bitchin'" very
quickly from spending so much time with Mai.

"Bitchin'!" Amir said, sticking his thumb up.

I heard a knock on the apartment door and gasped. Amir and
I rushed out of our room to see Aunt Fariba open the door for a
totally transformed Mai.

"Hello! I'm Mai Asano. You must be Soheila's aunt! I've heard
such wonderful things," Mai lied. But she did it oh so well!

"Hello," Fariba said, taking in Mai's long yellow summer dress
and the black cardigan that I knew was covering the tattoos on her
shoulder. Mai's hair was under a fashionable summer hat that hid
her purple streak. There wasn't a hint of makeup on her gorgeous
face.

"Please, come in!" Uncle Khosro said as he stood up from the
couch. "It is so nice to meet one of Soheila's friends!" He was being
kind. Everyone knew Mai was currently my only friend. "Please,
please, come in and have something to eat!"

"No, we'll be late for the movie!" I told my uncle. Why couldn't they just let me leave?

"What is this movie our little Soheila is so excited about?" my uncle asked Mai with genuine interest. It was the first time since my arrival that I had been excited about anything.

"We're going to see *The Muppets Take Manhattan*. You know, Kermit the Frog, Miss Piggy," Mai said cheerily. I bit back a laugh. I was sure I would enjoy watching the Muppets (I liked *Sesame Street*, which I watched with Amir), but I appreciated Mai's lie.

"We don't want to be late," I pleaded with my uncle.

"Okay, but be home before ten. Call us if you need anything." My uncle may have said more than that, but I wouldn't know because we ran out after the first word.

"How did I do?" Mai asked me when we were outside.

"You were good," I replied.

"Yeah. I've got grandparents from Japan. I get it. Kind of."

Mai led us to a blue AMC Gremlin parked down the street. A young white woman sat in the driver's seat, her window down to release the smoke from her cigarette. Her hair was dyed black and white. She reminded me of the skunk from Looney Tunes if that skunk from Looney Tunes never smiled.

"What the hell happened to you?" the skunk lady asked Mai.

"I'm trying out a new look. For one night only, thanks," Mai said, leaning in to kiss the skunk lady on the mouth. I tensed. I wasn't used to public displays of affection between boys and girls, never mind between girls and girls.

"I like the new look! All you're missing is a Members Only jacket!" A young white girl with a red bandanna across her forehead waved at me from the backseat.

"Wow! You weren't kidding, Mai! Your friend looks exactly like her," a black girl in preppy clothes added.

"Girls, this is Soheila. Soheila, that's Cecilia," Mai said, pointing to the youngest member of the group. "Janine." The blonde with the red bandanna saluted. "And my girlfriend, Genevieve."

"Gen," the skunk lady with the salty expression said. "Let's hit the road before we miss the show."

As soon as I saw Prince's silhouette bathed in purple light, holding a guitar onstage, I felt a rush of adrenaline that didn't leave me until the end of the film. When Apollonia appeared in the backseat of the taxi, worried about paying her cab fare, Mai and her friends all yelled and clapped and pointed to me, letting the rest of the packed movie theater know that they were sitting with the star of the movie.

I didn't see it. Apollonia was glamorous. She was sexy. She was a risk taker. I wasn't any of those things. And I definitely wasn't ever going to get naked and jump in a lake for a man. Even if that man was Prince.

I laughed during the scene when Apollonia got on Prince's motorcycle as one of my favorite songs, "Take Me with U," played. I didn't laugh because it was a funny scene but because I realized I hadn't thought of anyone back home since the movie started. Then I began to cry. I didn't care if any of my companions noticed.

After the movie, as we all piled into the car, Mai asked me if I wanted to audition for their band. "It'd be awesome! We do a little bit of everything. Funk, R&B, punk. Right now we do mostly covers and put a feminist spin on them," she said.

"Though I do hope we start doing more original songs," Cecilia hinted.

"Are you kidding? With Apollonia's doppelgänger, we'd get booked at parties and events so fast." Janine snapped her fingers.

"Let's see if she can sing first," Genevieve warned as she looked at me in her rearview mirror.

"What do you think? Would you like to try out?" Mai asked.

I didn't think about whether or not it was a good idea, if it was even possible for me to join a band since I didn't know when I would be going home, or whether I might be bad at singing their songs even though Mai said I had a good voice. I just thought of how music made me feel better. So I agreed.

"Soheila! Your mother is on the telephone!" Aunt Fariba shouted from the kitchen a few weeks later. She dangled the phone cord in her hand as though she couldn't be bothered to hold the actual receiver. I gently took the phone from her and nodded in appreciation, which I resented. Aunt Fariba's initial polite smiles had morphed into grimaces as the weeks wore on. I hated having to feel apologetic for taking up space. I hated having to make up excuses for coming home late with Amir when I took him to band practices. (I was now a full-fledged member of the Ovarian Cysters. I had asked Amir to translate what our band's name meant, but he had no idea.)

"Hi, Mom," I said quietly into the phone.

"Hello, my love."

I always took a deep breath after hearing my mother's voice. Everything would be okay as long as I could hear my mother breathing. "Your father says hello." We both knew that if my dad got on the phone, he would just weep with abandon and the phone call would last longer than it needed to. We were always mindful of my uncle's phone bill. International phone calls between the U.S. and Iran could get pricey.

"How are you?" she asked.

I wanted to tell her I had gone to see *Purple Rain* six times. I wanted to tell her that I was homesick but I had made some new friends who called me Apollonia and they were making things better. I wanted to tell her that I was in a band, but I knew she wouldn't approve. Good girls weren't performers. Only compromised women got onstage to dance for people, unless they became famous and rich; then it was okay. My mother might not feel that way herself, but her friends back home did, and she wouldn't want them to gossip or think badly of me when I returned.

"I'm fine." It seemed like the responsible and grown-up answer. "How are you? How is everyone?"

I heard her sigh.

"We are okay, but I have some bad news." I braced myself for something awful. Did someone die? "Kayvon," she began. Our housekeeper, Akram, had helped raise me, and her son, Kayvon, was like a younger brother to me. "He . . . he enlisted."

I gasped and sat down on the kitchen floor. I felt my eyes brimming with tears.

"But he's . . . he's only fourteen," I said, though my mother and I both knew boys as young as twelve were sacrificing themselves for the country. "Poor Akram." I began to cry.

"Don't start that! You have to be strong!" She wasn't going to tolerate any tears from me. I had to be a grown-up. I controlled my breathing and composed myself. "We tried to persuade him not to go, but there is all this pressure. We're losing so many young men . . . He didn't even tell his mother. He left a note."

"Give Akram my love." I didn't know what else I could say that would be of any comfort. "Mom? When am I coming home?"

"Can you tell your uncle to call me later tonight? Tell him he can call anytime—we will be awake."

She hadn't answered my question.

"I will tell Uncle Khosro to call you, but—"

"Don't forget. It's important. We have to say good-bye now."

"Okay. I love you. Tell everyone I am thinking of them."

"We know you are. But try not to think about us so much. Focus on your life over there."

She was commanding me to focus on my life here. I didn't know what that meant. I could feel Aunt Fariba's gaze on me when I hung up the phone. I turned around and offered a small smile, as though she were a prison warden that I needed to maintain a decent relationship with. I wanted her to ask me how everyone was back home. I wanted her to offer me some sort of affection. But she didn't smile back. She just nodded and asked me to help her with the laundry. There were chores that needed to be done here. I guess she thought there was no reason to worry about a place a world away.

"Okay, He-Man, can you hit the cowbell like this?" Mai asked, crouching down to Amir's eye level in the college practice room. She hit the bell with a drumstick in a quick one-two beat, and Amir copied the rhythm, excited to be able to bang something to his heart's delight. "Bitchin'! Watch me for when I want you to do that, okay?"

Gen, our bassist, had arranged for us to perform at an all-ages club in South Boston that night. I was nervous to sing in front of people, but Mai said we had to let the city know how good we were. I was planning to tell my uncle that there was a double feature of *Ghostbusters* and *Gremlins,* but first we had to practice our set. And as usual, I'd brought Amir with me.

"You better watch out, Janine. He-Man is going to replace you on percussion in no time," Gen threatened.

"Yeah, yeah, drummers aren't real musicians. Ha-ha already, Gen. He is missing something, though." Janine took off her red bandanna and tossed it to Mai, who tied it around Amir's head.

"Now, that's better! You're the coolest guy in the band. Don't grow up to be a misogynist and you'll be all right, kiddo," Janine said, twirling a drumstick in her right hand. I didn't know what a misogynist was, but I would remember to ask her after rehearsal.

Mai pointed her finger at Gen to start our cover of ESG's "My Love for You" with a kicking bass line.

"Now, He-Man!" Mai commanded.

Amir banged the bell in time, head-banging along. Next to me, Mai began to sing and I joined her, both of us dancing to the sick beat. Cecilia, who played the keyboard, had been helping me learn the lyrics.

When the song ended, I was out of breath.

"Awesome!" Mai said as we high-fived.

Amir kept hitting the bell, roaring intermittently at each of the girls.

"How much sugar has he had today?" Cecilia asked in genuine concern from behind the keyboard.

"Okay, let's take it from the top," Mai said. Gen started the bass line again.

"What do you think you're doing?" I looked up to see Fariba rush into the music room. She had asked me the question in Farsi. I froze, horrified. The band was the only thing that kept me going. She was going to ruin everything.

"Uh, can we help you?" Cecilia asked, not knowing who Fariba was.

My aunt must have followed Amir and me instead of going to work. How else would she know we were here?

"You can help me by telling me what my son is doing here," Fariba said in English, glaring at me.

"We're taking names and kicking ass!" Amir responded. He had heard Janine say it a number of times during our rehearsals.

Aunt Fariba's clawlike bangs couldn't hide how red her face was. "Amir! Soheila! Let's go! Now!"

Amir complied and walked to his mother. She ripped the bandanna off of his head and dropped it to the floor.

I hated that she felt it was okay to embarrass me.

I hated that she looked at my friends in the same way Mrs. Abney looked at us.

I hated that she didn't give me any of the affection my mother did but still expected me to treat her with the same respect I would give my mother.

"I'm not going," I said, gripping the microphone stand.

It became eerily quiet in a room that was always full of sound.

"What did you say?" Fariba asked in Farsi, slowly marching toward me. "Who do you think you are? You are a refugee. We have given you a life here, and you disrespect me by hanging out with these loose girls? You disrespect your uncle, who sweats and struggles to house you and feed you?"

She grabbed me by my hair. I screamed out in pain. Amir began to cry, and the rest of the girls yelled for Fariba to stop.

My aunt let go of me, her face crumbling. She looked like she didn't know where she was or how she got there. Her hands trembled and she looked at me in remorse. "I . . . I'm sorry," she said, turning around to pick up Amir. Her cheeks were red as she left.

The room became quiet again.

"Are you okay?" Mai asked me.

I wiped away my tears and took a deep breath.

"Let's take it from the top," I said.

$$\times \quad \times \quad \times$$

"It's a chick band? No way. I bet they can't play for shit," a young man with a Kajagoogoo haircut said a little too loudly backstage. Gen had failed to mention the show tonight was a contest. The winner of the battle of the bands would take home the grand prize of five hundred dollars. None of the other bands had women in them.

"A little warning would have been nice, Gen!" Cecilia said, peering out at the crowd of two hundred and fifty people.

"What? I didn't want you to feel pressured! Besides, we're going to go out there and show them we can play. Right, Apollonia?" Gen asked me. My hair was teased out and curly just like Apollonia's, and I was wearing heavy purple eye shadow. I wasn't going out there in lingerie though. I wasn't insane! I was wearing a black tank top and jeans with holes in them. Mai told me the holes had been deliberate, which I didn't understand. Why would someone put holes in a pair of perfectly good pants?

"Please put your hands together for the . . . You're joking with this band name, right?" the host onstage asked us.

"Just read the damn card," Janine yelled.

"Okay. The Ovarian Cysters, ladies and germs!" the host said to lukewarm applause. As soon as we took the stage, we were cat-called and whistled at.

"You ready?" Mai said, putting her guitar strap on her shoulder.

I was ready to kick ass and take names. I had a lot of shit I needed to let out.

Mai started to play the beginning of Siouxsie and the Banshees' "Happy House." The audience began to bob their heads, though some of the whistles persisted. Then I grabbed the mic and wailed.

I jumped up and down in between verses. My hair whipped side to side, and the more I poured all my rage, all my hurt, all my heartsick, into the void, the more the audience responded. The roar of the audience quieted the footage of the tanks, silenced my aunt's words, and briefly killed my worry about my parents and friends back home.

During that set, I was free to be whoever I wanted to be. Not Apollonia, not Amir's babysitter, not a self-conscious girl.

I was bitchin' and so was my band.

AUTHOR'S NOTE

When I was asked to write a piece for this anthology, I knew I would write a story set in the 1980s, which is to me one of the most fascinating decades of the twentieth century. While many may think of the '80s as a time of ostentatious superficiality or self-interest, I think of it as the decade that helped shape today, for better or for worse.

It was a decade that brought us the cell phone, the personal computer, video game consoles, MTV, credit card debt, primetime soaps that made audiences aspire to exorbitant wealth, Wall Street greed, the AIDS virus, global conflicts that are still being felt today, and global resolutions like the end of the Cold War.

There are some conflicts, however, that did not garner as much attention in the Western world as the Cold War. The Iran-Iraq War lasted from 1980 to 1988. Many lives were lost on both sides, and I often wonder if there was no oil in that area, how many lives would have been spared? How many families would be intact?

My grandparents lived with us for a year of that conflict in 1987, and while I don't remember much, as I was only three, I do remember the music of the '80s, particularly R&B and soul music. My parents had come to the States in the '70s, but a great deal of their American musical knowledge was based on pop radio, and while I didn't grow up listening to any of their old LPs, we listened to Rufus and Chaka Khan's "Ain't Nobody" and Michael Jackson's "Smooth Criminal." My mother tells me that when she was eight months pregnant with me, she went to see *Purple Rain* with my father. Apparently, I kicked hard throughout the movie. Not surprising, then, that Prince's music became a huge part of my life as well as the lives of so many others. I bet I kicked when Apollonia came on the screen, when Prince sang "Let's Go Crazy," and when Morris Day danced to "Jungle Love."

Soheila's story is a brief one, but it is a love letter to a time of sorrow and joy. A time of being in a new country and figuring out whether you can make that place home. The music helps her find her place as I think the music of the '80s helped us find ours without our really knowing it.

ABOUT THE CONTRIBUTORS

—

DAHLIA ADLER is an associate editor of mathematics by day, a blogger for *B&N Teens* by night, and a writer of kissing books at every spare moment in between. She's the author of *Behind the Scenes, Under the Lights, Just Visiting,* and the Radleigh University series, and a contributor to the historical young adult anthology *All Out.* She lives and works in New York City.

ERIN BOWMAN is the author of two Western novels for teens, *Vengeance Road* and *Retribution Rails.* When not writing about girls defying gender norms in the late nineteenth century, she jumps to science fiction, where she continues to feature female characters railing against the constraints of their societies. The Taken trilogy is available now, and *Contagion* is the start of a new duology. She lives in New Hampshire with her family.

DHONIELLE CLAYTON is the coauthor of *Tiny Pretty Things* and *Shiny Broken Pieces* with Sona Charaipotra and the author of *The Belles* and *The Everlasting Rose.* She has contributed to several anthologies, including *Unbroken: 13 Stories Starring*

Disabled Teens; Meet Cute: Some People Are Destined to Meet; and *Black Enough: Stories of Being Young and Black in America.* Dhonielle is chief operating officer of the nonprofit We Need Diverse Books and cofounder of the literary incubator CAKE Literary. She lives in New York City.

SARA FARIZAN is the author of the Lambda Award–winning *If You Could Be Mine,* the non-award-winning but super-fun *Tell Me Again How a Crush Should Feel,* and *Here to Stay.* She lives in Massachusetts, misses Prince and George Michael, and thanks you for reading her work.

MACKENZI LEE holds a BA in history and an MFA in writing for children and young adults from Simmons College. She is the *New York Times* best-selling author of *This Monstrous Thing, The Gentleman's Guide to Vice and Virtue, The Lady's Guide to Petticoats and Piracy,* and *Semper Augustus,* as well as *Bygone Badass Broads,* a collection of short essays about incredible women from history. She loves Star Wars, sweater weather, and Diet Coke. On a perfect day, she can be found enjoying all three. She lives in Boston, where she works as a bookseller.

STACEY LEE is the author of *Under a Painted Sky, Outrun the Moon, The Secret of a Heart Note,* and *The Downstairs Girl.* She is a fourth-generation Chinese American whose people came to California during the heydays of the cowboys. She believes she still has a bit of cowboy dust in her soul. A native of southern California, she graduated from UCLA, then got her law degree at UC Davis King Hall. After practicing law in the Silicon Valley for several years, she finally took up the pen because she wanted the perk of being able to nap during the day and it was easier than moving to Spain. She plays classical piano, raises children, and writes YA fiction.

ANNA-MARIE McLEMORE is the author of *The Weight of Feathers,* a finalist for the 2016 William C. Morris Debut Award, and of *When the Moon Was Ours,* a 2017 Stonewall Honor Book that was long-listed for the National Book Award. Her latest novels are *Wild Beauty* and *Blanca & Roja.* "Glamour" was written from her passion for magical realism and her daydreams about a queer Latina girl like her trying to find a place in the shimmer of Golden Age Hollywood.

MEG MEDINA writes fiction for children of all ages. Her work examines how cultures intersect as seen through the eyes of young people. She is the winner of the 2019 John Newbery Medal for her novel *Merci Suárez Changes Gears.* She is also the winner of an Ezra Jack Keats New Writer Award for her picture book *Tía Isa Wants a Car* and of a Pura Belpré Author Award for her young adult novel *Yaqui Delgado Wants to Kick Your Ass.* Her novel *Burn Baby Burn* was named the 2016 Young Adult Book of the Year by the New Atlantic Independent Booksellers Association (NAIBA). It was also long-listed for the National Book Award and named a Kirkus Prize Finalist. In 2014, she was named one of the CNN 10: Visionary Women in America for her work to support girls, Latino youth, and diversity in children's literature.

MARIEKE NIJKAMP is the #1 *New York Times* best-selling author of *This Is Where It Ends* and *Before I Let Go.* She has contributed to *Unbroken: 13 Stories Starring Disabled Teens* and to *Feral Youth.* "Better for All the World" introduces her first #ownvoices autistic character.

MEGAN SHEPHERD is the *New York Times* best-selling author of The Madman's Daughter series, the Cage series, *The Secret Horses of Briar Hill,* and *Grim Lovelies.* She lives on a historic farm in North Carolina and has been coerced into many Civil War history tours of Charleston and Savannah by her husband. She personally prefers haunted tours, pirate tours, or, even better, haunted pirate tours.

JESSICA SPOTSWOOD is the author of the historical fantasy trilogy the Cahill Witch Chronicles and the contemporary novels *Wild Swans* and *The Last Summer of the Garrett Girls.* She is the editor of *A Tyranny of Petticoats: 15 Stories of Belles, Bank Robbers & Other Badass Girls* and *Toil & Trouble.* She lives in Washington, D.C., where she works as a children's library associate for the D.C. Public Library.

SARVENAZ TASH is the author of *The Geek's Guide to Unrequited Love,* an Amazon Best Book of the Year; the Woodstock Festival romance *Three Day Summer; Virtually Yours;* and the middle-grade novel *The Mapmaker and the Ghost.* She received her BFA in film and television from NYU's Tisch School of the Arts, which meant she got to spend most of college running around making movies. Sarvenaz lives in Brooklyn with her family.

ACKNOWLEDGMENTS

———

Books are collaborations, and anthologies are even more so. Many people put their hard work and love into this project. I am tremendously thankful to the following:

Hilary Van Dusen, editor extraordinaire, and endlessly supportive. I have learned so much from working with you. Miriam Newman, associate editor, an incisive line-editing goddess, whose notes on my own story were immensely helpful. Copyeditors Hannah Mahoney and Erin DeWitt, for making sure the manuscript is consistent and anachronism-free. Nathan Pyritz, for the lovely interior design; Matt Roeser, for the beautiful cover design; and James Weinberg, for the stunning cover art. Jamie Tan, publicist extraordinaire, for helping to connect *Tyranny* and *The Radical Element* with readers and booksellers and social media influencers. Anne Irza-Leggat, for a wonderful Q&A guide, an amazing time promoting *Tyranny* at NCTE, and all the ways you help educators, librarians, and readers find this book. Candlewick has been the absolute perfect home for these anthologies, and I am so grateful to the entire team there.

Jim McCarthy, for championing this project and helping me find the perfect contributors. The North Texas Teen Book Fest, Texas Book Fest, McNally Jackson and NYC Teen Author Fest,

Curious Iguana Books, and especially my local independent bookstore, One More Page, for your support in highlighting women's historical fiction. Tiffany, Lauren, Lindsay, Robin, Miranda, Jenn, Jill, and Liz for always cheering me on and listening when I feel overwhelmed. One of the reasons I'm passionate about writing complex, fascinating, clever girls throughout history is that I'm surrounded by complex, fascinating, clever women I adore. My brilliant husband, Steve, for always reassuring me that I can in fact do all the things—just not all at once. And my family—especially my dad, who loves history as much as I do; my uncle Mike, who has painstakingly compiled amazing family histories; my Memaw, who first took me to tour historical sites and was an avid researcher of our family genealogy; and my Papaw, who loved to tell stories of World War II. They all woke in me a great curiosity for the stories history tells—and even more curiosity for the stories it can erase.

Dahlia, Mackenzi, Erin, Megan, Anna-Marie, Marieke, Dhonielle, Sarvenaz, Stacey, Meg, and Sara—thank you for sharing your beautiful voices and for trusting me with your stories. I am so glad to have worked with each of you, and so proud of what we've created.

And most of all, our readers. Thank you for reading. To those of you who feel like outsiders in your communities right now, we see you. We value you. Your voices are so important. We can't wait to hear and read *your* stories.

Another edge-of-your-seat anthology
edited by Jessica Spotswood

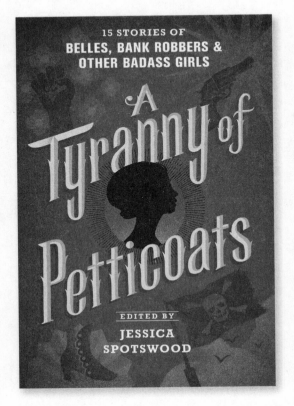

A THRILL RIDE THROUGH HISTORY WITH
AMERICAN GIRLS DRIVING THEIR OWN STORIES

★ "Historical fiction at its finest. . . . The heroines
are tough and memorable and full of heart, and the
concept is irresistible." —*Booklist* (**starred review**)

"Delightful. . . . These energizing, adventurous,
and occasionally somber tales will readily please
fans of historical fiction." —*Publishers Weekly*

Available in hardcover, paperback, and audio and as an e-book